My Heart Belongs in Deadwood

JEWELZ BAXTER
CYNDI FARIA
A.L. LONG
SHERI LYNN
SIDNEY PARKER
GINGER RING
TINA SUSEDIK
AARON VOLNER

My Heart Belongs in Deadwood
Copyright © 2022

All rights reserved under the International and Pan-American Copyright Conventions. No part of this book may be reproduced or transmitted in any form or by any means, electronic or mechanical, including photocopying, recording, or by any information storage and retrieval system, without permission in writing from the publisher.

This is a work of fiction. Names, places, characters and incidents are either the product of the author's imagination or are used fictitiously, and any resemblance to any actual persons, living or dead, organizations, events or locales is entirely coincidental.

Contents

MIDNIGHT JUSTICE by *Jewelz Baxter* 1

CAM'S STRAWBERRY MOON by *Cyndi Faria* 89

SILVER LINING by *A.L. Long* 143

THE SPLENDOR AND SECRETS OF SUNNY CREEK by *Sheri Lynn* 197

HUGS By *Sidney Parker* 271

I'LL FIND YOU By *Ginger Ring* 343

RESCUING ELIZA By *Tina Susedik* 403

THE GLASS WHISPERER By *Aaron Volner* 485

Midnight Justice
Deadwood Drifters Collection

Jewelz Baxter

Cooper Daly has spent most of his life drifting through the Dakota territory. A hired gun bouncing from town to town, he felt like an outcast, until one fateful night in the fall of 1876, when he stole into the bedroom of Cora Palmer.

It was a night that would change their lives forever.

CHAPTER ONE

Fall of 1876, Deadwood, SD
Cooper Daly

Three horses stood on top of the rise as the star-filled sky gave a hazy view of the town below. Cooper Daly leaned his forearm on the pommel of his saddle, studying one house on the edge of the cluster of buildings that made up the little mining town of Deadwood. The house was dark, showing no signs of life, telling him the owner was fast asleep.

"Not too many lights on down there," Emmett commented. "We can make it through town unseen if we stay clear of the saloons. Follow the creek around and camp out in the valley."

Howard nodded. "We can see him ride in from there. Sure 'nough."

"I'm thinking we hide out in town," Cooper said, still staring at the cabin below.

"What about that place?" Emmett jerked his head

toward the apparent ranch house tucked into the side of the mountain to their right.

"No," Cooper barked, nudging his horse into a trot. Without a word, the two men fell in behind him as they followed the well-traveled road toward the settlement. Before reaching town, he turned, leading them farther into darkness and slowing his pace until they reached a neglected barn stationed behind the very place he had zeroed in on.

"We can't just barge in some civilian's home and take over," Howard complained.

"You're not a marshal anymore, Howard. We're all civilians," Emmett reminded him.

"Dang it, boy! You know where I'm coming from."

By this time, Cooper was off his horse and leading it into the questionable structure. "You two put a lid on it. I'm going in to make our presence known."

"Hold on there. We all go in. How do I know you're not leading me into a trap?" Howard demanded.

Cooper whirled on him, anger flaming in his glare. "If I wanted to kill you, I would have done it on the trail, not wait for witnesses."

"I don't know who's in that house," Howard rebutted.

"That little lady is none of your concern," Cooper shot back.

"Look,"—Emmett stepped between them—"we're in this together. Now, put a cap on your differences and focus on what we're here to do."

Cooper turned and walked toward the door, trying the

handle. When it opened easily, he swore under his breath, shaking his head as he stepped inside. Leaving the door wide, he made his way to the only other room. Faintly aware of the two men behind him, Cooper focused on the door. Rather, the woman he had no doubt was sleeping behind that door.

Slowly, he eased it open. A plethora of thoughts filled his mind. *How would she react? Would she scream? Would she listen? Would she fight back? Would he feel bad for upturning her life?* The answer to the last question was 'no'. The only downside he could see, was that he was not alone.

He moved toward the bed as quietly as possible, studying the sweet face showcased by the moon peeking through the window nearby. So peaceful. Her long braid draped over her shoulder, a blue ribbon wrapped around the end. One hand was on her waist, the other resting on the pillow next to her ear.

In one swift move, he had her hands pinned at her waist and her mouth covered.

CHAPTER TWO

Cora Palmer

Cora Palmer's eyes shot open, and panic filled her lungs as she gasped, sucking in the woodsy scent of leather and horse but unable to push out a sound. Staring at the dark eyes above hers, she searched his face until recognition seeped in. Her legs relaxed first, no longer kicking at the quilt holding them hostage. Slowly, her resistance to his hands gripping hers faded. She knew this man. She had seen him several times since moving here, though she had never met him personally, let alone been properly introduced.

Why was he here, in her home? What did he want? Could there be a bit of truth to the sordid stories she had overheard? Something in his eyes soothed her nerves, even as he leaned closer.

"You can pretend to know me or take your chances with those two at the door." His voice was rough and demanding.

She glanced toward the men he mentioned, then back to him. Nodding against his hand still holding in her voice, she agreed to do as he said.

"Good choice," he whispered, releasing her.

Cora immediately gripped the covers to her chest and pushed her heel into the mattress, scooting to sit against the iron scrollwork of the bedframe.

"I didn't want you to wake up and be startled to find us sleeping in your barn." He straightened, tucking his thumbs in his gun belt.

"Okay," she whispered, still wondering why he chose her barn to use. As he turned away, she called out. "Cooper."

He turned back with a smug grin, causing her heart to skip a beat.

"Yeah?" he asked.

"I don't have fresh hay for your horses. I didn't know you were—" She cut her eyes toward the door.

"Didn't know I was bringing anyone with me?" he finished for her, covering his random stop.

"No, I'm unprepared for three horses."

"It's all right. We'll take care of it," he said.

"I… um… are you coming back inside?"

"Yeah," he assured her, holding in a laugh. "I'll be back to see you."

"No, we got your horse. Catch up with your girl," Emmett said, backhanding Howard's shoulder to follow him out.

"Well, I'll be. I was sure he was pulling a fast one on us," Howard said to Emmett as they turned.

"Howard, you're suspicious of everyone," Emmett said as their voices faded into the night.

Cooper leaned against the bare wall, crossing his arms. His head titled to the side as he studied the woman across the room, still clutching the quilt to her neck.

"So, you know who I am," he stated rather than asked how she knew.

"I've heard it," she admitted.

"Smart woman, Miss Palmer."

Her eyes widened at the mention of her name.

"Yeah, I know who you are. I've seen you walking the sidewalks, carrying eggs to the diner and on occasion to the hotel. You live here alone, selling eggs and taking in sewing to support yourself. Other than your close friends, which are few, you keep to yourself."

Her heart began to race. She blinked, glancing toward the window. Blackness with a faint glow of starlight gave no assurance to her doubts. Was this a dream? Surely, this man who she had admired from afar was not standing in her bedroom in the middle of the night as casually as if it were a common occurrence. Not to mention he knew her routines. Turning back toward him, she dared to ask, "What do they want?"

His laugh was deep and warm, setting something afire low in her belly. "You sure they're the ones to be leery of? You may be trusting the wrong man." He pushed from the wall, closing the distance between them. "Not curious why I claimed you? Why I'm here under the cover of darkness, hiding in your barn?"

The heat from her belly rose, and she realized the deep movement of her chest was not hidden by the bedcover she gripped as if her life depended on the hope that it never fell. She opened her mouth to defend herself, maybe to scream. She wasn't sure what she should do, her head and her body tugged in opposite directions.

Inches from her face, his hands wrapped around the iron scrolls above her head and his breath brushed across her cheek. "You should always lock your door. Now, sleep. We'll talk in the morning."

He turned and walked out, leaving Cora in a daze of emotions, tussling, playing with her mind for some time before allowing herself to drift back to sleep.

CHAPTER THREE

Cora

Cora rolled toward the warmth of the sun beginning to peek through her window. She stretched, forcing her eyes open. The thin lace over the windowpane seemed to allow more light in than normal. Squinting toward the sun hovering above the mountaintop, she snapped erect, her eyes widening in realization. The sun was up. Normally, when she awoke, it was only half visible, creating rocky shadows over the town. Scrambling from bed, she quickly dressed so she could begin her day.

Reaching for the door handle, a strong scent of coffee stopped her in her tracks. She didn't drink coffee. She kept none in the house. Her heart pounded. Last night was not a dream. She eased open the door, stepping into the main area of the home.

"Good morning," Cooper said, rising from his seat next to the table. "Would you like some coffee?"

"I don't have—" She glanced around the room. "I mean, I don't drink coffee."

"I hope you don't mind. I brought some in from my bag. Most days this is the only thing available to get the day started. Breakfast can be a luxury."

"I can whip up something for you. Biscuits, maybe?"

"I don't want to put you to any trouble," he told her, still standing behind the chair he vacated.

"Where are the others? Weren't there two men with you last night?"

"Yes, ma'am." He grinned. "They're outside. At least until you give the word they can come inside."

"You're inside," she dared to tell him, hoping to understand the situation better.

"If I waited to be invited, I would never make it anywhere. So, I go where I want." He moved toward her, placing his palm on the small of her back and guiding her toward the table. Pulling back a seat, he motioned for her to sit and leaned in, his breath brushing her ear. "And when I see something I want, I take it."

Shivers danced through her body as Cooper hid a smirk and stepped past her, dropping back into the seat where his coffee-filled mug sat. "Tell me, why are you so calm with the idea of three strangers taking over your dwelling?"

"Should I be afraid?" Her head jerked toward him, searching his face.

"You should always question people. Question their motives and guard yourself against the unsavory," he advised.

Clenching her hands under the table, she sat tall and

confident. She had dealt with a lot since being on her own. Men were usually more talk than action. But if need be, she had become familiar with a rifle by defending her chickens when larger critters came after them. "What do you want from me?"

His sinful smirk appeared again, amused by her attempt to stand against him. "Just your company while I hide out with my companions."

"Why must you hide out? Why here? Are you wanted?"

Heat filled her as the last of her questions spilled from her. Did she really just ask if he was wanted? Of course, he was wanted. By half the women in Deadwood and most likely ones from the other towns he visited. Her chin dropped a bit, pushing the thoughts from her mind. *Focus*, she scolded herself.

"Why hide out?" he repeated her question. "If I recall correctly, you were strolling along the sidewalk yesterday as I rode out of town. So, no one knows I'm here. I need it to stay that way, and I trust you will keep my secret, if for no other reason than to save your virtue. Now, for being wanted." His grin was hypnotizing as he paused. "Not by a single soul. That position is available. Are you offering to be responsible for me?"

Cora sucked in a breath as he leaned against the tall wooden slats of the chair, lifting the mug to his lips. "I believe you're past the age of needing a guardian. You're in no way a child searching for a home."

She could almost swear the devil flashed in his eyes as

they burned into her, mocking her lack of experience with men. "I meant to say, you're all man. No. You're…" Her words trailed off with a huff and a jerk of her head. Squeezing her eyes for a moment, she straightened, returning his gaze, although she was not as amused as he appeared to be. "That didn't come out right. Nothing is sounding right." Gathering her words, she tried once more, but her jumbled thoughts spilled out again. "Why do you want me? Please don't hurt my chickens."

His deep laughter rolled from him like thunder.

"I sound like a blundering young girl infatuated with her first beau." As the words slipped from her, they echoed in her head. Combined with the smug look he shot toward her, she felt the need to move away from him. "Oh, for heaven's sake! I didn't say that." Jolting to her feet, she stormed past him.

He jumped up as she did, racing to open the door for her. His hand on the handle, he cocked his head. "Do I make you nervous, Miss Palmer? Why would that be?"

She stood facing the door, wringing her hands, willing the confidence to reply. Her confidence failing her, she lifted her shoulders, biting her lips closed.

"Want me to tell you why?" he offered.

"I want… no, I need to go out," she said firmly, reaching for her wrap. Before her fingers touched the brown woolen strip, she dropped her hand to her side. The heat of embarrassment filling her body should be enough to keep her warm. If she was lucky, the cool air would bring some sort of sense back to her.

"Before you run and hide, do I have your permission to invite my companions into your home?"

"Did I give you permission to enter?" Her words sounded sharp, or at least she hoped they did. The smirk he shot her way told her differently.

"As a matter of fact, you did. Last night. So, I take that as I have your permission." He pulled open the large wooden panel and stepped to the side, giving her a wide berth.

CHAPTER FOUR

Cooper

Cora's brisk retreat amused him, and the sight of her striding across the yard held him captive. The skirt she gripped in her hands only tugged the material closer to her luscious, round bottom. He had many times admired her curves from afar. This? This was different. This was his first glimpse of her full shape. Lost to the images his head conjured, he was taken by surprise by a slap to his back.

"What's the ruling? We staying or going?" Emmett asked.

Cooper turned toward the two men awaiting his decision. "Of course, we're staying. We have the best view of the stagecoach, and I trust her."

"No way this will work," Howard complained. "Women gossip. She'll have some gal friends drop in or she'll run out and blab that three crazy old farts are hid out in her barn."

Emmett moved close to Cooper as they now stood in

Cora's house. "You sure you trust this woman? The dozens of times we've passed through here, we've not once stopped here."

"You been trailing my every move?" Cooper narrowed his eyes on his friend, his lips tight, forming a straight line. When no reply came, he walked toward the window, pulling back the curtain. "Look."

The men moved next to him, studying the view.

"The stagecoach stops at Thurman's Supply House. Right there." He pointed to a two-story building across the dusty road from where they stood, and not far down the way. "We'll see him when he disembarks, and after dark, we'll ease into the hotel and make our move. By morning, no one will know what happened, and we'll be on our way."

"I don't know about this," Howard commented, shaking his head. "That's against the law."

Cooper and Emmett whirled in unison toward the man they had agreed to help.

"There is no law here. You hired me to find him and put a bead on him. This is it. You follow up or leave now."

"Tell me this," Emmett spoke up. "You brought him in and what happened?"

Steam would have puffed from Howard's ears if he were a tea kettle from the anger boiling up inside him. He had arrested the man, expecting a fair trial. Instead, the trial was a lie, and he was set free.

"You tracked us down, not the other way around," Emmett reminded Howard.

"I tracked your reputation," Howard snapped in return.

"I have never killed a soul who didn't deserve it," Cooper said matter-of-factly. The room grew silent as the men stared past him. Cursing himself, he swung around, coming face-to-face with Cora.

She stood with her hand still on the door. Pushing it closed, she said nothing as she moved toward the small stove and grabbed the apron hanging from a nail next to it.

"Cora," Cooper said softly, forcing her to look up from tying the apron strings. "Sorry you had to hear that, but I'm sure you know my reputation."

"I heard nothing." Her smile appeared genuine and a bit of the nervousness that had overtaken her earlier had vanished. "I'm here to make biscuits for breakfast, but if you plan to stay long, I'll need to make a trip to the Supply House for some goods."

"All right." He turned, and they continued the discussion in hushed voices, confident her humming would block out any more unsavory details.

CHAPTER FIVE

Cora

Placing the meal on the table for her visitors, Cora wrapped a biscuit for herself in a handkerchief before easing through the back door. The chair that usually sat on the porch had been carried inside to accommodate her unexpected guests, so she settled down in a sunny spot on the edge of the wooden planks. The morning had half passed and she still had chores to do. Quickly finishing her little meal, she pushed to her feet, brushing the crumbs from her lap.

Walking into the barn, she slowed, studying the horses now filling most of the space. They were all magnificent creatures, but one stood out. She eased next to it, carefully stroking the solid black stallion. "I've seen you before. I don't know your name, but I have seen you. You're beautiful, and you stand as confident as your owner."

"Red."

Cora gasped at the nearness of Cooper's voice. His

breath sent the stray tendrils next to her ear in motion, tickling her skin. She didn't move. She couldn't. The heat of his body was burning through her threadbare dress without touching her. He stood so near, if she moved an inch, she'd bump smack into him. Her gaze strayed to his outstretched arm and traveled the length of it to focus on the broad, strong hand offering the horse reassurance.

"His name is Red. See his one red ear?" He ran a finger over the nearest ear, making it twitch. "He likes to be talked to. We have many conversations. Don't we, boy? He can keep secrets too."

"I'm sorry. I need to gather the eggs." She scrambled past the horse without looking back at Cooper. Forcing herself to focus on the task at hand, she moved toward the nesting boxes lining the solid wall of the small barn. Or maybe it was the other way around. Maybe it was three narrow stalls squeezed into the rather large hen house. Either way, she gathered the edges of her apron and reached in the first patch of straw, lifting two eggs, laying them into the apron hammock.

The chore did nothing to lessen the heat she had experienced earlier when she and Cooper were alone in the house. Now the hen house where he'd followed her. Especially when she turned to reach into the next nesting box.

"Oh!" She found herself face-to-face with him. The smirk he flashed was hypnotic, freezing her to the spot, forgetting her task.

"Eggs," he finally spoke.

"What?"

"This is the last of them." He lifted his hands, offering the eggs.

"Oh, thank you."

Adding them to the makeshift sling, he asked, "What else needs to be done?"

"I can haul water into the house if you like. I have a tub hanging on the back wall."

"Are you implying I smell?" His smile was slight at first but broadened at her reaction, growing until a laugh escaped him.

"No. Not at all." Her eyes popped wide. "You have apparently been traveling for some days. I thought it might be a refreshing pleasantry."

"Refreshing pleasantry, huh? Are there other refreshing pleasantries up for the taking?"

What else could he want? She worried her lip as she thought. "I can whip up a pie for dessert later."

He barked a laugh, the sound deep and thrilling. "A bath would be nice, but I will not allow you to haul water. We can wait until dark and take a dip in the creek. Our clothes could use a bit of attention too."

"Let me do that for you," she offered.

"Absolutely not. We have imposed too much as it is."

"Cora," a high-pitched voice echoed across the yard.

"Ellie," Cora whispered, jerking toward the open door of the coop and shoving him to the ground. Holding her apron tight, she scurried through the opening into the sunlight.

"Your door was locked," Ellie announced.

With a laugh she hoped didn't sound forced, Cora told her, "I may have forgotten to open it after my bath yesterday." Lifting a basket from the rear wall of her home, she placed the eggs inside. "Headed out to sell the eggs. Want to accompany me?"

"Of course," her friend accepted, looping her arm through Cora's.

Cora set the stride as they rounded the small structure toward Main Street. She had been deposited in this town by chance, and although this was not her ideal place to put down roots, she decided to make the best of it. And to her surprise, shortly after settling into her little log cabin on the edge of town, she crossed paths with Ellie and Alice, her two best friends. Actually, her only friends other than the sweet lady who helped run the general store near her home.

As Ellie chatted away, Cora's mind drifted back to the man she left in her chicken coop. Her mind bounced from hearing her friend's ramblings to the odd sensations she had felt since the arrival of Cooper Daly in her home. Reaching the back entrance of the hotel, she pulled them to an abrupt stop, not able to recall the short distance there.

"Is something wrong?" Ellie asked.

"Oh, no, not at all." Cora shook away the thoughts, conjuring a smile as she stepped over the threshold. "Hello," she called out as her gaze flitted around the kitchen.

"Good day," an elderly woman responded, dragging a cloth bag across the floor.

"Let me help with that," Cora said, hurrying to the

woman's side. She placed the basket onto a worktable. She twisted her hands in the sack of flour and tugged until it was in position to open and scoop the contents onto the long wooden table. With enough flour piled high to blend the ingredients together for bread, she tied the sack closed and returned it to the small pantry.

"You are a godsend, deary. Seth is out getting supplies, and I have run out of biscuits. The noon meal will be upon me in no time, and we must have some sort of bread to go alongside the soup today." She turned from the flour, wiping her hands in her apron. "Have eggs today, do you?"

"Yes, ma'am." Cora removed them from the basket one by one, placing them on the rolled-up cloth where Mrs. Foster kept them as she cooked. Most likely, they would all be gone by nightfall. The woman, in her slow movements she had become accustomed to, lifted a tin from a shelf and removed the payment for the eggs, dropping it into Cora's hand.

"Thank you, Mrs. Foster," Cora called as she rejoined Ellie.

"Do you imagine Alice is awake?" Ellie asked.

"It's early for her, but we can try. Maybe she's out on the balcony."

"All right," Ellie agreed and looped her arm with Cora's again as if walking alone would be the end of them. Somehow, the connection gave confidence to each of them as they navigated this town filled with lawless hijinks. The street was bustling with activity as they emerged from the narrow alleyway behind the hotel. Across that second busy dirt road, they could see the roof of the home they were headed toward.

A few blocks from Main Street, but not quite in the private home area, stood a pale-blue two-story. As they drew near, Alice was not on the balcony nor anywhere in sight. They only saw a man leaning his chair against the wall on two legs. Watching them approach, he dropped the legs of the chair onto the floor of the porch and narrowed his gaze on them.

"Looking for work?" he asked.

"We're looking for Alice," Cora said, ignoring his offer.

"Well, she's resting up for her evening shift. Now, if you were to work alongside her, you two could visit anytime you desired."

"I'm sure you want your girls to look their best. I was here to offer repairs or fittings if needed."

He studied Cora a moment. "You're the girl who does the sewing?"

"Yes, I am," she answered, standing tall and unphased by his uncomfortable assessment, feeling the extra squeeze of Ellie's arm through hers. "Would you please let her, or any of the women, know that I asked?"

"If I recall, when they rouse from their rooms," he finally agreed.

Chapter Six

Cora

Cora stared at the sparkles reflected from the fading sun across the shallow stream where it cascaded over rocks, sending a soothing sound through the breeze. This was one of her favorite times of the day. The chores were complete, and although part of the town came alive at dark, her little corner of the world quietened. No rushing stagecoaches. No galloping horses stirring up dust as they disappeared over the horizon. No children galivanting and searching out mischief to dive into. As the stars traded places with the sun, the sweet chirping of the birds bowed out, giving way to crickets and the occasional frog croak, which was music to her ears.

The moon now hung above the mountains surrounding the town. Closing her eyes, she inhaled deeply, enjoying the fresh fall air. Slowly releasing the breath, she stood and turned, lifting the bottom of her skirt to make her way from the stream back home to her surprise guests.

"Put this around you before you catch a chill," Cooper

said, approaching with her wrap in hand.

She spun, gripping the edges of the warm material as he draped it around her shoulders. She hadn't heard him come up from behind her, and welcomed his thoughtfulness. "Thank you."

"You spend much time out here?" he asked, adjusting his hat and taking in the beauty of the moonlit paradise.

"I like the evenings here. To be true, I fancy any time I spend here. It's like my own little corner of the world." She dared a glance his way to find him studying her. "Other than my friends, no one else comes here."

"A true escape from the beaten path," he agreed. "Now, I must be considered a friend."

"I'm unsure as to what you are," she admitted, bringing a deep laugh from him.

"You'll figure that out soon enough." He moved closer toward the stream and listened to the calming ripple of the water. "We'll be gone before daylight." He spoke without looking her way. "I want to apologize for the intrusion and offer my gratitude for the warm bed."

Cora twisted her fingers in the shawl, pulling it tight against her as she watched his silhouette in the moonlight. "Where will you be headed?"

"Far from here."

After a short silence, he turned, facing her. He swung his arm, suggesting a spot near a large shade tree. "Shall we sit?"

She glanced toward the spot she knew was hidden to anyone not searching for it. "That would be improper."

"Ah, propriety." He closed the space between them.

"Propriety is best saved for public appearances. What you do in private is just that, private. Privacy best reveals who a person is and how they feel. The art of propriety lies for many. If you are comfortable sitting with me and holding a general conversation, is there fault in that?"

"None I see," she admitted.

"Then why should it matter where that conversation takes place? Who is here to object?" he asked.

A faint smile took over her lips as she settled onto the cool grass, tucking her skirt underneath her legs to block the dropping temperatures. Straightening her back, she held herself confident and proper.

He dropped to the ground, removed his hat, and leaned against the wide tree trunk. "This is a quite soothing place," Cooper acknowledged, raising a knee and dropping his wrist to rest on it. "You must sit here often."

"I do love it. When the weather allows, I can sit here for hours mending clothing or other such chores that are not tied to one place. The chirping of the birds flitting around keep me company, and the everchanging sky sweeps away boredom that may attempt to set in. An occasional frog may join me, and although he doesn't reply, I carry on a conversation with him until he tires of me and hops away."

Staring through the darkness, Cooper spoke. "That's how I feel on the back of my horse. He knows my deepest secrets and carries me farther than I think I can go at times. When it's just the two of us under a clear sky, day or night, I feel free. No worries of the world that ceases to exist.

Stopping in a town from time to time pulls me back to ground."

"Is your plan to travel the west until you can travel no more?" She ventured a look his way.

A heavy breath escaped him.

She wondered if thoughts and dreams flashed through his mind. Maybe dreams of a life no one else would suspect from him.

"I have no plans. Day to day brings its own goals and adventures." He flashed a look of admiration toward her. "Do you ever tire of the mundane routine of small-town life?"

Cora relaxed at the image forming in her mind of her travels to and from the town she'd grown to love. "Oh, no. I find challenges and wonders filling each day. Just as you find each day a change of your surroundings, I examine wonders on a smaller scale. For instance, a toad joined me the other day as I sat here mending a dress for a client. While he sat basking in the sunlight, I wondered where he had been and where he may find himself by the day's end. Wonder can be found everywhere."

"That clearly is a unique take on life. I wonder how you ended up in a place as this alone."

"Originally, I'm from St. Louis. I agreed to travel west to assist my grandparents who had grown tired of the bustle of the city and went in search for a simpler life. My grandfather didn't make it here before falling ill and succumbing. Grandmother grieved so deeply that she gave into her sadness before I ended up here alone. Luckily, I met the wonderful older couple who run the small general store across the way, and they assisted me in settling in." For the first time, she twisted, studying him. Just looking at him demanded her heart to beat faster. Although the roughness of his days in a saddle were evident, his appearance sparked interest no other had before. "Where are you from?"

"Everywhere. Nowhere. I have no home. Not anymore." He pulled his gaze from the stream babbling by and cocked his head, intrigued by the fact this amber-eyed beauty saw things others take for granted. His gut told him she could detect things in him that he had kept hidden from his closest friend, Emmett, and even hidden from himself.

After a moment of silence, Cora told him about another wonder. "At times, I think I see a faint glow near the top of the mountain across the way. I've noticed it two, maybe three times. But I find myself searching for it as I venture here past dark."

"What do you consider the possibilities?" Cooper asked her.

"I mentioned it to Mrs. Thurman once."

"What did she tell you?" Cooper asked.

"A family owned a house there many years ago. The young son witnessed an intruder murder both parents. Such a sad thing." A sadness reflected in her voice as she told him.

"What did she say happened to the boy?"

"A couple in town took him in. But eventually, he ran away in search of the killers. She didn't elaborate on the details, but I wonder whatever became of the boy."

Cooper said nothing but stared, seeing only a veil of black hiding the house and its secrets.

"Will I see you before you leave?" she asked, rolling onto her feet and standing.

"If you want."

With a nod, she spun back toward the house and scurried inside, where the warmth of the unexpected fire greeted her.

CHAPTER SEVEN

Cooper

Cooper stood in the narrow alleyway with Emmett and Howard, watching the glow of the lantern in the window above them fade to black. "Ready?"

"He'll have a rude awakening if he's not," Emmett commented, cocking his head toward Howard. "Do as we instructed and there'll be no problems."

He swung his head between the men. "If I miss?"

"Then you'll have no more problems. He'll shoot you on the spot and have another notch on his gun. Remember, the skeleton key always hangs to the right side of the room boxes. Don't forget to put it back on your way out," Cooper told Howard. "Now, go, I'm not waiting here all night. I got you here, now you're on your own."

Howard, the ex-lawman, nodded as he checked his weapon and took the rope from Emmett, then eased toward the rear of the building. "I'll meet you men at the horses," he said and disappeared.

Cooper and Emmett stood under the window for a

time, listening for an altercation that never came. Minutes later, two small bags dropped to the ground from the window and Cooper scooped them up, shoving one into his pocket and tossing the other to Emmett before they moved toward the two horses waiting next to the rear of the hotel. Just as they were beginning to imagine the plan went awry, Howard snuck from the door.

"You must have more outlaw in you than you think," Cooper praised. "You pulled that off without a sound. Like a pro."

"Unless he abandoned his goal," Emmett accused, throwing his leg over his saddle, gathering the reins.

A nervous grin appeared as Howard's head bobbed. "I chewed on it a bit, but it's done now. And I understand the reason you insisted I be the one to do it. She was my sister he kilt. It was my deed to do, and it felt good." He climbed onto his horse and turned toward Cooper. "You know where I'll be if in you ever need me." Then, he kicked his mount into motion and headed from town.

"I'm stopping in Lead for a night or two then coming back through here," Emmett informed Cooper as he leaned onto the pummel. "Catch up with you on the trail." He gave a nod and urged his horse into motion also, quicky fading into the darkness.

Cooper turned and kept to the darkness as he strolled back through town toward the little cabin. Pushing open the door, the smoldering fireplace gave a soft glow to the room as he studied the place. He pulled the money from his pocket he had only minutes before received and tossed a few dollars onto the table. Then, making his way across the room, he stoked the flames, bringing them back to life, and bolted the front door.

Easing open the bedroom door, cold swooshed over him as he moved to stand at the foot of the bed, where he studied the woman sleeping. Her beauty caught his attention the first time he had admired her, but her kindness and unique outlook on life had him intrigued. Moving to her side, his gentle touch brought her eyes open and a sleepy smile to her lips. "You're cold, hun."

"Hmm," she murmured, still half asleep.

Dropping to his heels, he spoke again. "Why are you so cold? The fire does no good if you shut the door."

"I didn't know if you would be coming inside or not," she told him quietly.

He pulled the top quilt from the bed and flipped the covers back. Holding out his hand, he told her to come with him, and wrapped the quilt around her shoulders when she stood. Her trust of him punched him deep in an unfamiliar way as she willingly followed him in only her night clothes. Reaching the sofa, he dropped her pillow onto one end and guided her to sit. "Let's get you warmed up," he told her.

She tucked her feet underneath her and twisted to face him, holding her cover tight. He sat with a bent knee on the seat and a boot hooked under the leg firmly planted on the floor. The gentle touch of his hand against her cheek sent a tingle through her when he propped his arm on the sofa back.

"I can warm you much quicker if you allow me to hold you," he suggested, immediately chastising himself for asking permission, something he had never done before.

Wiggling to close the space between them, she leaned into his open arms, where her head rested perfectly against his chest. The pieced-together quilt may have blocked the crisp air, but it did nothing to block the heat radiating from embracing her. A heat that grew with each thump of his heart as he stroked her back.

The instant her palm slid across his shirt to stop at the small buttons she mindlessly toyed with, the tempo in his chest began to race. Shivers shot through her as his hand slid up her arm, stilling her fingers with his. His chest rose and fell at a greater pace than before, and the heat around them began to burn into his soul. "I must go," he forced out, low and raw.

In a single motion, he had them both on their feet and facing the door.

Still enveloped under his protective arm, she walked with him across the room. "What's this?" she asked, picking up the money he had dropped onto the table earlier.

"I pay my way. That's to replace the food we used."

He reached out, touching the braid hanging over her shoulder. His fingers ran down the silky strands of various browns that reminded him of a tortoise shell. Caressing it ever so lightly, he found himself becoming lost in her. The silky softness of her braid. The alluring softness of her full pink lips. The desire to taste her softness further was demanding to be set loose. Even the color of her eyes was a soft shade of amber, such as the honey he would steal from a hive when he was a boy.

The contrast of the pale-blue ribbon holding the ends together brought his hand to a stop. It matched the apron she had been wearing when she cooked and gathered eggs. "You fancy the color blue," he said softly, fingering the ribbon and bringing a smile to her face. "It's the perfect accent to your beauty."

CHAPTER EIGHT

Cora

The crimson creeping up Cora's neck and filling her cheeks was unmistakable, even in the faint glow from the fire as she glanced away. Heat surged through her at the nearness of him and the manipulation of her braid sent shivers down her spine. Mixed emotions filled her as she lifted her gaze to meet his.

Cooper's eyes were intense as the mahogany rings grew darker and the smirk lifting one corner of his lips cleared her mind of any thoughts she may have had. Held captive by his stare, she hadn't realized his hand had abandoned her braid until his thumb touched her plump bottom lip.

"Soft." The word drifted past her parted lips an instant before his mouth came down on hers. When he pulled away, his hand lingered on her skin until he regained his full height.

She tried to say something, but no words would come.

Her breathing was deep, and her body numb to move as she stood hypnotized by his sweet, stolen kiss. Only when he reached for the door did she break the trance and move. With his gaze still on her, she quickly removed the ribbon from her braid and placed it in his hand.

His lopsided grin returned, and with a wink, he turned and walked through the door.

For a long moment, Cora stood motionless, lost in the unfamiliar surges filling her. When she heard the whinny of the horse leaving the yard, she stepped to the door, locking it. Returning to the sofa in a daze, she curled up under her quilt, and with distinct images filling her mind, she drifted to sleep.

CHAPTER NINE

Cooper

Weeks passed by, and although Cooper's mind traveled back to his time spent with Cora, he hadn't returned until now. With Red settled in for the night, Cooper made a pass by the nesting boxes before stepping into the cold air. The moon reflecting off the light dusting of snow illuminated a figure on the porch abruptly coming to a halt. He paused to drop the latch in place before closing the gap between them.

"You should be inside keeping warm," Cooper said, guiding Cora back across the porch and through the door. He closed the door behind himself, removed his hat, and shrugged off his duster, placing them on nails in the wall as if he did this every day.

Cora looked up, smiling. "I thought I heard a noise and stepped out to check on my chickens."

Relief rushed through Cooper. The joy in her voice and the sparkle in her eyes assured him he was still welcome here, even after his lengthy absence. "Just old Red making his presence known," he explained.

"Would you like something to help you warm up?" she offered.

Smirking, he studied her bundled in colors of honey. "Well, that depends on what you're offering, honeybee."

"I purchased a bit of coffee, or I can warm up soup," the words rolled slowly from her.

He let out laugh, shaking his head. "How about a fire?"

"Oh, of course. Come sit down." Cora hurried toward the small sofa, unwrapping herself and draping the blanket over the end of the seat. She watched as he walked toward the fire and stoked it to a blaze.

"You have a man's coat hanging by the door," he stated, staring into the dancing flames.

"That's my grandfather's. It's big, but it's warm when needed. I dug it from my chest when the snow began. The boots were my grandmother's. I never understood her reasoning for wearing boots as such until I needed them for the chickens and to trudge through the snow occasionally. That's when I keep them by the door."

Finally, he faced her. "Am I making you nervous? Do the proper standards of society still burden you?"

"I recall being advised once that I should feel no shame for what my private life holds as long as I smile inside and can hold my head high. I answer to only God and myself."

"So, you've been thinking about me?" He grinned. "Along with taking my advice."

Color crept up her neck, spilling into her cheeks as she dropped her gaze to the fire behind him.

"Cora?"

Jerking up her head, she blurted, "Have a seat. Tell me where you've traveled."

Facing each other in the firelight, Cooper reminded himself to keep the distance he had not kept last time. Better yet, he should have passed through undetected. But the need to see her rivaled the need to breathe, if only for a short amount of time, so here he was. "We made a trip farther south, where it's not so cold on Red. Not warm either, mind you, but not bone chilling," he told her.

The conversation was the boost he needed to survive the lingering cold as he and Red drifted. Her innocent laughter and angelic eyes rooted deeper into his memory as once again they shared dreams and desires.

"I need to let you get some shuteye. I've kept you up too long," he said, rising to his feet.

"You can sleep in here," she offered shyly, unsure whether it was a good idea.

"That would be wrong, sleeping together under the same roof, alone."

"No one would know. You can sleep here." She patted the sofa cushion next to her.

"You need to rest there to stay warm," he told her. "I'll be fine with my horse."

"I trust you." The words tumbled from her lips.

An odd sensation washed over him. Trust. She trusted him. He nodded, considering her proposition. "You keep the sofa. I'll bed down on the floor here."

With a twinge of excitement, she bounced to her feet and disappeared into her bedroom returning with blankets.

Soon they were both settled in, and his breathing evened out quickly, as exhaustion from days of riding with little rest took over.

In the morning, he woke and came to stand over her. He ran his fingers through the loose hairs that had fallen from her braid, rousing her. "I must set out before I'm noticed." His voice was low and rough as he knelt next to her, feeling comfort from the smile on her face. "I'm only passing through. I'll be back this way in a few weeks. I'll drop in."

She blinked tired eyes at him. "Do you ever stay in one place long?"

"Not often. I'm not the sort of man most towns want settling down for long. Some consider me an outlaw or gunslinger. Both tend to bring the fear to surface, no matter it's warranted or not."

Hesitantly, she raised her hand and touched his face, bringing the corners of her lips higher.

He stood motionless as she explored, watching her, unable to look away. He had fought urges and won, keeping his hands to himself. But her touch coupled with the look in her eyes was wearing on him. He swallowed, bringing her attention from his beard to the movement along his throat. He should turn and walk away. She was not like the women he was accustomed to. A roll in bed would not be enough for her, and she would expect more. More than he knew how to give.

The touch of her hand seared through his clothing, burning into his chest. In an instant, his hands were holding onto her waist, pulling her flush to him, his mouth crashing onto hers in urgent need. Knowing in his mind that she had never experienced such a passion, he forced himself to slow down. Tasting her lips, coaxing them open, taking his time teaching her the erotic dance of their tongues. When he forced himself to pull away, his gaze fell to the heavy rise and fall of her chest. He pressed his lips to hers once more, then grabbed his coat and hat from their hooks and jerked open the door, walking out.

"To hell in a handbag," he mumbled to himself, kicking his stallion into a gallop away from her house. Far away. The farther the better. "I knew not to touch her, not to taste her. Damn it to hell!"

He never looked behind him. His mind drifted back to the warmth of her hand, the sweetness of her lips, but he rode in the opposite direction for as long as he felt comfortable to push old Red.

CHAPTER TEN

Cora

It had been days since Cora had seen Cooper. She sat on her porch wrapped in her grandfather's coat as she did many afternoons in hopes of seeing him ride into town. The sun hung high over the treetops blocking the view of the road coming over the mountain with its bright white rays.

"Good afternoon, Miss Cora."

She turned toward the man approaching. "Good afternoon, Henry."

"Mrs. Foster sent this over."

How sweet of her. She reached for the checkered cloth Henry held out. "She didn't need to do this. Tell her thank you for me, please."

He rubbed the back of his neck, shifting his feet. "I didn't mind bringing it over, ma'am." He looked up. "I'm here if you ever need anything."

He was sweet, but his company held no interest for Cora. "That's sweet of you, Henry. I'll keep that in mind."

He nodded and turned away. Shoving his hands into his pockets, he headed back toward the hotel restaurant.

Henry, among others, had at times, requested to escort Cora to events or take a stroll along the countryside. But none of their offers had interested her. She had been perfectly fine in her own little world. That was, until Cooper invaded her world that one night.

She smiled at the memory of her first time seeing Cooper. He was riding down Main Street on Red. She and Ellie were chatting as they walked toward the general store in search of thread to complete a quilt they were sewing as a gift for Alice. He sat tall and stoic as townspeople scattered from his path. He glanced her way and she believed that very day she lost herself in his eyes. They were dark and empty, Ellie had commented. But Cora saw something else. A deep passion.

Cora glanced down at the small loaf of bread she held. She had a good life. And good friends. Although Cooper sparked a new world of emotions in her, she understood her life had not changed outside of the stollen visits after dark.

The day was not over, and chores remained to be done. She pushed from her chair. One last glance through the blinding rays and she smiled, stepping into the house.

She would see him again. She felt it.

CHAPTER ELEVEN

Cooper

As much as he scolded himself for weakening against his desires, he was headed back to her town, back to her. That one kiss had doomed him, making it hopeless to stay away from Deadwood, from Cora. The taste of her and the undeniable trust she had in him was consuming him. The towns he had passed through in the couple of months since that night had proven that fact. His normal visits to brothels had changed. His nights were now spent in the saloons, not even noticing the saloon girls enticing the room around him. He focused on the card games at hand and fell into bed alone when the games ended.

Now, he sat at the same rise, looking down on the town just as he had that first night he'd invaded her home, disrupting her life. And his. With a deep sigh, he nudged his trail companion into a trot, and within minutes, he was stirring up dust along with dozens of others traveling Main Street. Amongst the bustle of the crowd, two women strolling side by side along the sidewalk caught his attention. He reached into his pocket and pulled out the pale-blue ribbon that was always there, rubbing his fingers over the smooth satin as he watched Cora laugh along with her friend, and trusting Red to carry him toward the livery from habit rather than guidance.

"Beginning to think you had abandoned me," Emmett commented when Cooper stepped from the building, slinging his saddlebags over his shoulder.

"Had things on my mind," Cooper confessed, wishing to avoid the subject. "I need to get a room and pick up supplies. What ever happened to Howard? You follow him on into Oklahoma territory?"

"Most of the way, before getting preoccupied." Emmett barked a laugh, joining Cooper's snicker, and walked into the hotel.

"I heard you might be arriving," the hotel clerk greeted. "Your usual room?"

Emmett's elbows hit the counter next to the registry book. He twirled the toothpick in his mouth as Cooper signed in.

Without a word, Cooper dropped the pen next to his name and grabbed the key, then headed for the stairs, followed by Emmett. He unlocked the door and tossed his bag into the only chair in the room.

Emmett bounced onto the bed, crossing his ankles as he threw his hands behind his head, leaning against the wall. "I noticed you didn't leave town same as we did."

Cooper shed his dusty shirt, popping the dirt from it.

"Well?" Emmett prompted.

"Well, what?"

"Tell me about Miss Cora."

"I believe I'm in need of a bath and laundry. Then a stop at the mercantile to refill supplies." His expression remained absent, knocking Emmett's boots to the floor.

"All right." Emmett chuckled, slapping Cooper's back as he stood. "Let's get presentable."

Copper

As Cooper moved through the dark toward the place they'd last sat beside the stream, his attention was focused on Cora, who was so caught up in the light show dancing about her, she seemed unaware of her surroundings.

"You do know lightning bugs use their lights to compete for mates."

Whirling on her heel, she crashed into his chest. "That's how they communicate," she corrected, her hands splayed on his chest.

"They're courting." His expression was unreadable under the shadow of his hat, but his thoughts were relayed by tracing circles on her back.

Her voice drifted out on a sigh. "Do you think we're interrupting their privacy?"

"Only if we're not joining in." His words faded into her mouth as he claimed it with a passion that took her breath away. Pulling her roughly against him, he felt shivers dance through her body, setting her heart to race and her fingers to dig into his sides. Kissing her filled him with heat, burning from the inside out. His fingers tangled in her hair, tugging, giving him access to pepper kisses along her jaw. The heavy rise and fall of her chest pressed her hardening nipples against his chest with each breath, bringing a soft moan to escape her. A sound so sweet and seductive, it slammed into his heart, slowing his demands, leaving a fire in them both.

Her hand flew to her swollen lips as he stepped back, studying her, gripping her hips as if he were afraid she'd bolt if he let go. His thumb nudged away her hand, tracing her plump lips. A faint glow from the moon gave evidence of the redness his beard had left behind.

"Shall we enjoy the light show together?" he asked, getting a slight nod in response.

Searching the ground around them, he located his fallen hat and dropped next to it. As she settled beside him, her full skirt bunched over his lap, giving the perfect opportunity to adjust himself before pulling her to him.

The silence returned their pulses to normal, or as normal as possible when they were together. As the lightning bugs faded in number, Cora leaned back her head, searching out his face. "I baked an apple pie today. Would you like a piece?"

His laugh was abrupt and low. "Yes. Yes, I would love some pie."

MIDNIGHT JUSTICE

Cooper

The next day, Cooper stood leaning against the display counter of the small general store talking with the owner when the bell above the door jingled. Without turning toward the swish of skirts and the faint click of dainty boots on the wooden floor, he felt Cora's presence. She and her friend. "Take care of them. I'm in no hurry," he told the old man before backing away to a spot across the store. The woodburning heater called to him, not for heat because it wasn't in use, but it held the best view of the entire store other than behind the display counter.

The women chatted as they gathered a few items, and Cora studied something in the glass case as Ellie counted out the coins for her purchase.

"Want to see it?" the store owner asked Cora.

"Oh." She shook herself, aware of the man talking to her. "No. I'm getting closer every day, but I haven't saved enough yet."

"Don't fret. I'm sure it will still be here when you're ready."

"I do hope so, but I understand it may not be." She placed her coins on the counter and took the small piece of lace in her hand.

"Look, Cora. New ribbon rolls. You can replace the blue one you lost or choose a new color."

Her fingers flew to the faded green ribbon holding part

of her hair twisted behind her head as she turned to examine the available colors with Ellie. A slight gasp escaped her an instant before her eyes filled with a desire he had witnessed up close. With his arms crossed over his chest and feet apart, he watched the light fade from her eyes and the enticing pink of her cheeks transform into a crimson heat of shame. He felt the hurt and the disappointment in her eyes cutting through him, although it did nothing to move the stoic expression he forced.

"What do you think about this?" Ellie held up a purple so deep, it would fade into the night unseen.

"I think I should head home now. I need to finish this dress for Alice." Cora touched a more appealing shade of yellow without acknowledging her friend's comment, then turned and walked away.

Finding himself alone with the owner once more, Cooper strolled toward the glass case, searching the spot she had studied. "What was she hoping to purchase?"

"You know Miss Palmer?"

Cooper cut a look toward the man, bringing a chuckle from him.

Sliding the back of the case open, he lifted a broach filled with colorful stones and placed it on top of the case.

"This the price?" Cooper touched the tag tied to the clasp.

The owner shook his head. "I doubled the price to dissuade buyers. When she arrived in town, unexpectedly alone, she sold what she could to settle here. This was a family heirloom and the single item of real value she had with her. I gave top dollar and now I'm holding it for her to buy back. She owes half that amount."

Cooper ran his fingers over the costly stones. He couldn't imagine her wearing something so stately. On the other hand, from their talks, he had come to know family meant a lot to her. This was a piece of her family, just as the tattered Bible threatening to fall apart that she kept on a small table. It was a part of her family she was not yet willing to replace.

Lifting the small cloth where it lay, he wrapped it and watched the man return it to its original spot in the case. "I need a length of ribbon. The yellow." The moment he was left alone, he stretched, reaching inside the case, snatching the jeweled pin. "I need a handkerchief also," he called over his shoulder, slipping the item into his pocket. Minutes later, with the ribbon and kerchief tucked into his pocket, he stepped back into the warmth of the sun, planning his evening.

Chapter Twelve

Cora

Cora awoke to the sun peeking through her window as it made its way above the mountains. She had slept through the night, restless but nonetheless through the night, with no visitors. After being shunned the day before, she locked her doors at bedtime just as he had been insisting. Stretching, she stood. She chose her dress for the day, a brown the color of her eyes with a tiny white pattern. Entering the main room of her home, a bright-yellow ribbon demanded attention from across the open space. It had not been there the night before. No, she did not own a ribbon so bright. Her heart skipped a beat as she pulled the chair back from the table, lowering herself into it, staring at the wrapped item tied with the ribbon. No question of where it came from, but many other questions instead bombarded her. How did he get in? Why would he not wake her? He had ignored her the day before, but he brought for her the very ribbon she had admired in the general store. Why? If he was done with her, why a gift? Was this a game to him? Something to amuse himself with as he passed through town?

Hurt or disappointment, she wasn't positive which, won the battle over curiosity. She pushed to her feet and jerked the pail from next to the sink and pulled open the door, headed into her day. Inhaling the fresh summer air, she admired the blue above her, soft and welcoming. Airy whisps of white danced along the breeze reminding her of the lace she had sewn into Alice's dress the night before. After her trip to the outhouse and to the chicken coop, she stepped inside, still avoiding the bundle occupying the center of her table. Pumping water into the sink, she glanced toward the smooth white cloth still hiding its contents.

Exasperation at her impatience escaped her and, drying her hands, she whirled toward the chair she had vacated earlier, dropping back into the seat. The ribbon was a beautiful color, she admitted, bringing the hint of a smile to her lips as she untied the bow. With it spread out to the sides, carefully, she unrolled the cloth. Shock came in a gasp. The very broach that had belonged to her mother and grandmother was in her hands. The smooth stones arranged together in shiny metal scrollwork felt heavy in her hand. How could she ever repay him for this? What must the Thurmans think of him purchasing her such an intimate gift?

After placing it onto the white cotton cloth, she sliced a piece of bread and filled a glass with water. Sitting at the table with her breakfast meal, her gaze never strayed from the piece of jewelry before her. Anxiety crept in, and taking one more sip of the water, she scooped up the gift and grabbed the pail of eggs along with a folded garment on the table, hurrying through the door. Once in the sunlight, the soothing sounds of summer invaded her senses, slowing her stride. Smiling at the birds swooping onto the green patch in front of her door where they hopped willy-nilly searching for a meal, she changed her path.

The eggs would wait until after she spoke with the Thurmans. Such an inappropriate gift would tarnish her reputation. She hoped to convince them to not divulge to anyone how she came to own this treasure.

The jingle as Cora entered the store brought Mrs. Thurman from a storage room. "Good morning," she greeted, stopping at the display counter.

"Good morning," Cora began. "I need to speak with you about the piece you were holding for me."

"You don't know how happy I was to discover you had picked it up after your final payment. I'm always hesitant to leave the store unattended even for a moment, but it was a quick delivery next door while the mister was delivering to the Harmons. I returned as Mr. Thurman was walking in. He's the one who noticed the money in place of your broach."

Cora glanced down at the broach in awe. Cooper had managed to do this wonderful thing for her privately, keeping her reputation intact.

"So, you have nothing to fret over. We did get the

money," Mrs. Thurman assured Cora.

"Thank you, again, for helping me when I needed it," she told the woman.

The woman's smile was genuine as she spoke. "Glad we could do it. I hope you know you can depend on us for anything you may need."

Cora returned her smile and rolled the jewelry piece back into its cloth. "I do appreciate all you've done. Well, I should be off to deliver my eggs and a bit of sewing. Have a blessed day."

As the door fell closed behind her and setting her sights on the day's chores, she picked up her step, heading for the hotel restaurant before delivering the mended garment to Alice.

Chapter Thirteen

Cooper

"A game of poker before you sneak off into the night?" Emmett joked, leaning against the post of the hotel. Townsfolk and visitors alike streamed in and out of the hotel for lodging and the food after a short-lived shower settled the dusty street without bringing mud to puddle in places.

"Let's see what we can rustle up." Cooper clapped Emmett's back as he stepped into the road. Navigating the traffic, they crossed the street, heading toward their regular poker spot when in town. Assessing the games in play and the possibilities of new takers, the duo chose a spot at the bar, waiting for a prosperous opportunity to show itself. As usual, the wait was short.

"I'm feeling lucky tonight, boys. Who's up for a game?" a voice boomed across the room.

Taking in the man, they glanced toward each other and strode his way. He was not a stranger to either of them.

Hank ran a local brothel off main street. He was known for duping women into owing him and working off the money. At times, Cooper had heard stories of the man using force or unsavory conditions to gain their employment. It was hearsay that he had no firsthand evidence of. And if he did, he would most likely look the other way as most did.

With two others recruited, they filled the seats around a table with drinks in hand. Hank smugly combed back his long, curly, dusty-blond hair and reached for the deck in the center of the table.

"Hank, what's got you so chipper?" asked the man sitting beside Emmett and across the table from Cooper, pulling his dealt cards toward him.

"Got a new girl today. Owee, she's a sweet thing too. You men should stop by and treat yourself," Hank boasted.

The proposition held no appeal to Cooper as he studied his cards and anteed.

The conversation fell away as the game progressed and the first player was forced out by losing his last bet. Shortly, the winnings were covering one side of the table with the opposite side dwindling. "This is my last go of it, men. Got to keep enough to take home for supplies," the man they knew as Frank, announced, pushing a small wager toward the center of the table.

"Up to you," Emmett informed Hank.

Hank studied the cards before him, then reached into his pocket. "I don't have the cash, but I have this." He tossed a jewelry piece onto the pile of money.

Cooper's heart crashed against his chest with rage.

Cora was over the moon when she received it only a day ago. He stared at the piece and recalled the words from earlier. Had Hank duped Cora into owing him? That was something he decided to deal with one on one. Cora's name was not being brought into a saloon. In a swift movement, he cut a look toward Emmett the same time he jerked a blade from his boot, slamming it into the table near Hank's hands. "Get that out of my sight and get out of here."

"No harm." Hank reached around the knife, retrieving the broach and dropping it back into his pocket. "I'm out of money anyhow." Gathering the few bills from the table in front of him, he stood and walked out.

"Let's see," Emmett said, hurrying the game to an end. All cards splayed on the table, Emmett congratulated the man to his left on his win and the piles were gathered, disappearing into their pockets.

"What's wrong with you?" Emmett complained, jerking the blade from where it stood upright in the wooden table. He glanced around the saloon, satisfied they had drawn no unwanted attention, and punched Cooper in the arm.

Cooper shot to his feet, demanding to catch up with the lowlife who had attempted to bet away Cora's prized possession. Dodging eyes and slipping into the darkness, he quicky explained the situation and caught up to their target.

Whistling, Hank stepped up to the rear door of the two-story home where he kept his girls. Unaware of Cooper and Emmett, he strolled inside and minutes later, a man the duo knew worked as a guard when Hank was away, stepped into the night and disappeared down the road.

Cooper burst through the door. "Where's the girl?" he demanded, his hands around Hank's throat, resting the blade of his knife against his skin. Adrenaline pumped through him harder than he could ever remember. "The new girl you boasted of."

"No need to get out of sorts. She's upstairs. Complementary poke just for you." Fear dripped from Hank's words as his body trembled.

"I got him," Emmett said, holding his gun on Hank and shoving him into a chair. "Go get her."

Cooper bounded up the stairs and one by one kicked open the doors. Of the four rooms occupied, men retreated from three, jerking trousers up as they ran, never looking back. Four shocked females screeched, clutching bed coverings to their necks.

"Last time I'll ask before ending you," Cooper growled, storming back down the stairs and into the room. "Where is she?"

"All my girls are upstairs in their rooms."

"Where's the woman you took this from?" He reached into Hank's pocket, jerking out the broach. "How did you get this?" he demanded, ignoring the frightened women huddled at the top of the stairs.

When Hank said nothing, Emmett clicked back the hammer. "All right, last chance."

"All right! All right! I stole it! I don't know where she is. What's it to you anyway?"

"You steal from these girls and force them to repay you. You steal from me, I demand repayment too." Cooper's fingers gripped the stones and gold so tight, it threatened to pierce his skin. Rage danced in his eyes as he whirled toward the women. "Who of you want to leave this place?"

"Now wait a minute! This is my livelihood," Hank yelled.

"Do you want to know what mine is?" Cooper leaned inches from his face, growling. "Maybe you're interested in my friend's livelihood?"

"Does anyone want to tell us what happened here today?" Emmett shouted toward the women.

Alice glanced at the faces surrounding her as she eased to a lower step. "She was here delivering a dress today she had mended for me, but she ran. He tricked her inside, and she ran, losing that when he grabbed at her." Her voice drifted down toward them.

She was not here. She was okay. Most likely safe in her home now.

"You want to leave here?" Emmett asked Alice, watching her nod. "Go get your things."

She turned on a dime, running back toward her room and quickly gathering her few things, shoving them into a pillowcase. Minutes later, she stood next to Cooper and Emmett, hugging the filled pillowcase like a lifeline.

"Can you guarantee me she's not harmed?" Cooper needed to know.

"Yes," Alice replied, blonde ringlets dancing about her nape as she answered.

Pressing the blade against Hank's throat once more, Cooper made the man a promise. "If I find she has been harmed in any way, I will return. No questions asked. No second chances. I will kill you, that you can bet on. Now, I'm taking this girl for the payback of stealing from my woman and the headache of dealing with you." He pressed deeper into the skin with each statement, bringing drops of blood as a reminder not to cross him. Then, he shoved, knocking the chair onto its back.

CHAPTER FOURTEEN

Cora

Slumped at the table in the center of her tiny kitchen, Cora dropped her head onto her folded arms. Everything around her seemed to be crashing. Cooper had shunned her, then slipped into her home undetected with a gift. A precious gift she had lost earlier when returning Alice's mended clothing. She knew she shouldn't have had the broach with her at the time. It held special memories and was to be worn only for special occasions. Plus, she doubted she would be permitted to visit her friend again. Her head jerked toward the jiggling of the rear door followed instantly by a pounding.

"Cora!"

She pushed from the table and scurried toward the door. The instant the bolt slid from its latch, she flung it open and was in Cooper's arms. He kicked the door closed and together they stood holding each other without a word. An unknown amount of time ticked by as Cora listened to the rhythm of his heartbeat pounding against his chest and matching the cadence of hers. Her eyes drifted closed, further blocking out the world beyond them along with her fears.

"It's okay. I'm here…" Cooper spoke softly.

Pressed against him, enveloped in his arms, his cheek resting possessively on her head, she savored the strong wall of protection and love surrounding her. Yes, love, she admitted to herself. She had fallen in love with this man who had toyed with her on his schedule. But he was here now, and the strength of his embrace confessed a fear within him that matched hers.

She pulled away enough to lock her gaze with his. "You shunned me. In the presence of others, you were ashamed to know me." As the words passed her lips, the hurt returned and brought tears for the first time.

"Shh," he coaxed, swiping the wetness from her cheek. "Is that what you thought?"

She said nothing as she watched his features transform into the intoxicating smirk she had come to adore, although a glint of sadness still haunted his eyes as he spoke. "Honeybee, do you know what I do? How many people could come looking for me at any time to take revenge? I refuse to let you into that crossfire. If no one knows how I feel about you, no one will target you to get to me. I couldn't live with myself if something happened to you."

Within moments, she found herself sitting on the edge of the table with Cooper standing between her knees, her hands limp in her lap as she watched him dig in his pocket.

The jewels had no shimmer in the faint light, although the beauty of the piece was unmistakable.

"Where did you find that?" she blurted, jerking her head up, searching his face.

"This was tossed into a pool of wagers tonight," was his only explanation. "Like to explain how it made its way there?"

Her lips trembled, not desiring to relive the horrid confrontation from earlier in the day. Averting her gaze, hope filled her that he would not push or scold her as she heard no accusations in his voice.

His finger, crooked under her chin, lifted her gaze back toward his. "You can't trust everyone. I understand how much you would relish a peaceful and trusting world to live in, but this is not the place for that. Evil lives everywhere. Just as I do."

"You're not evil."

"You don't know the things I've done."

"I know the person in here." Her palm pressed against his chest.

Her touch ignited a warmth that burned straight into his heart. No one since childhood had seen that side he kept hidden. The person he had so long ago thought dead.

"You're a good man, Cooper." She took his face in her hands. "I love you."

His lips twitched, even though he fought the reaction but failed. Caressing the back of her hands as her palms continued to admire the roughness of his facial hair, his focus grew more intent on her words while at the same time battling to move past the walls he had lived with for more than half his life.

"I can't say why I didn't refuse you to stay that first night, or the nights following, but a part of me anticipates the door suddenly swinging open to announce your arrival in the midst of darkness. You conjure feelings in me I have never imagined, and I imagine no other could. When you shunned my greeting, I felt my world, diminish."

His belly roiled learning she had felt unworthy when all he wanted was to keep her safe. "I fell for you the instant you relaxed against forcing myself into your home, your own private world. I had kept an eye on you for some time along the streets as you delivered your eggs and strolled along chatting with companions." Intertwining his fingers with hers, he lifted them, pressing his lips to her hand. "I love you too, Cora."

Abandoning her hands, he slipped his fingers into the brown silky locks that hung around her shoulders. He loved the sensation as he combed it from her face, his fingers tangling in the strands, holding her head where he wanted. He pressed his lips onto hers, gently savoring the softness for an instant before pressing, urging access to taste her, inviting her tongue to dance. Her mouth was warm and sweet and eager. Her touch sent electricity surging through him, and he felt as if he were soaring on a cloud as her faint moans filled his ears. Slowly lifting her skirt, he explored the softness of her legs, touching, caressing.

She moaned and leaned into his touch.

"I'm sorry." His mouth abandoned hers and he

dropped his head to rest against hers. "I can't do this to you."

Cora swallowed. "Do what?"

"You deserve better than this. Better than me." Cooper lifted his head and her chin, staring into the eyes that followed him everywhere he had travelled since falling into them all those months ago. "I want more. And when I get a taste of more, I'll want it often. You're not a passing whim and shouldn't be grasping at threads in hopes of a visit. Yet again, I can't put you in danger."

"How can I be in danger if you are here with me?"

Her smile brought hope to the uncertain thoughts trampling his mind. He had spent his life seeking revenge, for the death of his parents then for others who had sought him out for help. He had made many enemies. But with her help, her trust, her love, he envisioned a home. A home like the one his parents had given him for as long as they could. One filled with love and laughter, and children. Studying her, warring with the possibilities, the corners of his lips finally broke into a smile to reflect hers. "Marry me, Cora. I'll settle down. Here. With you."

"You wouldn't mind living in such a small home compared to the vast open skies you're accustomed to daily? Or bored in a mundane life?"

"There will be nothing mundane about a life with you. What do you say?"

"Yes. I say yes." Excitement bubbled from her, from the expression in her gaze to the hug she engulfed him in.

His lips recaptured hers in a slow, intimate celebration,

a kiss she melted into, pulling him to her and igniting the embers again until Cooper pulled away once more. "I'll head out to tie up business dealings I have, then in one week, when I return, we'll marry. Right here under our tree near the creek."

"That would be lovely. Just us and a preacher." Her eyes shot wide as saucers, darting toward his calm features. "Where are we to find a preacher so quickly?"

"You needn't worry your pretty head about a thing. Just be ready to bind yourself to me on my return. I'll handle the details."

Chapter Fifteen

Cora

Four days seemed to drag past in an effort to diminish the intensity of excitement that had settled in Cora's heart. But as their courtship had developed in private, she decided so should their engagement and nuptials. Even as she thought she may burst from hiding such news from her friends, she agreed to cherish the intimacy of the private union before sharing their time with others.

The bell above the door announced her arrival. She hoped to find a length of white ribbon along with what lace she had deemed necessary to transform one of her well-worn dresses to fit the occasion. Searching the available stock of notions, she chose only the ribbon for her hair.

"You have a telegram."

Her head shot up from sorting the coins in her small drawstring bag. "For me?" Curiously, she took the message and the ribbon, tucking the ribbon into her bag. "Thank you."

Upon hurrying into the brightness of the clear day to read the telegram, her pace seemed to slow. Heart racing, she unfolded the yellow sheet, staring at the two words. "Three days." That was it. No explanation. No name. Three days.

The disappointment of her dress situation disappeared, replaced with the reminder of the most important fact. Cooper loved her no matter what she wore the moment she married him, just as she had no cares of what he wore. Her smile brightened more than she thought it ever had as she imagined Cooper standing next to her under that tree dressed in his normal black attire, exchanging vows.

"What you got there?" Alice asked, breaking into her thoughts. "Must be something. You've been perched on the edge of the sidewalk ogling over that paper for a while. Enough time for us to walk from your house without notice."

"I didn't think you knew anyone outside of town to be receiving telegrams from," Ellie observed.

Folding the telegram, Cora held on to it, not willing to let go of the words. "Let's head back and visit. I must hear all about your adventures of striking out into your new life," she redirected the conversation by setting the pace toward her home, where they passed the afternoon filled with laughs and promises of future get-togethers.

Then, two days later, late that evening, a knock at her door startled her. With haste, she pulled the small pan from the oven and slid it onto the stovetop before rushing toward the door. She dusted her hands on her apron and patted it straight before pulling open the door and coming face-to-face with a young boy.

"Ma'am, are you Cora Palmer?"

"Yes, I am."

"This is for you." He held out an envelope.

"Thank you," she told him, taking the offered letter, but before her words fell silent, he had turned and ran back toward town.

A laugh escaped her as she watched the child sprint across the yard, jumping imaginary obstacles. Glancing at the plain sealed envelope, she flipped it over and pried open the flap. Bumping the door closed with her hip, she pulled the sheet of paper from its holder and unfolded it.

Dearest Honeybee,

I'm safely checked into the hotel and preparing for our day. See you at noon!

   All my love,
   Your Outlaw

A giggle escaped her. He had kept the message private, she imagined, considering the boy may have lost it or gotten distracted.

Tomorrow, she reminded herself, slipping the letter between the pages of her well-worn Bible. Tomorrow would begin a new life.

Chapter Sixteen

Cora

The day was perfect, Cora thought as she stepped into the sunlight. A cool breeze pushed wisps of hair into her face as she hurried to gather the eggs before turning her attention toward preparing for her wedding. Mindlessly, she filled the pail from the nesting boxes and carried them inside to the little corner shelf in the kitchen space. Her mind was sorting through the tons of questions bombarding her since waking. Would she be a good wife? What would he expect? Did she even know what she was doing? Which dress should she wear? Would she have time to gather a small bouquet of wildflowers? Tonight, she would be a married woman. Mrs. Daly. She came to an abrupt halt from brushing out her hair. Tonight. How would tonight be?

Cora jumped, startled by a knock at the door, and the brush tumbled from her hand, landing onto the wooden floor with a thud.

Her heart raced as she twisted her hands in her skirt and scurried to see if Cooper was here early. She cracked the door enough to see the woman standing there.

"Hello, Cora," Mrs. Thurman greeted as she held a bundle of cloth in her arms. "May I come in?"

"Of course." Cora pulled open the door for the woman whom she knew from the general store, easing the door closed behind her and hoping this visit would be short. Turning, she followed the older woman to the sofa. "What can I do for you?"

Mrs. Thurman's smile returned so bright Cora wondered if she had missed something.

"Cooper asked if I could lend you a hand this morning."

Cora froze. "With what?" she forced out, knowing they had agreed to keep this private until after the fact.

"I hope you don't mind, and please feel free to tell me if you do, but he explained you were alone here and may be in need of a mother figure today."

Cora's hand flew to her lips, too late to hide the shocked gasp that accompanied her eyes growing large. She stared at the beautiful lace-covered garment Mrs. Thurman was unveiling as she spoke.

"I don't have a daughter to pass this on to. So, when he came to me, I pulled this from the chest for you. Like I said, please tell me if I'm out of line. You may have one from your mother or grandmother."

"No. No, I don't," Cora interrupted, reverently tracing the edge of the neckline. "It's beautiful."

"Here, I have rose-scented bath oil to help you relax before dressing. And I'd offer to arrange your hair, but I was informed you like it down with a ribbon."

Throwing her arms around the woman, her fears were once again overshadowed by learning Cooper had thought of the tiniest details and handled the situation, as she imagined he would always handle any situation that arose. She had nothing to question or fear. "I would love for you to help me. I admit, a bit of anxiety had reared its head this morning."

"Honey, there is no need for you to go this alone. Let's fit the dress, so I can make any alterations while you soak in a luxurious bath. We'll talk and have you dressed and ready in no time."

True to her word, Mrs. Thurman accomplished the few small alterations to the dress while Cora soaked in the water they had heated on the stove and added the rose-scented oil to. Even though Mrs. Thurman had no daughters to have carried on this conversation before, she handled the delicate marital questions with ease and confidence. She also knew things about raising children and family life that she shared for future times.

Feeling more at ease, when the time arrived, Cora stood in front of her mirror, admiring the perfectly fitted dress. Part of her hair was held back with the white ribbon she had purchased, beautifully contrasting the soft-brown shades hanging in loose curls around her shoulders.

"I believe I'm ready." No sooner than the words tumbled from Cora did another visitor appear. "And just in time." She laughed, talking to herself. She glanced around the space ensuring it to be tidy for Cooper.

Mrs. Thurman cracked open the door, prepared to tell Cooper his bride was ready. Instead, her own husband greeted her. "Is she ready?"

Smiling as he stepped inside, Mr. Thurman shook his head in awe. "I must say I never thought I would see the day that man settled down. Much less settle here. My dear, you have accomplished a feat we have failed at."

The small handful of flowers that he offered her mixed their scents together, sending a sweet aroma to Cora as she admired them.

"Are you ready?"

Offering her his arm, she slipped her hand gently in the bend of his elbow and they set out together, toward that special spot under the tree.

Making their way across the yard, she was glad for the escort. Her gaze was fixed on the man standing facing her. Dressed in his usual black as she had expected, her breath caught at the sight. His hair, nearly as black as his attire, along with his beard, had been trimmed and neatly combed. His smile was mesmerizing as always, dimming the world around him.

Although she listened and spoke at the appropriate times, her heart raced, eager to be in his arms again, to experience his lips on hers.

When the vows had been repeated and the preacher requested the rings, Cooper produced a set of gold rings from his pocket. "These belonged to my parents," he whispered, slipping one on her finger and placing the other in her hand for her to do the same.

Minutes after the ceremony, Mr. Thurman spoke. "You made our day with this surprise, son." Then, he turned toward Cora. "Welcome to the family."

Her head jerked toward Cooper as he replied, smiling, "I could have done none of this without you two."

CHAPTER SEVENTEEN

Cooper

"Mrs. Daly, you are all mine now." Cooper swooped Cora off her feet and kicked open the door, carrying her over the threshold of the home they would now share together. With another kick, it slammed shut as they disappeared into the bedroom.

"How did you know the preacher would be in town?" she wondered aloud.

He let out a laugh, imagining her anxiety and hesitance. He knew how old women talked about sex. To most of them, it was an unpleasant chore, something he would make sure she never considered it. "I gathered him myself and brought him here. I knew it would take a week to retrieve the rings and gather the only preacher who I knew to be nearby."

Placing a knee on the bed, he gently eased her onto the mattress and toed off his boots to take his place next to her. "Any other questions?" His gaze never left her as he settled and rolled her to face him. Ever so gently, his lips brushed hers. "Questions before we make this little cabin ours and begin a family?"

"We'll need to keep the family small for the room," she observed.

"We have plenty of room." He claimed her lips again, pulling her flush against him, his fingers nimbly working the tiny buttons behind her. "Remember the house on the hill you have imagined being filled with tragedy? We will be replacing that tragedy with love." His eyes radiated the desire burning in him as he locked gazes with her. "And fill it with kids. I'm the little boy you heard of. I own that."

A laugh bubbled up from her in a confusing reaction to the news he had been reluctant to share.

"Does that give you a different perspective of me?" he gently prodded.

"I think it's an honorable past." Her eyes assured him, reflecting her words.

"Most consider me an outlaw and murderer for it."

"Then we must share the same twisted hearts, because I believe it's the most romantic story of family love."

"Honeybee, I knew you were perfect for me." His lips crashed onto hers, demanding as never before. Maneuvering the lace sleeves from her arms and bringing the satin bodice lower, her eager responses to his exploring touches surprised and aroused him more than he thought possible. In a matter of minutes, the dress laid piled on the floor, forgotten along with her undergarments, soon followed by his clothing. Each moan and slight gasp of pleasure that escaped her fanned the fire raging in him. Their bodies pressed together, finally succumbing to the passion that filled each of them and brought a new level of ecstasy neither had known.

And as the fading sun kissed the windowpane, a good night gave way to the darkness… a darkness filled with new beginnings.

THE END

If you enjoyed Jewelz's journey into the past, you can read more in her collection of historical western romance short stories releasing this fall. Be sure not to miss a release by subscribing to her newsletter at: https://mailchi.mp/c863678df1cb/jewelzjournal.

ABOUT THE AUTHOR
JEWELZ BAXTER

Jewelz Baxter writes MC romance. Her stories may take you on an emotional ride, but be assured she strives to leave you satisfied with the happy ending you desire when you close the book.

Jewelz loves spending time on the road with her husband. Many stories and characters have been born while exploring the backroads on their Harley. When not writing or riding, she can be found spending time with her grandchildren.

Jewelz would love to hear from you.
e-mail: authorjewelzbaxter@gmail.com
FB: Author Jewelz Baxter
FB Reader Group: Jewelz Baxter's Babes
Instagram @authorjewelzbaxter
Website: www.authorjewelzbaxter.com

Cam's Strawberry Moon
A Timber Cove Wolves MC Sample

Cyndi Faria

Cam Smultron crushed on me the minute I walked into the saloon, thinking I'd be his next hit. But he had me all wrong. I wasn't even human. Patrons howled. They always howled in Deadwood. Sexy Cam with the disrespectful hands needed to be taught a lesson. I'll be the woman to put him in his place.

One look at Pepper Ruslor and I'm setting up house, something I can't allow. They called me a drifter. But I'm an ex-Marine whose mistake led to my brother's death. Humor, meaningless flirtations, one-nighters hide my pain. Until *she* walked into the bar. I'll do anything to make her mine.

CHAPTER ONE

Present Day, Deadwood, SD
Pepper Ruslor
Prospect, Timber Cove Wolves MC

So much for my girls' night out. I'd suggested it to my pack the second we rode into Deadwood, South Dakota. It's the first time I've traveled anywhere from the Northern Pacific Coast. Can you blame me for wanting to ditch my older brothers? Maxon Salvador, my half-brother and VP of the Timber Cove Wolves MC calls the shots as Second in Command. It's been his goal to meet up with other packs during the Sturgis Motorcycle Rally, but the first stop is in Deadwood. After my fascination with the televised series, I couldn't come this far without checking out the sights. I thought I'd convince the women to break off from their mates and scout the nightlife, but Maxon wants us to stick together while enjoying the music inside Saloon No. 10. The wives agreed. Well, except for Eve. She's our youngest prospect member who turned twenty-one last week and, like me, isn't mated.

Eve wears jeans and a crop top, showing off her midsection. At least that which isn't covered by her cut. She's long-haired and even longer legged, with black hair and rich brown eyes. She scopes out a group of human males poking balls with their sticks at the pool table, her mouth gaping. "Look at all those silver belt buckles and Stetsons. I'd look good on a cowboy, don't you think?"

She clicks her tongue to the roof of her mouth as if pack law would allow such a coupling. I mean, it's possible to turn a human by biting them. But I've never seen it done. Rumor is most humans beg for death after they've been turned because it's so painful. There's no escaping the full moon and the change month after month. It would take a warrior's strength to survive the bone-cracking metamorphosis. In my book, I wouldn't want another's pain or regret on my hands.

But maybe it's the taboo that appeals to her. We're not much different. If I were looking. Which I'm not. Ok, I do steal a glance when I spot one of the men looking our way. But he's as human as the rest, older than me by half-a-decade by the look of him. I can smell the hint of his sandalwood cologne if I focus.

He winks in my direction.

I spin in my seat, facing forward. If I want that upper position with the pack, I have to follow the rules, even if I don't like them. I must continue to prove to Maxon that I put the pack first above all else, including my libido. Besides, a human can't give me what I really want. But I could use the practice… And those cowboys whooping it up, as if they're more bad-ass than a pack of shifters, could do me good.

They're a distraction. He's a human. Find a shifter to imprint on. Lots to choose from tomorrow…

"He's looking at you too." Eve nudges my shoulder with hers. "You'll know when the right one comes along if you listen to your heart."

My heart doesn't have a say. She can't until I lock in my position. "I don't need anyone standing in my way of securing my position as Secretary for the MC."

"Secretary? You're more important than a notetaker. Maxon obviously trusts you wholeheartedly. I think the tail gunman position suits you. You were amazing, and I felt safe riding with my back turned to traffic knowing you were keeping watch."

Maybe Eve is right, and I am reaching for a position that doesn't suit me. I don't know much about the secretary position other than it involves taking notes. I've kept a journal for as long as I can remember, but that's not exactly record keeping. Maybe Maxon has other plans for me. He put me in the rear of the pack, telling me he trusted me to have his back as a tail gunman, from California to here.

Glass shatters.

I nearly jump out of my seat, stretching my arms out and putting the pack behind me as I scope out the waitress who's bent over, cursing out her cracked bottles of beer. Naomi swears behind me, having toppled her drink. "Everyone okay?"

"We're fine," Naomi sings, tugging me back into my

seat. "Nothing a few napkins won't fix. Are you okay?"

"Good. Just jumpy." I pat my chest.

Maxon cups my shoulder before retaking his seat across from me. We're both protective of our family. It's just our way.

I wonder if Maxon is checking me out as the first female to score a top position, since our father was an Alpha of the Silver Bend Pack. Mostly, except when some A-hole tried to cut off the last few riders on our way here, I made sure the pack stayed corralled. Not one member complained. Unless you count Kayla—my brother Tavin's very pregnant wife—worrying about her water breaking, which it didn't.

She checks me, both of us learning the ropes as new members. Both of us are hesitant about leaving home when I'm about to come into my needing time. Maybe that's why I'm so on edge tonight. I've never wandered far from Timber Cove or Silver Bend. I've always worried about Tavin getting himself into trouble. But he's a changed man after imprinting and marrying Kayla. Who knew?

The sexy winking cowboy strolls past me, giving me a sideways glance.

Before I can acknowledge the look, Maxon knocks my chair legs with his boots.

"Don't bother with those rowdy humans," he grumbles. "Deadwood, as well as Sturgis, is full of other packs, not all of them rivals. You need to find a mate since you haven't imprinted on anyone back home. You have only a year left to fall pregnant."

I stiffen against a shiver and the reminder that if I don't break the curse that affects all she-wolves, I won't live to see myself sitting in the secretary position. "Excuse me for a moment."

I scout the bar, booths, and stage as I make my way to the bar, the cowboy having returned to his seat and not a wolf-shifter in sight, unless you count my pack. In fact, I haven't seen one shifter here that meets my qualifications. He'd have to be handsome, brave, a master at fighting, if needed, trustworthy, kind, compassionate, and want a child. The sooner the better. I grab several napkins to replace the ones Naomi used. I retake my seat, handing napkins to her. "Did you bring me along so I could find a mate, which has little to do with pack business?"

Naomi, Maxon's wife, pats my hand as she is sitting beside me, across from her husband. "I know you thought we'd stay behind in the hotel, and we don't want to be a buzzkill, but it wouldn't hurt to leave your options open. Your future mate could walk through the doors any moment. We're here to vet him ASAP."

Naomi is always the diplomat. She's also a fighter, strong and brave. She looks out for the pack as the female alpha. She left her pack–my old pack–and crossed rival lines to meet Maxon and saved our lives by proving virile males were out there. Apparently, I just need to find my match.

I don't want to seem scared, but maybe I am. I don't want to pick the wrong person and disappoint my Alpha. But maybe he's brought me along to observe me in action.

You know, in a pack family kind of way. "You're right. I agreed to mix business with pleasure, one big happy pack family."

Which I'll never do again. It's like having your parents on a date, only worse because Maxon is the VP, my Alpha, and in charge. He's tall, muscular, with a defiant edge. He exudes danger, and his wolf is alert in case he's called into action.

"I'm serious about you finding someone soon. I don't want to lose you," Maxon confirms.

I get his concern. But what kind of man is brave enough, or stupid enough, to hit on me with Maxon around?

I lean back in my chair, frustrated.

The microphone strikes up.

The twang of the steel guitar and nasal tones of the lead singer blaring out of the speakers positioned behind me sets my teeth on edge. The bar might as well hand out dog whistles as party favors, this dude is just that obnoxious.

I hope the business Maxon wants to discuss is worth it because the struggle to scrape any pleasure out of the evening is real.

I reach across the table and snag a handful of boiled peanuts out of the bowl. "Who picked the front-row seats?"

"It was the only table left." Naomi closes her fist, crunching the shell in her hand, and extracts the peanuts from inside before tossing the husks on the floor.

I cover my ears for a beat. "I'm beginning to understand why."

Naomi is as pretty as her twin sister Alina. Both are fair skinned with straight, onyx hair that falls mid-back. Both are moms, survivors of the curse. I'm lucky to have known them all my life and to have watched them find and fight to be with their mates.

I shift my gaze to Maxon whose brows are pinched together as he stares at the bowl of peanuts, the salty-dust and bits cluttering the table. I lift my glass. "I need a refill. Anyone else?"

Maxon must not hear me because Naomi elbows him in the ribs before she tips her beer back and drains the longneck bottle dry in one pull.

Maxon holds up two uncracked peanuts and pretends to stuff them into his ears. "You think if I cram these in my ears it will help muffle the sound?"

A giggle escapes me. I lean across the table and pull the bowl away from him. "Oh no, I don't think so, buddy. The two of you picked this tourist bar open mic night. You're going to sit here and suffer like the rest of us."

"Damn, Pepper. I would have shared." Maxon slams back his shot of tequila, sets the glass upside down on the table, and chugs his beer chaser. "Peanut earplugs. The next late-night TV infomercial sensation. Patent pending."

"Lawsuits too." Naomi slaps her hand on the table, laughing at her own snide remark.

This is what I want in a relationship. Two people finishing each other's sentences, laughing at their shared jokes, one the entertainment, one the cheerleader. I don't dare think of the consequences if I don't find a mate in the next year.

Naomi eyes me as she pulls a couple of twenties from inside her bra.

I've seen more than the near nip slip mid cash grab. Naked is nothing new for a werewolf. Good thing too, because otherwise the way her glossy pink lips part in a mischievous smile would make things awkward.

"I buy, you fly?" The bills swish against one another as she rubs them between her fingers.

"I've got this one." Eve swoops back in from her trip to the bathroom and snatches the twenties.

She's so quick, I barely see the unhuman flash of her hand. It seems that I'm not the only person eager to put some distance between themselves and the singer.

"Need a hand?" I clamp my hands around the edge of the table and start to push to my feet when she gives me a pat on the shoulder and her assurances that she can handle it.

"Nice try." Naomi crushes another shell in her hand and pops the peanuts into her mouth. "But you have to be quicker around that one or she'll outwit and out maneuver you."

Eve's one of the fastest runners in the pack. She's also part of the reason we're experiencing permanent hearing loss from some local yokel's painful rendition of Garth Brooks' "Friends in Low Places," as she recommended the saloon to Maxon, promising a one-of-a-kind experience.

She's loyal, hard-working, and puts the pack above everything else. She reminds me a lot of myself. Which is why I nominated her for the scout position.

Kayla's well into her third trimester and in desperate need of an assignment later down the line. She's a RN and helps with our pack if anyone incurs injuries. But she's also one full moon away from delivering babies in the middle of her watch. We need to find her replacement.

The sooner the better.

And despite Eve's poor taste in bars, she is the best candidate for the medic position as she's quick to think and act in tense situations.

"So, what do you think?" I lean back in my seat and prop my feet up on one of the table rungs under our six-seater table.

"About Eve?" Maxon scratches his fingers through his beard, watching her place her order at the bar.

I jam my thumb in the direction of the stage and the so-called country singers. "Well, I'm sure as hell not asking for a Billboard review. Is there an extended version of this song that I'm not aware of?"

"For his sake, I hope not." Maxon's jaw twitches as he grinds his teeth together. "Let's chat about Eve. You have medical experience. You've patched up your brother more times than I can count. Are you going to show Eve the ropes?"

Maxon isn't questioning whether I would step up to the plate and train Eve for the position. He knows better. He knows I want the best for the pack. It doesn't matter what the job is. If it needs doing, I get it done. Or I can train just about anyone.

What he wants to know is whether I think Eve is ready

for the added responsibilities when she's just coming into her needing period and still a bit aloof. To be a medic is selfless. She'll have to drop everything and focus on the emergency at hand.

I cross my arms over my chest. "If you think she needs training, yeah. I wouldn't have recommended her if I wasn't willing to teach her what I know."

"But you don't think she needs it." Maxon mimics my pose, shaking the table as he props his legs on the table brace. "Okay. I still say she's too young, but I trust your judgment, Pepper. I have since the first time we met."

I'm counting on his trust—Naomi's. If I can prove myself with the lower prospects, I might just score that secretary position after all.

But Kayla's mating and successful pregnancy is a painful reminder that I'm staring down the wrong end of my twenty-sixth cycle. The odds of surviving my twenty-seventh drop significantly without a mate.

Without a pregnancy, I'm as good as dead.

I haven't had much luck in the mate department. Not for a lack of trying. I just seem to attract the wrong guys. Or maybe *I'm* attracted to the wrong guys.

Either way, I'm starting to think I'm not relationship material.

And not being in a relationship is a serious problem for women of a certain age in our pack.

Twenty-seven is far from old. Werewolves live a long time, but it's a make-or-break moon cycle for mating and falling pregnant. Which is something I'm not sure I even want anymore.

But it's not just up to me. My wolf has a say in the matter.

My love-them-and-leave-them approach to relationships works for me. My wolf? Not so much. She doesn't want to risk dying. She wants to find her forever mate. She wants to make babies and be a mother. And the closer we get to the twenty-seventh cycle, the more vocal she is about it.

I'm taking her suggestions under advisement. I have a full year until my time's up.

But if I decide to take a mate and things go wrong—which judging by my track record with men, it is highly probable they will—Eve will be up for yet another promotion, and I might not be around to see her succeed because I'll be dead.

I shake my head at my inescapable predicament. "Eve's younger than me and needs training. I appreciate your vote of confidence in me. What about you, Naomi?"

"If you're willing to train Eve, she's got my vote too." Naomi groans when the band fires up for another song, making their way down Garth Brook's list of greatest hits. "A vote I'm going to repeal if she doesn't hurry back with my beer."

"Alcohol won't drown your sorrows or that godawful sound." I eye the boiled peanuts in front of me and pluck two from the bowl, considering shoving them in my ear canals. "Patent pending, huh?"

Maxon clears his throat and starts spinning an earplug pitch that would make any used car salesman proud, sending me and Naomi into a fit of laughter. He's the owner of a motorcycle shop, so he's a master of persuasion when he wants to be. I'm still wiping the tears from my eyes when Eve returns balancing a tray loaded with our drinks on one hand.

"What did I miss?" Eve sets the round of beers on the table, followed by four shots of tequila, lime wedges, and a refill of peanuts before sliding the plastic serving tray on a nearby table.

Naomi snickers as she reaches for her beer. "Maxon's impersonation of an infomercial host, selling 'high-end' earplugs. All he's missing is the argyle sweater vest."

Eve grabs the saltshaker and proceeds to lick, shoot, and suck, placing the rind in the empty glass. "Damn, why do I always miss the good stuff? It might be the tequila talking, but I have to say, what this place lacks in entertainment it more than makes up for in atmosphere."

I cast a backward glance over my shoulder and track her gaze to the group of guys amid a now heated game of pool. They're her age, fresh off the farm with their plaid shirts, tight jeans, cowboy boots, and Stetsons. Except for one…

"Why do you think I'm sitting in this seat? The view is spectacular." Naomi's ruby-red lips part in a grin that shows a hint of her canine teeth.

I don't get the lure. Well, not exactly. I have to wonder if my mating link is broken. Maybe if I picture myself flirting with the older cowboy who stalks his shot, lines up, and only shoots when he's sure. Grumbling about being a few minutes late and stuck within the booth with my back to the pool tables, I nudge Maxon's boot and plead to swap places. "Maxon, switch seats with me."

Maxon knits his brows together as he zeros his gaze on the humans. "Damn, are you all like this every time you go out together?"

I toss up my hands defensively. "I warned you I wanted a ladies' night out. Please, don't even pretend like you aren't drooling over every bitch you see when you're out with the guys. Don't like listening to the ladies ogle the fine specimens on display? Maybe keep that in mind the next time you go out drinking."

Naomi raises her hand for a hive-five and slaps her palm against Eve's.

I jut my bottom lip out in a perfect pout. "I'm not high-fiving anything until someone switches places with me."

"Turn that frown upside down." Maxon slides the salt, limes, and my shot glass closer to me. "You aren't missing much. Besides, those boys are as human as humans can be."

"Forbidden fruit." Naomi picks up a lime wedge and runs her tongue along the rind, trying to get a rise out of Maxon.

Which, of course, works like a charm.

But I'm not ignorant to what they've pointed out, even if my wolf stretches and lifts her head, curious. Because what if... What if I'm looking for a mate in the wrong place with the wrong species?

Maxon's nostrils flare and his rich forest-colored eyes shift to an amber hue as his pupils dilate. "It's not forbidden. It comes with great risks and responsibilities not many are willing to facilitate. You turn someone, he could go mad. I don't want that for you, but I do think you'd be woman enough to handle turning the right individual. He'd have to want it. He'd have to be sure. If ever a human like that exists and you find him, you're more than welcome to bring it up for negotiation at the next pack meeting if you come across a male worth turning."

My wolf shifts, adding a protective and somewhat repulsed growl. She's as cautious but as tempted as I am to have a taste at the older cowboy. But dating a human is like playing with fire. You're bound to get burned eventually. I don't have time to get burned. I have a year to find a mate. The thought of turning the cowboy roils the peanuts and alcohol in my belly. How could I sentence a non-shifter to eternal monthly pain? What if he regretted his decision and hated me? What if he left me mateless?

What if he's The One sent to save your life, if you turned him? What if he's real?

My wolf begs me to twist in my seat and sneak another look. I'm not sure why I find him so attractive. He could take one look at me and run if he finds out what I am.

He's not running. He's been looking at you all night.

The pack hasn't gone mainstream. I'm not sure if we ever will, even though being a shifter is accepted and protected by new laws. It's just not our way. We prefer the dense forests of the Northern California Coast. Spending too much time with humans risks exposure the Timber Cove Pack keeps in check. Mating with one of us? That's a threat of a whole other kind.

No Alpha in his right mind would approve a pairing that would jeopardize the bloodlines and weaken the pack. And as an Alpha's daughter, I'm the last of my bloodline, me and Tavin.

With Maxon's wolf close to the surface and his protective instincts in hyperdrive, it's time to change the subject.

Unfortunately for me—and quite possibly every other person in the bar—it appears one of the pool players has other plans.

The brim of his hat is pulled low, hiding his eyes from view, but from the strong line of his jaw and the angle of his nose, I can tell he's ruggedly handsome. The crooked smile he's wearing suggests he's also going to be trouble.

Heat pools low in my belly and my wolf sits pretty, as if showing off her peppered fur.

Too bad he isn't a wolf-shifter like me. Because he'd be exactly the kind of trouble I'd be looking for.

I'm known for keeping my cool and playing my cards close to the vest. It's why Maxon and Naomi trust me as a tail gunman. I have their backs. They can count on me to keep the pack safe when on our runs. Like the run we're on now, Timber Cove to Deadwood to Sturgis. My loyalty and pride are why I continue to rise in the ranks of our pack.

But there's something about this guy that keeps glancing my way. I can't quite put my finger on it. Whatever it is, it's got me hot, bothered, and ready to make some bad decisions.

Which is why I plan on sending him packing if he dares head my way.

Chapter Two

Cam Smultron

The bar is hopping for a Thursday night. Open mic night might be good for business but it's hell on my eardrums. After another long day harvesting a bumper wheat crop, all I'm interested in is knocking a few cold ones back with the boys.

And maybe taking a few of their hard-earned dollars at the pool table.

The music drowns out the crack of the cue ball as I break the racked resin balls, scattering them across the bright green felt. The three-ball drops into a side pocket, leaving two money balls on the table. With a clear shot on the six and nine, I'm about to run with this game and the stack of bills sitting on the edge of the pool table.

I line up my shot, stretch across the table to sink another ball along with any hope Haden has of winning, and that's when I see her looking my way.

She exudes confidence and grace in those skinny jeans

that hug her ass. It's not only her strawberry hair, or freckles that dapple her cheeks and nose, giving her a natural look that has me gaping. It's the way she carries herself and that self-worth has me considering my own.

I tip back my hat to the single most attractive woman I've ever seen in my life. She's a natural beauty. No makeup required. Seems we can't help but swap stares every couple of minutes.

She strolls to the bar and back with an air of confidence that says she's well aware of the curves of her body and the effect they have on men. Myself included. She's definitely not a local. I've never seen her before.

With a face like that, I'd damn right remember.

Long waves of hair cascade down past her shoulders in a shade that reminds me of wheat fields under a full strawberry moon. I can't help but wonder what that luscious mane would look like splashed across my pillow with her underneath me.

I don't know who she is or where she came from. Two things I plan on rectifying before the night is out.

My confidence slips when I see a guy give her his seat at the table in front of the stage. *Boyfriend?* It's too early to say, but the kick-ass look in his eyes puts a crimp in any plans I have for how the rest of my night is going to go.

If I learned anything from my time in the military, it was patience. I decide to take it slow and see how things play out with the guy at her table.

I pull my gaze away from the beautiful woman and back to the game in time to watch the cue ball chase the six into the corner pocket. Haden retrieves it from the other end of the table, sets up his ball in hand, and runs it on the table.

Which is fine by me. The stack of twenties on the ledge isn't the prize I'm after. Not anymore.

There's an empty barstool next to the rack of pool sticks fastened on the wall to the left of the pool table that offers a clear view of the sexy stranger. I claim the seat, ignoring Haden's nudge of the cue ball before he takes his shot.

I'm not one to let a cheater prosper, but I can't seem to take my eyes off this woman. The more time Haden spends taking shots, the more time there is for me to enjoy the view.

I let Haden win the game, along with the rights to defend the table and the cash prize before grabbing a refill at the bar. Weaving through the tables, I alter my route enough to put me within earshot of the alluring stranger and the group she's drinking with.

Or what would have been earshot if not for the Cattle Men's lead singer Jason's ear-piercing attempt to cover a modern-day country music classic.

Despite the off-pitch and off-tempo performance, I've got a little pep in my step and my hopes are on the rise.

Upon closer inspection, everyone at her table is squarely in the friend zone. Guys know when another guy is interested in a woman.

And this guy isn't interested.

Looks like he has his sights set on one of the women

in their party seated beside him, now that he's traded seats. I want to make my move, but my tongue is tied in more knots than my stomach. Lucky for me they're serving liquid courage by the shot glass. Besides, it seems like they're in the middle of a conversation that doesn't need interrupting.

The night is young. There's still plenty of time for introductions.

"What can I get you?" Mike, the bartender of the best bar within a fifty-mile radius of the farm I live and work on, is wiping out a glass beer mug with something that once passed for a dishrag.

"Double shot of whiskey." I set my empty bottle on the bar top.

"She's out of your league, Cam." Mike places a shot glass in front of me and fills it to the top with whiskey. "And I mean by a lot."

"Thanks for the vote of confidence." I raise the glass in a mock toast, slam the shot back, and tap the empty glass on the counter. "Hit me."

"I would if I thought it would knock some sense into you." Mike's party-keg belly shakes with laughter at my expense. "When she's through with you, come on back and I'll buy you a drink to ease the pain while you lick your wounds."

Mike shoves iced water toward me, as if I need to sober up. I've had a few beers. A shot or two over the past few hours. I may be buzzed, but I'm not blasted. I down the water and slide the empty glass toward him. "Damn, Mike, that's harsh. What's next, coffee and stroll around the parking lot?"

"Real funny, kid. But seriously, I need you to see this one with clear eyes. She's not your type." Mike uses the underside of the bar to pop the top of my beer chaser before handing it to me. "Word of advice, don't be yourself."

I pull back, insulted. I'm measured, focused, and master at any assignment, whether playing pool or driving a Farmall. What's so wrong with me to earn me his suggestion? I cast a glance back at the mystery woman's table before giving Mike my attention again. "What in Sam Hill is that supposed to mean? I'm a hard-working man just trying to earn a dollar."

"That right there is what I'm talking about." Mike tosses the dingy dishrag on the bar. "I raised three daughters. I've seen my share of hayseeds like you. You're used to the farmers' daughters fawning all over you while you're shirtless on the tractor. Nothing but working, drinking, and fucking. Nothing but a walk-a-way Charlie. But that one there? She isn't from around here, and she'll give you a run for your money. Mark my words."

I peek over my shoulder, rolling around all the labels Mike glued on me. Am I really that guy? Could I be more than a guy who hides his past behind shallow relationships? She's still sitting, chatting. Still as alluring as the moment she walked in the bar. In this tourist town, I thought I'd found everything I needed. But I wouldn't say I'm happy. Maybe Deadwood still has that cherry-on-the-top to offer me. Or maybe I need to stop waiting for something better to fall in my lap and go after what I want. "There was a time when I wasn't from around here either. Well, mark *my* words. Me and that beautiful blonde will be walking out of this bar together."

With a tip of my beer, I slide off the stool and head back over to the pool tables to win some of my money back.

"You just proved my point," Mike hollers after me.

He's wrong about me, but there's no sense in arguing with the stubborn old man.

Just because I come in here a couple of nights a week to toss a few back and blow off some steam with these so-called "hayseeds" doesn't mean I'm anything like them.

If I were, I'd be charging Mr. and Mrs. Jenkins twice what they're paying me to work the farm, and I'd have taken their divorcee granddaughter up on any one of her numerous offers to *give her a hand* in the hayloft.

The Jenkins are good people. They've got a good family and they welcomed me into it despite my unwavering efforts to keep to myself. I'm not taking advantage of them or their granddaughter.

My mother and the military raised me right. Only trouble is, that beautiful lady across the room has me thinking all kinds of wrong.

"You're up. Rack 'em," Jimmy calls out before tossing the pool rack toward me.

"What?" I dodge to the right in time to avoid being beamed in the head with the plastic triangle.

"Hell, Cam. You're supposed to catch it." Jimmy's laughing as he walks around the table to grab the small cube of blue chalk. "Are you going to stare at her all night or are you going to man up and go over there? What do you think, boys? I say he chickens out."

I've been called out in front of God and everybody. "Damn. Take it easy…"

Only Jimmy is right. Either I go talk to her or listen to their horseshit for the rest of the night. Jimmy's challenge is just the kick in the pants I need.

I'm not one to stumble or stutter around the ladies. Quite the opposite, in fact. There are plenty of notches in my belt. I can sweet talk my way into the arms of just about any woman. I've had plenty of time to perfect my pitch.

Before, during, and after the Marines.

Mostly after. I'm good at finding solace one night at a time.

But this one?

She's different from the string of small-town girls and one-night stands that led me to Deadwood, South Dakota.

Back in Spec Ops, I was the wild one. In it for the thrill of the hunt. No mission was too dangerous. I loved the rush. Until one mistake, one rash decision cost my brother his life. I walked away from everything. Turned my back on my family—blood and military alike.

I'm not that guy anymore. Not for a long time.

But damn if she doesn't have my blood pumping. My heart is pounding against my ribs and I'm running high on the rush of adrenaline. The closer I get to her, the more I'm reminded of the man I used to be.

I'm not sure if that's a good thing or a bad thing. Guess there's only one way to find out.

The sounds of hooting, hollering, and even a couple of

whistles follows me as I make my way across the bar to her table.

"Excuse me, ma'am." I sidle up to the table and rest my hand on the back of one of the empty chairs. "Is this seat taken?"

"No." She angles her head to one side and sizes me up with a glance of sapphire eyes.

Damn soul-piercing eyes that lock onto mine. "Well, then mind if I—"

"I do, actually." She hooks her foot around the leg of the chair and pulls it under the table.

I wouldn't be surprised if the woman spit ice cubes with the arctic chill in her voice, but I can see the fire raging behind her glare, telling me this is her flirty game.

Something tells me she's worth the risk of getting burned.

"This isn't a lame attempt at a pickup line. Trust me, I've got better moves than that." I jam my thumb over my shoulder in the direction of the pool tables. "We've got more people than chairs over there, and seeing as how you're not using this one…"

A hint of a blush warms her cheeks as she shoves the chair back out from under the table.

"Thank you kindly." I tip my hat and flash my signature crooked grin, enjoying the silver dollar-eyed looks of surprise on the faces of her and her friends as I lean the chair back on its hind legs.

I make a show of dragging the chair back to the far side of the bar and the rowdy group of farmhands who are just waiting to bust my chops over the apparent failure.

But quitters never prosper, and I'm not throwing in the towel just yet.

"All part of the plan, fellas," I reassure them as I settle into the seat with the scent of her perfume still permeating my senses. "Wait and see."

"Whatever. A snowball's got a better chance in hell than you do with her. You blew it. Just admit it."

Jimmy's bellowing laugh sticks in my craw, but I decide to let it slide. Guys like him aren't worth the overnight stint in the sheriff's holding cell. Which is a lesson I learned the hard way before landing in Deadwood.

The best way to knock that shit-eating grin off his face is by walking out of here with a beautiful woman on my arm.

Something I intend to do before the night is out.

I'm two shots away from winning my money back in another game of nine ball and strategizing my next move when an opportunity presents itself.

Out of my peripheral, I catch a glimpse of her making her way toward the bar. She seems oblivious to the men salivating over the sway of her hips as she weaves in and out of the tables that intersect her path.

Or maybe she doesn't care. I'm more than willing to bet the twenties stacked on the rail of the pool table it's the latter.

After sinking the eight and nine balls, I collect my winnings and prepare to make my move. I snatch the pile of cash and wave the bills in the air. "I got the next round, boys."

I set my sights on the blonde spitfire at the bar and take my place beside her.

She waits for Mike to finish pouring a draft while doing her best to ignore my existence.

As much as I hate to admit it, Mike's right. At least about one thing. I've gotten used to women falling all over me. A few drinks, a few laughs are usually all it takes. It's been a long time since I've had to work this hard to get a woman to pay me the slightest bit of attention.

But I'm up for the challenge.

Chapter Three

Pepper

"Another round of beers for me and the boys. And whatever she and her friends are having."

The cowboy calls out to the bartender before I can even open my mouth to place my order. I give him the cold shoulder and wave the barkeep over. "Thanks, but no thanks. Another round."

"I insist." He sets the cash down on top of the bar. "For the misunderstanding earlier."

I cock my hip to one side and lean against the bar. Is this how human men play the mating game? Yet, I have been checking him out. So maybe I need to see this through, just for the hell of it. Maybe show Maxon that I can take care of myself. "Oh, I think I understood you just fine. This good ol' boy routine might work with these small-town girls and horny, tipsy tourists, but I'm not falling for it."

"I think I'm the one that's falling, darlin'." He slides

the stack of bills across the polished wooden surface of the bar toward the bartender. "Drinks are on me."

I keep my focus on the bartender and do my best to ignore the relentless cowboy on my right. "Just put it on our tab, if you don't mind."

But damn if that lopsided grin and mischievous glint in his eyes isn't piquing my curiosity.

He seems like my type: fun for a night with no strings attached in the morning. Still, he's pouring it on thick. From the crowd in the back of the bar watching him make his move, I'd say there's a little wager going on whether he takes me home tonight.

For some reason, I just can't bring myself to give him the satisfaction of winning. No matter how satisfied I might be come morning.

Maybe it's the fact that he's human when I've never been with one.

Or maybe I'm just having too much fun knocking him down a peg in front of all his friends.

Either way, I'm sending him home. Alone.

"Wow." He tucks in his chin and shakes his head before reaching over and encircling my wrist in his hand. "I don't know who hurt you, but please, don't take it out on the rest of us."

I flick my gaze down to my wrist and back up to meet a pair of eyes that are a shade of blue so deep and rich they remind me of the Pacific Ocean adjacent to Timber Cove. But what he doesn't know is that I'm conflicted about him manhandling me. My wolf wants more. Me? Maybe I want to be the dominating force. "You're the one that's going to be hurting if you don't move your hand back where it belongs."

Everything about him is easy on the eyes. From his muscled physique, no doubt hardened from manual labor on a nearby farm, to his strong jaw and suntanned complexion. It's no wonder he comes off as confident. If I had to guess, I bet the women in Deadwood fawn all over him.

And from the side-eyed glares cast in my direction, it seems the local ladies are none too pleased he's got his sights set on me tonight.

They shouldn't worry their pretty little heads over it. I have no doubt he'll take one home to lick his wounds, and all that makeup and hairspray they've plastered on won't go to waste.

Out of the corner of my eye I catch Maxon moving. He's up out of his seat and ready to defend my honor. Which has nothing to do with whether I actually *need* help and everything to do with his Alpha tendencies being triggered.

Women in a pack are equal to the men in everything. Roles and responsibilities are interchangeable. Alpha and beta alike.

Except for one thing.

Our biological clock. Metaphorically and literally speaking. While the men enjoy living well into their silver years, our days are numbered.

Unless, of course, we procreate.

As archaic and twisted as the law sounds, it elevates women in the pack and in some instances makes us virtually untouchable.

The fastest way for an outsider to get their ass kicked is by disrespecting a woman in a pack. It's a coin toss on who gets to do the kicking—the guys or the woman in question.

In the cowboy's case, that'd be me.

With nothing more than a slight shake of my head, I let my friend know I've got this.

Maxon takes my cue. He stands down but doesn't sit. Naomi and Eve stand on either side, sandwiching him in the middle. Both are just as ready to square off as Maxon.

One wrong move from me or the country bumpkin with his hand wrapped around my wrist and Saloon No. 10 will go off like a powder keg.

I've got this whole itinerary for this trip. I planned it out weeks ago, and a bar fight with a bunch of farmers is definitely not on my list of things to do in Deadwood.

I lower my gaze to my wrist again.

He unfurls his fingers, but just when I think he's letting go, he switches his hold from my wrist to my hand and brings it up to his lips.

"I'm sorry, darlin'." His mouth curves into that damned crooked grin as he breaks the kiss and peels his lips back from the back of my hand.

"You're sorry all right," I manage to say through gritted teeth while jerking my right hand out of his grip, which instinctively curls into a fist to match my left.

I'm torn between punching him in the mouth or grabbing him by the shirt collar and pulling him in for a kiss. The odds of either option working as a method for shutting him up are pretty low.

Persistent son of a bitch.

If he was a wolf, I'd have put him in his place by now—flat on his back with me on top. Unfortunately for the both of us, he isn't.

That's an itch I'll have to scratch some other night with some other shifter.

"Forget the drinks." I pull a few bills out of what passes for a pocket in the pair of skinny jeans I'm wearing and set them down on the bar. "That should cover whatever's still on our tab. Keep the change."

I should wait for the cowboy to walk away, but instead I make the mistake of giving him my back. His hand connects with my ass with a smack that echoes around the world. The lingering sting is a promise of tantalizing things to come that sends a rush of heat through my belly and tightens my body with anticipation.

It takes a moment for me to bank the heat in my eyes before rounding on the cowboy to even the score.

I whirl around poised to land a slap of my own, but on a different cheek. My hand is mere inches from connecting with his face when he blocks the blow by catching my arm. He jerks me forward, pulling me against the hard planes of his body.

He's fast. And strong. He tightens his grip on my arm. Not hard enough to bruise, but enough to let me know he's a dominant male—in the bedroom and out of it.

If I didn't know better, I'd swear he's an Alpha.

There's a hint of darkness in his eyes. Not enough to send me running the other way. Quite the opposite, in fact. I'm a sucker for bad boys, and it only serves to pique my curiosity.

Maybe he isn't just another corn-fed cowboy after all.

Mike slams a chunk of a two-by-four against the bar, silencing the band and the patrons. "All right, you two, knock it off. Miss, looks like you and your friends were on your way out. I appreciate your business and hope to see you folks again. Cam, get your ass out of here and back to the farm before I call the sheriff."

"I'll save you the phone call." The cowboy named Cam releases my arm and points to the far end of the bar. "The sheriff is right over there."

The bartender and the sheriff exchange their first names and nod at each other in greeting.

"Need me to walk you out, Cam?" The sheriff swivels around on his barstool, sets one foot down on the floor as if he's preparing to stand, but the look on his face says he's hoping Cam sees himself out.

"I'd hate to put you out any more than I already have, Sheriff." Cam digs into his pocket, pulls out the wad of bills, and counts out a few twenties. "That should cover another round for the guys. Sorry for the trouble, Mike."

Cam's fingers graze my thigh, leaving a trail of fire in their wake as he brushes past me on his way out the door.

"What about you, missy?" The sheriff turns his attention to me, along with every remaining patron in the bar—my pack mates included.

They're ready to blow this joint and avoid drawing any more unwanted attention to us, or worse, our entire pack. Our pack chooses to live under the radar. Trust me, it's better that way.

For weres and humans alike.

I never intended to make a scene, but you know what they say about good intentions. The road to hell is paved with them.

For someone who's supposed to be keeping a low profile and enjoying her vacation, while watching out for my pack, I've done a fine job of making myself the center of attention, and thereby them.

Time to make an exit.

"No thanks, sheriff. Like the fine gentleman behind the bar said, my friends and I were just leaving." I wave Maxon and the girls over.

We don't waste any time getting out of the bar and across the parking lot to the bikes.

"I'll say this for you, Pepper." Maxon gives me a shoulder bump. "It's never a dull night when you're around."

"This is nothing." Eve wedges herself between me and Maxon and drapes her arm around my shoulders. "Girls' night gets pretty wild with Maxon around. We should do this more often."

"Then it wouldn't be girls' night." Naomi tosses Maxon the keys to their bike. "Well, we've outstayed our welcome at Saloon No. 10. Are we hitting another bar or heading back to the hotel?"

"I'm starving." Eve gives her stomach, which is growling loud enough for all of us to hear it, a reassuring pat and pep talk that pancakes are coming. "Naomi cleaned out the snack basket, along with the mini bar, and room service is closed."

I recall when planning our trip that a diner wasn't far from here. I lift my cell, checking the map for directions. "There's a twenty-four-hour diner not far from here. Like two minutes, I think."

"How do you know where everything is?" Eve rubs her rumbling stomach again. "Not that I'm complaining."

"Itinerary." Maxon chuckles at my expense. "Our little travel nerd here planned every second of this trip in minute detail the moment she found out we were coming to Deadwood."

I grab my helmet, reminiscing about my plans to sightsee the old mining town. I recall the series, the cowboys, the danger, the rugged history. Cowboys took risks to cross America to get what they wanted. "Damn right. You know how much I loved that show. I never missed an episode. And the diner is listed on all the brochures in the hotel lobby. You guys go ahead without me. I'm going to head back to my room and lock in plans for tomorrow."

"Come on, you can't quit on us now." Eve pleads with me to join them for a very early breakfast as she mounts her bike. "You can get a western omelet. You know, since we're in the Wild West."

I can't help but smile at her attempt to win me over with eggs and a side of home fries. My belly complains, but it's craving something else besides food. "That's tempting. But I've got a full day planned for tomorrow."

"More sightseeing?" Naomi groans over my early-morning plans. The nightlife and casinos are more her style, she's told me. "What's on the agenda? Abandoned gold mine? Local history museum?"

I'm halfway from shoving the rest of my hair inside the helmet when Naomi's response causes me to stop short. "A little of both actually. But my first stop is Mount Moriah Cemetery."

Naomi's brows pinch together as a look of genuine confusion settles onto her face. "You don't even know anyone from Deadwood. Who could you possibly be paying respect to in a cemetery here?"

It's all I can do not to devolve the conversation into a Discovery Channel documentary of the Wild West celebrity when it appears they don't recognize the name. "Calamity Jane. She's an original badass. Hung out with Wild Bill Hickok. Toured with Buffalo Bill."

"Never heard of her." Eve latches on to Maxon and Naomi, steering them closer to the bikes parked across from me. She shrugs. "But I have butter and maple syrup on the brain."

I laugh. "You're hopeless."

"Hopeful for a taaaaallll stack," Eve shoots back.

I watch them walk to their respective bikes and exchange promises to meet up tomorrow morning in the hotel lobby for the continental breakfast and coffee before I head out to hit the tourist traps.

It isn't until I straddle my bike and turn the engine that I catch the whiff of sandalwood and realize someone's watching me.

Not just anyone.

Cowboy Cam.

Ignore him, Pepper.

I should just kick my bike in gear and drive back to the hotel. I should do a lot of things.

But I turn off the motor, slip off my helmet, letting my hair fall about my shoulders, and dismount instead.

CHAPTER FOUR

Cam

This woman is hotter than hellfire and just as feisty. She may be immune to my charms, but there's no way she'll back down from a fight.

I crack my knuckles playfully. Here we go. I can't believe she's falling for my game—hook, line, and sinker.

She's marching a straight line from the motorcycle that's parked a couple rows behind my truck. "I've got to hand it to you, Cowboy Cam. Your balls are bigger than your belt buckle. Are you stalking me now?"

The motorcycle doesn't surprise me. Nor the pack that she rides with. I can tell when she decides to ride that things may get a little wild. I just hope her night's plans include riding me. Guess ol' Mike implying that I won't change strikes the mark.

But screw it. I want what I want. Right now, that's her. I push myself off the tailgate and drop down onto the ground in front of her. "Stalking implies I'm following you. You haven't gone anywhere. Seeing as how I walked out of the bar first and I'm just sitting here minding my own business until some of the alcohol wears off, maybe I'm the one who should be worried about having a stalker."

"Ha, that's a laugh. Me stalking you? You've been hitting on me all night." She steps forward, closing the small distance between us. "Clearly, you can't take a hint."

"Or maybe I can." I rest my elbows on the tailgate and lean back, taking pleasure in watching her gaze travel the length of my body stretched out before her. "Because here you are."

There's a fire in her eyes. One she's struggling to contain judging by the rise and fall of her breasts as she takes a couple deep breaths back-to-back.

Things could go one of two ways. She'll either hit me or kiss me.

If I was a betting man, and I am, I'd put my money on the latter.

I've been trying my damnedest all night. I'm feeling confident that my rugged looks and good old boy charm have finally won her over. Or it could be my tight-fitting jeans and the way they highlight certain features.

Either way, now that I've got her right where I want her, and she's positioned herself between my legs, I want it to be her decision.

"Goddammit." She wedges herself even farther between my thighs, fists her hand into my shirt, and jerks me to her with a strength and ferocity that hints at things to come.

She claims my mouth with a kiss, snaking her tongue across my bottom lip before giving it a little nip. Her hands find their way down my chest and around my waist as she swings one leg over mine. She's wrapping herself around me like she's climbing a fucking tree, and I'm starting to wonder if we'll make it out of the parking lot.

"Hey." I pull back, catching my breath, and it occurs to me that I still don't know her name. I run the risk of killing the mood, but the things I want to do to this woman are not meant for public view or closed-circuit TV. "This place is older than dirt, but Mike's got cameras. Installed them after a rowdy Sturgis bike run a couple of years ago."

"We can go back to my hotel." Some of the passion drains from her eyes and is replaced by something else.

Hesitation?

Whatever it is, it isn't regret. I've seen that reflected at me in the mirror and yeah, in the eyes of a couple of the women I've been with.

"How far is your place?" She kisses her way up my neck and nibbles on my earlobe.

I have no idea where she's staying, and I slide my hand over her hip and around her backside, cupping her ass and pressing her tighter against my leg. "Closer than your hotel."

"Your place it is." She grinds against my thigh before backing away and walking around to the passenger-side door. "You coming or what?"

She's in the cab of the truck as soon as I hit the unlock button on the remote.

"Not yet, but I'm getting there." After making a quick adjustment in my jeans, pausing for a moment to acknowledge I'm no longer buzzed, but damn focused on my next addiction, I climb in, fire up the truck, and tear out of parking lot in the direction of the two-bedroom house I'm living in while working at the Jenkins' farm.

I've been known to have a lead foot, but the fiery woman buckled into the passenger seat of my truck has me breaking all kinds of land speed records. If one of the sheriff's deputies catches me for speeding, they'll have to follow me to the farm because I'm not slowing down until I hit the gravel driveway leading up to my house.

She tugs at the seatbelt and repositions herself until she's catty-cornered between the seat and the door. "I'm Pepper, by the way."

"Of course, you are," I reply with a wink.

The name suits her personality. The smile my response garners sinks her hooks deeper into my heart. It occurs to me that I may have bitten off more than I can chew with this one.

I'm in trouble with a capital T.

We make it to the farm in half the time it would normally take. The headlights illuminate the small, one-story house. For the first time since I moved in, I find myself wondering if it's good enough.

Not for me.

I always travel light and never settle in one place for too long. The Jenkins farm is the closest thing I've had to a home in a long time. But I want it to be enough for Pepper. *I* want to be enough for her.

And that scares the hell out of me.

"This is yours?" She hops out of the truck before I can walk around and open the passenger door for her.

"Not all of it." I jostle the keys on the ring until I find the right one for the front door. "Not any of it, actually. The Jenkins brought me on to work the farm and fix up the place until they're ready to sell."

Suddenly, I'm all thumbs and fumble with the lock. It's not like me to fumble anything, especially when my dick is involved. Maybe it's the residual alcohol still parked in my veins. Or the fact that I haven't brought anyone here. No reason to with all the hotels in Deadwood, and without really taking a one-night to the next level. Hell, the next day. Or I'm too busy worrying about the fact that I have nothing to offer Pepper and I can't figure out why. I just met the woman tonight and only learned her name moments before.

But that kiss. The way her body feels pressed against mine. I'm beginning to suspect one night with Pepper isn't going to be enough.

Not nearly enough.

She's on me the moment I get the door open, and we're leaving a trail of clothes in our wake as we head to the bedroom. Pepper is even more breathtaking than I could imagine.

And I've got a pretty good imagination.

Pepper's long, strawberry hair swishes across the small of her back as she sashays down the short hall to my bedroom. She casts a backward glance over her bare shoulder and the come-hither look in her eyes is enough to do me in. I have to have her.

Here and now.

I reach for her, catching her by the hip, and ease her back against the wall. I slip off her skinny jeans, revealing a little thong that's more like a floss than a covering. I glide my hand down the smooth expanse of her thigh before I hook her behind the knee and hitch her leg up.

Pepper echoes my groan of pleasure, making quick work of my buckle, zipper, and pants. She wraps her hand around the length of me and guides me to her opening. She encircles my hips with her legs and locks them at the ankles as I bury myself inside her.

But the moment I'm enveloped by her burning heat, I realize how vulnerable I am because I don't want to rush this. I want time to stop when I know that's not how time works.

Damn if I won't make this night together unforgettable. I take her mouth with mine, savoring the taste of her, sweet from the citrus-flavored tequila, salty from the peanuts. Fucking delicious.

Her moan hits the back of my throat, and I think she may eat me alive. But I fucking don't care that she's taking charge, that she's the alpha in our two-some. I feel her tug my hair, rock her body, taking me deeper all on her own, and it's the sexiest thing alive. I'm harder than I've ever been. I'm also noticing the raw sounds she's making pleasuring herself, and that's a fucking turn on that tells me she's allowing herself to be vulnerable with me too.

I hike up her other leg and march to the bedroom, laying her down, both of us still holding on to each other, clinging for dear life. Both of us recognizing that this kind of instant attraction only comes once in a lifetime and neither of us is willing to quit what's happening.

"Harder," she manages between moans and buries her hands in my hair. "Don't hold back."

I groan, the sound coming from a place I don't recognize, deep in my belly. I'm more than happy to oblige her in this and any future request she might make. I just hope I get more than one night. Because connected as we are, I want her here forever. "Whatever you say, darlin'."

I'm a goner. Turns out I'm the one who's falling hook, line, and sinker.

I pick up the pace and the pressure, pounding my body against hers when I feel her tightening around me. She's on the edge and taking me with her. But it's at this moment, where normally I'd close my eyes, that I keep them open to stare down at this beautiful woman, her hair fanned across my pillow where no other woman has laid. "Look at me."

She opens her eyes, the haze of her pending orgasm giving her a drowsy edge. "Your eyes remind me of home…"

I nearly come undone, losing my rhythm. How can she feel like I'm feeling? What are the chances I've met my soulmate? I start to move inside her as I wedge my hand between us, finding her sweet little bud and feeling it bloom under my control. But isn't that a lie? I gave up control the moment I spotted her across the bar. She owns me, and I'm her very willing puppet. I've never wanted to pleasure anyone before myself. Not when I realized how short life is and how quick it can be snuffed out. But her? Pepper? I lose all thoughts of getting off before her. "You're beautiful. Special. Keep looking at me…"

She grips my arms, digging what feels like claws into the back, but the pain only heightens my desire for her. She's pain and pleasure. She's cracking the walls I didn't know existed.

"That's it, right there. Oh God, don't stop." She takes my face between her palms, locking her gaze on mine, and screams my name as she climaxes.

Hearing my name on her lips is sexy as fuck and it rips the best orgasm of my life from me. A climax that locks us together until my suspension above her buckles. I brace my arm against the headboard for added support, panting. "That was…"

"Intense." Pepper's breathing is as ragged as mine. Her hair is dewy around her forehead. "We should do it again."

I brush off the hair sticking to her face, thinking that this girl is just one surprise after the other, and I'm one hundred percent on board. "Can I catch my breath first?"

Her lips on mine are the only response I get.

The seconds it took to get from the hall to my room, to my bed to our first shared climax, are as much a blur as the hours we pass naked in my bed until sunrise. I've explored every inch of her body and it isn't enough.

It will never be enough.

I'm drifting off to sleep when I feel the mattress shift under her weight as she creeps her way to the edge and rolls off.

I rub the sleep from my eyes and throw back the covers. I can't remember the last time someone besides me ran for the hills the morning after. Usually, I'm the one scurrying around in the dark, quiet as a mouse, in search of an errant sock or, on the instances I didn't go commando, my boxers.

I'm not only falling asleep but falling for someone I just met. I don't know anything about her. Well, that's not entirely true. I know how and where she likes to be touched. What drives her wild and makes her scream my name.

Over and over again.

Thank God the Jenkins are both hard of hearing or the sheriff would have been out on the porch banging on my door. "Where are you running off to?"

She freezes briefly before reaching to the floor. Her hair tumbles down like a waterfall before she's back on the edge, sliding on one sock and then another. Nothing on but two socks, where the hell does she think she's going, looking like Lady Godiva? "I really should get back. My friends will worry if I'm not in the hotel lobby by ten."

I climb out of bed, check the clock on the bedside table, and realize ten is hours from now. I grab a pair of sweats draped over the side of the wicker laundry basket against the wall, forgoing underwear. "Were you planning on stealing one of the horses? I'd hate to have to report you to the authorities."

"I was going to call a ride and wait down at the end of the drive." She stands and turns to the mirror above the dresser and finger combs her hair, spinning around when she catches my amused reflection in the mirror. "What? What's so funny."

"You're about as rural as rural gets." I deflect the pillow she tosses at me. "I can't get a pizza delivered out here and you think you're getting an Uber?"

She flops down at the foot of the bed, rummages around, I suspect for her jeans, which are still lying in the hallway. "I've done the walk of shame before, but never a drive. This is embarrassing."

I shake off the dig. It's just like Mike pointed out. She's way out of my league, but I shove doubt away. We shared something special last night. I'm not the only one still feeling vulnerable, only I am the only one not running away from the foreign feelings. I know what I want. I just have to convince Pepper that I'm more than a one-night stand. That I'm worth her time, if she'll give it to me. That I'm a man of substance and honor. "Embarrassing would be explaining to sweet, old Mrs. Jenkins why you're loitering around her mailbox nude, except for the frilly socks."

"That would look bad…" She knots her hair into an impromptu bun, seemingly perfectly comfortable naked, and then returns to the bed, taking a seat on top of the mussed comforter.

I pull the drawstring on the sweatpants tight and loop it into a knot. I can tell she's conflicted, but hell if I know what to do. I've never begged anyone to stay. "Real bad if she shoots you first."

She pivots to look at me, twisting the comforter so it bunches around her thighs. "Mrs. Jenkins would shoot me without a conversation?"

I smirk at what gets done in these parts without a conversation, like fixing a neighbor's fence, or rounding up loose cattle. About her and me last night. "There wasn't much talking between us, and I did a lot of shooting last night."

She giggles, the perfect pitch the complete opposite of the Cattle Men's band last night. I need more of her smile, more of her period. She must be hungry after the workout we made lovemaking. "You like bacon, eggs, sourdough toast, and handpicked peaches?"

She shakes her head, and her shoulders round, as if she's having second thoughts about ditching out on me, or her predicament, rather than objecting to the breakfast menu. "Fresh peaches, you say?"

Hope warms my chest, but I tread carefully. I jab a thumb in the direction of the kitchen. "I picked them yesterday. Sweet and delicious right off the tree in the front yard."

"And coffee?" she asks with a resigned smile.

That warmth in my chest tells me that I'm getting hotter, saying the right things… If only she'll give me a chance, a conversation. "And coffee. All the coffee you want. Let me cook you breakfast."

She pushes off the bed and grabs my shirt off the floor, the one I wore last night, threading it on her little body. She buttons a few buttons, mid-shirt. Looking adorable, she comes to stand in front of me and flashes me an apologetic look. "I've never been one to stay."

My pulse ramps up, thinking this is it. It doesn't matter if she's wearing my clothes as a souvenir. Plenty of women have stolen my shirts. But not her. I can't stomach the thought of watching her walk out that door because she doesn't know how to take the next step. Hell, we're both novices in this department. But if I don't make a move, I'm certain I'll never see her again.

At that thought, my heart cracks, splits wide open. She's the kind of woman I need in my life—fearless and strong. The kind of woman who'll challenge and change me to be a better man. The kind of woman who can get me to stay put. Maybe I can be her reason to stay.

I hold her face, kiss her mouth, and she lets me in.

"I don't know how to do this, but I do like bacon. And I really like you…" she murmurs across my lips.

I've heard bacon makes everything better. I sure hope that goes for a broken heart too. Because damn, if watching her get ready to leave didn't rip a hole into mine, watching her walk out that door will kill me.

I take her hand and lead her to the kitchen, to a new day, to hope for something more, to an uncharted territory for both of us. I want to claim her for my own, but she doesn't seem like the type. I guess I'll have to prove I'm man enough for her until she claims me as hers. But we have time…and I have little doubt that we'll find our forever in each other.

THE END

The story continues with ***Cam's Strawberry Moon***, releasing fall 2022. Subscribe to Cyndi's Newsletter and never miss a release. https://dl.bookfunnel.com/h6jfaiaz77

Ready for more? Start the Timber Cove Wolves MC series with ***Maxon's New Moon*** by visiting Cyndi's website at https://www.cyndifaria.com/timber-cove-wolves-mc

ABOUT THE AUTHOR
CYNDI FARIA

Two-time *USA Today* Bestselling Author Cyndi Faria writes hot, heart-warming paranormal romance about fated mates, werewolves, vampires, shifters, fae, and magic! She also writes sexy contemporary romance. Her stories are well known for their twist-turns you'll never see coming and happily ever after endings you crave.

"Cyndi Faria. 5 STARS!!! Oh my goodness!!! (S)eriously one of the best romances I have read!! No joke. That very first page pulled me into their world. Cyndi painted me a world so amazing that I did not want to leave at all. The action in the book kept me on the edge of my seat and there was never a dull moment. Every page is filled with captivating words that will draw you right in. And talk about twists!! I must have said OH MY GOD more than a couple of times."
~I Love HEA Romance Book Blog

"(Cyndi Faria) has a talent for lovely happy endings and I'm so glad she does."
~Night Owl Reviews

Connect with Cyndi:
JOIN Cyndi's Facebook Readers Group:
Cyndi's Superstars
Website: www.cyndifaria.com
Facebook Author Page:
www.facebook.com/cyndifariaauthor
Instagram: @Cyndi Faria
TikTok: www.tiktok.com/@authorcyndifaria

Silver Lining

A.L. Long

Lainey thought she had done everything right until now. Her life had turned inside out and upside down because of her choice to save the two people who mattered to her the most. Having control over her future was no longer her own, and even though she would never regret helping her parents keep their restaurant, she regretted listening to her college professor. Keeping her promise to marry Spencer Nolan, Lanie loses more than her freedom; she leaves behind a future with the one man who could make her happy.

CHAPTER ONE

Present Day, Deadwood, SD
Lainey Park

I focused on the road before me as my death grip on the steering wheel tightened. It had been raining for hours with no sign of letting up. With the sound of the rain as my only companion, my thoughts drifted back to the mess I left in Minneapolis. When Phillip called me into his office to discuss the chance of a lifetime—as he more than enthusiastically called it—I should have run away. The funny thing was, that was precisely what I was doing. How could I refuse? I found my fiancé, the man who I was forced to pretend to love, having sex with Phillip's secretary, Carla Wentworth. No wonder she wasn't at her desk to greet me. She was screwing the man I was supposed to marry in less than a month, in my boss's office. Spencer Nolan was to be my loving husband, or so I thought. I sacrificed everything for him. *How could I have been so stupid?* There was nothing more degrading than to be treated as second best.

Everyone could hear the loud voices coming through Phillip's office door. Spencer and Phillip were arguing over Phillip's decision to send me to Deadwood, South Dakota, instead of him. Spencer might have been the better journalist, but I knew how to get things done. Phillip finding out that his top journalist was screwing his secretary probably didn't help Spencer's chance of getting the assignment either. A little birdie might have had something to do with that.

I shook my head and peered through the sleet. My once happy life was turned upside down and just like the weather, unpredictable.

I was tired of everyone telling me what I should and shouldn't do or how I should live. It was ironic that *Renegade Magazine* would be my only escape from a life destined to make me unhappy.

Truth be told, everyone deserved to be happy, me included. But anger and betrayal circulated through my bloodstream. Somehow, I was hoping Deadwood would give me the pick-me-up I needed, the happiness I was still searching for.

The rain came down even harder, breaking through my thoughts and switching my focus to the drive ahead. I turned my wipers up as high as they would go, but they couldn't keep up with the sleet pelting my windshield. The smartest thing would be to pull over and wait until the storm quit, but even that was impossible since I could barely see. The last thing I needed was to drive off the two-lane highway and get stuck in a ditch. When I left

Minneapolis this morning, the forecast called for light showers and scattered thunderstorms, none of which would hit the route I took until later tonight. I intentionally left early this morning to miss the forecast altogether. *So much for relying on the weatherman.*

The downpour caused my line of vision to become a complete blur. Without warning, a deer came out of nowhere and crossed in front of my car. Although the moment seemed to last for an eternity and everything was moving in slow motion, only a few seconds passed. My car slid sideways in my effort to miss the doe, and as I spun out of control, my life flashed before my eyes. At that moment, I wished I had hit the four-legged animal rather than swerved to save its life. The deer escaped, but I wasn't as lucky. My car came to a stop with the front end buried in the embankment.

I was jolted back, slamming my head into the headrest. I panted and adrenaline shot through my body. Still holding onto the wheel, my arms trembled with shock and the realization that I could have been killed sunk in. After I caught my breath, I released the wheel and rested my head on the headrest.

Could God have another plan for me? I thought I was going to die. Instead, I'm alive and well. My car, on the other hand, was a different story. It came to a stop, inches from a tall pine tree. It wasn't going anywhere without the help of a tow. I had only two choices: I could stay inside the car, dry, and wait for someone to find me, or I could brave the rain and go for help. Neither one appealed to me, so I grabbed my purse from the passenger seat and searched for my cell. The option of calling anyone for help was a no-go. There was no cell service.

Releasing a defeated breath, I turned on my hazard lights and continued to watch the drops of water come down. In reality, there wasn't anything else I could do but wait for someone to stop and rescue me. My father always told me that if I got into an accident or my car broke down, I should never leave the vehicle to get help, but wait for help to come to me. Then again, my mother had told me always to be careful, be aware of my surroundings, and, more importantly, trust my instincts. I hadn't seen a car for at least an hour. It could be hours before another vehicle came along.

Before pushing the door open and entering the storm, I slung my purse over my shoulder and reached behind the front seat to grab my umbrella. As I opened the door, it was my mother's voice that gave me the courage to exit the car. The stories she told me of princesses and unicorns when I was a little girl came to mind as I made my way up the muddy embankment with only my heels to grip the wet ground. The situation I put myself in was far from the fairyland places my mom's stories took me. This was reality and a fight for survival.

I made it to the road, mud covering my five-inch designer heels. Even though the rain still came down full force, at least I could see if anyone was driving in my direction.

I was only an hour away from Deadwood the last time

SILVER LINING

I looked at my GPS before Bambi ran in front of my car. The wetter I became with no civilization in sight, the more I regretted not stopping at the last town and waiting out the storm.

It seemed like all I did lately was make poor decisions. Even my decision to marry Spencer instead of telling my parents the truth about the real reason behind the marriage was a mistake. I should have never listened to my college professor who convinced me to take Alistair Nolan's offer and marry his son Spencer in exchange for saving my parents' restaurant. I should have seen the writing on the wall when Spencer and I first met. I wasn't the only woman in his romantic sphere. His sexual appetite should have been my first clue that I'd never satisfy his continual cravings. In my defense, I was young, and marrying him seemed like an even trade to save my mom and dad from losing everything they had worked so hard for.

Our wedding would have taken place on September tenth. I had sent all the invitations—my parents spared no expense for the marriage of their little girl. How was I supposed to tell them that the wedding was off? How could I tell them because of me they would lose the restaurant?

Cold and soaked from head to toe, my umbrella proved to be no use as I trudged forward. My feet ached, and every step felt like I was walking on a bed of nails.

The sound of a car coming over the pelting rain against the pavement caught my attention. When I turned around and saw two headlights coming toward me, I thought it was only my imagination.

My heart beat faster as I moved off the asphalt-covered ground to where the shoulder turned to dirt. The last thing I wanted was to get run over. As the vehicle came closer, I prayed as I dropped my umbrella and waved my arms above my head with everything I had.

My knees gave out with an overwhelming sense of gratitude when the truck came to a stop, and a man got out. *There are kind Samaritans still left in this world,* I thought to myself as I tried to remain standing.

"Jesus, lady, are you all right?"

I looked up to find piercing-blue eyes staring down at me beneath a black cowboy hat. My savior was tall, over six-foot something, wearing a light tan coat with a 'D' emblem and the words 'Dodd Ranch' embroidered on the front.

"Thank you so much for stopping." My teeth chattered together, reminding me how cold I was.

"My God," the man muttered as he reached for my hand. "Was that your car off the road a few miles back?"

"Yes." It was the only word I could get out before my legs gave way.

"Let's get you inside my truck."

Strong arms lifted me from my kneeling position and carried me to a black truck with the same logo as his coat on the passenger door. He held me close to his body as he swung open the door. Setting me gently on the leather seat, he removed his coat and draped it over my shoulders. "This should help keep you warm until we get to my ranch."

I wasn't sure if I heard him correctly, but I managed to

tell him, "I have to get to Deadwood."

"Sorry, lady, but you aren't going to Deadwood. The road is closed. This downpour caused the mountain to come down in a mudslide. The Department of Transportation road crews won't be able to get it cleared up until tomorrow at least."

I twisted my head over my shoulder. Maybe this was another sign. I needed to press forward. I needed to stop looking back the way I came. "You say you have a ranch?"

CHAPTER TWO

Lainey

I didn't know the man who'd rescued me from the storm after my car broke down from Adam. But I had no choice but to trust him. He pulled his truck away from the shoulder, and I watched my umbrella disappear in the side mirror. I should have asked him to go back for it, but I was only concerned about my car at this point. That I'd be stranded and completely dependent on this cowboy.

I adjusted my position, taking full advantage of the heated seat. "I need to call a tow truck to get my car out of the ditch."

"When we get to the ranch, I'll send a few of my men out to retrieve your car."

"Thank you," I said. "I really appreciate it."

Since there was no way to get to the hotel until tomorrow, I thought the considerate thing to do was call the concierge and let them know of my situation. Reaching beneath the coat he had placed over me, I found my purse and searched for my phone. When I found it, I turned it on, only to find I had no service. I held it closer to the window, thinking I would get a signal.

"Cell service is nonexistent out here." He smiled and shook his head. "Once we get to the ranch, you should have a signal. I'm Rohan Dodd, by the way." He held out his hand, waiting for me to shake it.

"That would explain the 'D' emblem I noticed on your coat," I said, accepting his greeting by taking his hand. "It's nice to meet you, Mr. Dodd. I'm Lainey Park."

The rest of the drive to his so-called 'ranch' was driven in silence, other than the sound of the wipers moving back and forth to clear the windshield of the rain that showed no signs of letting up. Rohan Dodd was a man of few words. When he drove through the log archway mounted high above the road, with the horns of what I bet was a longhorn, I, too, was at a loss for words. I wasn't sure what I had expected. Maybe an old farmhouse with a few cows roaming around in the pasture. This was nothing like that.

"Wow, this is your ranch?" I asked, taking in the large two-story log home with tall pillars wrapped in stone paving the way to the grand entrance and the wraparound porch.

"Yeah, I guess you could say it is." Rohan turned off the engine and got out of the truck. When he reached the passenger door, I was still staring at the large home in awe. Opening the door, he held out his hand. "Come on, let's get you out of these wet clothes."

Taking his offered hand, I climbed out of the truck. My

heels sunk into the wet gravel, reminding me of how badly my feet hurt.

Rohan must have noticed my discomfort. "Pardon me, ma'am," he said before lifting me once again in his arms and carrying me to the log house.

"Thank you again for helping me," I said as I wrapped my arms around his neck.

"Anything for a beautiful woman."

His smile was breathtaking and dangerous at the same time. Somehow, I felt that Rohan Dodd was a man to stay away from, regardless of his kindness. But I'd always been drawn to danger.

Lainey

I wrapped the blanket Rohan brought me tighter around my body and took in the fire's warmth. My luggage was still in the trunk of my car, and I was glad that Rohan gave me a T-shirt and a pair of sweats to put on. It was August, and under normal circumstances, the air conditioner would be running, but Rohan lit a fire for me because I had a hard time getting warm. Not even the hot bath I took seemed to stave back my chattering teeth.

Rohan brought me a large mug of hot chocolate a few moments later. "Here. Maybe this will help you get warm."

"Thank you," I said, accepting the mug.

The fire burned steadily as the logs crackled and

snapped. As I watched the flame ride up the chimney, I took in the breathtaking fireplace, which was made of stone, much like the stones that covered the pillars outside. There was a mantle made of polished wood that extended the length of the fireplace. On the mantle were candles and what appeared to be authentic Native American artifacts. As I continued to sip my hot chocolate, I took in more of my surroundings. Rohan's home was incredible. Sitting in front of the fireplace reminded me of the time a group of us from college went to Spencer's parents' cabin in Wyoming, near Jackson Hole. Back then, it seemed like life was simpler. That was before I got myself into this mess. Before Spencer used our friendship for something else. All he wanted was to gain control of *Renegade Magazine* and secure his inheritance. It was a stipulation to his grandfather's will that all the heirs be married.

"Are you getting warm?" Rohan rose to his feet and walked over to the fire. He picked up the poker and stirred the embers before adding another log. "I have requested Chin, my chef, to prepare something that will warm you. I hope you're hungry."

"Famished," I said as I watched him tend to the fire.

Taking a seat in the leather chair near the fireplace, he turned his head toward me, the light of the flame making his blue eyes more brilliant. "So, what is so important in Deadwood?"

Despite my near-death experience and a fuzzy head, I was reminded that I hadn't called the hotel yet to let them know of my situation. Avoiding his question unintentionally, I rose to my feet and said, "I need to call the hotel."

I placed the soft blanket on the cushion and walked over to the table where I had set my purse. I picked up my cell, and when I turned to face him, Rohan's gaze was on me, a grin from ear-to-ear splashed across his handsome face.

I felt my face turn red, and I was sure he noticed. Smiling because there wasn't anything else I could do, I brought up the number to the hotel and pressed send. After the young woman recited her greeting, I said, "Hi, this is Lainey Park. I have a reservation with you, but unfortunately, because of the weather, I won't be able to make it to the hotel this evening."

"Yes, I see that we have a reservation for you until next Saturday. The weather has caused some problems for travelers attempting to get to the hotel. Your room will be available until you can arrive," she assured me politely.

After I hung up, I looked down at the screen and noticed that only fifteen percent battery life remained. Thankfully, when I grabbed my purse from my car, I also grabbed my phone charger. Pulling the cord from my purse, I looked to Rohan. "Is there someplace where I can charge my phone?"

He rose to his feet and strolled toward me. Taking my cell and the charging cord from my hand, he walked back over to the couch. I wasn't sure how I'd missed it, but on the side of the couch near the armrest was a USB port.

I was just about to thank him when a short Asian man

appeared behind me. "Mr. Dodd. Dinner is ready."

"Shall we?" Rohan placed his hand on my lower back.

Something in his touch sent a current of electricity through my body. Never had a man caused my body to react this way from a simple touch. Rohan led me through two large pocket doors and into a beautiful dining room. A chandelier made of deer horns and candles was centered above the large table. It fit the theme of his home and matched his rugged personality.

As we took a seat at the large table, an older man no more than three-inches taller than me, with short dark hair and kind eyes appeared wearing a chef's jacket. He had come from the kitchen and held two white plates, each with a perfectly cooked chicken breast, some garnished asparagus, and a pile of oven-browned potatoes. The helping was more than I could possibly eat, even if I was starving.

Taking in the aroma of the well-prepared meal, I picked up my napkin and placed it on my lap. "This looks amazing."

"Chin is an excellent cook. I'm sure you will agree once you take your first bite." Rohan smiled and poured us each a glass of wine. "Chin has been the family chef for as long as I can remember. When my parents died, he was going to move on since it was my father who hired him, but I insisted he stay." "No one else could put up with Mr. Dodd? He is so demanding," Chin replied jokingly giving Rohan a wink before he left.

Was this man for real? Everything I'd seen so far about

him was perfect. I couldn't take my gaze off his. He was hypnotizing. Taking in more of his features, my sight fell to his smile and the well-groomed beard he sported. His hair was mussed, probably from the cowboy hat he had worn before taking it off once we were inside the house. The top two buttons on his shirt were undone, which allowed me to see a trace of hair on his chest.

"See something you like?" Rohan asked.

"I'm sorry. I didn't mean to stare," I admitted coyly. "It's just that you are unlike anyone I have ever met."

"And you, Mrs. Park, are unlike any woman I have ever met. What were you thinking, leaving your car in this weather?"

"It's Miss. I'm not married." I looked down at my engagement ring, realizing that I still had it on. Pulling it off my finger, I knew I had no reason to tell him about Spencer, but for some reason, I wanted to. "I was supposed to get married next month, but my fiancé thought that having an affair with my boss's secretary didn't count as far as marriage vows are concerned."

"He is a fool," Rohan growled. "He doesn't deserve you."

I didn't know what was going on with me, but his words hit a nerve. From out of nowhere, the tears fell. Spencer *was* a fool, but I was the bigger fool. There was an undeniable ache in my heart tormenting me for the decisions I had made. I thought we could actually love each other one day, but he wasn't even trying. He wasted his love on someone else. No matter what we agreed to, I couldn't live with his infidelity.

I shoved back my plate, unable to eat another bite. Rohan took my hand and led me back to the living room, where the fire was still burning. Instead of sitting in his chair, he sat next to me and pulled me close.

CHAPTER THREE

Rohan Dodd

"I shouldn't have said what I did. I don't know anything about the man you were supposed to marry."

I was an arrogant bastard. What made me think I was everything every woman desired, making every other man less than a granule of dirt on this earth? Lainey Park was every man's dream. She was beautiful, but there was a depth to her that I wanted to understand. Pain that I wanted to fix, in much the same way I'd helped Chin, I wanted to help Lainey. A voice in the back of my mind pictured her sitting by the fire in my home, our home, forever. She didn't know it yet, but soon she would be mine.

On impulse, I pulled her closer to me. Sharing her company was not only surreal, but unlike anything I had felt before. Over the past year, I had more women in my bed than I cared to count, none of which meant anything to me other than fulfilling my physical needs.

"You still haven't answered my question," I reminded

her. "What brings you to Deadwood?" I had to know if she was escaping her fiancé or if someone else had brought her to South Dakota.

As she leaned her head against my shoulder, the scent of her recent bath filled my senses. "I am a journalist for *Renegade Magazine*. My boss sent me here to do a piece on the bike rally taking place in Deadwood."

"Isn't Sturgis a better place to do your piece?" I questioned. "Bikers from all over attend the annual event." Even though Deadwood was a big tourist attraction, the big rally occurred in Sturgis.

Lainey twisted her body until her eyes met mine. "I thought the same thing, but Phillip is more interested in what takes place before all the riders meet up at Sturgis. The Legends Ride being one of them."

"I assume this Phillip person is your boss?"

"Yes. He runs the magazine."

I wanted to continue this conversation with Lainey, but unfortunately, we were interrupted by a knock at the door. Pushing to my feet, I left Lainey's warmth to answer it. Two of my ranch hands were standing on the other side when I opened the door. Jagger and Souley's expressions revealed what I had expected.

Jagger spoke first. "Sorry to interrupt your evening, Mr. Dodd, but the young lady's car is in pretty bad shape. We went ahead and pulled it into the barn, but it will need a new radiator and two new tires. It could use some front-end work too."

As Jagger handed me her keys, Lainey came up behind

me. My guess was she heard our conversation. "How am I supposed to get to Deadwood? I don't suppose Uber comes out this far?"

Hearing Lainey's words, I kept my gaze on Jagger. "Thanks for towing Lainey's car in. It's going to be a big day tomorrow. Get some sleep. I'll see you in the morning," I said before I closed the door and faced Lainey.

"Rohan, I need my car. I have no other way to get to Deadwood," she cried.

"That isn't exactly true," I began. "Jagger can take you wherever you need to go. I'll call for a mechanic tomorrow. It will be okay, Lainey. I promise."

I pulled her close, easing her worry. From the first moment I saw Lainey walking along the road, she drew me in. Not only did I want to help her, but I also wanted to protect her. Her tear-filled eyes pulled at my heartstrings. There was an unexplainable urgency to kiss her when she looked up at me, completely defeated. Lowering my head, I pressed my lips to hers. Instead of pushing me away, she parted her lips and let me into her warmth. As quickly as she allowed me inside, it was gone. Lainey pulled away, her stare on mine. "It's getting late. Thank you again for everything."

"If you'd like, I can have Jagger grab your things from your car." Even though I would love to see her in my clothes, I knew she would be more comfortable wearing hers. Your room is upstairs, the first room on the right."

Nodding, Lainey walked away from me. I watched her walk up the flight of stairs. I didn't want this night to end, but after everything she had endured, she must be exhausted. I can't remember the last time I didn't follow through with what I wanted. Lainey was unlike any woman that I had ever been with. So instead of allowing this night to continue, I played the part of a gentleman and a man I could respect.

When she turned the corner to the bedroom I offered her, I grabbed the handle to the front door and opened it. By now, Jagger and Souley would be in the barn where the hired hands slept. Instead of bothering them, I went in a different direction toward the larger barn where Lainey's car was.

I pulled open the barn door, and just as Jagger said, Lainey's car was in bad shape. As reported, not only would she need a new radiator, the front end of her car required some bodywork. Shaking my head, thankful that the damage she had done to her car wasn't any worse, I walked to the back of the car and opened the trunk. Inside was Lainey's suitcase and a computer bag.

Closing the trunk, I headed back to the house with Lainey's bags. Her scent still lingered within the fibers of my coat as I shrugged it off, reminding me how much I desired her. I was selfish, when I swore then that no other man would come near her.

Holding her things in one hand, I lightly knocked on her bedroom door. Nothing could have floored me more than when she opened the door. Wearing only my T-shirt, her legs were bare and delectable. For no reason other than my selfish need, I said, "I think you should stay at the ranch, at least until we can get your car fixed. You'll have a driver at your disposal 24/7. Besides, it makes more sense than trying to get a taxi to pick you up with the rally going on."

"I couldn't. You have already done so much for me." Lainey took her suitcase and her computer bag from my hand.

Little did she know that this was more for me than her. I wanted to keep her here at the ranch as long as possible. There was so much about her I wanted to know. "Please. It would make me feel a lot better if you stayed, at least until your car is fixed."

"It would be more convenient if I stayed. Can I sleep on it?"

There was only one answer that would satisfy me. Stepping closer to her, I leaned in and placed my lips on hers. "I will accept nothing less than a yes."

"I'll stay," she breathed, the kiss having changed her mind.

"Good. It's settled."

Rohan

The morning came too quickly, with plenty of work to be done. Lainey was still sleeping when I left the house and headed to the corrals. The 200 head of cattle I'd had delivered were already being unloaded and herded in the south pasture. I had a great bunch of guys working for me who were willing to go the extra mile should I need them. Most of them didn't have it easy growing up, but I believed in second chances.

Leaning against the fence next to Jagger, I looked out to the south pasture. "What do you think, Jagger? Do you think this herd was worth $500k?"

"Some of them are a little on the light side, but all in all, I think we made a good deal."

Jagger was my ranch manager, and he knew Black Angus better than anyone. The Dodd Ranch had been around way before Jagger could even walk. It was handed down to me by my father, and his father before him. Not too many people liked the Dodds, but it hadn't stopped us from being one of the largest ranches in South Dakota.

Patting Jagger on the shoulder, I pushed away from the fence. "Ms. Park is going to need a driver, and I would like you to take her wherever she needs to go."

"Why me, boss? Can't one of the other guys drive her?" Jagger pleaded.

There wasn't a single guy I trusted more than Jagger. The other guys were good ranch hands, but they had control issues when it came to women. I'd have done the job myself except I couldn't get out of an important teleconference from New York.

"Sorry, Jagger, but would you trust any of the other guys to drive a beautiful woman around?"

Leaving Jagger to his thoughts, I headed back to the house to check in on my gorgeous guest.

Chapter Four

Lainey

It was hard to explain, but I woke up this morning feeling more rested than I had in years. It had to be because of the country air and the stillness surrounding me. I pushed from the bed, took a quick shower, and headed down the stairs. I looked beyond the front window in the living room and saw that the sun had barely topped the horizon. I was sure that Rohan had already begun his day. This was a ranch, after all.

When I hit the bottom of the stairs, the house was silent. I thought I was the only one around, until I heard voices coming from the dining room. The minute I entered the room, Rohan greeted me with his beautiful smile. He couldn't have been more handsome, wearing a long-sleeved denim shirt and a leather vest. When he rose to his feet, my eyes fell to his Wrangler jeans and the way they fit him perfectly. Whoever said that a man wearing a suit was sexy as hell hadn't seen Rohan Dodd in jeans.

For a moment, we simply stared at one another, until Rohan walked over to me. Greeting me with a kiss on the cheek, he said, "Good morning. I hope you slept well."

"Never better," I answered as my eyes fell on the table. "Do you always have such a large breakfast?"

"Every morning. The guys work better on a full stomach." Rohan looked toward the dining-room door where six men who looked like lumberjacks were entering the room.

Rohan took my hand and led me to the table. As I looked at our hands, the warmth of his skin and the way he held my hand made our connection feel natural. The show of affection made me realize that I deserved more than Spencer could ever offer, no matter what the outcome. I meant something, and Rohan made me feel like I mattered.

The conversation was in full force as we ate the wonderful breakfast that Chin had prepared. The stories between the men kept my attention as they spoke about individual experiences on the ranch. The life of a cowboy was far from what I had expected. Operating a successful ranch required a lot of hard work and dedication.

Before we could finish breakfast, a call came through Rohan's phone. It was the mechanic he had contacted. He called to let Rohan know that a truck would arrive shortly to pick up my car. I had called the hotel to cancel my reservation earlier, but with the mechanic picking up my car, I was second-guessing my decision to accept Rohan's offer to stay at the ranch. Maybe I should have just called a taxi. Things were heating up between us, and I wasn't sure if I was ready to dive into another relationship, especially knowing what awaited me in Minneapolis when I returned.

Lainey

Leaving my thoughts in the dining room, I walked through the front door on Rohan's arm, knowing the weather would be kinder than the storm that greeted us yesterday. The sun felt warm against my skin, and the only sign of the rain was the damp ground and the scattered puddles here and there. From what I could tell, Rohan's ranch was massive, the pastures stretching out toward the distant mountains, cattle like tiny black dots that peppered the landscape.

I knew there were many ranches across South Dakota, but I wondered where the Dodd ranch fell size-wise. I looked around his property.

"How many acres do you own?"

"Last I checked, 3,500." Rohan grinned. "When my great-grandfather started the ranch, he owned fifty acres, had a hundred head of cattle, and ten working horses. The Dodd Ranch has come a long way in four generations."

I smiled, pleased at all he'd accomplished and watched a herd grazing in the pasture. "Exactly how many cattle do you own?"

"With the 200 delivered this morning, and the recent calf addition in March, somewhere around 400 head."

"That's all," I said jokingly.

Leading me away from the corrals, Rohan said, "Come on. I want to show you something."

I wasn't sure what he was about to show me, but I was excited to find out. We followed the gravel driveway past the main house toward a row of barns. As I looked around, I noticed a firepit surrounded by five chairs made of logs not too far from the main house. I smiled, wondering how many campfires Rohan had had with his men and whether they included music. I could imagine seeing them singing while someone played the guitar.

The gravel road forked in a different direction, leading to another barn. There were four total, but it was the bigger one that we headed toward. Before we reached the barn door, I heard horses whinnying and neighing. Rohan stepped through the open doorway first. The floor was covered in concrete, which had a slight shine to it. When I stepped inside, I counted twenty stalls, ten on each side. Horses only occupied a few.

I continued to follow Rohan until he strolled up to a beautiful brown horse with a white streak coming down between its eyes that reminded me of a lightning bolt. Rohan placed his hand on the horse's forehead and ran it up and down the length of its nose. Rohan kept his hand on the horse's forehead, soothing the animal with his gentle strokes. "This is Thunder. He is as gentle as they come."

"Hello, Thunder," I said, bringing my free hand up to the horse's head and placing it over Rohan's hand.

Tingles raced up my arm from touching the cowboy.

So much so that I removed my hand from Rohan's grasp. Suddenly, the simple touch was doing things to me I couldn't explain. Rohan must have felt it too, because he took my hand again and led me to the other side of the barn.

Scanning the rest of the barn, I asked with a shaky breath, "How many horses do you have?"

Rohan pulled me inside an empty stall, his lips on mine in an instant. "Too many to count."

His blue gaze was on me. With only his stare, he was doing things to me I never thought possible. My thoughts filled with possibilities, and my breaths became shallower. "Is this real?"

"I was just asking myself the same question." Rohan's eyes met mine while he wrapped a strand of my blonde hair around his finger. "Please don't tell me to stop. I've been waiting so long for you."

"I don't want you to stop, Rohan," I said as I pushed to my tiptoes and continued where we had left off.

My invitation was out in the open, and I wouldn't take it back for one second. Rohan pressed his body close to mine, and I could feel his need through the thick material of his jeans. Our tongues danced together, and everything around us disappeared. It was as though we were the only two people on earth. I had to be crazy to get into another relationship, knowing what could happen.

With Rohan, it was different. I wanted him more than anything I had ever wanted in my life. My troubles in Minneapolis were miles away, and I only wanted to focus on him and this moment. Melding into his body, I deepened the kiss, bringing his body closer to mine. Nothing mattered except how good Rohan's lips felt on mine.

Rohan lowered his hand between us, capturing my heat through the material of my skirt. I bent my knees slightly, giving him access. I felt his calloused hand glide up my leg and beneath the waistband of my panties. I gasped as he pressed against the very top of my womanhood. A pleasure I had never known soared through me. His touch was soft at first, then building faster and harder. Every emotion I had kept hidden away exploded, and my body shook out of control.

Rohan held me in place until my body relaxed. Freedom washed over me, and for once, I felt reborn.

CHAPTER FIVE

Lainey

"How the hell did you find me?" I stared at Spencer as he stood arrogantly at the front door of Rohan's home.

"Phillip told me. He was worried that you wouldn't get the piece on Deadwood for *Renegade Magazine* done in time to make the scheduled press." Spencer moved closer to me, moving a strand of my blonde hair behind my ear. "I've missed you, Lainey."

Spencer didn't miss me. He just wanted me to seal the deal he made with his father. "Don't use that as an excuse, Spencer. It was clear what your choice was when you decided to screw my boss's secretary."

In the distance, I could see Rohan riding in. The last thing I wanted was to make him a part of my problem. Luckily, I didn't have to. Jagger pulled up to the house in an SUV with the Dodd Ranch logo on the front doors. "If you'll excuse me, I have to do the job Phillip sent me here to do. You can let Phillip know that I have everything under control when you see him."

"Answer me this, Lainey." Spencer took hold of my arm as I walked away, pulling me to a stop. "Does Rohan Dodd know about how you got the job at *Renegade* or your commitment to me?"

All I saw was red as my hand met Spencer's cheek. He had no right to use our arrangement against me. I wanted to beat him to a pulp. Fortunately for him, Jagger got out of the SUV and headed toward me. "Is everything okay, Ms. Park?"

"Just dandy. Mr. Nolan was just leaving." I stepped away and walked toward the SUV. When I got inside, I held my focus on Spencer as he strutted to his rental car and got inside. It was only after he drove away that I released the breath I was holding.

Jagger opened the door, looked at me, and smiled. "Where would you like me to take you?"

When we got to Cadillac Jack's, I got out of the SUV while Jagger went to park the vehicle. I wasn't sure if he would join me inside or wait until I needed him. Either way, it didn't matter. As long as he didn't interrupt my work, it was fine.

When I entered the hotel's lobby, the first place I went to was the casino. It was a sure place to find biker gangs milling around, testing their luck. There was one biker in particular that I was looking for. Declan McKee was the leader of Skeleton Four and the one person who would be willing to give me an interview, at least according to Phillip.

SILVER LINING

As I headed inside, I kept my eyes peeled for the signature logo of the Skeleton Four biker gang. It wasn't hard to miss. They were the only gang that used the skull of a longhorn and the state flower as its logo. I wasn't sure where the name came from, but I guessed that there were only four members before the gang grew. Instead of changing the name every time they initiated a new member—like Skeleton Five and so on—they kept the name where it was.

As I looked up and down the rows of slot machines, thoughts of Spencer came to mind. Even when things got bad, my mom always said there was a silver lining. Maybe Rohan was that silver lining. Perhaps it was what brought us together.

Hidden in the corner playing a machine, I noticed a large-built man wearing a leather vest with the Skeleton Four logo on his back. I wasn't sure if it was Declan McGee, but it had to be him based on Phillip's description. I made my way between the machines and the players to the corner. Tapping the man on the shoulder, I waited for him to turn toward me.

"You aren't the waitress," he said with an annoyed look on his face.

"I'm not, but if you could answer a few questions, I'll buy you a drink," I said, ignoring the way his eyes were scanning my body from head to toe. "Are you Declan McGee?"

"That depends. Who's asking?" he asked smugly.

"My name is Lainey Park. I'm a journalist with

Renegade Magazine. Phillip Dunlap gave me your name."

"Phillip Dunlap. I'll be damned. How is the old bugger?" Declan said, shaking his head in disbelief.

I smiled at Declan's description of Phillip. He was far from being an old bugger. "Phillip is fine. Is there somewhere we can talk?"

Lainey

The interview with Declan McGee went better than I'd expected. Underneath that tough-guy exterior, he was actually very nice. His life didn't revolve around a biker gang. Declan was an insurance adjuster with a wife and three kids. As a matter of fact, most of the members of Skeleton Four were law-abiding citizens with families. They were nothing like the bad rap bikers usually got.

When I looked at my watch, I noticed it was one o'clock in the afternoon. The thought of having lunch with Rohan crossed my mind. Pulling my phone from my purse, I brought up his number and waited for him to answer.

"Hello, beautiful," he answered. "How did you know I was thinking about you?"

"That's easy: because I was just thinking about you." I smiled at the prescience. "I was just thinking how nice it would be to have lunch together. Can you come to Deadwood?"

I held the phone to my ear as I stepped out of the hotel.

While waiting patiently for Rohan's response, Jagger pulled the SUV to the front entrance. The back passenger door swung open, and to my surprise, Rohan was sitting in the back seat. I ended the call with a smile on my face.

Rohan held out his hand for me to take, which I did, and climbed into the vehicle without hesitation. He had changed from earlier, wearing a freshly pressed white shirt and a black sports coat. His Wranglers were also black, and so were his Justin boots. Other than his Wranglers and boots, he didn't fit the part of a rancher.

Once I closed the back passenger door, Rohan's lips were on mine. I wasn't one for PDA, but with Rohan, it felt right. When he broke the kiss, his eyes were on mine. "I have the perfect place to have lunch. They serve the best clam chowder in South Dakota."

As we headed inside the small restaurant, Jagger remained with the vehicle. I was glad that Rohan didn't invite him to join us. I wanted it to be just the two of us sharing lunch.

The afternoon sun brought so much warmth that we chose to eat outside on the back deck. When I stepped outside the door, several tables with umbrellas were tastefully positioned on the wood deck. Rectangular boxes filled with colorful flowers hung over the railing, welcoming customers. I understood why Rohan picked this restaurant. I had a feeling it wasn't because of the chowder.

While we ate our lunch, the truth of what Spencer said entered my mind. If Rohan knew the truth about my past, what we had would end. I could quit *Renegade Magazine*, but that would mean my parents would lose everything they worked so hard for to make their restaurant a success. My only option was to marry Spencer so that he could honor his grandfather's will and get everything he wanted and my parents could keep the restaurant. I couldn't let Spencer ruin everything by revealing my past to Rohan. Maybe I could make another deal with Spencer's father—one we both could accept.

Rohan's hand fell upon mine, distracting me from my thoughts. "You seem to be miles away. What are you thinking about?" he asked, bringing my thoughts back to us. "Is it the chowder? If you don't like it, I can order you something else."

I glanced down at my chowder, noticing that I had hardly eaten a bite. "No, the chowder is wonderful. I was just thinking about the magazine." It was a lie, but the only thing I could come up with.

I couldn't believe that I was gullible enough to trust my college professor seven years ago, or the Nolan family. If I hadn't trusted him, I wouldn't be in this mess. But how could I blame him. Professor Adams was taken advantage of just like me. He owed Alistair Nolan his life. From what I gathered he and I weren't the only people at Alistair's command. As far as my parents knew, I got the job at *Renegade Magazine* on my own merit. Little did they know it was only an added bonus—and incentive. At the time, I thought I could live with myself. Marrying Spencer Nolan wouldn't be so bad. I really felt that I could learn to love him, but after today, I knew I was wrong. He didn't care about me. If he had, he wouldn't be using our arrangement against me, nor would he have slept with Carla, Phillip's secretary.

Rohan's eyes were on mine, and he didn't believe me from what I could see. I had to give him a distraction from my change in attitude. Switching gears would accomplish that. "So, what is on the agenda for the rest of the day?"

"I was just about to ask the same thing." He smiled, taking another bite of his soup.

"I would love to see more of Deadwood." It was a historical town, and with so much to see, I could get a feel for Rohan's world. Minneapolis had its advantages—the shopping was amazing, not to mention the theaters and the festivals. Not one day went by that there wasn't something going on. There were also disadvantages. With the higher population, there was higher crime and a higher poverty rate. But every town had their skeletons. To embellish my article, it would be great for Rohan to show me Deadwood. Everything I had seen of the small town so far made me want to stay and never go back to Minneapolis. If only there was some way I could free myself from the Nolans.

CHAPTER SIX

Rohan

As we rode back to the ranch, I wanted to ask Lainey about the man who came to see her this morning. I didn't have to, though. I knew who he was. When I asked Jagger, he told me that Lainey called him Mr. Nolan. I did a little investigation of my own. Spencer Nolan, the man who broke her heart. The man I hated, yet thanked for his infidelity bringing Laney to me. Jagger heard little of the conversation between them but knew that Spencer upset her enough to warrant a slap across the face.

What Jagger heard was somewhat disturbing. Everyone had a past they weren't proud of, me included. I've done some inexcusable things and have hurt many people. I couldn't imagine that Lainey's employment at *Renegade Magazine* wasn't more than a competition of the fittest.

Fifty minutes later, Jagger pulled up to the ranch. I promised Lainey that I would show her more of Deadwood, and that was what I planned to do. When we strolled inside the house and went our separate ways, Lainey headed up the stairs to change her clothes. I made my way to the library where I did most of my work.

I removed my Bugatchi sports coat and placed it over the back of the leather chair facing my desk. I knew I had a little time before Lainey finished changing. It felt like I was invading her privacy, but I had to know more about the woman I was falling for. I couldn't chance making the same mistake twice. Before I gave my heart to another woman again, I needed to know all her secrets. Never again would I be blindsighted with lies and deceit.

I brought up my laptop and continued where I had left off. Just as I was about to continue my search, I noticed an envelope in the lower right-hand corner of my screen. It was a notification that I had a new email. At first, I didn't think anything of it, but as I hovered my mouse over the envelope, I saw this notification wasn't for the ranch but for me. Normally, I wouldn't have thought it strange, but I hadn't used this email address in three years, and very few people knew of it.

Before I could open the message, Lainey appeared in the doorway. She had changed into a pair of blue jeans and a casual top. I hadn't seen this look on her, but it suited her. She was beautiful in her dressed-down outfit.

"You didn't change?" she said as her eyes set on me with confusion.

I rose from my chair and began unbuttoning my shirt. It took all of five seconds for me to pull another shirt from the closet and put it on. "There, I'm changed."

I walked toward Lainey, stopping only inches from her. Her beautiful green eyes met mine. Lowering my head, I placed my lips over hers. "Are you ready to go?"

I helped Lainey inside my truck before getting behind the wheel. There was so much to see in Deadwood that I didn't know where to begin. I let Lainey take the reins on where she wanted to go first. "What would you like to see first?"

"Can we see Mount Roosevelt?" she asked. "When Phillip first told me about doing this piece, Mount Roosevelt appealed to me when I researched Deadwood."

I looked down at her feet and was thankful she wasn't wearing heels like the ones I found her in when I picked her up on the side of the road. Instead, she was wearing ankle boots with a low heel. I turned on the engine. "I think we can do that. I hope you are in good shape. The view at the top of the monument is spectacular."

As I drove away from the ranch, I was consumed with all the things Lainey had made me feel. Not only did I have a successful ranch, I had a successful business—not in Deadwood, but in New York. One could say that the Dodd Ranch was more or less a hobby and a way to be someone else other than Rohan Dodd, entrepreneur and risk-taker. The more money I had, the more power I gained. When my father passed away and left me in charge of the Dodd Ranch, I didn't see it as a curse but as an opportunity. I was meant for more. I never thought that the Dodd Ranch would be the means to my success. Even though South Dakota would always be my home, it wasn't where I belonged.

With all the success came women, but none of them mattered. They always wanted more than I could give or wanted to take what I worked so hard for. I had never been interested in developing a relationship, but there was something about Lainey that made me want to. When I saw her walking on the side of the road, something told me to keep going, but when she turned and I saw her face, something in the way she looked at me caught me off guard. She was the most gorgeous woman I had ever seen, but also on the inside, her heart was pure. All I was going to do was help her out, but when she spoke, I wanted to do more. *Thank you so much for stopping.* Those simple words had me hooked. She wasn't like the rest.

Rohan

Come on, Lainey, we have a lot to see," I said as she stopped at the edge of the trail to take pictures of Mount Roosevelt with her phone.

"I'm coming, Rohan. Just a few more."

I waited at the top of the hill, smiling at Lainey. She reminded me of my childhood and the first time I had seen the monument. It seemed like a lifetime ago. Life was simpler then, and even though my dad was hard on me, I now know it was because he wanted to give me more than he had growing up.

Lainey met up with me minutes later, and we walked up the cement steps and entered the monument together. Even though it was warm outside, the inside of the monument was cool—probably due to the lack of windows. As I looked up the spiral staircase, I knew I would never forget climbing these stairs twenty-some years ago. Smiling to myself at the memory, I took hold of Lainey's hand. "Are you ready?"

"More than ever," she said as she gave my hand a light squeeze.

We ascended the stairs together, stopping for a moment to look out the small windows carved within the stone wall. The steps themselves were steep, but Lainey had no problem keeping up. When we reached the top, the climb was well worth it as a 360-degree view of the Black Hills came into view.

If I knew that we wouldn't have company, I would be making a new memory with Lainey. Since there were other hikers behind us waiting to see the monument, my only choice was to pull Lainey near and hold her body close to mine. When her eyes came to mine, I lowered my head and kissed her soft lips.

I wanted this moment to last longer, but I could hear voices coming our way. Breaking our kiss, I touched my forehead to Lainey's. "I wish we could continue this a little longer, but I would hate for the people coming up the stairs to enjoy the show instead of the view."

Lainey looked at me and smiled. "Then we better continue this at the ranch."

"I thought you wanted to go sightseeing?" Nothing would please me more than to have Lainey all to myself back at the ranch.

"I did, but that all changed when you kissed me."

We waited for the young couple to reach the platform of the tower before we made our way back down. Lainey's hand felt right in mine, and I refused to let it go as we walked down the trail back to where I parked my truck. My cell vibrated in my pocket as I helped her into the truck. I thought for sure there would be no cell service out here. If I had known, I would have turned my phone off. Looking at the screen, an unknown numbered appeared. Instead of answering it, I let it go to voicemail. Whoever it was could wait.

When I pulled up to the house, something was off. Usually, the SUV Jagger used to drive Lainey around would be parked in front of the main house. It was only used for guests; the ranch hands had other transportation.

Unaware of what was going on, I rounded the front of my truck and opened the passenger door. "Go ahead and go inside. I have something to take care of first."

"Is everything all right?" Lainey said, placing her hand on my bicep.

"I'll know in a few minutes." I kissed her on the cheek and watched her walk toward the house.

When she was safely inside, I headed toward the barn where the living quarters were for the men. I opened the door, and only silence hit me. As I looked around, I realized I needed to remind the men that even though this was their space, the least they could do was keep it clean.

I closed the door and searched the rest of the barns, finding no one around. Worry consumed me, and rightly so. In the distance, I saw Jagger riding toward me at lightning speed. There was only one reason he would be riding his horse that fast. Something was wrong.

I sprinted toward the fence enclosing the south pasture. Jagger came to an abrupt stop, and instead of dismounting his horse, he looked down at me. "The fence on the other side of the pasture was tampered with. About two hundred head got loose. The other guys are working on rounding them up."

"What do you mean, tampered with?" I asked, still trying to wrap my head around what he said.

"Yeah, the barbed wire was cut and pulled back, giving the herd a clear exit." Jagger pulled his cowboy hat from his head and wiped away the sweat. "Do you know of anyone who would have done this?"

I was clueless, but it didn't mean I wouldn't find out. "I'm not sure. There is no reason for someone to do that."

I was on good terms with the rest of the ranchers in the area. No one that I knew would do such a thing. "I'll let Lainey know what happened and saddle Thunder."

Jagger rode off as I headed to the house. Whoever released my cattle did this to get back at me. I just needed to find out who and why.

Chapter Seven

Lainey

When Rohan told me what had happened, I couldn't believe it. *Who would want to do this?* As Rohan continued to explain what happened, I wondered if this was Spencer's doing. It was a stupid thought. I doubted he was smart enough or had the guts to do something like releasing Rohan's cattle.

"I'm sorry that we won't be able to continue where we left off." Rohan reached for my hand and gently ran his hands up and down my arms.

"Do what you need to do. I'll still be here when you get back."

Before Rohan left, he reminded me of what would happen when he returned. The kiss was soft, and his lips felt perfect against mine.

My heart pounded with anticipation of his return as I watched him mount Thunder and ride away. The thought of what would happen later swirled in my head. If I wanted to clear my mind of all that was Rohan, I needed to concentrate on something else. The interview I had with Declan McGee was a good place to start. I pulled out the notes I took during the interview, glanced over them, and then retrieved my laptop.

I wasn't sure how long it would take for Rohan and his ranch hands to round up two hundred head of cattle, but I was certain it would be more than a couple of hours. I booted up my computer and focused on my emails first. Most of them went to my junk folder, while others were potential pieces Phillip wanted me to work on. He must have thought I was Wonder Woman. *Does he not realize that I can only focus on one story at a time?*

When I came to the bottom of my emails, my anger rose as I saw an email from Spencer. I almost sent it to trash, but then I remembered he also worked for *Renegade Magazine*.

I clicked on the email and began reading his message.

Lainey,

It was a surprise to find you staying at Rohan Dodd's ranch instead of the Iron Horse. I know you are angry, but you need to remember our marriage will be one of convenience and not love. Don't forget about your contract with Renegade Magazine and what it will do to your parents. You've had your fun. I will give you until the end of the week to come home. If you don't, your parents will suffer, and Mr. Dodd will know the truth.

Forever,
Spencer

Seeing fire, I slammed my computer shut. I had never wanted ill will for anyone, but right now, I wished that Spencer Nolan would fall off the face of this earth. The truth was, I had no one to blame but myself.

I inhaled and thought about Spencer's words and wondered if he would carry out his threat. Maybe I had underestimated him and his father. I could never repay Alistair Nolan, and Spencer knew it. Even if it broke my heart, the only way to save my parents was to do as Spencer asked. I had to go back to him.

Wiping away the tears that had fallen, I pulled myself together and called for a taxi. If I left before Rohan came back, I could avoid telling him why I had to leave.

The tears were still falling as I headed up the stairs to pack my things. The taxi cab company said they had a driver in the area, and he would be at the ranch in thirty minutes. The timing couldn't have been better. Thankfully, the Iron Horse still had my room available, even with the rally going on.

Lainey

When I reached my hotel room, I first called the mechanic Rohan had contacted to fix my car. According to the mechanic, other than the bodywork, it was ready to go. Since the mechanic knew nothing about bodywork, he offered the name of someone who could fix the front end, but that was the least of my problems. The only thing I cared about was getting to Minneapolis so I could confront Spencer and man-up to my obligation to the Nolan family. Once there, I could find a body shop and have the work done on my car.

As I sat down on the bed the only thing I could do was stare at my cell. I should have left Rohan a note, but I couldn't bring myself to tell him why I had left. Instead, I left his home like a scared rat. Soon, he would return to the ranch and find me gone. *How was I going to explain why I left? How could I expect him to understand that I had to marry Spencer without telling him the truth?*

Lost in thought, I debated calling him, until his name appeared on the screen. I could have let it go to voicemail, but I knew he would continue to call until I answered. Holding the phone to my ear, I answered. "I know what you are going to say, Rohan, but let me talk first. I can't do this. I'm not ready for any kind of relationship. I should have never led you on the way I did. I think it's better if we stop seeing each other." With every word, my heart shattered a little more. All I wanted to do was crawl beneath a rock and die.

"Where are you, Lainey?" Rohan's voice cracked. "I need to see for myself that this is what you want. I need to know that you don't want us."

Telling him a lie was easier than telling him the truth, but I knew he would come if I told him where I was. He would see the truth and see that I was lying. "There is no us. It's over, Rohan." The tears I tried to hold back rolled down my cheek. "I have to go. Goodbye, Rohan."

"Wait, Lainey."

I ended the call, and my heart broke in two. In my heart, I knew this was the right thing to do. I would marry Spencer Nolan, and my parents' restaurant would be safe. Tomorrow, I would be on my way back to Minneapolis, and South Dakota would be forgotten. It would be nothing more than a description in an article. But I would never forget Rohan Dodd. He would forever be in my heart. At least Spencer could never take that from me.

THE END

Rohan's and Lainey's story continues in the full-length novel *Red Heaven*, releasing fall 2022. Find out if the obstacles Rohan and Lainey face prevent them from being together. Will Spencer Nolan succeed in destroying the love they have for one another?

If you liked this story, please leave a review on A.L. Long's Amazon Author page: https://www.amazon.com/kindle-dbs/entity/author/B01AYG4TZQ.

Subscribe to A.L. Long's newsletter and get the inside scoop on new releases and upcoming events.
https://bit.ly/3jo8VZo.

ABOUT THE AUTHOR
A.L. LONG

Award-winning Author of the Independent Press Award and NYC Big Book Award, A.L. Long is also the National Indie Excellence Award recipient.

Some would call me a little naughty, but I see myself writing spicy thoughts. Being a romance writer is something that I never imagined I would be doing. There is nothing more rewarding than to put your thoughts down in words and share them. I began writing in 2013 and have enjoyed every minute. When I first started writing, I wasn't sure what I would write. It didn't take me long to realize that romance would be my niche. I believe that every life deserves a little bit of romance; a little spice doesn't hurt either. When I am not writing, I enjoy the company of good friends and relaxing with a delicious glass of red wine.

Visit me at www.allongbooks.com for all of my new releases and book signing events.

Keep up with all A.L. Long's latest releases:

Twitter: twitter.com/allong1963
Facebook: www.facebook.com/ALLongbooks
GoodReads: www.goodreads.com/ALLong
BookBub: www.bookbub.com/authors/a-l-long

The Splendor and Secrets of Sunny Creek

SHERI LYNN

Sunny creek is spectacular and enchanting. It carries many secrets. Secrets that flow continuously like the creek. Secrets that unlike the creek, run deep.

In 1878, Winfred Harrison resides on a ranch. Two hours away in the rough and unlawful town of Deadwood, Margaret Jean Miller gets separated from her parents and group traveling to Oregon. Mistaken for Winifred, she endures scandalous abuse before escaping and finding refuge in the home of the very woman she was mistaken for.

In 2022, Jeannie learns she is a descendant of deeded property in South Dakota. And there are more revelations awaiting her.

CHAPTER ONE

Fall 1878 Southwestern Dakota Territory
Margaret Jean Miller

One would think the appreciated sounds of a nearby town, of people, their laughter, and energetic activity would alleviate Margaret's angst. Especially after another long day of grueling travel under the eyes of those who remained hidden. Her pa had warned her to be on the lookout for bandits and natives who concealed themselves in the surroundings waiting to strike and steal. She'd done her best to keep watch. But journeying into the Black Hills altered her range of sight, as well as her pa's because they no longer had unencumbered views provided by prairies. No. There were trees and ridges. Were they being watched and followed? She felt an uneasiness deep in her bones.

The endless snap of twigs and the crunch of disturbed rocks signaled danger in every direction. She couldn't separate the sounds of her group, critters, or potential attackers.

Normally, they would've made camp before sundown,

but the men decided to continue in the hopes of finding a post to restock their provisions and handle necessary repairs. She prayed Pa would rent rooms and she could sink into a tub of hot water.

All day the sun teased them, concealing itself until it lowered hours earlier, and no moon appeared. Low clouds overwhelmed the skies challenging the group to progress in unsympathetic darkness. Margaret knew she would never feel safe again.

Ma and Pa were ahead of her by a good distance. Pa handled a four-horse team hauling a wagon carrying Ma and another woman along with her seven children. Having been an only child herself, the constant bickering and whining had her escaping the commotion and taking to her mare's needs. Pa adamantly refused her request to distance herself from them, until she produced tears and sobbed into his broad chest as he hugged her. He might have been a big man, but George Miller was a gentle, compassionate man of God.

A few weeks shy of her eighteenth birthday, Pa decided to leave Brainerd, Minnesota and relocate to Oregon. He planned to build a new church and deliver his lively and poignant sermons to others who went west hoping to start a new life. The bulk of his congregation hated to lose him and decided to go with them fifty-six days ago. The longest part of the trek still lay before them.

The closer they came to the settlement ahead, the stronger a sense of discontent infiltrated the group. Children began wailing. Horses became nervous. People started voicing their concerns to one another. As structures and light came into view, gunshots rang, and chaos ensued.

Yells and slapping reins commanded the horses to move on. Individuals on foot ran in every direction. Margaret's mare charged straight into the center of the action. Until it decided to make an abrupt halt and throw her.

The jolting impact of her body with the hard ground expelled all the air from her chest and left her wheezing. She worried she might die. Closing her eyes, she allowed herself to slip into a state of nothingness.

When she came to, the back of her head ached, and piercing pains repeatedly assailed her right shoulder. Shifting her hips and repositioning her legs, she luxuriated in the comfort of having an actual mattress beneath her, which slammed a bolt of awareness through her. She wasn't on the trail any longer.

"There you are. We were getting rather worried over when and if you would decide to greet us," a gentle, soothing voice purred from her left.

Margaret's eyes shot open. Light from a bedside table temporarily blinded her, triggering her to shut them again. Squinting, she saw a woman sitting on the bed beside her. She had a pretty, but tired, pale face framed by a massive array of unruly and undone black curls. Her breasts protruded over and out of her indecent garment.

Had she died? If so, she should be in heaven not in some sinful hell. Pa would be appalled.

"Bess, hurry your pretty self on outta here. It's high

time I speak to Miss Harrison."

The announcement came from a tall, dark-haired man standing in a doorway. Noticing his narrow black eyes and a long scar beneath his scraggly beard, Margaret shivered. He embodied the image of true evil.

Gripping the quilt, she pulled it to her chin. Where were her parents?

Hopping from the bed, the seemingly kind woman stumbled before righting herself in front of the menacing man. Lowering her head, she pleaded, "Johnny... Mr. Burns, do you think the doc should take a look at 'er. She took an awful hard fall—"

The man, Johnny or Mr. Burns, lifted his boot and kicked the woman's legs out from beneath her. She collided with the floor in a thump. "Get outta here. Go run her a bath and gather something for her to wear tonight," he grumbled.

Scrambling to her feet, the woman rushed around him and from the room, leaving Margaret alone with the vicious man. Her heart pounded in her chest and ears. The thought of attempting to explain her situation to him...whatever that situation might be, terrified her. So, she remained quiet.

Johnny clutched a chair at the dressing table and dragged it slowly across the room to beside the bed. The lengthy scraping and bumping of the wooden legs on the rough floor had her grinding her teeth and her breath hitching.

Twirling it with the back toward her, he straddled the

seat and leaned close. He glared at her before speaking. "It's gutsy for you to enter Deadwood at all knowing that Swearengin is interested in your land adjacent to the creek. Could be that's what got your father shot. Poor Horace Harrison and his heathen friends might have kept the property, but he won't be reaping any benefits now that's he's dead and buried. And you, riding in here at night thinking you don't have a worry in the world...plain stupid."

She opened her mouth to object, but he raised a hand and waggled a finger at her.

"Your mere presence reminds him of your pa's refusal to allow us entry on your property. Sure, Swearengin is profiting from his Gem Theater, but now with your pa all dead and gone, ain't much holding him back from taking what he wants. The Gem always needs fresh gals. Seems only fair since you offered yourself, we don't miss this opportunity to gain from a treasure your pa didn't care to share."

Offered herself. Land. Deceased father. Gem. This man believed her to be someone else. A woman who owned property wanted by a Mr. Swearengin. A woman who lost her father. Margaret had to find her party. She didn't want to lose her father. What did this man intend to do with her? Gain from a treasure? Her life depended on finding her party. She mustered the courage to protest. "I am Margaret Miller. I am traveling with a group from Minnesota to Oregon. We were riding into town, but amidst the gunfire, we split up. I am sure members of my party are still here.

They will confirm my story."

Her words fell upon deaf ears. Mr. Johnny Burns robbed her of everything. He struck her in the mouth after her initial and futile defense of her mistaken identity. She fought him and screamed, but to no avail, and he punished her worse. Afterward he cursed himself for blemishing her face because no patron would pay as well for her. For four nights and three days, she suffered his harsh and disgusting abuse. And he stole her will to live.

She couldn't survive it.

One of the working girls came that fourth night and told her Johnny requested she dress and join them downstairs. He expected her to entertain and accept pay from men in exchange for sex. She would rather die.

Traipsing down the stairs and through the raucous common area of the sordid establishment, her presence garnered little notice from the drunken men or the other girls. A few of them displayed evidence of beatings they received from a guest, Johnny, or his cruel associate, Dan. The cries, the arguments, and the threats she heard coming from outside her room haunted her. It would never end. The women were punished if they tried to leave and were frequently reminded that they had no money to get anywhere else and no one there or anywhere wanted them.

Reaching out for the doorknob, the familiar and forceful gruffness of Johnny Burns silenced the piano and the crowd. "Where does the lovely Miss Harrison wish to go? And without a chaperone."

Her fingers twitched as she willed them to grasp the

doorknob. The thump of his boots as he banged them on the floor caused a shiver to race up her back into her hairline. She squeezed her eyes closed, refusing to acknowledge him.

"Seeing how I'm a bettin' man… I would wager it all on the certainty that one of you fine gentleman will escort Miss Harrison outside for evidently a necessary breath of fresh air," Johnny boasted.

She didn't wait for a reaction from his audience. Clutching for the knob, the room filled with rowdy cheering which almost stifled her determination. She managed to crack the door open enough that she could slide through. Behind her the clamor of wood being destroyed as chairs were discarded and tables overturned immobilized her. If she ran, they would catch her. She couldn't endure any man's touch again. She wanted to die. She wished she was stronger. But what were her options?

She had limited time. Within seconds, any of the men leering near her or one from inside the Gem would constrain her. Then they would return with her upstairs. Or even Johnny or Dan themselves—again.

A man on a horse trotting up the road to her right urged his horse to a gallop and headed straight toward her. A stumble. One stumble would place her underneath its pounding hooves. But would she die instantly? Would she feel anything?

Closing her eyes, she surrendered herself to the decision. Arching her back, she abandoned her fears and embraced impending peace.

"What the hell do you think you're doin'? You truly are a dumb fragile li'l flower," a female berated. The woman had a hoarse, masculine tone, but still distinctly female.

Margaret couldn't distinguish reality from illusion. Or delusion. Had she died? Did she arrive in heaven or hell? The air whooshing in and out of her torso and mouth in unison with the bruising pummeling in her abdomen shook and loosened her garbled notions.

Fingers clamped into her armpit, yanking at her. "It's your decision. You can either ride as you are and regret it tomorrow... or offer a li'l assistance and get your ass up on the horse with me," the female scolded.

Yep. She didn't die. A woman on a horse stole her. It's not as if that detail made her situation any better. The gals at the Gem were as deceitful and greedy as the men. Another crash of her ribs against the pommel of the saddle had her scrambling to aid her captor in adjusting her upright on the charging horse.

Encircled by arms holding the reins of an enormous and swift animal, Margaret breathed deeply. It's not as if she could or would do anything. Why take the risk of injuring herself and not killing herself? Too many variables at stake. If she tried to escape, she could get caught in the reins and dragged. What if she slid to the side and the horse ran her into a tree?

Quick and painless. Please.

The unknown rider behind her wore trousers. And a man's coat. Yet they had thin, long fingers and narrow wrists.

"Where are we going?" Margaret muttered.

Slowing the horse, her companion's arms slackened. She lodged her chin into the back of Margaret's neck, and warm breath heated the area with each word spoken. "I'm taking you home. I don't know why you were at the Gem. And I don't want to know. I won't imagine any of it."

Margaret would never forget what occurred at the Gem. "I don't have a home," she muttered. Why did Pa not come for her before anyone spoiled her? She could never return to her family.

The strange woman's fingers clenched the reins. "What sort of crap are you saying? I promised your pa, my friend—may you rest in peace, Horace Harrison—that I would keep your property and you safe until Will arrives. Somehow, I failed on protecting you, but I damn sure ain't gonna lose you your land. Let us pray Will gets here and marries you before Swearengin believes he stands a chance and acts."

This person mentioned the name Harrison. As Johnny had. Another case of mistaken identity? "I don't know any Horace Harrison, Winifred Harrison…nor you. I am Margaret Miller," she declared.

The woman raised her fingertips to Margaret's lips, shushing her. They were rough, scabbed, and swollen. But those wounds would mend. They were physical. Nothing could or would ever heal her soul. It died.

"I honestly do not know these people you mention and—"

"Lay your head back and rest. Please. By the looks of it, you need it," the woman interrupted. She placed her hand over Margaret's, inciting an involuntary but immediate recoil. "Damn it, Winifred. You knew better. Why did you leave your property?" the rescuer empathized.

Margaret experienced safety in those moments. Her eyes were heavy. She rode with someone who wouldn't hurt her. A person who obviously cared for her. Someone who wished to protect her. But no, not her... Winifred Harrison.

Margaret

"Jane? What has happened? You demanded I remain here on my property, and you would be in contact, but not for weeks. Has Will arrived?"

The frantic appeals of a different woman had Margaret bolting upright and out of a restless slumber and away from torso of the female rider behind her. She saw light from inside the windows of a small home and a lady pacing in and out of an open doorway.

The woman behind her pulled the reins, bringing the horse to a halt. She addressed the woman on the ground, "I can't say I have a clear enough understanding to explain it myself, Winifred. I thought I seized you away from the Gem and had you in front of me," she replied. Dismounting in a fluid, confident leap, the woman reached up to Margaret. "Apparently, I didn't rescue Winifred. Let's get you down and get to the bottom of this."

"Hurry up and get inside. Were you followed?" the lady in the doorway, evidently Winifred, pressed.

"No. And I took the southern route in and out of the ridge as a precaution." The oddly dressed woman gestured for Margaret to go inside and followed behind her. Perhaps the three of them could unravel the apparent confusion. Did it even matter?

Entering the residence, Margaret stepped into the eating space and kitchen. An attractive, younger man came out of the darkness from the left, buttoning his shirt. Their eyes caught before his face reddened. He lowered his head and skulked around the table, addressing his additional unexpected guest, "Jane. We weren't expecting you—"

Circling, Margaret took her first good look at the woman who brought her there. She could certainly be mistaken for a man. Tall. A very tall woman. Removing her hat, she tossed it in the center of the table. She wore her dark hair tied back away from a sunned face which didn't flaunt the softness and beauty of a typical lady. Swinging her coat open, she placed her hand on her holster and tapped her fingertips on the gun. "That's damn obvious, Jesse. I can breathe easier learning that Winifred didn't fall into the hands of those at the Gem," she stated. "But I damn sure can't admit the same for riding in to discover this. You and Winifred sharing a bed now?"

The young, intimidated man swallowed hard.

Margaret watched his jaw tighten and his throat

constrict and struggle. She escaped a horrific situation only to enter another troubled one. But she wouldn't go back to the Gem. She had nowhere to go. She had no one.

Winifred slammed the door and dashed around Jane, positioning herself between the displeased woman and the man to blame for her upset. "I am to blame for it, Jane. Not Jesse. Pa would understand. Jesse was his best hand. I was scared to be alone after someone shot Pa. I missed Pa, and Jesse and I became close."

"Winifred, you're to marry Will. Another trusted hand of your father's. What if it had been him who rode up tonight and not me?" Jane bellowed. She dipped her chin and shook her head. "Jesse would have a gut full of lead. It ends now. I won't betray Horace's dying wishes. I agreed to protect you and the ranch until the rightful inheritor arrives. And that's Will Havely. Not Jesse."

Winifred started to cry. And Margaret did too. She couldn't control her emotions.

"Oh, good Lord. Not only do you resemble one another, but you both blubber like brats." Jane stomped to a cupboard and retrieved a bottle and a glass. Circling, she paused. "Should I grab a glass for everyone?"

Both sobbing women gathered their composure and regarded one another. They looked alike. They could've been twins. Both were close in age, of average height and weight with blonde, curly hair and large light eyes.

Slumping into the most convenient chair to him, Jesse answered, "One for me please. *We* love each other, Jane. Winifred doesn't love Will Havely. She's never met him."

"She loved Horace too. There's more at stake here than

her childish whims of the heart," Jane asserted.

Margaret and Winifred ignored the conversation. They scrutinized one another. "Who are you?" they questioned in unison.

Neither answered. They remained fixed where they stood eyeing each other. Both jumped when Jane returned and banged glasses and the bottle on the table. Yet they never broke focus.

"Who are you?" both repeated.

Jane poured and threw back her whiskey, and Jesse joined her. One or the other refilled the empty glasses and they drained them again.

"I am Margaret Jean Miller. I am from Brainerd, Minnesota on my way with a group to Oregon. Johnny Burns believed I am…you, I suppose. Winifred Harrison?"

A glass slid across the table, losing only a few drops of the brown liquid, and stopped within reach. Margaret had never taken a drink but decided if she ever had an occasion to indulge in one, now would be that time.

Relaxing her throat, she poured it inside her mouth and swallowed it all. It burned. And she gagged and coughed.

"Hear ye, hear ye, well done, our fair lady," Jane hailed, lifting her glass in a salute of sorts.

Winifred's color drained from her face, and she faltered on her feet, swaying over the table.

Somehow, Margaret managed to get her to a chair.

Planting her elbows on the table and burying her face in her hands, Winifred wept, "Johnny thought you were me. Your face. I'm sorry. He is a monster."

Margaret forgot about her abused appearance. Since

her first beating, she avoided the mirror. The bruises and cuts hurt far worse than they appeared. She hadn't run a brush through her hair. She hadn't eaten. Johnny was a monster, and the Gem his domain.

Leaving his chair, Jesse knelt in front of Winifred and embraced her. He kissed her face. "You didn't place her there. You weren't aware of any of it." Cupping his hands around her chin, he pulled her lips to his in a lingering and sensual kiss before continuing. "Jane rescued Margaret, and she is here. She is safe now. We will atone for this awful mistake as best we can."

The scene affected Margaret entirely. They were in love. They were caring and concerned when she doubted ever experiencing genuine kindness again.

"I'm thinkin' you should have another drink, Margaret Jean Miller. Cause you're gonna need it," Jane exclaimed. Gripping the bottle, she marched over and refilled Margaret's glass. Eyeing Winifred, she encouraged, "Put some distance between you and Jesse."

Jesse rose.

Jane waited until Jesse returned to his chair before continuing, "From the way you've been sniveling and carrying on, I think you need this."

Pinning Jane with a wet, incensed glare, Winifred snatched the whiskey out of her hold and took several gulps before firmly placing it on the table. "Don't you be condescending with me." She stood and trudged into the other room, returning with a shotgun. "Get your gun, Jesse. I'll sit watch on the south ravine, and you go east."

Throaty laughter erupted inside the otherwise grave gathering. Jane slapped at her thigh and stamped her foot in unmistakable and perplexing delight. Solemnly pausing, she sarcastically remarked, "There's the Winifred I've come to respect. But you ain't going anywhere with Jesse. I'll go out with Jesse. You stay and get Margaret settled in."

CHAPTER TWO

Current day
Winifred Jean (Jeannie) Scanlon

Damn if Jeannie could muster any excitement or enthusiasm over her week vacation to a place most likely named appropriately—Deadwood. Deadwood, South Dakota. She had never heard of it until three weeks ago. And now, she had paid accommodations and airfare for her and a guest courtesy of a William Havely to not only somewhere unknown, but a place she supposedly had family history with.

"Why you gotta be such a 'Debbie Downer'," Chelsea griped. "I swear if judging by your scowl and discouraging remarks…one would think we were attending a funeral."

Jeannie sighed and fell onto her bed. The open and overfilled suitcase regurgitated some of her garments as she bounced on the mattress. How many times did she have to explain this? She'd never been on a plane. She'd never been anywhere out of Alabama that you couldn't reach within a couple hours of driving. And she always imagined if she did get an opportunity to fly anywhere, it wouldn't be to Deadwood, South Dakota.

Nope. It would be a tropical paradise. With hot, cabana boys offering you endless drink service and begging you to give them the privilege of rubbing sunscreen all over your exposed areas.

Honestly, what single, ready-to-mingle, twenty-three-year-old wouldn't dream of a tropical paradise vacation. Who used any of their vacation time on going to some rinky-dink Ol' West town? Unless they were a history enthusiast or a biker. She happened to be neither. Knowing she had indeed googled the place but lied about doing so to Chelsea, she stiffened her chin and rocked herself from the mattress into a sitting position and delivered the most obvious of arguments. "Whether I own a smidgen of land or not near this *Deadwood*... I don't intend on keeping it. Why you and Mr. Conrad insist I see it before selling is completely a waste of time."

Stomping her foot and groaning, Chelsea reached out and shoved the suitcase off the bed. "You really are a pain in the ass," she grumbled. "I'm excited about this trip for a lot of reasons. People pay good money to buy those ancestry reports and you had one fall into your mailbox. And...and it's interesting as shit."

Boy, talk about the brutal truth smacking you in the face. Jeannie might need a plastic surgeon after Chelsea's verbal assault. And she recognized she deserved it. Basically, she won the lottery. Mr. Conrad, the attorney she worked for, validated the information she received and advised her of the financial gain she had in the property. He demanded she view the area and the plot in person before she made a final decision on whether to hold onto it or sell it. And she trusted him. He warned her that she would regret it if she didn't go, and he couldn't with good conscience allow her to make any rash decision.

After listening to several communications between Mr. Conrad and Havely's representing counsel and reviewing the supporting documents, even if Mr. Conrad hadn't pressured her to go, it intrigued her. Her mom loved genealogy and submitted an ancestry DNA kit years prior. Supposedly, it didn't yield much information other than what she learned from her mother and grandmother. Which she complained was little to nothing. Prior to that, she submitted the few facts on many family tree sites and communicated with several people, but still came up empty-handed.

Jeannie didn't understand her compulsion with it all. Maybe they weren't supposed to know beyond Jesse and Winifred Price who resided in Alabama in 1879. That's where her mother met a dead end. What if their parents were slave owners? Their fathers might have fought in the Civil War for the Confederacy. Either way, there could be a reason—a detestable reason—they renounced their pasts and those before them.

Either Mr. Havely or another family member found her mother's ancestry research online or were directed to her through the DNA test database. She wondered why they didn't contact her mother, but her mother remarried, and she and her new husband didn't stay in one place for long.

Jeannie should inform her mom of the recent developments, but she despised her parents. They divorced five years prior, and her high school graduation and college transition became a tug-of-war. Dad wanted her at his house. Mom at hers. The predictable and dreaded disputes over tuition and books prompted her to get out on her own. She worked and attended classes, but it became too much. She dropped out of college.

Four years ago, Mr. Conrad took a chance and hired her. She lacked office experience and had no knowledge of litigation law. He became her mentor and a father figure. He praised her when she earned it and criticized her when she deserved it. The discovery of one of her maternal grandmothers living in Deadwood over a century ago and of possibly having kept company with the infamous Calamity Jane fascinated him. Every single day for the last three weeks he stood waiting for her when she entered the office, a new batch of property records and maps and legends in hand.

"I'll be waiting in the car if you wish to join me. We need to leave ten minutes ago," Chelsea blustered as she whirled toward the door and marched out of the room.

Suck it up, buttercup. Now or never. Saddle up and embark on an adventure.

THE SPLENDOR AND SECRETS OF SUNNY CREEK

Jeannie

The Atlanta and the Minneapolis airports were how Jeannie always imagined airports would be. Large, overpopulated, busy, confusing, and a lot of walking. These are not her favorite things.

They downsized planes and entered a smaller airport with men in cowboy hats strutting with unhurried gaits. There's a big difference between a cowboy and a redneck. So it seemed. The men in Alabama she knew didn't wear cowboy hats. Everywhere she looked, she saw an honest to goodness cowboy hat. Obviously being country didn't always equate to western as it did in music. She came from the country, but it seemed she knew little to nothing about western.

"Are you awake now? You slept the entire flights. As in each and every flight. All three of them. And Steven is lucky he scooped me up and made me a wife and mom before I had the opportunity to come out here," Chelsea stated while ogling an attractive guy in an SUV pulling up in front of them and waving at another super smokin' cowboy.

Dropping her head, Jeannie reread the text message advising her of who would be picking them up. She scanned the few vehicles and no black Cadillac Escalade came into view. She saw either the typical SUVs or trucks. Who the hell were these people who presented her with an all-expenses paid trip, drove Cadillacs, and claimed she owned a parcel of their property? She did know they managed a ranch and owned thousands of acres.

None of it made sense. There had to be a hitch. Nothing in life is free. And from what she knew so far, she didn't fit in anywhere in South Dakota. She didn't fit in with the Wild West fanatics, bikers, or the hoity-toity folk.

When the sidewalk emptied of arriving passengers and it seemed as if no one intended to show, the sleek, luxury vehicle came into sight. It sped up, paralleling within inches of the curb, causing her to step back believing it might jump it.

A short, wiry guy jumped out of the driver's door and rushed them. Between his incessant apologizing, his flitting with the fob to open the trunk, and flinging their bags inside, she stood there and compiled her first impressions of Boulder Harrison. From her observation, his parents made a good decision on altering the spelling of his name from Bolder. She assumed they named him after the city, but he was anything but bold. She found him to be dismissive. And she didn't like him.

She observed insincerity in his over-exaggerated excuses and erratic motions. As if he allowed himself to slow down for a mere few seconds, she would see straight through him. Dressed in an ugly, preppy sweater, with a scarf tied around his neck, and in seventy-degree temperatures were unnecessary. And unattractive. As was the countryside. They left the airport, and she surveyed the landscape. What happened to the trees? To green? Everywhere she looked, she saw flat land. Brown land. So boring compared to Alabama. Alabama is trees, grass, green, even in the winter you see green.

Boulder rambled about the winter months. Which he claimed lasted from September until May. He mentioned blizzards. Closed roads. Additional upkeep to any homestead during the cold months.

"My attorney told me it's raw land. So, any upkeep is minimal compared to a residence," she challenged.

"Yes, yes, it is. All true. And I understand you aren't interested in maintaining a home in this area. So, a no-brainer, you'll be selling the property." He drummed on the steering wheel, increasing her annoyance.

"But land is king," she retorted. Odd how that phrase popped out of her mouth. Her great-grandmother preached that to her until the day she died. Jeannie swore those may have been the last words the strong, sweet lady spoke to her.

Her emphatic statement shut him up for a while. Not nearly long enough. He attempted to spook them with ghost stories and folklore of the region. As if she believed in ghosts or yetis.

The countryside altered as they neared the Black Hills. Trees dotted the slopes. Turning the vehicle into a Travelodge, he stopped at the front entrance. Boulder offered but delivered more of a gloated semi-apology. "Sorry we didn't put you up on Main Street, but this is the beginning of peak season, and we couldn't get you in anywhere else."

"How far are we from the thick of things?" Chelsea asked. Odd that Chelsea hadn't spoken a word during the forty-five-minute drive until then.

Waving his arm behind him, he answered, "That way…just down the hill. About a mile."

Snatching the door handle, Chelsea stepped out of the vehicle, but not before emphasizing, "A mile ain't shit. We brought walking shoes because we have land to walk." She closed the door behind her with a forceful shove.

Jeannie swore she heard Boulder grumble under his breath before he spoke clearly. "Let's get your bags and get you checked in. I'll be back at eleven in the morning to drive you to the ranch and meet with my uncle."

"Sounds good." And did it ever. The sooner they got away from him, the better. She feared now that Chelsea had found her voice again, she would use it. Too much.

They were checked in quickly without any additional comments between the three of them, and the girls were in their room within ten minutes. Those ten minutes were evidently strenuous for Chelsea. The moment she rolled her bag across the room, she whirled around to Jeannie and ranted. "What a prick. What is his deal? He didn't have one positive thing to say. He wants your property. And now I am super interested in it. And putting us up in this?" She fanned her arm and spun in a circle. Her scrunched lips and her disapproving expression supported her words and her unhappiness.

"Since when did you become high maintenance? There is nothing wrong with this hotel. It's clean. It has everything we need."

"But for some rich dude you've never heard of to contact you about property deeded to you… then offer to set you up because you wish to come and view it, and he puts us up here and not in one of the swankier hotels downtown rich in history is beyond me. They are driving home a point. And I don't like it," countered Chelsea.

She agreed but didn't see any reason to harp on it. The two of them had an opportunity they never had before. Get out of Alabama. Together. A little vacation combined with an adventure. And she planned to take advantage of it. Now that they were there.

"Shower, or don't. Change clothes, or don't. We are headed out," Jeannie announced.

They hit the town. The town might have hit them harder. The history alone did. Honest to goodness sharpshooters inhabited the area in its beginning. And the famous death of Wild Bill Hickock at a poker table. Yet, they experienced friendliness. The entire atmosphere welcomed them. They shopped at the "tourist traps." They drank. They gambled. And as they rounded the corner back to the Travelodge, they came upon an Irish pub.

"One more before our treacherous trek up the threatening, wannabe hill," Chelsea announced.

Honestly, one more. She shouldn't. They both already drank multiple beers and numerous shots. *When in Rome...* or Deadwood, behave as the current or past inhabitants. Neither were over-intoxicated. They had eaten a little. They split a few appetizers.

What the hell. Why not? Jeannie accepted, "One more. Of each. Then we are outta here."

Chelsea chuckled. "So, that's one more beer each and

another shot each." Throwing her arm around Jeannie's shoulders, she hugged her into her side. "I told you not to pass on this. Already it's a trip to remember."

The lights were dim. The large space consisted of multiple tables and chairs, several big screen televisions airing baseball games, and a huge bar on the entire back wall. They took seats on the right end of the bar. A handful of others were inside. A couple sat at a table, oblivious to their surroundings and one another as they stared at their phones. Two guys stood playing darts. Another couple and a man off to himself also sat at the bar.

An attractive, dark-haired, possibly of Asian descent girl about their age approached and placed cocktail napkins in front of each of them and smiled. "What can I get you?" she asked.

The single man across from them on the opposite end of the bar suggested, "Maybe these lovely ladies wouldn't mind a recommendation." He had a masculine voice. Yep. A manly, assured, assertive voice. It grabbed her, seizing her focus. She couldn't recall ever being attracted to a voice, but she couldn't describe the affect his had on her any other way. Her body responded to it. Her pulse quickened and her stomach fluttered.

"Does your recommendation come with a complimentary sample," Chelsea snickered. Even the wedding ring on her finger didn't deter men from hitting on her. And that evening had been no exception. She possessed striking beauty, a magnetic personality, quick wit, and whether because she had those traits or not, killer confidence.

But the guy with the captivating voice had his eyes on Jeannie. He had short, dark hair and a matching groomed beard. Until his lips slowly lifted into a knowing grin, she didn't realize she stared at him. And he had a gorgeous, kissable mouth. Dropping her eyes, she felt her face heat. Oh, good lord, he made her blush. She wasn't a blusher. How humiliating. If she took a guess, she would estimate he had at least a decade on her. At least. And her traitorous reactions had her giving the impression of an infatuated schoolgirl.

"You ladies beer or wine drinkers? There's plenty of local ones to choose from. He stood, his beer in hand, and grinned again. Damn if her entire neck didn't warm and radiate. Lifting a black cowboy hat from the barstool beside where he sat, he strutted over to them. "I suspect you are tourists."

"So, you're a local?" Jeannie blurted.

"Was. Might be again someday." He winked at her, and damn if her heart didn't skip a beat. He spoke to the pretty bartender, but hell if Jeannie heard a word. Sure, she listened. Okay, maybe she didn't. It's not as if she could escape the effect his voice had on her or her body's response. She shifted in her seat. Unbelievable. This guy turned her on. As in *big time*.

The bartender placed a tall, sweating glass of beer in front of her. "This is one of our local pales. If you don't like it, let me know and I'll get you something else." She delivered one to Chelsea and the hottie next.

Studly stuff picked his up from the bar and came around behind her, taking the stool to her right. "I'm Dane," he said, holding his glass out in front of him for a cheer of beers.

This man completely unnerved her. Her hand shook as she reached out for her glass. Raising it to his, she looked into his eyes. Brown. A deep, warm, smoldering shade which promised both sensitivity and intensity. "I'm Jeannie."

Thank goodness Chelsea didn't rely on her for attention and entertainment. She did her own thing while Dane and Jeannie immersed themselves in one another. They talked about music. He actually put some songs on the jukebox, and they danced. Just the two of them. And she never felt self-conscience. They laughed. A lot.

The dude oozed charisma. She'd heard the metaphor before, but she had never experienced it firsthand. Between his big, tall tales and amazing bone structure and stunning good looks could any woman not be overwhelmed by him? He weaved stories as if he were a part of them. The legends of Deadwood. Wild Bill and Calamity Jane. And he delivered them with infectious enthusiasm and a startling amount of animation.

She didn't quite know what to make of him. On one hand, she found his overzealous narrations and reenactments unusual. If she didn't enjoy his company, she would describe him as over-the-top. She dropped her beer on the bar when he vaulted out of his stool, knocking it to the ground, and proceeded to perform a monologue of a gunslinger spouting threats. Not the type of guy she would normally be attracted to. But he had the whole sexy cowboy persona going on. And she didn't want the night to end. If only she could stop staring at him. His beckoning eyes. His beard. Her fingers twitched, yearning to caress it. It looked soft. It probably smelled good. Aftershave?

Finishing another round of darts and winning, Chelsea pranced over to them. "I'm sure neither of you are aware, but it's almost two in the morning. Amy, our glorious bartender, stayed open for us…or rather for Dane." She held her near-empty glass over her head and curtsied toward the bar. "Love you, Amy. Practice tomorrow and you might stand a chance at winning a game against the champion."

"It's past time to call it a night—" Jeannie started.

Dane took her hand in his. "I want to see you again. Tomorrow?"

She opened her mouth to speak, but a puny sigh released instead. Closing her eyes, wishing she had an ounce of dignity in his presence, his warm fingertips cupped her face. His lips were on hers. They were magical. Everything she imagined they would be. Hot. Soft. Patient. Affectionate. Heated. Aggressive.

Chelsea loudly and exaggeratedly cleared her throat. "Sorry, but I need to start walking back while I can."

"I'll drive you where you are going," Dane stated. "Where are you staying?"

"The Travelodge," Jeannie answered.

Taking her hand again, he paid their tab and led them to his Jeep. The cool kind of Jeep. No doors. No top.

"Tomorrow? What time can I pick you up?"

"I have an appointment in the morning. I'll give you my number. You can text me."

CHAPTER THREE

1878
Margaret Jean Miller

It didn't take but a couple of days for Margaret to determine that her life as a pastor's daughter was over and living on and running a ranch were exhausting endeavors. They were up each day before the obnoxious rooster crowed. And they never stopped. She lived in a cycle of obtaining milk, eggs, and vegetables from the garden. She cooked. She canned. She fed animals. She cleaned stalls and pens. At sundown, the three of them returned to the house, cleaned up, and ate. They shared trivial conversation about their day and discussed the next day's chores before retiring for the evening.

Winifred and Jesse accepted her into their home and their lives. She learned and assisted as needed around the ranch. She couldn't stay there without contributing. It occupied her body and gave it purpose. Her mind and her heart suffered. She missed her ma and pa. Any impulse to ride into Deadwood and make inquiries about them or her group, she quashed. It could never be. She couldn't look into Pa's eyes after what happened at the Gem. Her gaze would transmit her shame and desecration. And he would never look into hers with adoration again.

How long could she stay there? Jesse and Winifred had not discontinued their relationship. They were very in love. Margaret heard Winifred crying at night and Jesse's attempts to soothe her. What would occur when Will Havely came? They never spoke about these things. They worked, they lived, and they existed under a cloud of dread and uncertainty. From the very first night when Jane and Jesse left to go keep watch for any unwanted visitors and Winifred suggested they rest, she slept in Mr. Harrison's old room. They woke, they labored, they ate, but not once did anyone mention how she came to be there and what would transpire and result for any of them.

The weight of it all became too much. When Margaret stretched out in the bed at night, the memories of the Gem consumed her. Being around Jesse and Winifred and witnessing their tenderness and devotion to each other reminded her of what she would never have. She had no future. And she couldn't continue to live at the ranch. She didn't belong there. She didn't belong anywhere.

On a sunny afternoon, she saddled a horse and rode. To nowhere in particular. She would know when she got there. She crossed fields and hills and meandered in and out of groupings of trees. Coming to the top of another incline, she gazed upon a section below cluttered with trees and color. It stood in contrast to the brown and rocky expanse encompassing it. Sweat beaded on her forehead and trickled down the back of her neck. The temperature seemed unusually hot for a day in May. But she wasn't in Minnesota.

Heading down the slopes, she entered the trees and a cool breeze greeted her. She closed her eyes and listened as it rustled through the branches and tickled the damp hair along her face. She found a sanctuary. A blessing in the otherwise demanding and unkind region. And she heard the delightful ripples of water.

Dismounting, she strolled through the trees. She extended her arms and touched the trunks of the trees as she wandered. Ahead of her, sunlight spread, indicating she reached the end of her woodland refuge. The rays beckoned her as if she were coming upon the gates of heaven.

Maybe she had. She stepped up to a sparkling creek. Rays of light danced upon the current. It twinkled, and beneath the steady stream gold glistened. Taking a seat on the bank, she removed her shoes and stockings and placed her feet in the cold water. Leaning forward, she dipped her fingers in and watched the shiny flecks flow through them.

She now knew the secret of Sunny Creek. Swearengin wanted it for profit. In bed at night, she overheard Winifred and Jesse talking and learned Horace Harrison appreciated and respected the gifts of the land as the Lakota did. He wanted it because of its beauty and wished to honor it. Winifred wanted it because Jesse first kissed her there.

Removing the knife from her apron, she positioned the blade on her left wrist. Tilting her head back, she closed her eyes and breathed deeply, prepared to exert pressure and prayed the Lord would forgive her.

"Winifred! Don't. Please."

Dropping her chin, she opened her eyes and saw a man on a horse across the creek. He had a dark, full beard and stared at her intently. Before she could react, he jumped from his horse and trudged through the water, stopping in front of her. Turning his palm up, he placed it between them and nodded once. His eyes were the color of rich soil. The foundation necessary for seed to take root and thrive.

"I am sorry about Horace. And I'm sorry it took me so long to get here," he expressed. "But I'm here now, and I promise I am here to stay. I will do all I can to provide for you and protect you and fulfill your father's visions."

She believed him. And she wanted him to. She wanted him to do it for her—with her. His words, his gaze, and his evident dedication stirred the dead parts of her. Raising her arm, she placed the knife in his hand.

Sheathing it in his belt, he clasped her wrists and pulled her into his chest. It had to be triple hers in width. He stroked her hair. He kissed the top of her head.

And she cried. She cried like a shamed child. She trembled like a frightened one.

He took her and sat cradling her in his lap. He held her and comforted her. "I've seen a lot of country in my life, but this is by far the most beautiful." He caressed her cheek and chin until she met his eyes. "And you are more breathtaking than Horace described. You are exquisite." Pressing his hot, soft lips to her forehead tenderly, he rocked with her. "We haven't been formerly introduced. I am Will, William Havely, your intended. We will wed in the morning before the men arrive with the cattle. And if I discover that your pain is due to anyone having harmed or threatened you, it will be the last wrongdoing of their lousy life."

Her face heated. She couldn't marry Will. She shouldn't welcome his consoling. She averted her gaze. "I apologize you found me in such a state."

"Don't you apologize to me. You lost your pa. You were burdened with a lot for a young woman who grew up in the East under the care of a wealthy aunt until a few years ago," he sympathized. "Horace was tickled to death when he set down roots and you decided to join him here. You are to never contemplate self-harm again. You will speak to me if you are troubled. I pray it wasn't marrying me that brought you so low."

Jerking her head upright and staring into his gorgeous face, she noticed the creases in the corners of his eyes. She figured he had to be close in age to her father. "No. It wasn't."

He grinned. "Good to hear. Now, let us head to the house and you can introduce me to Jesse. I need to see if the fencing is complete. And complete any pertinent tasks prior to the drive arriving."

Margaret

Will gripped both of Margaret's hands in the center of his abdomen. Her breasts pressed into his large back as they rode from Sunny Creek. It felt good. It felt right. But she couldn't avoid the inevitable. As in how to navigate the introductions at the ranch and the tales she began spinning. She hadn't lied. She just didn't correct him in his assumption.

Intuition drove her. She had an opportunity to possibly bring happiness to them all. Unsure how exactly, she relied on her gut instinct. Winfred loved Jesse. Will and Winifred were to marry. He thought she was Winifred.

Before Will showed up, she wanted to die. All of it had her head and her heart racing and her stomach rolling.

Hammering. Not her heart or her head, but Jesse hammering on the stable behind the house alerted her of their proximity to the homestead and how crucial it became for her to gather her wits.

Catching sight of Winifred as she sprinted from the side of the house, Margaret announced, "Will found me, Margaret. He surprised me at the creek." She knew she spoke, but her voice and her words were unrecognizable to her. Best she continued her deception before her newfound courage deserted her. "Will, this is my cousin, Margaret. She came upon hearing of Pa's death, and she and Jesse have since married."

Unfortunately, the effect her admission had on him shocked her. Bounding from the horse, Will charged Winifred, jabbing his unyielding finger into her collarbone repeatedly. "How is it you come here to comfort and support my fiancée while she grieves, yet I find her at the creek alone with a blade at her wrist?" Will hollered.

Crossing her arms over her chest to ward off any additional finger stabbing, Winifred's knees buckled. "Until the mare came back to the barn, I didn't know she left. Jesse and I were getting ready to ride out." Her eyes were wide and wild with remorse and confusion.

Once again, Margaret's heart broke. Winfred didn't deserve his wrath. Though unnecessary, Will's protectiveness bewildered and moved her. She couldn't allow Winifred to accept it. "Stop," she screamed, scrambling from the horse to her feet.

Jesse ran up and observing Winifred crumpled to the ground with a big, irate man towering over her, he fisted his hand and swung at Will.

Ducking, Will popped up and gripped the wrist of his opponent. "Enough," he snarled, wrenching the thin, shorter Jesse to him and daring him with a dauntless scowl. Jesse stepped back and dropped his arm, but Will didn't release it.

Judging by what occurred, she made the right decision. If Will learned of Jesse and Winifred's relationship, he certainly would kill the young man. He took loyalty and his word seriously. As any decent man should.

Will's eyes and jaw softened. He apologized, "I behaved disrespectfully. You, on the other hand, behaved as any man should if he witnessed any individual berating his wife. I apologize to you and Miss Margaret and wish to make amends."

Shaking loose, Jesse knelt to Winifred and whispered to her until she stood. He rose with her. Shifting his focus to Margaret, he furrowed his brow before responding, "You must be Will Havely. It is a pleasure to meet you. Mr. Harrison spoke highly of you."

Margaret's heart stopped. She swore it did. Intervening, she suggested, "I can serve us something to drink."

Winifred regarded her hesitantly. And Jesse's focus alternated between her, Winifred, and Will questioningly.

"I believe there is a slice of pie or two left. Margaret, come with me. Jesse, Will and I will marry in the morning. Show him to the bunkhouse where he will stay tonight and let him wash up before you join us," Margaret added.

Please, please let Jesse decipher my clues.

Winifred hustled over and they went to the house. The moment they were inside, Winifred fretted, "What have you done? Have you gone mad? You meant to kill yourself? You are pretending to be me?"

Snatching Winifred's upper arm and demanding her attention, Margaret snapped, "I'm pretending to be his fiancée. Unless you have had a change of heart and desire to be his wife?"

Her retorts sobered and subdued the otherwise

overwhelmed woman. Taking a visible and audible deep breath, she croaked, "Why would you do it? Any of it? I had no idea you were so unhappy and would rather die—"

"I don't understand either. I have nowhere to go. I can never seek out my family. Not being tarnished as I am." Unaware of the pressure she exerted on Winifred's arm until she saw and heard her wince, Margaret instantly let go. "Pa would try to accept me. And he would. But he sees only good and evil. And I would serve as a reminder to all that is corrupt. I would taint his perceptions and cause him suffering." Retreating and busying herself with boiling water, she added, "We aren't resilient. And we weren't prepared for the ruthlessness we would encounter."

Walking to the cupboard, Winifred retrieved cups and sugar and stressed, "You claim you aren't resilient, but you are. You have worked beside us. You are willing and agreeing to fake being me. You will sacrifice yourself for mine and Jesse's happiness?"

It's not as if she had anything to lose. Until Will, she had nothing to live for because everything inside of and about her perished. "I hope we all receive joy and live out our remaining years happy, prospering, and setting examples of good people."

It took the men much longer than she expected to come to the house. As in after sundown. During that time, Jesse and Will apparently became friends. They entered the home teasing one another and laughing ridiculously.

"All right, you two. It appears Jesse introduced you to the ranch and his flask," Winifred scolded. "You both sit your bottoms down and drink some coffee and eat something."

Jesse slurred his response, "Winni… fr, Margaret, we made him proud. Will agrees that Horace is smiling down upon us."

Winifred banged the cups and plates on the table and scowled at Jesse. "As if it was ever doubted. We have two hundred heads of cattle arriving tomorrow. We also have more mouths to feed. It pleases me you two are satisfied with the preparations, but…" she paused. "W… Winifred is getting married in the morning. And she and I are trying to make a list of staples we need from town," she pressed.

"Besides me, there will be four more," Will informed.

"We're low on basically everything. Jane brings us the bare minimum, which we are grateful for, but it's been a few weeks," Winifred stated.

Margaret's anxiety increased. Getting married meant going to town to see the preacher. Not a one of them should go to town. What if they ran into Johnny or Jane? Will could discover the truth. She suspected he wouldn't take kindly to their deception. And what if he learned about her time at the Gem?

Glancing at him, her heart hurt. It shocked her. She didn't want him to discover her identity. She didn't want him to discover that she wasn't a virgin and the vile circumstances causing such. Regardless of his intoxicated state, she found him appealing and craved his affection and protection.

He slumped into a chair, lifted his legs, and dumped his boots on the edge of the table. "So, Miss Jane kept her promise to Horace. Damn woman is a foul-mouthed rascal, but she's got a huge heart and a quick draw."

"Get your nasty feet down. Now," Margaret reprimanded. Her sudden boldness surprised her. His reaction thrilled her.

Swinging his legs to the ground, he caught her wrist and pulled her onto his lap. He hugged her and peppered her face with kisses. "Don't be cross with me, Wini. Tomorrow is a big day for me too. I never thought about taking a wife until Horace rambled on about you. I never thought I'd want to settle down in one place." Placing his fingertips lightly under her chin, he guided her face in front of his. "I can't imagine not doing those things now. With you." His lips came to hers in a sweet, assuring kiss.

And she enjoyed it. She wished it never ended. Dare she dream that Will could love her? Could her lies be forgiven in the eyes of the Lord? Would she one day meet her ma and pa again beyond the gates of heaven?

CHAPTER FOUR

Current Day
Jeannie

The alarm went off at ten a.m., but both Chelsea and Jeannie groaned at it. They were out until after midnight which neither usually did.

Getting out of bed, Jeannie went to the small coffee pot and began brewing each of them a cup. She thought about Dane. Then she wondered if he texted her. Certainly not. He probably went home and crashed just as they did.

Jeannie delivered the first cup of the hopefully potent liquid to Chelsea. Then, to check her incoming texts, she grabbed her phone. The screen indicated she did have a new text message from a number unknown to her. She swiped and read the message.

"It's Dane. Had a great time and can't wait to see you. Text me when you're available." The timestamp read 2:10 a.m. Right after he dropped them off. He probably wouldn't text again. They were two people who happened to meet and enjoy themselves. Could've been any chance meeting. She shouldn't expect anything. But she impatiently wanted to complete her meeting with William Havely and get back to see Dane again.

"You really liked him, didn't you," Chelsea asked, interrupting her silent reverie.

Her first instinct of downplaying it and mocking the suggestion burned in her throat for release. But she doubted she could succeed at either. She really did like him. Rolling her eyes, she shrugged. She admitted, "I did. I do. But it's all so silly. Honestly. I don't do relationships. And I certainly don't do long-distance ones."

Propping up the pillows and sitting up in the bed, Chelsea eyed her. "Yep. You don't do relationships. Or booty calls. Or dates. But you like him. It's more than your norm. Long distance could be the answer."

True, Jeannie didn't do relationships of any kind. She'd witnessed enough of the bad shit between her parents. She couldn't deny the attraction between her and Dane. It felt comfortable. Good.

They showered, dressed, and were downstairs waiting. But no Boulder. Jeannie repeated to herself while Chelsea bitched that it didn't matter if Boulder peeled into the parking lot thirty minutes late. She wouldn't let anything dampen her good mood.

After another full minute, sure enough Boulder showed up, parking at the curb. Wearing another awful sweater, he darted out of the vehicle and scrambled to open the passenger door and the back passenger door. He advised, "You ladies need to get a fresh drink or use the restroom before we head out. It's a good thirty-minute ride."

Chelsea snapped, "I think we handled it all…again, since we were given substantial time to do so. Within the last thirty minutes."

Thankfully, he didn't engage them in any frivolous or unfavorable conversation during the drive. Jeannie stared out the window in awe of the beautiful landscape. It still consisted of pastures, but she viewed trees, not just a grouping here or there, but thick sections, and the rolling hills, not just flat land, reminded her of home.

Taking a right off onto a narrow lane, she saw wide, tall stone columns on each side holding elaborate iron work. The Double H Ranch.

How could she not assume the Havely's had money? But she didn't foresee visiting a ranch which rivaled the one on Yellowstone. The house stretched out atop a vast elevated area. Meadows surrounded the estate. And yes, she would describe it as an estate.

"It is impressive, isn't it? I've been visiting or living here since birth," Boulder bragged, as if he had something she wanted.

To hell with him. She wasn't some money-grubbing gold-digger. They contacted her. She wouldn't give him any satisfaction by responding. She couldn't object. It was impressive.

Boulder pulled in the circular driveway and stopped in front of the massive dwelling where a man greeted them. He opened the passenger doors.

Chelsea introduced herself before he could. "Mr. Havely, I'm Chelsea. I can't thank you enough for paying for me to come here with Jeannie."

Boulder laughed raucously. And insultingly. "That's not my uncle. That's Malcolm. Your basic caretaker of the residence."

Bubbling echoed in her chest and ears. The bubbling of her blood boiling. Yep. His rude comments and pretentious attitude infuriated her. But the tall, slender, elderly, impeccably presented man ignored Boulder. He even went as far as to ridicule him by stating, "You are late. I think it wise you exclude yourself from here on. Unless it is your goal to kill your uncle. He received implicit instructions from Connie to avoid stressors of any form."

Mr. Havely had health conditions? At the age of seventy-five, he probably did. Those considerations didn't resonate with the young. Her grandmother had her fair share of issues, but nothing yet that diminished her quality of life. She continued to live in her mother's house after her death. She cooked Sunday dinner for Jeannie every week.

The caretaker, or Malcolm, escorted them up the front steps of the mansion and into a beautifully marbled foyer with a curving staircase enclosed with black wrought iron. The stairs, doors, and trim were all dark wood. The high, tongue-and-groove ceiling in matching dark wood enthralled her. The space combined modern, grand elements with rustic, natural ones. They blended perfectly. The huge window on the back wall of the second floor allowed enough light in to prevent the area from feeling dim and closed in.

Leading them to an opened, arched double door on the left, Malcolm announced, "Your guests have arrived, William. I advised Boulder to get lost."

Stepping out of the way, Jeannie got her first look at William Havely. He chuckled at Malcolm's statement and presented her and Chelsea with a dashing smile. He didn't appear ill or unwell. Dressed in black slacks and an eggplant-colored button-down, he appeared downright debonair. And extremely handsome. He had a tanned face, but not overly. Almost as if recently returned from a lavish, tropical vacation. He had a head of thick, salt-and-pepper hair.

Walking over, he shook their hands and gestured them inside a gargantuan, expensively decorated, but comfortable formal living room. "I do apologize for foisting Boulder on you as your shuttle driver. But he is my nephew. And he is a decent man beneath all his haughtiness. He does have a mind for business and is a wonderful father."

A middle-aged blonde, who obviously spent money on her appearance and took care of herself, sauntered through the French doors on their right and went straight to the bar section of the room. She poured herself a generous drink. Raising the glass, she pivoted and greeted them. "Jeannie…and Chelsea, if I remember correctly from the information provided for travel arrangements, it is a real pleasure to meet you both. Can I offer you a drink?"

Chelsea uttered, "Yes, please."

"A girl after my own heart." The beautiful blonde

winked and turned to pour another. "And what about you, Jeannie? We have so much to discuss. I am sure neither Boulder nor William showered you with any details. Nope. They would've let sleeping dogs lay. But I love astrology and genealogy and any real good story."

No words came. This woman, who she instantly liked, blew her mind. She didn't mince words. Twice, Jeannie's mind had been blown in twelve hours.

"I'm Constance Havely. The second and best wife to the love of my life, William Havely, IV." Handing off Chelsea's drink, she tapped their glasses and gushed, "He indulges me and my *wild* fantasies. But even he can't negate the treasure trove I've unearthed."

"Connie, I've only had a few minutes with them before you gusted in here," defended Mr. Havely.

Tipping her glass and finishing her drink, Connie huffed, "As if Boulder is ever punctual. Not unless it means money in his pocket."

"Connie," Winston cautioned.

Connie grunted, returned to the bar, and poured another drink. "Do you wish to see the property before we continue? Or would you prefer we sit? You must have a million questions."

How did one answer that? She did want to see the property. She did have questions. But where to start. "According to the documents provided, a William Havely and Winifred Rose Harrison Havely willed a portion of your property to one of my ancestors, Margaret Jean Miller. You learned more than my mother did during her searches because I've never seen or heard of any relation to any Millers."

Connie nodded. "I probably had more information to go on. And what a blessing it is that your mother did delve into her lineage. It certainly made my job a little easier. Your mother's quest stalled at Margaret Jean and Jesse Price. Neither were native to Alabama. They went there in 1879 and had one daughter who married a Jones."

As she had since they first contacted her, she wondered why they bothered with any of it. They could have easily and legally discounted an over a century old bequest. Heck a one hundred and forty something year old legacy. "And you believe this Margaret Jean Miller is my…however many greats grandmother, Margaret Jean Price?"

One of Connie's perfectly contoured eyebrows lifted above her hazel eye. "I know it is."

"Mom, the verdict please," urged an oddly familiar voice from behind her. She blinked a few dozen times. Sure, she did. Rotating only her head, she shut her eyes tight, dreading reopening them. He either hadn't noticed her, disregarded her, or focused on his mother.

His mother?

Dane spoke again. "I don't know why you insisted I handle this. I understand omitting Boulder, but you have other capable hands. You always bitch at me to put myself out there, and I did. Don't make me fuck this up before it even gets going."

She froze and her chest, her abdomen, and her core tightened and throbbed. Her damn face heated again. That damn voice of his. Could it all be a fucking outrageous coincidence? Or some weird swindle. As if she had anything they'd want.

Except the property. The property. Had they planned to use Dane to woo her out of it?

"Wah, wah. Stop whining. You remind me of Boulder. Let me introduce you to the true heir of Sunny Creek." Constance sauntered between them and gestured. "This is Winifred Jean Scanlon. She prefers Jeannie."

Turning her head in the opposite direction of him, she dreaded the entire awkward sort of re-introduction. She didn't trust any of it.

Chelsea's laughter invaded the uncomfortable situation. She laughed. And laughed. Loudly. "Hi, Dane. Great to see you again. Is this all going to end in some story about how Dane and Jeannie are related?"

"No. They are not," William Havely interjected.

His statement hushed the room. Chelsea appeared mortified. "I'm sorry. I didn't really mean it would be funny. Because it's not."

Oh, good golly. Could they be related somehow? They linked her to the property. Did they link it through DNA too? Was Margaret blood-related somehow and that's why she owned land there?

"Relax. They are not related. Winifred was a Harrison," Connie declared.

Jeannie couldn't bring herself to meet eyes with any of them. She stared at the geometric pattern in the tiles. She knew Winifred was a Harrison. A Harrison who married a Havely. That's how the ranch got its name. The Double H for Harrison and Havely. And Winifred and Margaret crossed paths at some point.

"Jeannie is the owner? I should have asked the name of the woman you brought here."

She saw and felt his hand slide over hers, intertwining their fingers, but she stayed focused on the floor.

"Jeannie," he murmured, "I promise you I had no idea you were the one Connie found and—" he paused before blaming, "insisted this entire venture wouldn't conclude in a debacle."

"Why don't we all simply leave this alone for now. I'm sorry, Dane. I never imagined the girl you met last night might be Jeannie," Connie empathized. "This is a lot to take in. We've all just met, and here I am cramming a bunch of farfetched but accurate history at you."

Dane squeezed her hand.

Did she have any mind remaining to be blown? The entire past connection. The mere fact that Dane told his mom about her. He said he didn't want to fuck it up. But Constance couldn't be his mom. She must be his stepmother? Right? She couldn't be older than fifty-five. She could be his mother. She might have had him young. After she married Havely. No. The records indicated she married Havely twenty years ago in 2002. So. Just because they weren't married at Dane's birth didn't translate as he couldn't be their child.

Tugging on her hand slightly until she met his gaze, he explained, "Seems as if I get to kill two birds with one stone. In the best possible way. Connie recruited me to escort the owner of Sunny Creek to the property. And because I'm such a good boy, I couldn't and wouldn't disappoint her. Even if it meant I wouldn't see you again until I did. And here you are."

He called Connie by her name that time. So, she had to be his stepmother. His lips curled into a calming grin. Paired with his relaxing brown eyes, it slowed her overwrought mind.

"I have horses ready, but something tells me that isn't your preferred travel method." Dane pulled her out of the room and out of the house. "We aren't going on horseback, are we?" he questioned.

"What's the alternative? It's not accessible by car?" she asked.

"It's way beyond what we ranch, so no access roads. ATVs then. You ever drove one?"

She chuckled. At his question and his excitement. She jogged to keep up with him. "I'm from the country. I'm familiar with four-wheelers."

"Four-wheelers it is. Hope you can keep up."

"What about Chelsea? I shouldn't leave her behind," she worried.

"I think Connie can keep her entertained." He took them behind the house and to a giant metal building beside a huge stable. "Let me just make sure they're gassed up and we can be on our way." They didn't just store four-wheelers inside, but snowmobiles, and more off road vehicles. She watched him retrieve a gas can and fill the tanks. She watched the shirt tighten across his muscular back. She watched his gait. And his nice derriere. She watched his biceps flex as he pulled the thick chain and opened one of the oversized doors flooding the garage with sunlight.

He cranked the machines and motioned for her to take a seat on one. She let him lead since he knew the property. They drove alongside the fence for a while. She admired the horses. She viewed cows. Tons of cows. Reaching open fields, he increased his speed. She did the same. They raced and cut up and laughed.

They slowed and talked. He informed her that his father met Connie three years after his mother died. They married when he started high school. His mother died when he was seven. He credited Connie with breathing life back into not only his father, but him, and the Double H. After his mom's death, William allowed the Harrisons to step in and take over a good portion of the ranch duties.

His next comment shed light on his exuberant personality. "And I never took interest in running or managing the ranch. I reckon I inherited my mother's love of the theater, and with Connie's encouragement, I pursued it."

Admiring his handsome features, she agreed he had the looks for it. "Anything I should recognize you from?"

He laughed. "Nah. I doubt it. I do perform in the reenactments during Wild Bill Days in Deadwood. I travel the Northwest and have recurring roles in small theaters. I didn't put all my eggs in one basket, let's say. I have a degree in marketing and found myself enjoying and developing graphic art."

Interesting. He lived a colorful life. Probably why she

dreaded him asking about her life. Which he did. She delivered a condensed version. Not that there happened to be much more to it.

Her skin prickled. The hairs on the back of her neck stood. Ahead she saw a cluster of trees on the greenest grass she'd ever seen. Braking, she shut off the motor. Stepping inside the oasis, she twisted in and out of the trees. A sweet breeze rustled the grass and leaves, and she breathed deeply, inhaling the beauty and the peace.

Gripping a trunk, he swung in front of her. "Why are you stopping here?" he asked.

"This is it. Isn't it? This is mine."

"What gave you that indication?"

"It did," she replied emphatically.

He gazed at her in disbelief. His brown eyes bristled with excitement. "Connie is going to have a field day with this."

"Because I'm right," she stated. She'd never been a believer in the occult or déjà vu. Or even love at first sight. In that spot, in those moments, her entire world shifted. Insane and silly. Could it be that she just got caught up in the splendor and tranquility of it? She owned a hidden gem in the otherwise rocky and dry terrain. And the beautiful man in front of her rivaled it.

He grinned at her as if her reactions were precious and he didn't want to break the spell. In the distance, she heard the flow of water. "Is there a creek?" she asked.

Taking her hand, they strolled through the trees and exited to a wide stream. Immediately, she rolled her jeans up to her knees and removed her shoes. Dane did the same.

The frigid water numbed her feet. Even in winter, she doubted Alabama waters were ever as absurdly cold. But the edge was clear and shallow, and the pebbles were visible and beautiful underneath the surface. And it was speckled with gold.

It's speckled with gold.

Bending forward, she fanned her fingers through the bottom. *It can't be gold. If it is gold, why would they...who in their right mind would relinquish it?*

"Yep. It's gold. But Mom needs to explain it all to you. Not me," Dane said.

She stared at him with a thousand questions penetrating her mind. They both grabbed at each other, and their lips met. And she saw stars. He kissed her firmly, but tenderly while their hands roamed and somehow, they ended up naked on the bank. It was perfect. They made love and frolicked in the water. They learned about each other, not just sexually. They shared all of themselves. Nothing in her life ever felt as right. It all seemed too good to be true. It probably was.

CHAPTER FIVE

1878
Margaret

Today Margaret married. The day on the ranch started as the ones before it. They woke. They completed their morning chores. Except they had Will assisting, and he worked fast and hurried them along. He insisted they get to town, marry, purchase supplies, and return before noon. She dressed in a lovely, pristine, light-blue skirt and jacket and pulled her hair back with a matching ribbon.

She was excited. Her heart raced and her legs were uncooperative. It didn't help that the hem of the dress rested beneath the soles of her boots and every step she took she heard it rip. But Will wanted to marry her. And she wanted to marry him.

It happened quickly and dully. Until he pressed his lips into hers. Could one person transfer their confidence into another? She believed they could. She inhaled his strength. She savored his gentleness. He kissed her long and sincerely with one hand on the back of her head and his other at her lower back. He held her possessively and protectively. She wished those moments could last forever.

But they couldn't.

He scooped her up in his arms and carried her out of the church and to the wagon. He lifted her on the bench and jumped up beside her.

Winfred and Jesse climbed in the back.

"Don't look so petrified. I know you've stayed away from town, but I'm with you. Ain't no one gonna bother you. The scoundrels need to see you with your new husband and know they better keep to themselves," Will assured.

Taking the reins, he directed the horse away from the church on the edge of town. The noise of horses' hooves, people shouting, and the clanking of metal erupted in her ears and chest. It compounded the banging of her heart. The street was messy and muddy and busy. There were people everywhere she looked. They were looking at her. Weren't they? They recognized her. They would expose her dirty truths.

"Don't say anything. Keep your eyes down," Winifred urged from behind her. She had moved into a crouching position at the bench and leaned over it, whispering at the side of her head. The side opposite Will.

He stopped them in front of the general store and helped her to her feet. Jesse did the same with Winifred. Hooking her arm inside of Winifred's, she insisted, "Let's make this fast. Get what we need and leave." Winifred nodded.

Once they were inside, they made quick time of it. Jesse and Will stood in the doorway blocking anyone trying to enter and keeping watch over the ladies. Seated back in the wagon, she sighed a breath of relief.

"Who da hell would've believed there were two blonde beauties hiding out on Harrison's land?" Her spine stiffened hearing the raspy voice of Cruel Dan from the Gem. "Imagine the two-fer deal Swearengin could've gotten with them."

In a flash of movement, Will stood towering over Dan with his pistol cocked and centered in the monstrosity's forehead. "I don't need a reason," he growled. "You are speaking about my wife and her cousin. I don't take too kindly to any man disrespecting women. Especially when one of those women is mine."

She couldn't read Dan's expression. Not that she made any effort to do so. A part of her hoped Will shot the loathsome man.

He did not. Will tilted his gun and fired into the air above Dan's head. "You tell everyone that Will Havely has arrived. Any man caught badgering these women or stepping on the Harrison land will be killed," he yelled.

Clapping sounded across the street. Twisting her head, Margaret saw Jane leaning up against the building with her feet crossed at the ankles in front of her. She continued to clap, drawing the attention from everyone in the otherwise silent crowd. Dropping her hands, she bounced forward and swaggered toward them. "Will Havely, you never did know how to announce your presence without causing a ruckus." She circled the wagon, exchanging solid pats to the back with Will.

"You lookin' mighty pretty, Miss Jane," he greeted. He grinned and winked at her. "I appreciate you checking on the girls until I could get here. Horace would've too."

Removing her hat, she lowered her head and closed her eyes. "God rest his kind soul. You gonna need some help once the drive gets in?"

"I will never decline an offer from you. Come on and stay for dinner. The girls got a real nice meal planned." He climbed up on the seat beside Margaret. "I assume you never found out who put the bullets in Horace's back?"

His inquiry rattled Jane. At his mention of the girls and a nice meal, her eyes darted from him and onto Margaret and Winifred. Her mouth opened to comment but his remark about Horace suppressed it. Margaret mumbled a prayer before announcing, "Will and I married this morning. I know Pa is at peace. It's what he wanted. We will build the ranch he dreamed of."

Fidgeting with her hat between her hands, Jane narrowed one eye at her. "Yes, you will." Switching her focus to Will, she confessed, "I have come up empty on who murdered Horace. It's not from lack of investigating and roughing up several for information."

"I didn't expect anyone to own up to it. I less expected anyone to offer up their life by snitching." He took Margaret's hand and squeezed it. "See you afterwhile, Jane."

The ride home consisted of laughter and stories. Will

told stories about when he first met Jane and of their outrageous antics. Seemed both enjoyed playing pranks. Margaret couldn't believe she was a married woman. She couldn't believe they went to town and not only returned with their lives, but she and Winifred returned with their secrets intact.

At the ranch, once they unloaded the wagon, she and Winifred went straight to the coop and garden. Tonight, in addition to biscuits and the newly purchased potatoes, they would dine on fried chicken and peas. Because of the oven and stove, the heat inside the house surpassed that of the sweltering outside. She fanned herself with her apron.

Hearing footsteps on the porch, she looked over her shoulder and saw Will. "Jane is here. She rode out and scouted the drive. We have a couple of hours still before hell breaks loose." He cocked his head and smiled at her. "Mrs. Havely, will you take a ride with me?"

She scanned the table and the counters that were all covered in bowls and knives and spoons. She couldn't leave.

"Go," urged Winifred.

"I can't leave all this on you—"

Swatting at her with a towel, Winifred stressed, "I won't let you if you keep standing there and don't go."

Fumbling with her apron ties, she finally freed herself of it and draped it over a chair as she skipped to her husband. *Her husband.*

She held on to him tightly as the horse galloped them across fields and over hills and along trees. The bright sun illuminated it all. It heated her face. She doubted any of it could rival the brilliancy in her heart and soul. She knew where he planned to take her. The very place where she chose to end it all. The very place where he rescued her and gave her a reason to live again.

Weaving in and out of the trees, they came upon Sunny Creek. It was extraordinary.

Standing on the bank, they held hands and gazed at the clear water and the twinkling within. "Horace never out and said anything about gold being on the land. But I understood. He told me about the Lakota he encountered back in '72. How they ate and hunted together. How they predicted this land would be taken. He appreciated it as they did. He promised to preserve it and keep a friendly and reciprocal relationship with them." He tugged her hand, pulling her to face him. "You probably know all this."

No, she didn't. Winifred might. She didn't. Lowering her eyes, she prayed for strength and forgiveness. She hated lying to him. But it went too far now.

Lifting his hands to her hair, he removed the combs letting it fall loosely to her waist. He splayed his fingers through it and rubbed it. "So beautiful," he murmured. His lips met hers.

Every negative notion disappeared from her mind. Actually, her mind deserted her. Her heart and her body controlled her. And she gladly surrendered to them. What began as a sweet, chaste touch of mouths became demanding and frenzied.

Pulling away, Will stripped himself of all clothing and waded in the creek. "The day is hot, and your kitchen is as if you entered hell itself. Come on. Let's cool off."

Her fingers trembled, but she removed her garments. She chose him. She chose this. She would be his wife in every sense of the word. Happily.

Margaret

Margaret thought the ranch required a lot of time and sweat before the cattle arrived. She had no idea. In the first few months after they wed, she saw William at supper and in the bedroom. Two of the hands chose to stay on at the Double H. Which she and Will appropriately named for Harrison and Havely. And she supposedly was both. Her days and nights were filled with purpose, motivation, and joy.

Winifred and Jesse sat her down one afternoon and gave her heart-wrenching news. They were leaving. To go South. To easier winters. They yearned to rightfully marry. Margaret couldn't deny them the happiness she found.

"Never forget this is the Double H Ranch. Continue as you are and persevere. Build and maintain my father's vision. It's all I ask," Winifred insisted when the two women hugged good-bye.

Tears leaked from Margaret's eyes. "I promise. This land is yours. Always."

Dabbing at her eyes, Winifred surmised, "I appreciate it. But it hasn't been since Pa died. Honor him." She chuckled and hugged Margaret as they both sniffled.

"We will both have babies," Winifred beamed through tears. "Then they will have babies. I only hope my father is never forgotten."

"It's my promise to you, I will never forget him or what you've done for me," Margaret promised. Sunny Creek is yours forever. It will belong always belong to your or your children."

CHAPTER SIX

Current Day
Jeannie

The afternoon at Sunny Creek changed Jeannie's life forever. At least she thought it did. What did a twenty-three-year-old know about forever.

She did know that chance encounters possess the ability to alter one's future. Reluctantly, she and Dane returned to the house after their first afternoon together after dark. Chelsea and Connie were on the open deck sitting around a built-in firepit.

Dane easily persuaded her, with hidden grabs and touches, to accompany him inside to eat and grab an alcoholic beverage. "I told you Chelsea would be fine with Connie. Unfortunately, I suspect they've had a lot of alcohol."

Whether they did or not, it wouldn't have mattered. The bizarre story she heard from Connie left her speechless.

"I have Margaret Jean Miller's Bible. It's been passed down from generation to generation. Because we all get consumed in our own lives, no one truly studied it. Not the scripture itself, but the personalized pages. I sincerely can't imagine not one of the previous descendants questioned it, but I went further and analyzed it," Connie divulged.

The Havely's had a Bible which belonged to one of her ancestors? If Margaret Jean Miller and Margaret Jean Price were indeed the same woman. It kind of made sense. Didn't it? Her greatest grandmother and one of theirs obviously knew one another. Why else would she be heir to a parcel of land? She shook her head, faking understanding.

"Jeannie, get your head out of the clouds and join me in what will surely blow your mind," Constance urged.

They all laughed. Jeannie witnessed firsthand the magnetism Connie and Dane shared. How fun it must have been to have known Connie during his pivotal years.

"Margaret Jean Miller was the daughter of a preacher. No way she would ever leave her Bible anywhere. And that, my dear friend, is why I had a DNA specialist examine the sample your mother supplied through an ancestry database against the Harrison's DNA." She rocketed out of her seat and waved her hands in the air. "Lo and behold, Little Miss Margaret Jean Price wasn't only Margaret Jean Miller, but she was Winifred Harrison."

Too much. Too fast. The martini Dane fixed her, which she accepted without intent to drink, tasted fine as she drained it.

"Connie, you're getting ahead of yourself…well, Jeannie," Dane warned.

"What are you trying to say exactly," Jeannie asked. And what did it mean? Nothing really. One of her ancestors lied about their identity. It's not as if it affected anything currently.

Or did it? Were she and Dane blood related? No matter how many generations removed it might be, did they share blood?

"I can only guess. Sometime after Horace Harrison's death, Margaret and Winifred encountered and befriended one another. I don't know why they switched identities. But they did. The Bible includes handwritten notes of Margaret's early years in Minnesota with her parents, George and Sarah Miller. It also includes later entries in which she listed her name as Margaret but marked through it and wrote Winifred. It's all been analyzed and judged as the same penmanship. It records the births of her and Will's three children. There is also an entry about remorse and how she prays for Winifred's well-being nightly," Connie elaborated.

"This is beyond…beyond—"

Lifting her out of her seat, Dane straddled behind her, settling her into his lap. "It is. But if you put the pieces together, they form a perfect puzzle," he maintained.

"Winifred Havely, or the woman who claimed to be her, had it documented and stipulated to her children that Sunny Creek belonged to Margaret Miller. The Havely's have honored this through the generations. I initially wanted to uncover the relationship these two women had and why it meant so much to Winifred to hold Sunny Creek for Margaret. I never imagined I would learn that they switched roles and became one another." Connie bounced in her seat. "It's an amazing tale don't you think?"

Amazing? Perplexing. "So, I am related to the Harrisons. Margaret didn't marry Jesse, Winifred did."

Connie nodded and grinned. "Yep. Makes sense she held onto her true name by passing it down to her daughter. And her daughter...and so on. She also used Margaret's middle name." She shrugged. "And you even share the name, Winifred Jean."

"But I'm a Harrison. And Winifred married a Havely—"

Dane interrupted, "No... Margaret married a Havely. We share no DNA, Jeannie."

Right. Right.

"William and I are delighted to not only fulfill the wishes of Winifred Havely, but to know Sunny Creek truly remains with its rightful owner. A great granddaughter of the true Winifred Harrison," Connie gushed.

Jeannie

The incredible account—well obviously truth if it's supported by DNA—astounded Jeannie. All of Deadwood did. Sunny Creek did. Dane did.

The remainder of her trip, she spent hours with Connie and William at the ranch. William shared information he had on his great-grandfather Will Havely. He explained that Margaret and Winifred most likely fell victim to trouble in or from Deadwood which drove them to abandon their names and assume the name of the other. The murder of Horace might have been a part of it. All Horace had wanted was to settle down with his daughter on beautiful land and expose her to a simpler life. A life in which you reap what you sow. A life filled with beauty, accomplishment, and respect. Financial profit wasn't his goal. He wanted to teach her to appreciate the land, hard work, and the rewards.

And Margaret had been on her way to Oregon. Something happened that estranged her from her parents. They told her many stories they knew of both women who were known and loved as Winifred.

They welcomed her into their lives, their hearts, and their home. So long, Travelodge. She and Chelsea moved out of the motel the day after the "big reveal." Dane had been crashing with friends, but once Boulder left, he joined them. Seemed he and Boulder had never gotten along well.

Dane took the girls on tours of the surrounding area. The quaint Old West town of Keystone located truly in the center of the Black Hills quickly became one of their favorites. It had a spectacular setting as it sat low surrounded by the high hills embedded with trees. They visited Mount Rushmore.

Often, they went back to Sunny Creek. On horseback. She loved it. Yes, it terrified her. But it also felt right—appropriate and meaningful to access it as Winifred and Margaret did. Dane urged his horse into a gallop as the creek came into view. She did the same with hers. She ignored the instantaneous terror and basked in all of it. Him. The scenery. The history. The profound connection she had with all of it.

She found love. She loved Dane Havely. It happened quick. Too quick. Some would call it "instalove." And she saw all the red flags. His age. His gypsy spirit. She certainly thought if she ever met a gypsy, it would be a female one. Not that she even envisioned herself with a free spirit. After prolonging her trip an additional week, she cried when Dane dropped her off at the airport. Already he had a flight booked to Alabama in ten days. He promised they would make it work.

And she believed him. Sunny Creek was magical. Winifred and Jesse, Margaret and Will, and now Jeannie and Dane found love there.

Horace Harrison found an extraordinary piece of property. Jeannie vowed she would protect it and honor him and share the stories of it for generations to come. And it would start with hers and Dane's children. A Harrison and a Havely as Horace intended.

The End

ABOUT THE AUTHOR
SHERI LYNN

Sheri Lynn is a *USA Today* best-selling author. She also writes as Sheridan Knight. She writes romance across several genres-contemporary, vampire, Western, futuristic/post-apocalyptic, historical fantasy, and a few novellas included in anthologies she categorizes as historical suspense. She's a hopeless romantic and can find a happily ever after in most situations and settings. First published in 2015, she has followed with over thirty additional single or anthology titles with many more coming.

Growing up an Army brat, her childhood consisted of moving every three years until her father retired to Alabama while she was in high school. Currently she splits time between Alabama, Florida, and Wyoming with her husband, two Golden Retrievers, a chihuahua, and a turtle.

Needless to say, she keeps herself surrounded in inspiration.

Where to find her:

Social media:
twitter.com/sherilynnauthor
www.facebook.com/sherilynnauthor/
www.amazon.com/-/e/B0182IRER8

www.bookbub.com/profile/sheri-lynn
www.instagram.com/sherilynnauthor/
www.facebook.com/groups/SexyScintillatingRomanceby
SheriandSheridan/
www.goodreads.com/author/show/14678523.Sheri_Lynn
www.amazon.com/-/e/B0182IRER8
www.amazon.com/Sheridan-Knight/e/B07RMKMQRP

Contact information: https://sherilynnauthor.com/
Email: sherilynnauthor@yahoo.com

Sheri's Newsletter signup:
mailchi.mp/sherilynnauthor/sherilynn-sheridanknight

Hugs

SIDNEY PARKER

A gift from her beloved grandmother and the chance for a fresh start has Blaze Blackwell, a single mom, driving cross country to Deadwood, South Dakota, and a new life. Everyone welcomes her and her little girl with open arms. Everyone, that is, except the one person who wants her to go away and is determined to make her life a living hell.

White Knights are not just for fairy tales. Sometimes a knight in shining armor comes to the rescue in a pair of faded blue jeans.

Chapter One

Present Day, Deadwood, SD
Blaze Blackwell

"Well, baby girl, I don't think we're in Kansas anymore."

I glanced down at my child and then at the house in front of me. A run-down, older than dirt, little tiny house, set back from the main road and surrounded by ten acres of dust. Welcome to Deadwood, South Dakota.

No matter how much I loved coming to visit my grandparents every summer when I was a little girl, I never though the fates would decide this is where I was meant to live. But then there were a lot of things in my life I never dreamed would happen.

Theadora pulled at the hem of my T-shirt, the one I'd been wearing for the last three days as we drove from Miami to Deadwood. Outside, I glanced at the dirty brown that surrounded me, the lack of color and the dust that swirled from the land up into the air when the wind scooped in and took it for a ride. I saw the nothingness. But where there is nothingness, there can be change, and I needed changes—big ones.

"Momma, hungry."

Reality snapped me back and I picked up Thea, snuggling into her face with mine, making her burst out in a fit a giggles. Theadora Rose, my entire reason for being and the reason we needed to get out of Florida and come to the only safe place I knew of, giving us a fresh start. Deadwood, South Dakota…our new home.

Balancing Thea on my hip, I grabbed the key my aunt left tucked above the light by the front door and let myself inside. The furniture was old but looked to be in good shape. It was obvious my aunt, Cathy, had been here cleaning because I couldn't see a trace of dust anywhere inside the house. The refrigerator had been stocked, along with the pantry, and I even found a cookie jar filled with fresh chocolate chip cookies inside. I felt the tears filling my eyes as I remembered that very same cookie jar, Winnie the Pooh, sitting on the kitchen counter when I was a little girl. My grandma always had fresh cookies ready for me too.

Thea was perfectly happy with eating a cookie first while I whipped her up a peanut butter and jelly sandwich, the crusts removed, for lunch. Hopefully, a nap would soon follow so I could unpack my truck with what little I brought with us. I purged before we exited Florida. Since the universe decided to kickball all the plans I had made for my life to the far left field, I decided to leave the excess baggage behind me as well. It made leaving a lot easier.

Two hours later, I checked on Thea, who was still sound asleep. She never made a sound as I hauled in the boxes and set them in my soon-to-be bedroom and in the corner of the living room, respectively, everything had labels. To say I was overly organized was an understatement.

My phone vibrated from the back pocket of my jeans where I had shoved it earlier. I smiled as I saw the name that came up.

"Hey, Aunt Cathy. Everything looks amazing, and you even made Thea cookies."

"Oh my sweet Blaze. I'm glad everything was okay. I sent Sam over there this morning, just to double check one more time. And every little girl should have cookies waiting for them. I can't wait to get my hands on that little cherub of yours. God never gave me any girls, just my three crazy boys, so your little one is getting some spoiling."

My aunt rarely took a breath between her words. She never had. I remembered how much she spoiled me during my summer visits to see my grandparents. Cathy's husband, Sam, was my dad's youngest brother. Sam and Cathy had three boys, and my uncle George and his wife had four. My parents just had me, and I was the only girl on both sides of my family. Now there was Theadora, and yes she would be spoiled—spoiled with the love of everyone in the bunch.

Cathy went on. "I think you have everything you should need, or what I thought anyway. I stocked the pantry with the basics. I wasn't sure if you were into all that healthy stuff the co-op in town carries, but I figured you could pick that up yourself. I can come over in the morning and sit with Thea if you need me to. I'm just dying to get my hands on the little darling."

My daughter was definitely going to be spoiled.

"That would be great, Aunt Cathy. I want to grab some fresh vegetables and fruit, though if you have things to do, I can take her with me. I'm used to having Thea attached to my side these days." I laughed.

"No, no. I have nothing else to do but help you get settled. I was thinking of having you two over this weekend. Get the boys and their significant partners over for a little welcome celebration for you and Thea. We can talk about it in the morning. Do you need help with unpacking? Sam can run over and do the heavy stuff."

"I'm good. I didn't bring more than what fit in my truck. I got rid of most of the junk I had down in Florida. This is our fresh start, thanks to grandma."

I purged everything. The rental house where my dreams of happily ever after blew out the door with a slam the night I announced we were having a baby, the dead-end job managing a fast food place with a bunch of privileged brats who didn't understand the meaning of hard work. But most of all, I purged the mindset I was carrying around that I needed a prince charming to rescue me and take me and Thea off on a giant white horse to a castle high up the hills.

My answer came from my boot-wearing, hard-working, cuss-like-a-sailor, do-it-herself grandmother from Deadwood, South Dakota.

She was my queen.

Chapter Two

Blaze

Cathy was on the floor with Thea in the living room, a box of toys already scattered on the rug, showing my daughter all the miniature farm animals she had found and the noises they made. Thea's happy giggles were making it easy to slip out the door to run some errands while leaving her with a relative stranger, even if they were family. I wasn't sure I would even be missed. Just as I was climbing into my truck, someone came barreling down my dirt driveway, fast enough to send a giant cloud of dust flying into the air.

A black Escalade appeared behind me when the dust settled and a man stepped out. From the expensive cowboy boots that first hit the ground to the jeans with a harsh crease pressed into them and the black ten gallon hat that partially hid the man's face, I felt like someone wanted to intimidate me.

"Who the hell are you?" boomed out a harsh voice with a nasty edge to it.

No hello, no welcome the neighborhood, no introduction. Just a demand. I had enough of that kind of treatment to last me a lifetime. No more.

"Well," I said, "who the hell are you?"

"I'm the man who owns the land you're standing on, missy." His voice was loud.

"That's impossible. My grandmother owned this land and she left it to me," I retorted.

"She was selling it to me. I own everything around you."

"Well, she didn't. It's mine, and I'm not selling, so get the hell off my property."

I stepped closer, planning on going nose-to-nose with the old jerk.

He sputtered and stamped his foot, his fists clenching at his sides and his face turning even redder. I heard the front screen door bang open behind me and Cathy's voice start hollering.

"Patrick O'Connell, you get your hind end back in that vehicle and get on out of here. I just called the sheriff and he's on his way. You've been pulling this crap for years. Give it up. Emma Rose wouldn't sell you her place if you were the last man alive. You leave my niece alone and get out."

With a few choice words I couldn't make out, he got back into his Escalade and backed it up, running over the flowers planted on the edge of the front yard, and hit the gas full throttle going out the long driveway. I started coughing from all the dust flying at me. I turned and looked at my aunt, and she started to laugh.

"Your white T-shirt isn't white anymore," she said.

I looked down and the dusty brown splotches covering my shirt. I imagined my face looked the same.

"I think I made an enemy already, Aunt Cathy."

"Maybe, but Patrick O'Connell is a pain in everyone's backside. He makes a lot of noise, but for the most part, he's harmless. Your grandmother loved to yank that man's chain every chance she got."

Great, I thought. My grandmother may have left me a house of my own, but she also left me an arrogant, asshat neighbor who didn't seem to want me here.

"I hope you're right. I really need a peaceful environment, especially for Thea. We've been through enough already."

Cathy patted me on the shoulder affectionately.

"You'll be fine, and so will Thea. Life may hand out a few bumps along the road, but things find a way of working out for the best when you just go with it. I mean, just take a look at the last few months. Did you ever think you'd be living in Deadwood? Now you have family close by to help you where, in Florida, you were all alone," Cathy pointed out.

That was true. I had wanted to live by the ocean ever since I went on a vacation there at age twelve. That was my one main goal in life. I chose my college because of the location, and I stayed even when I had great job offers in the Midwest. I wanted that giant body of water close by. The truth was, especially after Theadora was born, I rarely had time to walk on a beach, much less enjoy the water.

Now I was living in a dust bowl with lots of time at my disposal.

"You're right, Cathy," I agreed. "Everything happens for a reason. Where's Thea?"

"She just fell asleep in the middle of the living room floor. She moved all her animals onto the blanket she pulled off the couch and started singing to them. She fell asleep mid-song. So precious." Cathy glanced back at my daughter.

I raced into town to pick up the few things I still needed, after changing my shirt. Then, with Cathy's help, I had most everything unpacked and put away. The only thing left was my office. I was going to use the little room between the living area and Thea's bedroom. The room was tiny, but it would be fine for what I had in mind. And I would be able to listen when Thea was napping.

Once Cathy left, I scooped up Thea and set her on her bed. covering her with a light quilt. I pulled the curtains closed to dim the sunlight and quietly closed her door. I was surprised at how well she was adapting to a new home. The move didn't seem to faze her at all.

Back in my office, I looked around. I had already hung my white board and the matching cork board. The shelves were up, and I set my boxes of books below them. It took me less than an hour and I had my computer up and running and my drawing desk organized just the way I needed it.

I had earned my bachelor's degree in fiber arts, with a minor in design. Being a single mother, I was always afraid to take the leap and become completely self-employed. I needed the benefits my lousy job had given me, and I wanted some kind of security as far as a paycheck went.

When Grandma left me her house and a small monetary inheritance, I jumped. My clients assured me they would help spread the word, and my website was ready to go live as soon as I hit the button. Now I just prayed jumping wasn't going to land me in a dark, murky pond.

Chapter Three

Blaze

"Momma, cows."

Thea stood in the doorway of my office.

"Moooo."

I glanced over at her and smiled.

"Cows do say moo, Thea. Very good," I praised her.

"No, cows," she insisted and pointed at the living room.

I didn't have time for this. I had just sent off pricing information to four new potential clients. And I had several more emails to answer. My website had only been out there a week and already the inquiries were coming in almost daily. I gave a quick thanks skyward to the heavens.

"Thea, is there a cow in the living room?" I asked, and she giggled.

"No. Cows." She reached for my hand and pulled me toward the front of the house where the windows were wide open and the curtains billowed from the breeze. I glanced around the room, at the toys scattered about, but I didn't see her cows. I looked at her, but her gaze was directed at the window.

At first, the sight outside my front window didn't register. Not until a loud moo had me clearing the hardwood floors beneath my feet. There had to be a dozen cows or more in my front yard. I raced over and opened the front door, only to slam it shut again when I came face-to-face with a cow on the front steps. While I was standing there, back against the front door, freaking out, my daughter was clapping her hands and squealing with delight over a bunch of cows in our front yard.

Since I really didn't know who else to call, I called my aunt and uncle's place, though they were a good twenty miles away. My uncle Sam answered on the third ring.

"Hi Sam, it's Blaze. I seem to have a small problem over here," I told him.

"What's up?" he asked.

"I have a frigging front yard full of cows."

"You what?"

"My front yard is full of cows. There are at least a dozen, and one was right outside the front door on the steps. What do I do or who should I call because I'm not feeding them and they are wrecking the front yard." Not to mention cows probably pooped all over the place, and big cows pooped big. Not a place for Thea to be playing. Yuck.

"They are probably O'Connell's cows. That's the only place around you. In fact, his land completely surrounds your property. Not sure how they got through the fence in the first place. Do you have his number handy?" Sam asked.

"Nope," I replied, seething. The crabby-assed neighbor. Just the man I wanted to deal with. And what did Sam mean his land surrounded mine? Could the jerk prevent me from getting to and from my own house? I was seeing a lot of drama possibilities in the near future.

Sam gave me the phone number, and when no one answered, I left a message. Short and sweet. Come and get your damned cows out of my front yard. Thea and I waited, and waited, and waited. Two hours passed and no response. While Thea was completely enchanted with a yard full of moo-cows, as she called them, I was not. And furthermore, I was not going to be the one to pooper-scoop up all the fresh manure now stinking up my yard.

It was five minutes shy of three hours when a bunch of whistles and ye-haws suddenly filled the air. Thea started squealing and clapping her little hands from her front-row window seat she had been glued to since the commotion started. I stepped outside as the cows were being directed by a couple of guys on horseback toward the rear of the yard where there seemed to be a gap in the fence. A rather large gap. A truck pulled into the driveway—a red one this time—and two men jumped out, nodded toward me, and gathered what appeared to be fencing material from the back and followed the receding cows.

Thea slipped out the door behind me and stood by my side with her arms wrapped around my legs. I wanted to follow the men to see what was happening, but I hesitated to walk through the long grass. I hadn't taken the time to put shoes on, and the fear of stepping in fresh poop kept me on the front porch.

"Horsy, Momma, horsy." Thea's little voice grew even more excited than she was about the cows. I was about to tell her the men on horseback were taking the cows home, when I realized someone was riding up the dusty road at a full gallop toward us. Thinking it might be that crabby O'Connell man again, I turned and picked up my daughter and moved toward the front door to go inside. She didn't need to hear her momma cuss anyone out, and that was what I planned on doing momentarily

A gorgeous black quarter horse came to a stop just below the front step of my house, snorting a breath and glistening from the hard ride. The man on top removed his aviators and hopped down to stand before me. It was not Patrick O'Connell.

"I am so sorry about the cows, ma'am The boys and I were fixing fencing up on the north end, not realizing there was a problem over this way. I do apologize." His voice was like a smooth whisky over ice. Gentle yet rough, sending warmth from my head to my toes. It took a moment to find my voice.

"How did you find out?" I asked. "I left a message for Mr. O'Connell several hours ago."

"Margie, the housekeeper, heard it. She took one of the four-wheelers out trying to find us and get us over here. It just took her a while to find us. She's not real adept at driving a four-wheeler. Patrick—that's my father—is out of town for a few days picking up more livestock. We're a bit shorthanded as some of the boys went with him to Wyoming. Again, I do apologize, and the boys will be cleaning up any messes in your yard from the cows. I see a little one peeking from behind you, and I'm sure you don't want her running through any cow patties, ma'am."

I turned and check on Thea to find her playing peek-a-boo with this strange man from behind me, a huge grin covering her little face.

"I'm not ma'am. I am Blaze. Blaze Blackwell."

He stepped forward. His sandy-blond hair curled over the collar of his shirt and flipped around his ears. His cobalt eyes twinkled and his smile was flirty and Thea stepped in front of me to get him. He went down on one knee and gave her his hand.

"Hi, pretty girl, My name is Dusty O'Connell, and you must belong to the beautiful Blaze Blackwell."

Thea giggled but stayed silent as she put her hand in his.

"This is Thea. Theadora, my daughter."

"Pleased to meet you, Miss Theadora. When you grow up, will you marry me?"

Her response was another giggle.

"I'll remind her of your proposal when she gets a bit older," I joked.

Dusty O'Connell gave me a million-watt smile and stood up.

I'd never been a believer in love at first sight, and I'd never been rendered speechless by a man before either, but I was now. My mind was a complete blank and I couldn't seem to form any words that sound remotely intelligent. All I could do was stare at the man in front of me. It's a good thing most of his attention was on my three-year-old who had suddenly mastered the art of flirtation. All I knew was I could watch these two all day long for the rest of my life. Me. The one who said never again, had just fallen hopelessly in lust with a stranger that just happened to be the son of the man who didn't want me here in Deadwood.

True to Dusty O'Connell's word, there was not a trace of cow poop left in my yard by late in the afternoon. It was not a job I would have cared to do, and the guys thrilled Thea as they moved about cleaning up the messes while we hung out on the front porch. Even at three, she had discerning taste when it came to the opposite sex. While she smiled at the men as they worked, she saved the brightest ones for Dusty. He hung around and helped patch up the fence and then had to leave. I couldn't make out the conversation that was going on by the fence post from where I was, but Dusty did not look happy and left shortly thereafter.

I asked one of the guys if the cows had knocked the fence down and if he thought it would become a problem in the future, but he evaded answering. He just said Dusty was taking care of it so it wouldn't be happening again.

CHAPTER FOUR

Dusty O'Connell

"What the hell are you thinking?" I shouted at my father through my cell phone when I got back home. I was pacing back and forth in the mammoth kitchen of my father's house. My house, too, as I lived here, but hopefully, not much longer. One of us had to go, and the old man was not budging.

At one time, the house was warm and inviting. It smelled of baking bread and fresh flowers. Laughter was the most common sound inside these walls. That was until death decided to invade this sanctuary, devastating my father and turning him into a heartless, nasty old man. The house lost its beauty when my mother passed and it's never been the same.

"You may not have cut that fence yourself, old man, but you paid someone else to do your dirty work and that's the same thing as doing, in my book."

"Is not."

The man was an ass. He sounded more like a five-year-old than a grown man in his late sixties.

"You're going to cut this shit out and you're going to apologize to her."

Cold chance in hell, but I had to say it. My father owed her an apology. His response was to hang up. Later he would claim the phone accidentally disconnected.

Blaze Blackwell. Emma Rose Blackwell's granddaughter. I wondered if she had her grandmother's spunk. That woman would go toe-to-toe with my father, never backing down, no matter what he did. I think I had more respect for Emma Rose than I did the good Lord in heaven. She was tough and she was kind. She detested my father as much as she loved me and my brother. Especially after Ma's passing. She made dealing with my father bearable by giving us a safe haven to run to.

Mitch had mentioned his cousin inheriting the house a month or so ago when I was over getting my truck worked on. I kind of remembered there was a girl, younger than me, that would come to visit Emma Rose in the summertime. If I had it right, the granddaughter was the only girl in a family of a lot of boys. When I heard she was moving here from Florida, my mind conjured up a princess. The salon-streaked hair and makeup perfect, dressed to the nines type of woman.

What I met was down to earth, natural, and stunning in an old pair of cutoffs and a Rolling Stones vintage T-shirt. Her hair was in a messy tail, and there wasn't a stitch of makeup on her face. She was beyond angry when she stood on the front porch and chewed me out. The woman literally took my breath away. When her little girl stepped out behind her, I was a goner.

Dusty

I pulled into Mitch's driveway two hours later, parking my truck by the open doors of the garage that housed his business. The music was blasting, and I could just make out a pair of scruffy work boots peeking out from the underbelly of a car.

"Be with you in a minute," Mitch called out.

I heard a wrench clatter on the cement floor and a few impressive cuss words before the dolly he was laying on, slid out easily from under the car.

"Hey, Dusty, what's up?" Mitch grinned. Ever since he met Delaney and moved her up from the twin cities, the man was always smiling. I'd known Mitch since grade school. He was a super athlete, until a lousy play in a football game in high school ended that dream. He had a hard time for a while and made some bad choices back then, but life was really good for him now.

"I was in the area and I thought I'd stop by," I lied.

Mitch just chuckled. He walked over to his refrigerator and pulled out two beers, handing me one. He leaned back against the edge of a work bench with his legs crossed, opened his beer, and waited.

"Okay, maybe I wasn't exactly in the area, but I was close," I admitted. "I met your cousin earlier today."

"Blaze? I heard she was here. How did that go?"

"It would have been better if my dad hadn't given her a bad time before he left for Wyoming and the stock auction. He had someone cut the fence bordering the property line so she had a yard full of cows this morning. I can't prove it, but my gut says he did it."

Mitch spit out a mouthful of beer.

"What the hell!" he exclaimed

"Yeah. My old man is a first-class asshole."

"What did she do?" he asked

"Left a message at the house for someone to come and get them damn cows." I chuckled. "She was not happy, but at least she was nice. Is it just her and her child?"

Mitch grinned. "A bit awestruck are we?" he teased.

I could feel myself getting red. I'd never had a problem where women were concerned. I usually just let them chase after me, have some fun, and move along. I hadn't thought much about settling down, but lately, after watching some of my closer friends start having families, the thought crossed my mind occasionally.

"She's single," Mitch told me. "According to my mom, Thea's father was nothing more than a sperm donor. He hit the road as soon as she found out she was pregnant. My aunt and uncle wanted her to come back home, and Gran offered to have her move here to have her child, but she stuck it out down in Florida on her own."

"That couldn't have been easy," I commented.

"No, but Blaze is a worker and she can take care of herself. Always been an independent little cuss, even as a kid, and she had no problem keeping up with all us boys. She was the only girl out of all the cousins."

"Her little girl is a sweetheart. I think she loved the cows in her yard." I chuckled.

"She's a head-turner. She has the biggest eyes I've ever seen. Mom said she's three and skipped over the terrible twos completely. Always happy. Her mom was like that too. I never remember her giving any sass like the rest of us. She was a gorgeous little girl too. Now she's a gorgeous single, grown woman." Mitch grinned at me.

"So…if I ask her out, it's okay with you? I don't want to get my ass kicked or step on any toes here."

"Go for it," Mitch said. "Just make sure you treat her like a gentleman. Any complaints and I'll come looking for you, friend or not. Besides, first you have to convince her to go out with you. She's met your old man, remember?"

I was trying to keep that thought out of my head. Hopefully, she wouldn't hold that against me. Otherwise, I had a lot of convincing to do because I was nothing like my old man. Not at all.

CHAPTER FIVE

Blaze

The good thing was I hadn't run into Patrick O'Connell all week. The even better thing was I seemed to run into his son, Dusty, almost every day.

Thea and I went for a long walk the day after the cow incident and ran into Dusty while he was out checking the fences. Then I ran into him at the grocery store in Deadwood a few times. I'd been working on stocking the pantry with the items I used a lot of so I didn't have to go out as much, but I was almost starting from scratch. Every time I went to pull something out for dinner, I'd find I was missing a few ingredients.

I was delighted there was a grocery in town that stocked a large assortment of organic foods, and a co-op just on the outskirts. The farmers market on Saturdays was still going strong, too, but the vegetables were getting scarcer as the season came closer to ending. I did manage to pick up a bushel of tomatoes and a feed sack of corn that

I was going to spend the day blanching and freezing for the winter months.

I ran into to Dusty just as I was trying to maneuver my vegetables and Thea into my vehicle. He took over and arranged everything so nothing would topple over while maneuvering the twists and turns of the road leading back home. Then ten minutes later, I even ran into him at the gas station when I pulled in to fill up my truck. Before I was even out the door, Dusty was reaching for the handle to the pump.

"I know how to pump my own gas," I told him

"I'm sure you do very well at it, but why would you want to smell like gas when I'm offering to do it for you?" He grinned.

He had a good point. I hated the smell of gas.

I thought about inviting him over for dinner. I mean, after all, he seemed to be helping me every time I ran into him, but I didn't want to seem forward. Maybe he was this nice to everyone. I hadn't been on a date since before Thea was born. And since the last date I was on happened to be the no-good jerk who shared my child's DNA, I'd concluded I was not the best judge when it came to the opposite sex. I was still trying to get my nerve up when I ran inside to pay for my gas. By the time I came out, Dusty was getting back into his truck. With the tip of his hat he was gone, and I had lost my chance.

Thea and I headed back home, her chattering to her rag bunny all the way while I berated myself on my lack of confidence. When I pulled up next to the front of the house,

HUGS

I noticed a large box on the front porch by the door. Jumping out, I quickly unbuckled Thea from her car seat and set her and the bunny on the ground and we both raced to the front door.

"We got yarn!" I exclaimed while clapping my hands. Thea clapped and spun a circle.

"Yarn bunny. Got yarn," she told her doll as she danced behind me while I wrestled the large box through the door and into the middle of the living room.

My plan, if the stars were all aligned, was to start selling my knitting patterns online. I designed mostly children's clothes—sweaters, hats, mittens and more. I also did some adult styles, but mostly children's. I had a few sewing designs as well, usually to compliment whatever I'd knitted. I'd earned some money selling the clothing, but I felt I could do much better with selling my custom patterns and offering knitting classes online.

Grandma Emma Rose turned me on to knitting back when I was nine years old. All summer long we would knit in the evenings. She was the one who taught me everything I used today. And it was the inheritance, along with her house, that was allowing me the chance to start my business. I had enough to live on, frugally, for the next four years. It should be enough time to build the business enough to support Theadora and myself.

"Look at all these pretty colors, Thea." I showed her the soft earthy tones from the first bag I thought would be great for fall. The second bag had bright shades of red, blue, hot pink, and purple. My mind was already going in every direction on the sweaters I had drawn up. It's a good thing Thea liked clothes because she was my primary model for all of my designs. Especially the hats. The child would wear a hat in the dead of summer with a heat index of one hundred degrees.

Thea and I made quick work, moving all my new yarns into my little office and putting them on the shelving unit I had set up. All yarns sorted by color, contents, and weight. I worked only with natural, organic fibers. Especially designing for kids; they hated anything itchy.

In my office, I had my laptop on the desk right by the window so I could look outside, alongside a small drafting table. Two walls held shelving, and the last wall I had my sewing machines sitting on my grandmother's antique cabinet where she once had her machines. Everything was all set to go. One of the best perks was the venders I recommended in my patterns for a specific yarn I used were keeping me well stocked. They sold the yarn from the patterns I designed and I knit, almost for free. It was a win-win for sure.

I could see Thea's eyes drooping as she curled up on the rug in my office with her bunny held tight and her thumb tucked into her mouth. Another blessing. The child loved her naps and she could fall asleep anywhere, usually within minutes of lying down. I closed the blinds completely to darken the room more and let her sleep where she was on the cream fur rug. I left the door ajar as I moved toward the kitchen to get started on preserving the vegetables I had picked up when out of nowhere there was a knock on the front door.

I opened the door and my sunny mood started to sour.

"I thought you would have hightailed it back to where you came from by now."

Patrick O'Connell stood on my porch. Bow-legged, dirty, muddy boots, and an ancient cowboy hat that had seen better days. In his mouth was the worst cigar I had ever smelled in my life. I started coughing and waving the smoke away as it haloed around him.

I pulled the door closed behind me and moved toward the man, forcing him to back up until he was down the stairs and on the grass.

"That thing smells awful and I don't want the fumes near my house," I told him.

"You can't tell me what to do, missy!" he shouted.

"I can tell you to get off my land."

"It should be mine," he growled.

My finger jabbed into his chest. "I'm calling the cops and filing a complaint on you. This is harassment. It's my house and my land and you are trespassing."

The man just glared at me and stomped off. He left a cloud of dust when he gunned his truck out of my driveway once again.

My first call went to the police department, which promised to send someone out right away. The next was to my aunt's house. I needed advice on how to deal with this jerk.

CHAPTER SIX

Dusty

I pulled into the driveway of my father's house pushing fifty up the long driveway. I slammed on the brakes and skidded to a stop, missing his rig by a few feet, barely. I slammed to door behind me and took the stairs two at a time and swung open the front door, not caring if it hit the wall or not. I found the old coot sitting calmly in the kitchen eating a plate of spaghetti, mopping up the red sauce with a chunk of garlic bread.

"What the hell?" I yelled.

"Don't talk to me that way in my own house."

"When you treat people the way you did Blaze, I will talk to you any way I want," I came back.

"Who the hell is Blaze?"

"Our new neighbor. She's Emma Rose's granddaughter. And I will not let you keep harassing her."

"Sounds like you're getting soft towards the enemy, boy. Better know who your loyalties are with if your living under my roof."

He'd just threatened me. I couldn't believe my ears. Me, the one who ran this place of his and kept his employees from walking out on a weekly basis. My anger hit an all-time high.

"I can leave anytime. And along with me will be most of your ranch hands. They only stay because I'm here. You treat people so lousy that no one can stand being around you. It's getting worse every day. What the hell crawled up your butt and laid eggs, old man?"

His face turned purple and he threw his plate across the room at me, missing by a large margin.

"Then get out. Don't come crawling back when you're starving either. You're just like your damned brother. No respect."

"Don't forget, Dad, you only own a third of this place. Eric and I own the rest. The land was in Mom's family, not yours, and she left a third to each of us when she died. She must have known what an ass you were even back then. You just try and do it yourself because when you fail, and you will, it will be you moving off this land."

I slammed the front door hard enough to knock a picture off the living room wall as I stormed out. I'd be back later when I calmed down to get my stuff. Part of me want to go over and check on Blaze, to see if she was still upset like Mitch told me. Who was I kidding? I wanted an excuse to see the woman I had been running into almost daily for a least a week or more. Since I wasn't purposely following her, it had to be a sign. I just prayed my father's harassment didn't make Blaze hate me too.

Mitch had been the one to take Blaze's call to his

parents earlier. As soon as he figured out what had Blaze so upset, he'd called me to give a heads up. The bad thing was my dad as the most stubborn old man the Lord ever created, and I couldn't see him giving up any time soon. He harassed Emma Rose for at least ten years, and I think he harassed her husband, too, when he was still alive.

I passed the sheriff's squad car, heading to the ranch. My first thought was stay out of it, but that only lasted a few seconds before I spun the truck around and followed him up to the house.

"Hello, Dusty." Sheriff Todd had been at the job for at least the last eight years. He was a fair man but didn't put up with much. "I'm here about your father."

I nodded.

"I'm here to back you up," I replied.

He just looked at me and waited.

"The old man is crossing too many lines. I've asked him to stop, but he hears nothing he doesn't want to or isn't in agreement with what he wants."

Bill Todd just nodded and headed toward the front door. Patrick O'Connell pulled it open and stepped outside, slamming the door behind him and making it clear the sheriff was not an invited guest.

"What the hell do you want, Todd?" he bellowed.

"To inform you to stop harassing one Blaze Blackwell. You are to stay off her property and away from her and her child. No more threats or intimidation. Is that clear?"

The old man just stared back, saying nothing.

"Patrick, if you continue to bother the girl, I will arrest

you and put you in jail."

"Don't threaten me." But the bluster wasn't quite there.

"I'm not. That was a promise. Any more trouble and you're spending time in county lockup. I'm going to be keeping an eye on you."

His glare was lethal. Then, noticing me for the first time standing by my truck, he let out an impressive string of cussing.

"Thought you left, boy. Are you crawling back already?"

"Nope, I just wanted to see if you got handcuffed and stuffed in the back of a squad car. A boy's got to have some fantasies."

A chuckle came of Bill Todd as he climbed into his car. I followed right behind him down the drive. Down the road about a mile, just beyond the property line, he motioned for me to pull over. I rolled down the window as he walked toward me.

"Do you think your dad's going to be a problem? He seems to be getting worse as he ages. Maybe he should get checked out or something," he said to me.

"Good luck with that one." I laughed. "He's a stubborn ass, and yes, he's getting worse. He threw me out this morning when I told him to leave Blaze alone. He's going to have a hell of a time running this place himself. I'm betting most of the hand walk within the week."

"Then what happens? Do I need to keep checking on him? Where are you going to be staying?"

"He'll figure it out. My brother and I own two-thirds

of this place. We're not going to let it go under or let my dad destroy what we've built up. He just needs some lesson learning about how he treats people. He's been this way since my mom died."

Bill nodded. "You got a place to stay?" he asked.

"I'll either stay to one of hotels in town or at Eric's place. I'm leaning more towards town. A week or two of room service and cable television sounds nice."

"No cable at home?" Bill looked shocked.

"My father." It was all I had to say. "For all the money he has stashed, he's the cheapest man I know. There are no luxuries like cable at the ranch. Even the meals he likes are meat and potato's basic. Once in a while he likes spaghetti, but when the Margie see's the mess he made, throwing a plate of it at me, she won't be fixing him anything with a sauce for a long time."

Bill laughed long and hard at the picture I just gave him.

"Ornery old cuss," he commented.

"Every single day," I replied with a grin.

Chapter Seven

Blaze

I needed a change of scenery. We'd been sticking close to home the last few days while I worked on a few designs and got the website up and running for the patterns business. I decided Thea and I were spending the afternoon in town at the beautiful park located in the middle of everything. They had a fun play area for children, which I noticed Thea staring at longingly every time we drove past. She had been such an angel with everything I was trying to finish that she deserved lots of playground hours.

There were a few toddlers already there when we arrived. Being a school day, I figured it would be quieter. I sat on the bench right between the giant sandbox and the swings. She went right for the sand and the other kids, sitting right in the middle with them. Thea loved new friends. I made a mental note to stop and get a few sandbox toys at the five and dime on our way back home as I watched another little girl hand her a shovel to scoop the sand.

I couldn't have been sitting there more than ten minutes, alternating making notes on my tablet and watching my child, when the sun that was heating my face suddenly was blocked.

I looked up and there stood Dusty, once again.

"Are you following me?" I joked.

"Not really, but I do seem to run in to you a lot these days." He chuckled.

"Not working today?" I asked.

"Kind of. I'm actually living at the Deadwood Grand across the street for a few days, and I saw you and Thea from my little balcony, so I thought I'd walk over and say hi."

He must have seen the questions forming on my face. I would not be a good poker player as my thoughts and emotions had always been very easy to read.

"I had a bit of a falling out with my dad recently. I'm giving him time to cool off and think more rationally," he explained. "Then maybe he will understand boundaries."

"Oh, does this have anything to do with me?" I hesitated. I didn't want to be the cause of trouble for Dusty. His father, Patrick? I couldn't care less. That man was the ultimate jerk.

"Partly. My dad has been an ass ever since my mother passed away years ago. The problem lies in the fact he is getting worse. And I can't live under the same roof as someone who thinks he can act the way he does."

"But don't you help run the place?" I asked.

"Yes, and most of the ranch hands will probably quit by the end of the week."

Dusty didn't seemed bothered by this, which led me to believe he'd been down this road with his father before. I simply nodded.

"My brother, father, and I own equal shares of the place. The land belonged to my mother's family. I won't let anything happen to the place. I'm just giving my dad a little kick in the ass to get his mind on the right page and adjust how he treats people. No worries."

Talk about family dynamics. I was glad my family didn't act that way. I couldn't have done the last few years without their support. I may not have lived close by, but just hearing my Mom or Dad's voice made all the difference when things were rough.

"So are you just eating takeout then? I mean if you're staying in a hotel you probably don't have a kitchen, right?"

"The restaurants, some fast food. If I get desperate, I will visit my brother and his family around the dinner hour." He laughed. "Eric's wife is a fantastic cook, so it not a hardship to eat at their place."

Guilt hit. I was sure my dealings with Patrick were a big part of their riff, and I hated the thought of it. I was sure Dusty had dealt with his father for years, like he said, but I still felt like I caused some of this. It also gave me a perfect excuse to invite him over. Let's be honest, the crush wasn't dissipating. In fact, the more I saw of Dusty O'Connell, the more impressed I was.

"Would you like to come over and have dinner with

Thea and me? I mean I'm not a fantastic cook or anything, but I do okay. I just think a steady diet of takeout would get old pretty quickly. I tend to keep our meals organic when I can get the right food."

"I would love to," he replied with no hesitation whatsoever. "So organic, huh? Are you vegan? My brother and his wife tried that one for a while, but he said he missed his steak way too much to keep going with it."

"No. I like meat, but I try to buy it grass fed with no hormones. My fruits and vegetables have no pesticides, and I stay away from processed. The food industry has modified so much of what we eat with chemicals, and I just don't want to put that into my body or that of my child's," I explained.

I wasn't fanatical about my diet. On a rare occasion, I pulled into a drive-through and grabbed a burger, but I didn't, as a general rule, eat fast-food. Plus, dining out was a luxury I couldn't afford when we were living in Florida.

"What can I bring?"

"Just yourself"

Thea ran back toward me and I scooped her up onto my lap.

"Did you have fun, baby girl?" I hugged her and made kissy noises into her ear, making her squirm and slide back to the ground. She looked up at Dusty and hit him with one of her heart-melting smiles. She pointed toward the swings.

"Do you want me to push you on a swing, Thea?" Dusty asked her, and she nodded.

Taking her little hand in his, they walked over to the

swings as I trailed behind. This was new. Other than family, Thea hadn't been around many men. Usually, she hid behind me until she got to know someone.

Chapter Eight

Blaze

I was not going to overthink this. I invited a man to dinner, the house was clean, and the aroma coming from the kitchen was homey and inviting. Slow roasted chicken with root vegetables. I had made bread yesterday, and everything I needed for a fresh salad was already chopped and ready to mix. There were several kinds of dressings in mason jars, labeled and in the refrigerator, which I made over the weekend.

I glanced around my house. Other than a few toys scattered here and there, it looked fine. I always liked my place to have that put your feet up and relax feeling. Not the be careful where you sit in case your body has any specks of dirt. I never understood white carpeting or white furniture in a home where children lived. It was their home too.

On one side of my living room was a giant dollhouse my father built for Thea. The men in my family all had a talent for woodworking, so every stick of the furniture was handmade. Between my dad, my brothers, uncles, and cousins, every room of the dollhouse was filled. My mother and I made miniature pillows and quilts, and my aunt, Cathy, even upholstered a little couch and two chairs. It was a dream house for a little girl, and Thea spent hours playing with it.

Just off to the side of the fireplace, I had my spinning wheel and a basket full of fiber. There was another basket by the couch containing my current knitting project: a colorful sweater for Thea with a matching hat for the soon-to-come snow season. I draped a new quilt my mother had sent us across the back of the couch and updated the room with a scattering of fun pillows I had found.

My house may not be fancy but it was home and it was all mine, in spite of whatever crazy ideas Patrick O'Connell might have. I secretly hoped Dusty wasn't playing me to help his dad, but both Sam and Cathy said he was a good guy, and my Cousin Mitch thought a lot of him too, so I refused to worry about it. Besides, the man was hot and I thought my little girl was crushing on the man too. Just like her mom.

"I have not eaten a meal like that since my mother passed away. Thank you. The food was wonderful." Dusty slid his chair away from the table and patted his stomach as he complimented dinner. "Thea? Is your belly full like mine?"

Thea giggled and patted her tummy.

"I full up too," she told him.

"Too full up for strawberry sundaes?" I teased.

"Yes!" She let out an ear-piecing squeal. Strawberries on ice cream was Thea's favorite.

"I think there's a little room left for something like that, right, Thea?"

The evening was perfect. Thea showed Dusty all her babies, one by one, and her dollhouse. He gave each baby a hug and had numerous conversations with the make-believe friends in Thea's world. He marveled at the intricacies of her dollhouse, and he was amazed that everything was made by my family.

"Where did they find the tiny crown moldings?" he asked, his head almost inside the dollhouse, checking the detail.

"I think my cousin used a lathe. The guy is an artist with wood," I told him

"I know Luke. His work is fantastic. Someday, when I get a home of my own, I want to commission him for a few of the furniture pieces. The dining room set he made for Mitch is a work of art."

Later, after Thea was tucked into bed, Dusty was the one to read her two stories as, tonight, Mommy wasn't the right one for the job. I opened a bottle of wine and we settled in on the couch to enjoy adult time, the first as Thea had always been by my side.

The bay window in my living room faced the west. I could see the sun starting to go down and the sky was washing with every shade of orange and red known to man. The sight was breathtaking.

"So how do you like Deadwood so far?" Dusty asked

me quietly.

"It's a lot different than Florida. I'm starting to like it more and more each day. I know I loved coming here as a kid to stay with my grandparents."

"You had no idea Emma Rose was leaving you the place?"

I stiffened for a moment, hesitating before I answered him. He jumped in right away.

"I'm not asking for my father. That thought didn't even cross my mind. I don't agree with him or his actions towards you and this place at all. I loved your grandparents, especially Emma Rose. After my mother's death, she was wonderful to me and my brother, Eric. We preferred to spend our time with her rather than with a father spiraling out of control with grief."

"Has he always been the way he is?" I asked

"You mean an ass?" Dusty laughed. "No. He had always been on the rough side. A stickler for discipline with us boys, but my mom brought out the softer side of him. So did my little sister. He thought she hung the moon, just like my mom. Her name was Lisa."

"Was?" I asked softy.

"Yeah." Dusty grew quiet for a moment and his eyes teared up. Quickly, he wiped the moisture away with his hands.

"Lisa was not quite there when she died. Almost the age of Thea. In fact, your daughter reminds me a lot of Lisa. She got some crazy virus that went through the area. Most people just got sick for a few days and they were fine. It hit all of us. Even my dad spent hours puking his guts out. Lisa went to sleep and never woke up. My dad blamed himself because he was too sick to realize how sick my sister was. Four people here in the valley died from that virus.

Then my mom got cancer about ten years after. By the time they figured out what was wrong, she didn't have much time left. She never complained. Not once that I remember. Your grandmother spent a lot of time with her towards the end. My dad worked himself half to death, denying what was happening. When she passed, we were all there with her. Dad snapped and he has never been the same. The grief killed his heart and all that lives in his body is the anger."

That's so sad. It made me have a little compassion for the man, and understanding. I still thought he was a jerk, but at least now I realized why.

"How is the place doing with you gone?" I asked

Dusty laughed.

"Half the men walked out by day three. I give it two more days and I'll be back over there. The old man will probably leave on a vacation of sorts while I get things back under control. It's not my first rodeo with him this way. I just wish he'd think about retiring before the job kills him. He's in his mid-seventies and I keep thinking heart attack or a stroke with his blood pressure.

"Enough about a crabby old guy," he changed the subject. "Tell me about you. What was your life like in Florida? And how do you feel about dating?"

I almost spilled the glass of wine in my hand.

CHAPTER NINE

Dusty

I did not mean for those words to escape my mouth. They were supposed to stay in my head for a while longer. For the last several hours, it's taken everything I had, not to stare at her lips. They were the most perfect rosebud lips I had ever seen. Just a natural pout, luscious and plump. Whatever gloss she swiped across them after dinner made them glisten. If I could just lean over and kiss those lips, I would die a happy man.

I just hoped Blaze didn't realize I'd become a bundle of nerves just because I asked her out accidentally on purpose.

"I didn't mean to say that. Not yet. I mean, I do want to ask you out…on a date, but…shit. I can't believe I'm blowing this so badly. I'm just going to shut up and listen for a bit."

I was making a total fool out of myself, and over a woman.

The shocked looked that passed over Blaze's face turned to a twinkle, then a laugh. I could feel my face turning red and warm. In fact, my whole body suddenly became really warm.

"I haven't really gone on a date since before I had Thea, so I'm not sure how I feel about dating, but I would love to go on a date with you if that's what you're asking."

"Yes," I managed to choke out. I took a deep breath and tried to calm my racing heart. "Let me start over. First, would you have dinner with me?" I asked again.

"Yes," she answered with a grin.

"Next, tell me about you, your life in Florida, and how it was different. I want to get to know you." Maybe if I didn't have to come up with a coherent sentence for a few minutes, I could get it together and not come off like a bumbling idiot.

"Well, I moved to Florida because I wanted to live by the ocean. I wanted to walk on the beach every day and fall asleep listening to the sound of the waves each night. I chose my college because of that one desire. I lived close to Miami for almost seven years. In that time I finished school, met a jerk, got dumped by a jerk, had a baby, and worked a few dead-end jobs to support my baby while I also tried to work on my passion. My passion besides Theadora, that is."

"And what is your passion?" I asked her.

"I'm a fiber artist." She motioned toward her spinning wheel.

To be honest, I thought it was sitting there as decor. I

never knew anyone who ever used one before. I turned back to her.

"So you make yarn?" I asked.

"That's part of it. I dye the fiber and spin it into yarn. Sometimes, I just buy the yarn and create designs. My business is more the designs, the patterns. I just started a website selling the patterns, and I've teamed up with some of the yarn vendors to recommend their products. I've sold stuff I've made—hats, sweaters for kids, that kind of thing—but I can't live off that. It takes too long to actually knit the project. It's far more lucrative to sell the patterns and help people to knit my designs themselves. At least I hope it will be," she explained.

"Wow, I'd like to see some of your work. I've never known someone who makes a business out of knitting. My mom knitted washcloths and an occasional scarf, but that's about it. I thought most of that kind of stuff came from machines."

"A lot does. The cheaper stuff for sure. Hand-knit takes a lot longer. So it costs a lot more. Come on, I will show you." She got up and walked toward a room right off the living room. Once inside the door, I saw a wall of shelving filled with more yarn than I'd ever seen, even at Walmart.

"That's a lot of yarn," I said. "Did you get it at the store here in Deadwood?"

Somehow, I didn't think so, but I honestly wanted to know more.

She laughed. "No, most of this came from the vendors

I use. I haven't found a yarn shop in town yet. Hopefully, there will be one someday, or in one of the towns close by."

"Walmart?" I joked.

She shuddered.

"I'm a true yarn snob. I only work with natural fibers, and they don't sell those except at specialty shops. The acrylic is okay for some projects, but over the years, I've gotten used to working with only the really good fibers."

She turned on her laptop and scrolled through something, then turned the machine so the screen faced me. There were hundreds of photos of Thea in beautiful little sweaters, dresses, matching hats with scarves. Pictures from when she was a little baby up until just recently. Not one thing looked simple. The designs were amazing and colorful with intricate flowers and leaves woven into the designs on most of them.

"Thea is my primary model, especially for children clothes. I have another file with adult sweaters and hats too. I keep adding more to my website each week, and they are selling."

The excitement in her voice was catching.

"That's so cool," I told her. I meant it. She could have let life destroy her. Being a single mom was one of the hardest jobs I could ever imagine. It's hard enough with two parents. But instead of just getting by, she was going after her dreams and caring for her daughter at the same time. Blaze had both confidence and grit inside that little body of hers. I wasn't sure if she realized it, but there was a lot of her grandmother in her.

Closing the door softly, we walked back out into the living room. I didn't want this night to end yet. It was still early for me, but I was being selfish. She might have to be up at the crack of dawn.

"Are you getting tired?" I asked her. "Do you want me to leave?"

"Nope, the night's still young. I usually don't go to bed until midnight. I get most of my knitting done at night when Thea is sleeping. She loves to help and it's not always beneficial with knitting. Do you want to watch a movie? I'm into comedies more than horror so the selection may be slim, depending on what you like."

"Comedy is great. I'd rather laugh than cringe. I had nightmares over scary movies when I was a kid so I like to avoid them when possible."

"My lips are sealed. I won't broadcast your fear of scary movies."

I hesitated. "Can I ask you something?"

"Yes." Her lips went naturally pouty, a shape that invaded my mind multiple times day and night. Before I could change my mind, I leaned over and covered her lips with mine, gently sucking that beautiful pout.

Blaze let out a moan, but before I could pull back, her fingers raked through my hair and her lips demanded more. Every nerve in my body exploded. My tongue explored, my fingers explored, and my senses memorized the sounds she made as her body molded to mine.

Chapter Ten

Blaze

One night suddenly became daily stops for coffee, dinner at five thirty, and bedtime stories, for both my child and myself once she was fast asleep. I couldn't get enough of Dusty O'Connell, and while it scared the daylights out of me, it just felt so normal, so right. Just like a pair of soft, faded, well-worn blue jeans.

All we'd done was cuddle and kiss, but I swore it was the best cuddling, and by far the most delightful kissing I'd ever done before. My lips were permanently swollen, and there was a red patch on my chin from his whiskers. The man could kiss for hours on end. I didn't think he'd left before midnight the last three nights.

He's back on the ranch at his family home. His dad seemed to have backed down for the time being, which was good, but then, we both kept guessing how long would it last. I didn't know the man, and then again, I wasn't sure I wanted to. Given the fact I was spending most of my evenings kissing his son, I may not have much of a choice.

Thea sat by the window in the front of the house with her babies and watched for Dusty each day too. I was pretty sure the child was enamored with him. I wasn't sure how this happened so fast. Most men I'd met in the past had disappeared before we even got to the first date when they discovered I had a child. Or it's all about them, what they wanted, what they liked. Self-centeredness was not a quality I was attracted to in a man, or anyone, for that matter.

Dusty just kept doing everything to help me and Thea. He mowed the lawn, did some repair work around the house… He even changed the oil in my truck when I said I was going to make an appointment to get it done in town.

I mentioned him to Aunt Cathy when Thea and I went to Spearfish for the morning to visit.

"He's such a nice boy," my aunt told me.

Uncle Sam was walking through in time to catch her comment. "You thought Ted Bundy looked like a nice boy, too, Cath," he joked. I must have looked startled because he patted my shoulder and said, "Just kidding. She looks at the best in everyone. Except Patrick O'Connell. She can't find the good in that man."

"I don't care for him either, but his son has been coming around a lot, and he has been really nice. Almost too nice."

"There is no such thing as too nice. There is nice and not so nice. You're just not used to a guy treating you like a queen, Blaze. Talk to Mitch. Dusty was pumping him for information on you recently. According to Mitch, Dusty's got it bad. He is completely taken with you and little Theadora."

I blushed.

"Well, Thea and I like him a lot too. It's just that it's happening so fast."

Sam chuckled. "Sometimes, it works that way. Your aunt, Cathy, knew she wanted me within five minutes of meeting me," he bragged.

"You mixed that one up, buddy. It was the other way around." She looked at him pointedly. Then turned to face me. "He started chasing me from day one. I had a boyfriend already, and Sam here scared him away. He chased me for six months, until I finally agreed to go out with him."

"She wasted time, is what she did."

I loved spending time with my family. Everyone had so many stories to share, and for the most part, we all got along great. All my aunts and uncles were still married and they had been for years. Death do us part seemed to be the normal for us. It's what I wanted for Thea and me. I just hadn't been lucky as far as love went.

The door between the garage and the mud room shut with a bang and I could hear the sound of boots stomping.

"Hey, shake off the dirt before you come in," Cathy yelled out.

"Sorry."

Mitch and his girlfriend, Delaney, came walking into the kitchen.

"Hey there, sunshine." Mitch scooped up Thea and

twirled her around the room. Then he started two-stepping while singing a little country ditty as Thea squealed in delight.

I remembered Mitch as the quieter of the three boys, more reserved, especially after his accident and having to go to jail. It took him a long time to become part of the family again and to find his way. Cathy told me Delaney was the best thing that ever happened to Mitch and he was like a completely different person since she came along.

"How's everything going, cuz?" he asked me. "Is Dusty treating you good?"

I laughed. I figured the whole family must know about Dusty by now. "He's great. He adores Thea."

"Thea? You like your uncle, Mitch much better that ugly old Dusty don't you," he said to Thea, and he continued to dance with her in his arms.

"Dusty!" She let out a squeal and clapped her hands, wiggling to get down, and then raced to look out the window. When she found nothing, she turned to Mitch in confusion.

"Where Dusty?" she asked.

We all laughed and I picked her up. "Dusty's at work," I explained.

"Cows," she replied.

Mitch looked a bit dejected that Thea obviously seemed to like Dusty more.

I patted his arm. "Don't look so blue, Mitch. A three-year-old has a fickle heart. They go for whoever has the best toys to share. In Dusty's case, he has cows, and not even I can compete with cows."

HUGS

We stayed for another hour. I talked to Delaney about the new yoga studio she was opening in Spearfish, promising to sign up for classes after Cathy said she could watch Thea for me. As much as I loved working from home, I was starting to crave some companionship of the female kind. I needed to make some friends, and I figured exercise classes would be a good start.

I knew Dusty was delivering cattle east of the Black Hills today, so I took my time on the way home, making a few stops to check out some of the stores I hadn't visited yet. It was after three when I pulled into my driveway. Thea was sound asleep in her car seat, and it was a good thing as I was about to come unglued. Once again, my yard was full of cows.

CHAPTER ELEVEN

Blaze

"Yep"

That was how that jerk answered his phone. Yep. I was standing outside my truck, on my cell, trying not to scream so I would not wake up my daughter. I growled into the phone.

"Hello?" he said this time, irritated.

"Your damn cows are in my yard again," I said, my teeth still clenched.

"How do you know they're my cows?" he asked, laughing at his own humor.

"Come and get your cows out of my yard and bring a pooper-scooper with you, old man," I demanded.

"Just shoo them out of there. They'll leave on their own, and I don't pick up cow shit."

I was going to lose my mind. I looked in the truck and, thankfully, Thea hadn't woken up yet. My self-control was going to snap and soon. I walked around the house to look at the fence in the back, stepping around poop piles. The cows must have wandered in just after we left. My yard was a mess, and what flowers I had left were gone.

"Get your damn cows out of my yard. I can see the fence is open again, and I know you had something to do with it, O'Connell. Otherwise, I'm calling for help, and all these cows will be mine." I disconnected the call and started walking back to my truck. I made another call.

"Mitch," I said when he answered. "Do you know anyone will a cow trailer that will hold a dozen cows and a place I can stash these things?"

I had to wait for him to stop laughing.

"Are the cows back?" he asked while still chuckling.

"Yes."

"Okay, hang tight. It may take an hour, but I have an idea."

I moved a sleeping Thea inside and into her room and covered her up. Leaving her door ajar, I sat down with my knitting in a chair that I turned to face the front window. And I waited. I knitted to keep my mind busy and my hands from grabbing something and throwing it against the wall.

It was exactly fifty-five minutes and a few seconds when Mitch's big black truck came barreling down the drive, followed by a red Dodge I instantly recognized as Dusty's. He was pulling a giant silver trailer behind him. Two more guys on horseback came from each side of the back yard, herding the cows toward the trailer that Dusty and Mitch were opening up in the back.

"Momma?" I heard Thea behind me. She climbed up

on my lap to watch the commotion going on outside. "Cows," she whispered contentedly.

They were down to loading the last two cows when the Black Escalade came screaming into my driveway, driving like Satan was right behind him. Jumping out before the vehicle came to a complete stop, Patrick O'Connell ranted and screamed for the boys to stop.

"I warned you!" Dusty yelled back at him and motioned for the boys to load the last two.

"What are you doing with my cattle?" he raged. He was so loud I could hear him clearly from inside. Not wanting to miss a word, I stepped out onto the porch, Thea still in my arms.

"My cousin warned you what she was going to do and you just kept playing your games." Mitch stepped up to get into his face. Dusty moved in beside him.

Patrick O'Connell bounced from one foot to another, his hands clenched into fists on each side. His face was turning purple, as his anger rose.

"This. Is. My. Land!" he screamed, enunciating each word.

"No, Dad, it's not. It never has been, and Emma Rose was never planning on selling it to you. She left it to her granddaughter, Blaze, so she would have a safe place to live and raise her little girl. You need to come to terms with that. The land is not yours." Dusty calmly tried to talk his father down, moving toward him.

"But,"

"No buts, Dad. It belongs to Blaze and her little girl.

Look up on the porch, Dad. There she is. Both of them. You are scaring that beautiful little girl. What would Mom say if she were here, huh? I don't think she'd be very happy with you right now."

I watched Patrick O'Connell turn and walk toward the front porch. The closer he moved toward us, the slower he walked, until he came to a stop ten feet from the steps. Everyone was silent. Even the cows seemed to sense something was happening. I held onto Thea tighter, standing my ground. His eyes squinted and his clenched fingers loosened. He took one step closer, then another. The expression on his face was confusion. He was looking at Theadora, not me. I watched as his face softened and his body relaxed its stance. A tear rolled down his weathered cheek. Then another and another.

Thea pointed a finger at him, then looked up at me.

"Who dat?"

"Mr. O'Connell," I replied. "He has the cows."

She wiggled, scrambling to get down and walk toward him. I held my breath and she stopped in front of Patrick. Slowly, Patrick bent down, placing one knee in the grass, before Thea and gently held out a hand.

"What is your name, little one?" he asked softly. More tears streamed down his face. "I don't believe I've ever met you before."

"I Thea. Why you cry?" her little voice asked him.

"I'm crying happy tears right now, Thea. You remind me of another little girl from a long time ago. A little girl I still miss so much," he told her as he wiped his face.

Thea leaned forward and patted his arm.

"No cry…" she soothed him, and without warning, wrapped her arms around his neck and gave Patrick O'Connell a hug.

My own tears joined those coming from Patrick O'Connell. The angry old man who wanted me gone, disappeared. He was replaced by a gentle soul, corralled by a three-year-old's hug and memories from the past.

EPILOGUE

6 months later

Dusty

I never thought I'd have my father back. Not in a million years. I was now running the whole operation, while my father spent most of his time a willing slave to a three-year-old—almost four, as she liked to remind us. My soon-to-be stepdaughter. But in all reality, she was mine, from the moment I met her and her mother. We may have different blood, but as far as I was concerned, Theadora was my child and her mother would be my wife. I gave both of my beauties rings three months to the day of when we all met.

When you know, you know. And I knew. Blaze and Thea were the part of me I had been missing. We were planning a small ceremony on the ranch with family and a few close friends. Home cooking and a barn dance afterward. It's the way we did things out here on the plains. Blaze didn't want to wait, and she was fine with whatever

I wanted to do.

For the time being, we were going to stay in the house she inherited from Emma Rose. That is, until we grew out of the place. At that point, my dad wanted to switch and let us have the big house. All he asked in return was to live close enough to spend time each day with Thea and any more grandchildren we planned on giving him.

I still couldn't believe the change that came over my father that day in Blaze's front yard. The day little Thea gave him a hug. Blaze's explanation was simple: Hugs could create miracles.

THE END

ABOUT THE AUTHOR
SIDNEY PARKER

Sidney Parker is a Minnesota born and raised author who resides in the Twin Cities with her two rescue pups. When she's not dreaming up new stories you can find her out on ones of the surround lakes sailing or paddle boarding in the summer time and hiding under a blanket with a book by the fireplace in the frozen months. Sidney writes romantic suspense and women's fiction.

Join her readers group on Facebook at Sidney Parkers Pearls Facebook author page:
www.facebook.com/sidneyparkerauthor
Instagram @sidneyparker921
Twitter:@sidneyparker921

You can continue the romance blossoming in Deadwood with "Deadwood Dreams", released in 2021 and "Deadwood Nights" coming summer 2022

I'll Find You

GINGER RING

Elizabeth Stratton never intended to make Deadwood her home. But when she inherits a business from a relative, it was an offer too good to resist. It was the chance for a new start, a new venture, and when she meets fellow traveler, Garrett Anderson, maybe even a new love.

Garrett Anderson's only focus was getting to the Black Hills and starting up his smelting business. That is until he laid eyes on the pretty young woman next to him on the train. When they parted ways at their destination, he swore there were tears in her beautiful eyes.

Elizabeth feared she'd never see him again. But the only thing that gave her hope was Garrett's last words. "I'll Find You."

Chapter One

1889, Dakota Territory
Elizabeth Stratton

Elizabeth Stratton struggled to stay awake with the soothing sway of the train. The last thing she wanted was to miss her stop in Deadwood, but that was still a day or so away. There were funds enough in her purse to cover a sleeping cabin, yet it was best to save every coin she had until she reached her destination.

Fortunately, for the first day of the trip, an elderly couple had shared the nearby seats. They were kind enough to keep an eye on her belongings when Elizabeth needed to stretch her legs or get a bit of shut eye. It was with much sadness they bid their farewell early this morning.

The whistle blew as the big steam engine came to a screeching halt in another of the many small towns it would stop at. Travelers from all walks of life filtered through the doors and took their seats. Soon the cabin was full, except for the seat next to her.

She relaxed at being able to stretch out a bit. The bench

seats were both narrow and hard.

"I'm sorry, Miss, but is this seat spoken for? The porter said I could find a place to sit in this car, but this is the only one I see."

Elizabeth gazed up at the most handsome face she had had ever laid eyes on. She guessed his age to be around the mid-twenties. His blue eyes still held that devilish glint of a young man mixed with the sadness of one that'd seen hardship and pain. Who didn't? The civil war had ended years ago, but its effects still lingered.

Setting her handbag on the floor, Elizabeth motioned with her gloved hand for him to join her.

"Thank you, Miss. The name's Garrett Anderson." He removed his tan cowboy hat, placed it in his lap, and smoothed his dark brown hair in place.

"Elizabeth Stratton."

"It's nice to make your acquaintance, Miss Stratton."

"Please, call me Elizabeth, Mr. Anderson." The man beside her smelled fresh and clean as if he'd just left a bath house.

"Only if you agree to call me Garrett." He chuckled.

Her cheeks flushed at his bright-white smile. Every day in the store, people addressed her by her first name, while she respectfully addressed them more formally. Old habits die hard.

"Yes, of course." Her gazed dropped to his hat, and she admired the tan skin of his hands. The few callouses spoke of hard work but not of their trade. She looked up to see him studying her as openly as she was him. "Where are you headed, Garrett?"

"Heading to Deadwood to start a gold smelting and mining operation."

The gold rush seemed to be over, but smelting was successful in many areas of the country for finding what couldn't be mined with a pick or pan. "That's ambitious. I've heard the profits are great, but the work is hard."

"Hard work never scared me." He stretched out his long legs.

The man appeared tall. How much more than her was yet to been determined, but she guessed he was a good head taller. "And yourself? Are you traveling with family?"

The wounds of emotional pain made their presence known again as she shook her head and frowned.

"I'm sorry. I didn't mean to pry. I just finished my time in the army. It was a long ride here, and it's a long trip to Deadwood. I've spent a lot of time by myself or with soldiers, so I forgot how to mind my manners."

"That's all right. I'm traveling to Deadwood, so I look forward to having someone help pass the time."

Heat flooded her skin under his gaze. She grew up around men, so his nearness was nothing to get flustered about. Yet he was different. He sat strong and lean, and his shirt and pants were taut over firm muscles. His features were similar to other men she'd known in Minnesota. High cheekbones, straight nose, and a shadow of whiskers on his firm jaw.

"To answer your question, I am traveling alone." He remained quiet, so she continued. "My father recently passed."

Garrett nodded. "You have my condolences. I have no family left, so I know how that feels."

"I helped him run a general store for years." She'd been so busy working for her father, it had left little time for gentleman callers. At her age some would consider her an old maid. "I just recently found out my uncle also passed. He ran a store in Deadwood and left it to me. I don't know what to expect. It could be prosperous or a small hole in the wall, but I don't have anything keeping me back home."

"That's very adventurous of you. I'm sorry to hear about your uncle. He had no other family?"

"No, he was a bachelor. Apparently, he was also an admirer of my mother. The brothers had a falling out. He drifted for years before settling in Deadwood. A lawyer contacted me." She pulled a weathered newspaper from her handbag. "He sent me this advertisement of the place."

He took the ad in hand. "Stratton Dry Goods. Looks like they have quite a selection there. I'll be sure to stop in and get everything I need."

The fact that he could read when so many couldn't endeared him to her even more. It was a comfort to think she might know another person in the new city she was traveling to. Elizabeth crossed her ankles and turned his way. "That's wonderful. I look forward to seeing you around town. You mentioned mining? That sounds dangerous. Digging underground, using dynamite and such."

The deep rumble of his laughter drew her closer. Just

the sound of his voice sent shivers down her spine. What was happening to her? Never had she responded to a man like this.

"I promise not to handle any dynamite," he assured her. "I will be working with men who have years of experience."

Elizabeth wasn't usually so nosy, but she enjoyed hearing him speak. "Are you from Deadwood?"

"I'm from Galena, Illinois. People have mined ore there for years. A close friend from home told me I need to come out and share the wealth." He handed back the paper.

Bandits, accidents, and number of things could happen out in the middle of nowhere. "Still, be careful. I've heard where gold is involved, things can get dangerous for more reasons than one."

"I'll be careful, so don't worry your pretty little head about me."

He thought her pretty? Elizabeth turned her gaze at the passing landscape. They were in prairie land now, with miles and miles of grassland. "Do you have a sweetheart back home?" As soon as the words left her mouth, she wished them back. What must he think of her?

He chuckled. "No, do you?"

"Me?" She twisted to stare up into his beautiful blue eyes. "No, my father kept me very busy. There was no time for a beau." A frown crossed her lips. "I feel like a spinster some days. I'm way past the time I should be married, but it is one of the reasons I had to leave. It was time to see the world, even if I had to do it all alone."

"You are far from a spinster, and I fear that as soon as

we reach Deadwood, you'll be surrounded by men asking for your hand. The next time I see you in town, you probably won't have the time of day for me."

"I don't know about that, but I hope I can make some friends and do well at my new job."

"You have a friend in me already, and I haven't a doubt that your establishment will be very successful."

It seemed too good to be true that a strikingly good-looking man was not only sitting next to her but talking to her and saying he was her friend. The first glimmer of hope that her future might include more than work filtered in.

"You are too kind." Her gaze dipped to his lips. At the age of twenty, she'd yet to even have her first kiss. Taking a deep breath, Elizabeth shifted in her seat and stuffed the newspaper back in her bag.

"I'm also hungry. Can I bring you something from the dining car?"

"I, ah. Yes, that would be nice." She reached for her handbag for some coin.

"No, it's on me."

"I couldn't. I don't want to be any trouble."

"No trouble at all. Just don't give away my seat." He winked, and the flutter in her stomach started again. Garrett was not only handsome but kind. Her mouth dropped open, but no words came out.

"Is there anything special you want or don't like?"

"No, I'm not fussy."

"I'll be right back, Lizzy."

Lizzy? She felt dizzy. Hugging her purse to her chest, Elizabeth sighed. It was not hard to miss the admiring glances from the other women on the train as he passed. One even narrowed her eyes at her. The man was just being nice. That had to be it. Although she had years of experience working around men in her father's store, none of them ever made her feel the way Garrett did and in such a short time. It was as if she were special in some way, and not just because she was a hard worker.

Resting her chin on her fist, she counted the hours until they'd arrive at their destination. Even if he was only being polite, it was a chance to enjoy the company of a nice man for the limited time they had together. A man like him would have any number of women more than willing to share their bed with him, but that was not the kind of woman she was. There would be many lonely days and nights in her new home. At least she'd have the memories of their time on the train to keep her company.

She already felt the loss of her companion as he left the car. Funny how one didn't miss the things they never had, but having a glimpse of something that could be, made one yearn for more. All her life, Elizabeth had been too busy to think about marriage and children. It hadn't dawned on her how alone she was until her father died.

Garrett soon returned carrying a basket full of food. A porter followed behind with a small table he set up before them. "I wasn't sure if I could carry a tray and not spill everything, so I had them pack it in here." Several fellow travelers turned their way. Most went to the dining car to eat their meal. Garrett had brought the dining car to her. It might have seemed forward to dine with someone she didn't know, yet here they were.

She widened her eyes. It must have cost a fortune. The basket was filled to overflowing.

Garrett set the basket on the floor between them and handed her a plate, utensils, and a cloth napkin. He soon filled her plate with chicken, boiled potatoes, beans, and some warm buttered bread. There was even an apple pie in there.

How would they eat all of this? She couldn't help but grin at his generosity. "This is too much."

"Don't worry. I have a big appetite." He dug into his potatoes and moaned. "I love a good meal but can't say I am much of a cook."

They chatted throughout their meal. Garrett asked her about aspects of her life back home. The man seemed genuinely impressed with her knowledge of politics and what was going on in the world. In the past it seemed to put off any man showing an interest in her, but her father insisted she be well-educated.

The train traveled through the night, and it was morning before they disembarked. She was surprised when they ended up taking the same stagecoach to Deadwood. It was as if they were meant to be together. At least she hoped it was. The last part of the trip was dangerous, and as much as she wished to have more time with Garrett, he rode up top to help keep an eye out for bandits. When he pulled the guns and holster out of his bag and buckled it around his hips, she almost swooned. What girl wouldn't want a man who could protect himself and her.

The hills were dark with evergreens, and the pine smell

refreshed her tired spirit. It'd been a long trip, and she couldn't wait to take a hot bath. She poked her head out the window as soon as they arrived in Deadwood. The town bustled with horses, wagons, and people.

The stage stopped at a hotel.

Garrett helped her with her bags but didn't go in. He pulled the dusty cowboy hat from his head and held it in front of his chest. "I'm afraid I can't stay any longer. I have to leave for the site, and my friend is leaving soon."

Her lower lip quivered. The fact that she was now going to be alone in a strange town overwhelmed her. "Oh. It was a pleasure meeting you, and I wish you much success with your claim."

"I'll be back soon." He took a step back. "If it's okay, I'd like to see you again. Take you out to dinner."

Her heart soared. "Yes, I'd like that."

Garrett grinned as he put his hat back on.

"When will you be back?" she asked.

"Soon." He retreated but kept his eyes on her.

"But what if I've failed and the business is gone? I'm not sure where I'd go." What if it was all a farce and she had to leave in shame?

"Don't worry, I'll find you." Garrett promised and was gone.

CHAPTER TWO

Garrett Anderson

Garrett had only said good-bye to Elizabeth a couple of hours ago and he already missed her. Not to brag but Garrett had never lacked for female companionship, but Elizabeth was somehow different. There was a quiet strength about her. She'd known death and hardship like himself and many others, yet there was no doubt in his mind she would help anyone in need. How did he know that? Because when he was down to his last penny, he learned real fast who to ask for help.

Fortunately, through hard work, he didn't have to worry about pennies anymore. He wasn't here to work a claim. Garrett was there to work *his* claim. Years ago, he'd come to Galena with only lint in his pockets. Hungry and thin but not afraid to work. A surly shopkeeper hired him after kicking his last employee out the front door of his store, literally. The guy landed on the ground in front of

Garrett's feet. With nothing left to lose, he entered the shop and asked for a job. Mr. Henderson gave him one, and after a week of showing up on time every morning after sleeping outside in an alley, his boss gave him a cot in the back room. Soon, the grumpy man's wife was sending her husband with an extra lunch to share with Garrett. Without having to pay for a room and not much for food, Garrett was able to save money. A lot of money.

What Mr. Henderson lacked in personality, he overcompensated in making good investments. When his boss suggested the youngster devote part of his weekly pay in stocks for the railroad, Garrett listened. Actually, he put most of his earnings into stocks. In a matter of years, he'd earned a very substantial amount of money. Enough to pay the man what he wanted for the business so the Hendersons could retire in comfort. A year later he sold shop for double that.

He loved his time in Galena, but with the smallness of the area, his fame and fortune caused all the ladies to seek his last name. Garrett wasn't ready to settle down, and it was time to see more of the world. When he heard about the Black Hills of South Dakota, it was time to hit the road. A mining friend from Galena headed out first to search and purchase a parcel.

Again, his thoughts turned to Elizabeth. To her he was just a drifter from out east starting a new life in Deadwood, just as she was. Hopefully, she was settled in now. It was with much regret that he had to leave her where she stood.

Elizabeth wasn't his, and he would be overstepping his bounds by pushing any further. Once he was settled, Garrett would send a trusted member of his team to town and check on her, just in case.

How many hills and valleys had he ridden before finding the spot that was his? It took hours, and he was starting to mistrust the map he checked. Thank goodness, his horse wasn't easily spooked. Even though he'd made a quick stop at a bath house and changed clothes before leaving town, the dust was again clinging to his clothes. Hopefully there was a spring near camp so he could clean up again.

"Calvin." He waved at his partner from Galena as he rode into camp. Garrett had cut him in for a large percentage of the profits for all his hard work in finding the place, getting a crew, and starting to mine.

"Garrett, it's good to see you, old friend." The man ran over and held out his hand.

At ages twenty-seven and twenty-six, neither was old, but they'd known each other for years. Once off his horse, Garrett grabbed his hand and pulled him in for a hug. He thought of him as a brother and was the only family he had. "Find any gold yet?"

Taking his hat off, Calvin shook his blond head. "Nothing yet, but I know it's here. I can feel it. We simply haven't had much time to dig."

"Why not?" Garrett gazed at the entrance to their mine.

"Bandits, bad weather, you name it. I have men, who

should be working during the day, guarding the place at night. It's putting us behind."

Garrett blew a frustrated breath. But he had an idea, just as the store owner had needed a helpmate. "Then hire more workers and guards."

"I'll see what I can do. I was waiting for you to arrive." Calvin motioned to the mine. "I didn't want to leave the place without you here."

With a studying glance, Garrett took in the site. The mine opened into the side of a steep hill nearby a small open field. Multiple tents were scattered about, and he could hear the snores of men who must have had night watch. Handcarts, lanterns, buckets, picks, and other mining equipment sat near the opening of the shaft. The scent of pine mixed with that of sandstone and dirt. "Thanks. From what I heard in town, Deadwood is a pretty rough area."

"You got that right." Calvin kicked at the earth gone bone-dry from the summer heat. "With people still panning for gold, men are right on top of each other. If it gets out you struck it good, the worst of the worst comes to steal it from you. Even families just trying to cross the area are getting robbed."

Garrett gave his hat a good dusting on this thigh, and his horse nodded as if agreeing that Deadwood was a disagreeable place. "That's what I learned from the stagecoach drivers. I rode on top to help keep watch. I'd have much rather spent time inside the stage talking to a certain lady."

"Really? Anyone I know?" Calvin took the reins of Garrett's horse, and they walked toward the lean-to where the others were stabled.

"No, we met on the train. Pretty woman headed to Deadwood."

"Married?" Calvin's forehead wrinkled in question.

Garrett smiled and puffed out his chest. "Nope."

"She wasn't a working girl, was she?"

Garrett felt gut-punched and pulled back on his horse, his mood quickly turning to defensive anger. He tightened his fists. Elizabeth a prostitute? There wasn't a sweeter girl he'd ever met. "What? If you weren't my friend, I'd punch you in the face right now

Calvin tossed up his hands. "I meant no disrespect, but I've heard rumors of young women coming here hoping to take jobs but then ending up working in the brothels because there was nowhere else to turn."

"That would never happen to Elizabeth. She's too smart to be fooled. Besides, she inherited a business in town after her uncle passed. I even saw the business listed in a newspaper."

"Really?" Calvin cocked his head. "What was his name?"

Garrett shared the rest of the story and the name of the family business.

"Well, that sounds better. I know the place well. I purchased all our supplies there." Calvin scratched his head. "I guess I haven't been in there for a month or so.

The man appeared in good health the last time I saw him. Shame. As soon as you got here, I was planning to go back for more goods."

Garrett missed her already. "I could do it."

"You just got here. Do you have any idea what we need?" Calvin raised his eyebrows.

Garrett exhaled and shook his head. She'd made him insane. Or rather the fact that she could need help with the store and might fall prey to some wayward gunslinger. What if she hired the wrong kid, not someone like he had been, but a thief? No. He told himself. He'd met her. Spent long hours with her. She wasn't so naïve that he had to worry. Still there had to be something he could do to help...

"How about you write a letter or give me a message for her?"

Was she even thinking about him? He should be focusing all his attention on the mine. "I might."

Calvin shook his head. "I can't wait to see what she looks like. I can't remember you mooning over a gal before."

"I can't either. Not sure it's a good thing." There was so much to do. The last thing Garrett needed was to be distracted. This was dangerous business. Men could get killed when others got careless. They were working with dynamite, in close quarters, not to mention outlaws and thieves. "No, I need to work here. Tomorrow, you head to town. Hire more men and get more provisions. Once things are settled, I might think about a woman, but not now."

"Suit yourself, but if she's not a working girl and not spoken for, she will be soon. A good woman is harder to find than gold out here, and there will be a lot of men taking notice."

Garrett rubbed the knot forming in the back of his neck. It was probably from sleeping upright too many nights and not the thought that he might be letting the best thing to come into his life in a long time slip through his fingers.

Voices of their men echoed in the background.

His shoulders slumped. He had responsibilities right now. The miners gave up their time, families, and jobs to work the claim for them. He owed them first. For now, he would have to remember their time together, and hopefully, when things settled down, Garrett could get to Deadwood and see her again. If they were meant to be together, they would be. "I'll have to take my chances. We have much to do here first."

"Well, if you change your mind. I leave bright and early in the morning."

"I won't." Garrett removed the saddle and bridle from his horse and set the animal free in the penned-off area.

"Suit yourself. Let me show you around."

Calvin spent the next hour giving Garrett a tour around their camp. The mine had been partially completed before they bought it. The previous owner had died suddenly. He drowned while taking a bath in the river. Had he been drunk or held under the water? Who knew? The price for the claim was reasonable. From what Calvin had said, others were scared off from buying it, thinking the land surrounding it was bad luck. They had a limited crew, but now that he was here, things would change.

The camp was nice as outdoor accommodations went. In addition to the tents, there was a good-sized shed where the workers bunked, and the horses had a fenced-in lean-to so they could stretch and lay down, roll, sleep. Calvin had slept in the foreman's cabin, but he insisted Garrett take it now.

They even had a cook who was currently fixing lunch and handed Garrett a surprisingly good cup of coffee after they were introduced. The pair left to survey the surrounding area. It was good to meet their neighbors, others looking for gold, so that they'd know who was supposed to be in the area and who wasn't. Garrett also took a trip down into the mines to see the progress. The walls had some pretty good seams. Calvin assured him that it was just a matter of time before they would be mining full time.

The day had gone quickly, and it was a lot to take in. Garrett's legs were tired as he walked to his cabin after saying good night to his partner and the crew. He was optimistic. Calvin could be trusted and knew prospecting. It was only a matter of time before they struck gold and could start smelting.

As Garrett undressed and settled down on his cot, it wasn't visions of gold floating in his mind. It was a pretty girl with blonde hair and blue eyes, but he planned to wait a bit before going to town. There was too much to do, and this was no place for a lady. Besides, she had a lot to sort out with the store. Garrett had told her he wanted to court her, but he was needed here for the time being. His men depended on him. He would wait for her, but would she wait for him?

Chapter Three

Elizabeth

As much as Elizabeth hated to admit it, she missed Garrett. He already felt like a friend, and the sense of being totally alone surrounded her as soon as he had left. If only they'd had another hour or two to chat before he had to leave so suddenly. Not to mention the fact he wanted to court her. Why did she say yes? Sure, he was kind, handsome, and seemed trustworthy, but when would he be back? A girl couldn't wait forever.

Her trunk was left at the hotel for now until she talked to the lawyer and knew where she was staying. He was supposed to have made arrangements for her here but that wasn't the case. She placed her gloved hands on the counter, leaning toward the man pouring over paperwork. "Sir, are you sure?"

The hotel manager raised his gaze from the room ledger. "Sorry, Ma'am, but I have no rooms. Maybe later, but we can keep your belongings here for a bit."

"I just need to find where Mr. Grimm has his office. He's a lawyer here in town."

"Two blocks down on the right. Big sign above the door." He pointed his pen-filled hand to the left.

"Thank you. I'll be back for my trunk as soon as I meet with Mr. Grimm."

"It will be here when you return."

Elizabeth nodded and headed out the door. The town was busy with people going to and fro. She stayed close to the buildings to keep from be trampled by all the horses and wagons crowding the rut filled street.

Elizabeth passed restaurants, shops, and more hotels. A few ladies nodded in greeting as they passed. Some wore colorful and expensive dresses, while others were dusty and worn.

Shading her eyes from the sun, Elizabeth finally spotted the sign for Zavier Grimm, Esquire. Opening the door, the smell of old books and cigar smoke hit her nose. The room was indeed full of books, lots of them. Many huge and well used.

"Can I help you?" A slender man with slicked black hair, round glasses, and a fancy suit approached. The smell of smoke was even stronger now. He had a narrow mustache and beady eyes.

"I'm looking for Mr. Grimm. Mr. Zavier Grimm." It was a good chance he was standing right front of her, but she hoped to be wrong. Just being in his company made her nervous. She stayed near the window.

"At your service." He folded his hand across his chest and did a slight bow. "Miss Stratton, I presume."

"Yes, how did you know?"

"Your uncle showed me a photograph of you. You're quite remarkable. Even more so in person." He roamed his gaze up and down her figure.

She shivered but stuck to business. "I'm here to take over his store. If you could point me in the right direction, show me the books, and give me the key, I will be glad to be on my way."

"Of course. We can go there now." Zavier grabbed a skeleton key from his desk drawer and opened the front door for her. "After you."

Her uncle's store was on the other side of the hotel. The location right in the middle of town was a blessing. Mr. Grimm unlocked it and showed her around.

"It's been closed since Mr. Stratton passed, but I've opened it up for deliveries each day. You can find them in the back room."

The front of the building was like any other dry goods store: full of merchandise with the most popular items up front. Specks of dust floated in the air where the sun shone through the window. The place would need a good cleaning after being unused for so long. She followed him to the back. It was full to the ceiling with barely room to move.

"I have been signing for the deliveries, but you will need to start settling up with your debtors as soon as possible. There are living quarters upstairs. Since your bills are quite high, I didn't want to add to them by booking a room at a hotel, but I will get your luggage brought from there."

It had slipped her mind that he would still be receiving

merchandise ordered before his death. "Bills?"

"Yes, here are the books. Your uncle did a good profit but being closed for a month is going to make things difficult." He walked over to a desk and opened the large ledger sitting there. Again, his eyes seemed to linger where they didn't belong, namely on her chest.

She coughed, hoping to distract him. Elizabeth had never backed down from a challenge. "Difficult? I will open tomorrow and get things going as soon as possible. Paying for the supplies shouldn't be a problem."

"That's where you're mistaken. Things are at a premium here. Your being closed for even a day, let alone a week, will cause others to do their business elsewhere. Hopefully, the clientele will be back, but one never knows. Since your uncle put me in charge of the finances until you could arrive, I've had to take care of paying all the bills. I'll have the total for you tomorrow, with interest, of course." He smiled.

A lump formed in her throat. Without customers, how would she pay? "With interest? How much will that be?"

"I'll get back to you tomorrow. Perhaps we can do lunch." He arched an eyebrow.

"Thank you, but if I have to make a profit, I won't be able to close for even an hour until I can find help." Any excuse to not have to spend any more time with the man.

"I'm sure I can find someone to help you."

"No, please, you've done more than enough, and like I said, I want to make sure you are paid for your services as soon as possible." She wandered to the door, hoping he'd follow.

"I'm not concerned in the least. If you can't come up with the funds, I'm sure we can make other arrangements."

A sickening feeling started to seep in. "Arrangements? What kind of arrangements?"

"I'll let you know. Good day, Miss Stratton." He tipped his head.

After Mr. Grimm left, she quickly locked the door. What good would that do though? He probably had his own key. As soon as she retrieved her belongings she was inquiring about a locksmith. She wouldn't feel safe until the locks were changed. All of them.

Elizabeth

Everything was expensive in Deadwood. Not wanting to owe any more to Zavier Grimm, she hired a couple of men to carry her trunk upstairs. Her accommodations weren't too bad, but the place was still filled with her uncle's things. Removing them would have to wait for another day. Thankfully, the building was in an area that had running water, so her first bath in several days was heavenly. After changing into one of her plainer dresses, Elizabeth began to clean the place while the locksmith worked on the front and back doors. With the windows open to air out the place, it was soon dusty, noisy, and hot.

After a quick sweeping, scrubbing, and washing of the

store area, she brushed her hands off and headed to the back room. Her plan was to unpack and put out as many items from the boxes as possible before opening early in the morning.

Most of the crates held dry goods, but as she got closer to the bottom of one stack, a putrid smell became stronger. Holding her nose, Elizabeth carefully opened it. Inside were rotting eggs! Who would have dropped eggs off and not taken care of them? Picking up the box, she took it outside and threw the mess of moldy and cracked eggs into the ditch. The wood box they came in stayed outside. At least it was the only one with decaying items in it.

Thank goodness she had experience and knew about pricing and merchandising, only taking a quick break to clean herself up and dine in a nearby restaurant. After she was done eating, Elizabeth strolled down the street a bit to stretch her legs and take a break. There were other shops in town doing a booming business. Hopefully, once her mercantile was up and running it would be also. Wandering farther down, the buildings seemed to appeal to a shadier clientele. Gambling, drinking, and brothels were available everywhere.

"Miss, are you lost?" a young lady with rosy cheeks and a low-cut dress asked.

"I, ah, just arrived and was taking a stroll around to get familiar with the town."

"Well, you don't want to get familiar with this part of town." She looped her arm with Elizabeth's and turned her around.

"Why not?" She had a good idea but wanted to hear

why this woman was there.

"This part of town is called the Badlands. Things happen here that you don't want to be a part of."

"Then you should come with me." Elizabeth patted her hand and smiled.

"I wish I could. I came here with a good prospect for a job, but the job was for was working in a brothel."

A gasp escaped from Elizabeth's lips at the girl's admission. "Surely, there was other work you could do. I could hire you," Elizabeth offered, even though funds were tight.

"Thank you, but I'm indebted to the man who paid my way here." She stopped and looked the woman straight in the eye. "And if I don't pay, he'll kill me."

"What?" Her heart stopped. What kind of place was this? "How much do you owe?" It couldn't be that high, could it? But the amount she admitted to was staggering. The brothel owner not only charged her for her trip out west but also charged the women a colossal amount for their room and board while forcing them to work on their backs at the brothel. It was shocking, and Elizabeth thanked her lucky stars her trip here hadn't ended up the same way.

"I don't know what to say. That is horrible. I wish there was something I could do. What is your name?"

"Mary. Thank you for your kindness, but there is nothing anyone can do. At least I am in one of the better houses. Some are even worse." Mary turned her head and glanced down the street.

How could they be worse? "I'm Elizabeth Stratton."

"Nice to meet you, but don't think you need to say hello if you pass me in the street. I just didn't want you to be in danger." She had a kind smile lighting up her face. Any man would be proud to have her on his arm, but her chances of finding a husband after working in a brothel were not good. Then again, women were not plentiful here.

"I will definitely say hello to you. I own Stratton Dry Goods. Please stop in anytime. It will be open tomorrow."

"I'd like that." Mary frowned. "I must be getting back."

They parted ways. Elizabeth worked until well past midnight before turning in. Even though she wasn't located next to the area Mary had spoken of, the music and shouts from downtown could be heard even upstairs.

The nights were cool up in the hills. She'd have to make sure the stove was working before winter. Fluffing the pillow under her head, she wondered where Garrett was. Was he sleeping under the stars? Pulling a blanket higher, she hoped he was warm. His smiling face was the last thing she saw before slumber swept her away.

Elizabeth

Elizabeth rose early, and the rigorous work from the day before could be felt in every bone in her body. One would think she'd have something to eat in her store, but it was one of the things she was lacking. Fortunately, the restaurant next door opened at the break of dawn for all the miners.

Taking a seat, the stares of every man in the place turned in her direction. Quickly eating a hearty plate of eggs, bacon, and potatoes, she decided to buy a few items for the day. She purchased a loaf of bread and cake for lunch and returned to the store.

After putting the food in the back room, she pinched her cheeks to add color, and wrapped an apron around her waist.

She left the door open and wrote 'OPEN' on the lid of one of the boxes, which she set out front. Elizabeth stood just inside the door ready to welcome the first customers of the day. After the first hour of no business, she finally pulled a chair outside and called out to people as they passed.

"Shovels, pans, and all the tools you need for prospecting."

"Fabrics and soaps for the ladies."

"Powders and oils for what ails you."

Still, no one came in but entered her competitors' establishments instead. Finally, at around one o'clock, a man stopped his wagon out front and entered the shop. She calmed the urge to cheer when she saw his list.

"Hello, Miss," he greeted while brushing the dust from his trousers. "I'm here to pick up some things for the camp and to give you this."

Her fingers trembled as she opened the letter he said was from Garrett. He wished her well and said to give word to his man if there was anything she needed. It was a comfort to know he was thinking about her, but it was void of anything romantic as she hoped. She folded it and stuffed it in her pocket. "Please tell Garret that I am well and looking forward to seeing him in town. What can I help you find?"

For the next hour, Elizabeth found about ninety-five percent of what he needed. Better yet, he paid with gold, not credit. It would make a healthy dent in what she owed Grimm. But she needed more than one customer.

The next few hours were spent straightening shelves and rearranging things. Why were people not stopping in? One would think they would at least be curious about the newcomer in town. They certainly were at the diner this morning. From what she'd heard, her uncle had done a booming business.

As if her first day couldn't get any worse, Mr. Grimm paid another visit. "Dear Elizabeth, how was your day?" the man had the nerve to ask. "Profitable I hope."

It was painfully obvious the place was empty. "Tomorrow will be better once word gets out that I'm here."

"I'm sure it already has." He smirked. "I was hoping you would join me for dinner this evening."

The impulse to vomit came out of nowhere. There was something sinister about the man. Despite his clean appearance, she felt dirty just being in the same room as him. His eyes seemed to twitch at times, and he wore way too much cologne. "Thank you for the kind offer, but I'm exhausted from all the work involved getting the place ready."

"Such a shame. I was hoping to go over your finances again. It looks like there is a delay in getting your funds deposited from your father's will."

Her fists tightened. What! He was overstepping his bounds. "Excuse me, I'm not sure that is any of your business, and what do you mean about my finances?"

"Since I handle your uncle's will here, I had the lawyer taking care of your father's affairs send me those records as well. Looks like you are to become a wealthy woman once all is settled. Not to mention"—he motioned with his hand at their surroundings—"all that you have here."

She remained silent. Yes, there was a lawyer managing the sale of her father's estate back home, but she'd yet to find out all the details.

"Did you know you have to marry before you can inherit?" He strolled around the room. "I could help you with that, as well as other things."

The suggestiveness in his voice made her flesh crawl. Inhaling, she spoke in a firm voice and tried to hide the fear flowing through her body. "I was not aware of that, but no need to worry, I have a beau who will be in town soon. He's at his claim right now."

He narrowed his eyes. "Oh, really? And who may that be?"

She stiffened at his intrusion. "Again, I don't mean to be rude, but that is none of your affair."

"I disagree. I was put in charge of your uncle's store until you can take care of it. If today is any indication." He raised an eyebrow and taped a fingertip on the glass countertop. "Well, let's just say, a single woman, running it alone would not be in the best interests of the business."

She opened her mouth to disagree as a customer came in the door. As she turned, Elizabeth recognized Mary from their meeting yesterday. "Hello, Mary. Welcome. What can I help you find?"

"Miss Stratton, I must say." Grimm stepped near, and she refused to retreat. "You're consorting with whores? Obviously, you care nothing about your reputation in town. It's like you're making this so easy for me. Good day." Grimm shook his head and walked out.

Elizabeth slammed the door behind him. "The nerve of that man."

"I'm sorry, but I saw him come in and didn't want you to be alone with that monster," Mary said as she wrung her hands.

"Thank you." She massaged her temples. "I don't know what I'm going to do. This seemed so easy and exciting. Travel to Deadwood and claim my uncle's inheritance while waiting for my father's business to sell. Now Mr. Grimm said I could lose everything."

"I'm so sorry." Marry patted Elizabeth's arm.

Elizabeth slumped her shoulders. "Well, unless I get married before the end of the month, I'll lose it all."

"Let me guess. He offered to marry you?" Mary tilted her chin up.

Tears threatened to fall. But she'd taken care of herself her entire life. Mr. Grimm would never get his wish. No matter how hard he made her life. "I would die first. How can things get any worse?"

"I hate to tell you, but if you marry him, they will get much worse. The evil man I told you about, the one that owns the brothel and all the women there?" Mary pointed to the door. "That was him."

CHAPTER FOUR

Garrett

It'd been a week since Calvin returned with the news that Elizabeth was safe and running her store. Everyday he'd hoped to visit her and make sure it was still the case. Unfortunately, it had been one crisis after another. A few of the men had fallen sick, so he was stuck playing nursemaid and doing their work in the mine as well. He went to bed exhausted every night.

Garrett sent a second letter to her with one of his crew who he'd sent to town for medical supplies. The young man had not been exposed to the other sick men, so he felt it safe for him to deliver it and pick up medicine at the same time.

Elizabeth had sent a generous number of tonics, and salves for their chests. It was most likely a bad case of bronchitis going through the camp, but they wouldn't be allowed in town, or near others, until everyone was better. With the arrival of the medicines, the health of everyone greatly improved. Another week and he would be able to see Lizzy's beautiful face for himself.

It concerned him that the young man who delivered his post mentioned her establishment was empty. With all the people in town, and not that many businesses such as hers, it should have been booming. Leaving her alone was the biggest mistake of his life. What had he been thinking? He hadn't. She had him flustered like no woman never before. Thankfully, he'd been able to put his words to paper and tell her how he felt. Just the short time they'd been together, he could tell she was the one for him. It was killing him not to be there to court her and help with her store.

He wanted to take care of her, so she'd never have to work a day in her life, but Elizabeth was like him. There was no way she would want to sit home and do needlepoint. It was one of the things he loved about her. Love? How did one fall in love in a such a short time? They'd need to get to know each other better first. Flowers, dinner, and going on picnics. In a week, it should be safe to go to town. The last thing he wanted was to make her sick.

At least working in the mine had helped to keep his mind occupied. Calvin said they were near the vein, and any day now they'd be millionaires. He'd believe it when he saw it, but the guy knew mining, so who was he to argue.

Garrett

A week later, Garrett stood next to his saddled horse and gave Calvin last-minute instructions before traveling to Deadwood. They'd hit pay dirt just like the man said. Thank God he had hired extra men for security the first week he'd arrived. They would need it as soon as word got out they'd hit gold.

Calvin's eyes widened as he stared at something behind him. Garrett twisted to see a young woman riding into camp.

"What is this, Garrett? It isn't safe to have a woman in camp."

From the low cut of her bodice and the bright rouge on her cheeks, it was a good bet she was a working girl. "I didn't invite her."

Calvin brushed the dust from his shirt and pants before marching over to greet her. Taking his hat from his head, the man smiled. "Hello, Miss. Are you lost?"

"I'm here to see Mr. Garrett." The smile dropped from Calvin's face as he led her limping horse over to where the boss stood. "Are you Garrett?"

"Yes. Who are you?" He shaded his eyes with his hand. The young lady was pretty, but he couldn't place her.

"Mary. I know Elizabeth. She needs you."

A chill ran down his back. She needed him? "Is she all right? What's happened?"

"Well, it hasn't happened yet, but it will soon." Mary went on to tell him the story of what Elizabeth had been dealing with in town. "I'm afraid my horse threw a shoe a mile back. Would one of your men be able to help with that?"

After hearing the disastrous turn of events, he scolded himself and apologized for the profanity. But this was Mary. He'd left Elizabeth all alone in Deadwood, so close to the Badlands. He should have been there to protect her, but he was on his way now. That's what mattered. "Yes, of course. Cal, can you see to Miss Mary's horse and make sure she gets safely back to town?"

Now the grin returned to Calvin's face as his friend was obviously smitten with the working girl. She'd be safe with him, so his only concern now was getting to Deadwood and his Lizzy.

Garratt mounted his horse. He took off at a gallop but soon had to slow due to the rough terrain. The hills were rocky, and the last thing he needed was to have his horse go down on slippery pine needles. Yet it was killing him to think he might not get there in time. What a fool he'd been to leave her side. If she'd have him, he would never leave her again.

Mary said Elizabeth finally agreed to marry Grimm after he threatened to kill her. Mary pleaded with her not to do it. She even threatened to kill herself before she would let her friend marry that monster. Grimm warned Elizabeth that he'd burn the brothel down with all the women inside if she didn't go through with the wedding

Elizabeth would never let someone be hurt or killed because of her. If Garrett didn't get there in time, her life would be over. He even feared she might do something to harm herself. There were rumors in camp about what a cruel man Grimm was, but it'd never dawned on him the madman was her lawyer. After an hour of riding, he slowed by a creek to let his steed get a much-needed drink.

Dismounting, he stretched his tired back. The feeling of being watched trickled into his mind as he circled his horse to survey their surroundings. A flash of white caught his eye in the nearby tree line. Taking his pistol from the holster and keeping his horse in front of him, Garrett paralleled the river before circling back through the trees.

At first, he thought it was a child, but nearing the item, Garrett was relieved to see it was just a doll. The white came from its porcelain face, but what was it doing out here? Was there a lost girl around? His horse whinnied and swung around. The last thing he saw before everything went blank was a man dressed in black.

CHAPTER FIVE

Elizabeth

"Are you sure Garrett knew when the wedding was?" Elizabeth cried as she stared at her reflection in the mirror. A marriage ceremony should be the happiest of times, but all she wanted to do was throw herself off a cliff. The guard outside the door would put a stop to that.

"Yes, and he left to come here as soon as I told him." Mary paced the floor while biting her nails. "I don't understand. His friend, Calvin, told me himself that all the man talked about since he arrived was you. He rode back with me, and we didn't see Garrett on the trail. He had to have come here."

The bride sank into a chair, not caring in the least if the gown was crushed or wrinkled. It should be black and not white, as it felt like a funeral. The fact that Garrett hadn't arrived worried her even more. Something had to have happened to him. If it had, it was all her fault. She'd reached out to him via Mary and involved him in her mess.

Tears threatened to fall, but there were none left to shed. At least Grimm had allowed Mary to stay with her. Their friendship was just another tool he used to control her. The fear of what her life would be from now on paled in comparison to the thought of sharing a bed with the devil tonight.

The room spun and she couldn't breathe. Not being able to keep anything down for days, Elizabeth was weak when she needed to be strong.

Mary held a glass out to her. "At least drink some water."

She reluctantly drank the whole thing.

A knock on the door announced their time was up.

Her tummy rolled as she was led outside toward the altar. It wasn't a real wedding. There were no guests, only a few witnesses, Mary, and one of Grimm's henchmen. The service lasted a mere four minutes before a pen was shoved in her hand to sign her life away.

Choking back a sob, Elizabeth straightened her spine. Her life hadn't gone as planned, but she wasn't going to go down without a fight. She was going to do everything she could to help Mary and the other women at the brothel.

"Thank you, everyone." Grimm took Elizabeth by the elbow. "I no longer need your services as I will be taking my new bride out to dine."

The other witness left the room, and Mary gave her a quick hug.

"I'm not really hungry." Elizabeth wiggled out of his hold.

He sighed. "I don't care."

She drew a deep breath, willing her strength. She had to find a way out. "Let me change first."

"No, I want everyone to see you in your wedding dress and to know you and everything you own are now mine." Grimm grabbed her again.

She gritted her teeth, protesting as she squirmed in his greasy grip. "So, you had this planned the whole time?"

"As soon as I saw your photograph. Believe me when I say I could get any woman in town I want. In fact, I have a whole house full of women I can have any time, any place, and any way I want. So don't think you can hold, or withhold, anything from me that I can't get somewhere else."

Elizabeth shook her head. "Then what is this all about?"

"Money and property. The building your uncle owned is in a prime location. I plan to make it into a grand hotel. Something to rival the biggest and the best of establishments this side of the Mississippi. With all that and a beautiful bride from out east at my side, my reputation in town will rise as well."

"I married you under duress." She gritted her teeth together.

"Do you think anyone cares?" His beady eyes twitched, and his breath smelled of whiskey. "Now we are going out to dinner so that everyone will know you are now mine."

Elizabeth folded her arms over her chest. "I will never be yours."

"On paper you already are, and that's all that matters to me. What's yours is now mine."

Her jaw dropped open. Had her uncle died of natural causes or had Grimm had his hand in that as well? It broke her heart to think that he might have been an innocent pawn in Grimm's schemes.

They were seated in one of the fanciest restaurants in town. The food looked amazing, but it tasted like chalk. Would she ever enjoy a meal again? Elizabeth went through the motions as she was introduced to different important people in town who stopped to say hello. After she refused to smile at the first couple, Grimm painfully twisted her wrist under the table. "Do that again and I break it."

The smile on her face probably looked like a grimace, but from the pitiful glances she was receiving, it was a good bet most of the citizens of Deadwood knew what was going on. The looks of sympathy thrown her way proved they knew she was a victim. Another tragic casualty of this evil man.

Chewing in small bites was the only way she could get food down.

Grimm was losing patience. "You've had enough. It's time to go."

So much for appearances. He pretty much dragged her through the room and out the door. They stopped at a few other establishments on the way to his house, again to show his dominance over his new bride. Grimm lived in a large house perfect for a family, but the only way she would be bearing any of his children was if he took her by force. It was dark when they finally reached her new home, but as soon as they entered the house, someone knocked.

"What is it?" Grimm barked as the housekeeper hurried to open the door.

"Sorry to bother you, but there's trouble at the, ah, at one of your businesses." The man pulled off his hat and held it in front of his chest as soon as he saw Elizabeth.

"What kind of trouble?" Grimm grumbled as he poured himself a whiskey.

"Not sure, sir, but they said it was urgent."

"Fine." He slammed back the drink and headed for the door. "I'll be back. Then again, maybe I might stay there awhile. I'm sure the company will be much more to my tastes." Grimm narrowed his eyes at her before leaving.

If she could throw a dagger into his back with her eyes, he'd be dead. If only it was that easy. She didn't know how long she had before Grimm returned, so she needed to use her time wisely and quickly. Could she poison him? Make it look like an accident? Did she have it in herself to murder someone or should she just take a horse and slip out of town? There had to be something she could do, but what?

CHAPTER SIX

Garrett

Garrett rubbed the lump on his head where he'd been hit. Luckily, Calvin had found him in the woods after seeing Mary safely back to town. He'd been in and out of consciousness for days. It killed him to know that Elizabeth was in the hands of a lunatic, but they had to do things carefully or Garrett would lose her forever.

He'd watched from a distance as Grimm showed his new bride around. A woman Garrett had hoped to take as his bride.

Calvin was taken with Mary and, after seeing her safely returned to Deadwood, they'd made plans to meet again. That was how they were able to keep Garrett up to date with what was happening and to make the necessary arrangements.

The girls at Grimm's brothel were in on the plan to keep him away from Elizabeth and get Grimm to come to the brothel. The women sent word with one of the bartenders that they were refusing to see any customers until Grimm agreed to their demands. Garrett also bribed the guards who worked there with gold to close the place and disappear for the rest of the night.

The time had finally arrived to free Lizzy. Garrett watched from the second story balcony of the brothel as Grimm entered the establishment. The man's face was red with anger, just how Garrett expected. Emotion was liability when going into battle. His mind was clear and focused.

"Where the hell is everyone?" Grimm yelled as he breached the front door.

"Come find us." A woman stood at the top of the stairs before hurrying away.

"Have you all gone mad? I demand to know what is going on." Grimm ran upstairs where Garrett greeted him before he could reach the top.

Garrett held his hand over his holster. He didn't trust Grimm to play fair. "We finally meet."

Grimm flicked his gaze to the weapon. "Who the hell are you?"

"You don't remember the people you attempt to kill and leave out in the woods?" Garrett took a step forward, towering over the shorter man.

"I have no idea what you're talking about."

"Name's Garrett, and you're going to pay for what you did to Elizabeth, Mary, and everyone else you've hurt."

"I don't think so." Grimm pulled out a gun, but Garrett was too fast.

I'LL FIND YOU

Garrett pushed the guy's arm up in the air as the pistol went off. The bullet went through the ceiling. He hoped no one was up there, but he couldn't worry about that now.

They struggled back and forth, but Garrett was the larger, stronger man. He managed to get a couple good hits to Grimm's face before the guy lost his balance, pulling Garrett with him as they fell down the stairs.

Garrett's head spun, but he recovered quickly as Grimm struggled to rise. Grabbing Grimm by the lapel, Garrett pulled the bastard to his feet and hit him in the face.

Grimm pulled out a knife, but Garrett jumped back, narrowly missing a swipe of the blade.

Grimm wiped the blood from his nose with the back of his hand. "I'm going to enjoy cutting you to pieces before heading back to my new bride."

"I heard you got married. Too bad she'll be a widow soon." Garrett lunged, shoving his nemesis against the wall with such force his head made a dent.

The knife fell from Grimm's hand, but he surprised Garrett with a left hook.

Garrett was caught off-balance.

Grimm reached for the gun he'd dropped when they tumbled down the stairway.

They wrestled back and forth before Garrett pounded Grimm's fist so hard the weapon dropped free. Garrett wrapped his hands around Grimm's throat and squeezed while Grimm used his hands to claw at Garrett's face and eyes.

Grimm somehow wiggled out of the hold and tried to crawl away. Garrett reached for the man's head and twisted, snapping his neck. Grimm dropped to the floor. Garrett, breathing hard, stood and took a step back.

Calvin was waiting below and nudged the guy's ribs with his boot, but he didn't budge.

Mary and the other girls cautiously peeked out of their rooms then hurried down to the stairs.

It was never a good thing to take a life. But in this case, it was justified. Grimm almost killed him in the forest, he'd been lucky to survive the crack to his skull. What he'd done to ruin the lives of all the woman in this building was heinous. The risk he took in the man's demise was still up for debate. Would he now go to jail for saving the one he loved? If so, it was worth it, but he wasn't ready for the handcuffs yet.

"Get some whiskey," Garrett told Mary, and she rushed behind the bar. As soon as she handed it to him, Garrett sprinkled it over the dead man's clothes. "Poor guy drank too much and fell down the stairs. Right, everyone?"

They all nodded or replied yes.

"It was bound to happen one of these days," Mary remarked while another girl added, "I saw him fall. He was sauced for sure."

"Calvin, get our guys in here. Mary, you call the sheriff. Let's get this over and done with."

They all hurried to do his bidding and make things appear as normal as could be. The man was a terror, and no one was sad to see him gone. Even the sheriff made no mention of the bruises on Garrett's face, obviously glad to be rid of the foul man.

CHAPTER SEVEN

December
Elizabeth

This time her dress was burgundy, perfect for a Christmas wedding. She'd waited six months to wear it—more than enough time to mourn a husband she hated. He was found dead at the brothel the night of their wedding, and she couldn't have been happier. The sheriff declared it an accident. His body somehow disappeared, but his hat was found near a pig pen in the Badlands part of town.

Thanks to Grimm's timely death, she'd not only inherited her uncle's and father's wealth but Grimm's as well. Elizabeth was now one of the wealthiest people in town. Her store was crowded with customers now that Grimm could no longer threaten people if they shopped there.

Garrett's smelting company and mine was flourishing, and he was even wealthier than her. Together they were helping as many people as they could. The brothel Grimm had run was now a boarding house for travelers run by some of the women who had been forced to work there. Others had been given funds to travel home to their families, and others found husbands. Mary being one of them. Not wanting to wait, Calvin and she had married months ago.

The kind woman had blossomed as a married lady, and they were hoping to start a family soon.

"Are you ready?" Mary popped her head around the opened door.

"More than ready." Elizabeth picked up the bouquet of roses. Garrett had them sent special from down south.

Calvin greeted both ladies at the top of the stairs. "You look stunning, Lizzy."

Garrett's nickname for her had been adopted by everyone.

"Shall we go?" He held out his elbows for each woman to grab. The large man wouldn't let either one of them fall.

Once they were at the bottom, Mary led the way to the parlor where the guests were gathered. Garrett stood tall, dressed in a blue suit and black tie. Even though Calvin was to walk her down the short aisle of the large room, Garrett met them halfway.

Whereas her other wedding had been a blur, Elizabeth enjoyed every second the one with the man she loved. After Grimm's death, she'd learned the full story of what the fiend had done to Garrett. Thankfully, he had survived and came to her rescue.

Later they celebrated at the largest hotel in town. They

dined and danced with their friends until late into the night.

Elizabeth felt light on her feet. But even more, her heart thrummed with a love she'd never thought possible. "I can't believe we met on a train and now we are married. There were times when I didn't know if I would ever see you again."

"Never fear, Mrs. Anderson. I said I would find you, and no matter where we go or what we do, I always will." His lips touched hers as the rowdy guests cheered.

Gazing up at her handsome husband, her trip to Deadwood certainly hadn't turned out like she'd planned, but she would haven't it any other way.

THE END

ABOUT THE AUTHOR
GINGER RING

Ginger Ring is an award-winning author with a weakness for cheese, dark chocolate, and the Green Bay Packers. She loves reading, watching great movies, and has a quirky sense of humor. Publishing a book has been a lifelong dream of hers and she is excited to share her romantic stories with you. Her heroines are classy, sassy and in search of love and adventure. When Ginger isn't tracking down old gangster haunts or stopping at historical landmarks, you can find her on the backwaters of the Mississippi River fishing with her husband.

Website: Gingerring.com
Facebook author page:
www.facebook.com/romancewritergingerring
Instagram: @ringginger
Pinterest: GingerRing
Twitter: @GingerRings

Please check out these other great books by Ginger Ring available at fine online bookstores everywhere.

Love is a Dangerous Thing series
The Gangster's Kiss
The Gangster's Woman
The Gangster's Hand

Genoa Mafia Series
Madison's Mobster
Crossing Roman
Escaping Ryan
Taken to the Cleaner
Destroying Dominic
Playing Jasper
Chasing Arlo

Coulee Bluff Series- coming soon
Custom Made For You
Cheers For You

Standalones
The Pink Rose of the Prairie
Red Roses, Black Orchids

Rescuing Eliza

TINA SUSEDIK

Deadwood, South Dakota is teeming with history, both good and bad. When the area was overrun by those seeking gold, they were followed by men wishing to find riches in other ways. One of those men was Al Swearengin, who brought women to service The Gem, a place for entertainment, both upstairs and down. Al didn't always get his girls in the proper way. Trickery, lies, and outright kidnapping filled his brothel with "Spoiled Doves."

In 1877, when the town was barely a year old, Eliza Pringle is sold to Swearengin by her father. When reality of what her job at The Gem is to be, she seeks to escape. With the help of those who don't believe in prostitution, she is rescued, only to be hunted down by The Gem's owner.

Will Eliza stay safe in the hands of Wade DesForge or be forced back into Deadwood's seamier side of life? Find out in "Rescuing Eliza," a short story that is part of "The Darlings of Deadwood" series.

CHAPTER ONE

May 1877
Outside Galena, Illinois
Eliza Pringle

"Girl, get down here, now."

Eliza Pringle sighed. What did her stepfather want now? She pushed herself up from the bed and climbed down the wooden ladder from the loft she shared with her four sisters and three brothers in the log house on her family's farm. At the bottom of the ladder, she drew in a deep breath before facing the man who had caused her no end of grief since he'd married her mother twelve years ago when she was six.

Hank Olson slapped a newspaper against his leg and rested his elbow on the table. "You took your sweet time, girl."

She didn't bother reacting to his nasty tone, which would only make him mad, something she definitely didn't want to do. "Yes, sir?"

He grumbled under his breath.

She'd never called him father, or papa, or dad like her siblings did, since he'd only remind her he wasn't any of those things.

Her mother stood at the stove, her back to the room, shoulders scrunched to her ears.

He glared. "I found you a job, girl."

A job? Until she heard what it was, she'd contain her excitement over the chance to leave this place and a family who hated her because she had a different father. It didn't matter if her mother and father had been married and he'd died; they treated her like a bastard. "What is it?" She tried to keep her voice neutral.

"When I was in town, I met a Mr. Swearingen from Deadwood in the Dakota Territory."

She hadn't heard of the man, nor the place. "What kind of job?"

"He said being a waitress or a cleaning lady at his establishment. I guess cleaning would be the best for someone worthless like you."

She'd heard this so many times, he was probably right. Plus, since all she did on the farm was cook, clean, and watch the younger kids, it was all she could do. If it got her away from her awful existence, she'd muck out horse stalls.

"You'll be leaving tomorrow. He'll pick you up on his way back to Deadwood." He pointed a finger at her. "And you'd better be kind to him. Mr. Swearingen is paying for your travel expenses, plus new clothes."

Eliza glanced down at her skirt rising above her ankles and too-small blouse stretching across her breasts. Anything would be better than what she was wearing. "Do you know what time?"

"No. You just be ready at dawn, or you'll be sorry." He put on his battered straw hat, rose from the table, and slammed the door behind him.

During the entire conversation, her mother had stood motionless, as if she were one of those statues in Old City Cemetery where her pa was buried.

"Ma?"

Her mother sniffled but didn't turn. "You best do as he says."

"Ma, how come you let him treat me like he does? Do you hate me so much?"

"I don't hate you." Her mother glanced at her over her shoulder, then the front door. "In fact, I love you more than any of my other children."

"Then why don't you stand up to him?"

Her mother sighed and pulled back a curtain to look outside. "Is anyone upstairs?"

"No."

Her ma leaned against the counter and folded her arms across her chest. "When your father died, I had no idea how I would support both of us. You were only four. Since my parents didn't want me to marry George, they forbade me from returning. When Hank came along, I thought he was an answer to my prayers. He had this farm and was hard working."

Her mother paused.

"But?"

"The first few months were fine. He treated you as his own, but when I got in the family way, he changed and said he was going to raise his real children, not the leavings of another man. After David was born, he poured all his energy into him. It was as if you didn't exist."

She had vague recollections of David's birth, and how Hank pushed her away whenever she came close. It only got worse as the next five were born, until she was nothing more than a pesky fly to him.

"I'm so sorry I didn't protect you, but whenever I brought up his behavior . . ." She rubbed the side of her cheek. "Well, it's best you're leaving."

Tears filled Eliza's eyes. She didn't want to leave her ma, but deep down she knew it was for the best.

Her ma peered out the window again. "Now, come here and let me give you a hug before Hank returns."

It had been so long since she'd been in her mother's arms, she never wanted to let go. Memories of sitting on her lap brought more tears to her eyes.

Hank's voice brought her back to reality.

Her mother kissed her cheek, pushed her away, then turned back to the stove.

"Get upstairs before he comes in. Make sure you're ready in the morning."

CHAPTER TWO

Two Weeks Later
Eliza

The coach rocked from side to side. Eliza peered out the window. Her stomach rolled. They were going downhill at breakneck speed. Were they going to tip over and roll down the hill into the buildings visible in the valley? The girls across from her grabbed on to each other and screamed. Even though she'd love to huddle with someone, she wasn't about to act like a ninny.

The coach careened around several curves before finally hitting a straight path and slowing.

Eliza took a deep breath and wiped sweat from her forehead. The three coaches carrying fifteen girls had arrived alive and in one piece. She gasped at the sight outside the coach's tiny window. This was Deadwood?

Men, appearing as if they hadn't shaved or washed in years, lounged against the walls of buildings looking as if a spring breeze would topple them over. Horses, pigs, cows, and men mucked through thick mud. Piles of wood littered the edges of the street.

From what she'd seen so far, the town sported banks, a tin shop, restaurants, newspaper offices, a hardware store, a dry goods store, liquor stores, livery stables, several saloons, and a jail. And there were men. Hundreds of men. No, maybe thousands.

A shiver ran down her back. Why were there so many men here, and why didn't they look rich like one of her traveling companions had said? Where were the women?

The men whooped, hollered, and raced toward the coaches as they passed.

Eliza dropped the fabric curtain and shrank back. Why were they charging the coaches?

The driver halted the mules, and someone threw open the door.

"Well, look who we have here."

Eliza recoiled at the man's fetid breath and the dirty hand he held out.

"C'mon, darlin.' Let me help you down."

"Charlie, leave the ladies alone." Mr. Swearingen appeared in the doorway. "Let me get them settled first."

First? What did he mean by first? Like the cows following the lead cow to the barn, Eliza followed the others to a three-story wooden building with a balcony across the second floor. A sign reading *Gem Theater* swung from beneath the balcony. Thankfully, they didn't have to walk in the muddy street as the coaches had stopped before an actual boardwalk.

"Quit gawkin,' girl, and get a move on." The tallest, most muscular man she'd ever seen gave her a shove, nearly sending her into the girl before her.

She bristled at being called *girl*. And here she thought once she left home, no one would call her that again. It took a minute for her eyes to adjust to the dim interior of the building, but when they did, dismay washed through her. Where was the fancy restaurant and hotel?

They passed a bar running the length of one wall, rows of chairs facing a stage, and men lounging at tables calling out to them as they headed up a stairway. Some reached out and touched them, but the burly man, who Mr. Swearingen called Johnny, knocked them away, telling them they had to wait.

Johnny herded them up the stairs to the third floor where they walked down a hallway and were assigned a room for four. Thankfully, she was with the girls from her coach. Before closing the door, Johnny told them to not leave the room.

It was large enough, but barely, to hold two double beds, two bureaus with mirrors, and a chamber pot. Bare wood covered the walls. Eliza swore light came through cracks between the boards. At least there was a window, but no curtains. She glanced out the window to view a crooked building surrounded by barrels of empty bottles.

One of the girls dropped to the edge of the bed. "What are we doing here? I was told we'd be working in a fancy hotel. Nothing I saw so far looked remotely fancy."

Along with the others, she had no idea what was going

to happen to them. For the next hour, Eliza chewed on her fingernails as they tried to guess. Every so often, they jumped at loud voices coming from downstairs, yelling from outside, and the all-too-frequent sound of gunfire. Eliza was tired, hungry, and scared. What had Hank gotten her into?

Eliza

The next day around noon, Johnny appeared at the door, entered without knocking, and tossed in several dresses. "Get changed," he ordered before slamming the door closed. "You have fifteen minutes, then I'll come in and help."

His chuckle sent shivers down Eliza's back.

They scrambled to help each other lace up dresses so short on the bottom and low on the top, she'd have so much skin showing, she cringed. She tugged at the top to cover her breasts and let a tear roll down her cheeks. Her mother would be appalled.

The door flew open and a young woman wearing a purple dressing gown stepped into the room. "I'm Sapphire. C'mon, ladies. Johnny and Mr. Swearingen will be wanting to see you in the dining room."

Eliza took up the rear as they entered the hallway and were joined by the other women wearing clothes every bit as scanty as hers. Some of the women were crying.

Her stomach growled. Were they going to be fed?

She'd never eaten in a dining room before. In her mind, a dining room was something fancy with brocade curtains, a long table set with expensive dishes, and candelabras lighting up the room.

Sapphire opened a door at the end of the hallway. "In a moment, Jonathan and Mr. Swearingen will be coming in. Then we will eat, and you will go downstairs for the evening."

The dining room was as far from what Eliza had in her mind as a pig was from a hummingbird. Yes, there was a long table, but it was made from rough-hewn wood with benches of the same. If they weren't careful, they'd get splinters when they sat. Bowls and cups were chipped; silverware tarnished. The walls were bare and the room so hot, whoever made the soup probably hadn't had to use a stove. Platters with loaves of bread were placed up and down the table.

"Ladies, line up behind the benches." No sooner had Sapphire uttered the words than the door opened and in strode Jonathan, Mr. Swearingen, and another large man. They closed the door behind them.

"Welcome to the Gem Theater," Mr. Swearingen walked in front of the ladies on the other side of the table. "This is one of the best entertainment places in Deadwood Gulch."

One of the ladies caught a hitch in her throat, drawing everyone's attention.

Mr. Swearingen stopped before her and lifted her red hair. "Beautiful. You'll be sought after by many."

The woman jerked away from him, only to have him grab a handful of hair and tug her to him.

"Don't you ever do that again."

Tears ran down the girl's face.

Bile rose in Eliza's throat. Why was he being so mean?

Swearingen let go and moved down the line of women, eyeing them from the tops of their heads to their toes. He adjusted their dresses to expose more of their chests.

A shiver of nerves skittered across her skin when he rounded the table and came down her side. His perusal reminded her of going to a cattle auction where men moved up and down rows seeking the best.

"Well, I can certainly see I've purchased an interesting lot. Some of you will do and some will be working behind the scenes."

Eliza gave a sideways glance at the girl next to her. "Purchased?" she whispered.

"Quiet!" Jonathan's booming voice shook the windows. "Do as Mr. Swearingen says. He paid for your trip and your new clothes. He expects to be paid back in full."

Eliza's knees nearly buckled. How much did she owe him, and how was she supposed to pay him back? She released a pent-up breath when Swearingen stopped briefly before her then moved on without touching or saying anything to anyone before the men left the room.

"Okay, ladies." Sapphire clapped her hands. "Be seated. Supper will be served shortly. Then you'll retire to your rooms and prepare for the evening."

CHAPTER THREE

Eliza

While growing up, Eliza had heard adults say how days or weeks were from hell. She thought it was blasphemous, but now she understood. Each night they were paraded downstairs like horses at an auction. The loud, male voices, their laughter, and their smelly, sweaty bodies were revolting. Their touches made her stomach spin, making her turn inward. Except for her roommates, she didn't say a word.

Jonathan accused her of being touched in the head. If men thought that of her and left her alone, so be it. For, one by one, the women who came with her were led upstairs by men, doing things making them cry at night.

Word got out that the tall, dark-haired one was "tetched." Mostly it made the men wary of her, but there were those who thought since she didn't talk, she was stupid, and they *could* touch her however they wanted. If she narrowed her eyes and growled, they tended to leave her alone.

But there was one man, short, bald, wearing loud clothes, who wouldn't take no for an answer. Each night, his pestering grew bolder, until she hated the thought of going downstairs.

Mr. Frawley ran his fingers down her arms, offered her drinks, whispered in her ear what he wanted to do with her, and constantly explained how he was one of the richest men in Deadwood.

She didn't care if he were the richest in the territory, his fetid breath, white hair, and bulging stomach were enough to make the staunchest woman faint.

Sapphire stood next to her. "Eliza, I got word from Jonathan that tomorrow night is your night. Mr. Frawley has already paid for an evening with you."

Eliza's breath caught in her lungs and her stomach clenched.

"Listen," Sapphire whispered. "I know you can talk. I've heard you with the other girls in your room. I've also heard how Frawley treats the girls. He can be mean. That's why only our most hardened girls take care of him. But he believes since you don't talk, no one will hear your screams."

A sob lodged in her throat. She turned her head to hide her exchange with Sapphire. "What do I do? I can't. I just can't."

"You remind me of my youngest sister, and I'd do anything to help her. If Frawley gets his hands on you . . . Well, let's just say I'm afraid you won't survive. He tends to get rough with the girls. We've lost a couple at his hands."

Eliza gasped "But wouldn't someone help?"

Sapphire shrugged. "Jonathan follows Swearingen's orders, and all Al cares about is making money."

The fear knotting in her stomach nearly made her knees buckle. "I have to get out of here. Can you help me?"

"I'm not sure. Let me think about it." Sapphire brushed a feather from her red boa off her shoulder. "Now, go about your work like you do every night."

Would this be her last night in this awful place? If she knew for sure, it would make getting through it easier.

"Good evening, my dear." Mr. Frawley ran a finger down her bare shoulder. "You look lovely as usual. Has Sapphire told you the good news?"

Goosebumps covered her skin, and it took everything in her power not to shake him off. The last time one of the girls did that to a customer, she'd sported a black eye the next day. No one knew who gave it to her, but she thought it was Jonathan. But could it have been Mr. Frawley? Keeping up her persona as someone who didn't speak, she nodded.

"I'm fairly certain you've never been with a man." He kissed the back of her neck. "I'm looking forward to teaching you how to pleasure me. Now be a good girl and fetch me a whiskey and one for yourself."

Leaving the man's side brought a wave of relief, even if it was brief. The bartender handed her a glass filled with the amber liquid for Mr. Frawley and a watered-down version for herself. Mr. Swearingen didn't want his girls drunk.

The night dragged. The only good thing about

spending all her time with Mr. Frawley was not having other men paying attention to her. But after listening to the man drone on and on about himself, his riches, and what he had planned for tomorrow night, maybe another man would be preferable to this puffed-up toad.

Finally, at one in the morning, Jonathan stood by her side. "Sorry, Frawley, time for Miss Eliza to head upstairs."

Frawley sipped from his glass and looked over the rim at Jonathan. "Ah, c'mon, Johnny, old boy. Give a guy a break. I want to spend more time with this lovely gal."

Jonathan pulled her up by the arm. "You'll have plenty of time tomorrow night." He glanced at his pocket watch. "I guess that would be tonight, wouldn't it? She needs to get her rest. C'mon, I'll escort you to your room."

Huffing out a sigh of relief probably wouldn't bode well for her, but it was hard to hold it in. If she had to listen to the man's whiny voice one more second, she wouldn't be responsible for her actions.

Jonathan stopped at her room. "I was serious about getting your rest. You'll need it. I don't like Frawley, but he paid a pretty penny for you, so you'd best be good to him." On that note, he opened the door and pushed her in.

Sleep was hard to come by. She tossed and turned until Delta finally slapped her on the arm.

"Will you lay still? Worrying isn't going to make things easier." Her bedmate punched her pillow. "Just remember. Moan a little. Sigh a little. Wiggle. And pretend you're somewhere else. Like the rest of us, you'll get through it."

Well, if Mr. Frawley was going to be mean to her tonight, she'd fight tooth and nail against him. What did she have to lose? A frightening thought crossed her mind. Maybe her life?

CHAPTER FOUR

Eliza

Eliza sat at the empty dining room table. It was early so everyone was still asleep. She cupped a chipped mug filled with cold, bitter coffee. She never enjoyed black coffee, but evidently milk was hard to come by in Deadwood. With all the cows roaming the streets, why didn't someone corral and milk them?

A door at the end of the room opened. Sapphire stepped into the room and crooked a finger at Eliza. "Follow me," she whispered. "Hurry."

Eliza put the cup of unfinished coffee in a pan for dirty dishes, followed the woman through the door then gasped as they entered a second room.

On the other side of the door was one of the nicest rooms she'd ever seen. A four-poster bed with a lacy canopy filled much of the room. The walls were covered in rose brocade wallpaper. A dressing table was crammed with bottles and jars of various sizes and shapes. Feather boas, ones she'd seen Sapphire wear at night, were draped over one side of the mirror. Doors to a large armoire stood open, revealing gowns of every color of the rainbow.

"Quit gawking. I was a madam at a brothel in Chicago. When Swearingen tried to get me to come out here, I insisted I have a room of my own, decorated to my tastes." She lifted a pair of trousers and shirt from the bed. "Here, put these on."

"But those are men's clothes."

"Can't get anything by you, can I?" Sapphire paused. "Sorry, didn't mean to sound nasty. We don't have a lot of time to get you out of here." She tossed the clothes to Eliza. "Now get changed. I'm taking you out of this hellhole while everything is quiet. Even Jonathan has to sleep sometime."

Eliza tore off her clothes and donned the over-large shirt and pants.

Sapphire tossed her a rope to tie around her waist to hold the pants up.

"Where are you taking me?" Eliza knotted the makeshift belt.

Sapphire put a wide-brimmed, scruffy, brown hat on Eliza's head. "Tuck your hair inside the hat then put on those boots and coat."

Both the hat and coat stunk of . . . skunk? She wrinkled her nose. She didn't want to think about who had worn them, or whose feet had been in the over-sized boots. "Ugh."

"I know they smell. I was in a hurry." Sapphire wiped

a finger over the black soot from inside an oil lamp on her dresser.

Eliza jerked back when the woman reached out her dirty hand to her face. "What are you doing?"

"I'm going to disguise your face." After wiping her cheeks and nose, Sapphire stepped back. "This will have to do. Now, when we leave the room, I want you to act drunk."

Having seen her stepfather in his cups, it would be easy to do. Sway and stumble. Maybe sing a dirty song. "All right."

"Just don't lose your hat." Sapphire pulled it lower over Eliza's face. "And whatever you do, don't speak."

So much for singing a song, which, now that she thought about it, would give away her voice not being deep enough.

"Let's go." Carrying an empty basket over one arm, Sapphire pulled her through the door. "Remember, you're drunk."

They didn't encounter anyone as they passed through the building. After a week of being inside the Gem, the bright sunshine nearly blinded her. She squinted, kept her head down, and staggered against Sapphire.

"Not so hard. You nearly knocked me over."

Eliza squinted past the brim. "Sorry, I can't see. Where are we going?"

"I'm taking you to Haywood's Dry Goods store."

A dry goods store? Would she be sold again, only in a different fashion? "Why?"

"They're going to help you escape."

Eliza stepped around a large pile of horse manure. "Why would they do that?"

"Because they're kind people and don't adhere to what goes on at the Gem and other saloons."

Eliza weaved, stumbling over her roomy boots. "Have you helped other girls escape?"

Sapphire stopped and let two nice-looking men, who tipped their hats at her, pass. "Yes, you're the second. As far as I know, the people helping got her safely away. Now hush up with your incessant questions."

Compared to her arrival, the town was relatively quiet. Women, accompanied by men, carried baskets, probably heading to the stores. The rowdy men must be sleeping. Sapphire opened the door to a building in better condition than others.

Eliza took a moment to let her eyes adjust to a dim interior. Shelves behind the counter held canned goods, shaving equipment, and stacks of fabric. Whatever the barrels placed around the room held was a mystery. Wide, shallow pans hung from nails, and pickaxes and other tools she didn't recognize leaned against posts. A tall, slim man with dark, curly hair had his arm around a petite blonde woman nearly a foot shorter than him. They smiled as Sapphire and she approached.

"Colin and Sadie, this is Eliza, the girl I was telling you about. Is everything ready?"

Sadie came from behind the counter and shook Eliza's hand. "I'm pleased to meet you, but we have no time to spare."

She had no idea women shook hands like men. "I'm happy to make your acquaintance. You have no idea how much I appreciate your helping me get away."

Colin walked to a curtained-off room. "Think nothing of it. Come this way."

She followed Colin, Sadie, and Sapphire to a back room filled with boxes and crates. A grizzled-looking man stood beside a table where a pile of clothes was stacked.

"Eliza, this is Gustavus Field. He's a friend of ours and has agreed to help."

The man had to be fifty if he was a day. He was about as tall as she was, thin, with a gray beard trailing down his chest. A few strands of gray hair covered the top of his bald head. His jeans were frayed, flannel shirt faded, and boots worn to the point of non-existence. At least he didn't smell.

He struck out his hand. "My friends call me Gus, and you must, too."

His cultured voice surprised her. The voices of the men she'd seen so far tended to match their appearance. Clipped, uneducated, and filled with cuss words. She took his large, rough hand in hers. Immediately, warmth and safety filled her.

"Sadie, I must be getting back to the Gem before I'm missed." She put her hands on Eliza's shoulders. "Good luck. Do whatever they tell you and you'll be safe." Without another word, she left the storeroom.

Colin kissed his wife's cheek. "I'll go with her to help her fill up her basket with food to take back to the Gem."

"Here's what we're going to do." Sadie tipped her

head to the old man. "Gus has a gold claim about a mile from town. You're going with him and help him work it."

With this old geezer? Was she going from the pan into the fire? "Won't they think a girl looking for gold odd and make it easy to be found? Besides, I know nothing about hunting for gold."

Sadie smiled. "But you're not going as a woman. You're going as a young boy, as an apprentice to Gus. As an apprentice, you won't be expected to know what to do. As a teenage boy, people will assume your high voice means it hasn't changed yet."

"But I already have these clothes."

Gus laughed. "Do you know how bad you smell? Woohee, kid, you're making my eyes burn. Besides, you might have been seen in that outfit. If anyone noticed you come in here with Sapphire and leave with me, they may put two and two together."

Sadie handed her the clothes. "These should fit you better, too. Now go behind those boxes and change. Leave your hat off so I can cut your hair."

"Cut my hair?" She removed her hat and let the long strands flow down her back. She'd never had her hair cut before and it reached nearly to her backside. "But . . ."

"Do you want to get caught?" Sadie slapped her hands at her waist. "What if your hat should fall off and your hair be exposed? We can't take the chance of some man realizing you're female and either tell Swearingen or use you for himself."

But her hair? It was the only thing she had to be proud

of. But as the saying went, 'pride goeth before the fall.'
"All right."

Since she was small on top, the baggy, dark blue shirt and vest would hide her being female. Plus, binding her chest with the strips of flannel provided would flatten and disguise her breasts even more. The boots were her size, and the pair of socks would make them comfortable. She stepped from behind the crates.

Sadie walked around her. "Except for the hair, I'd say you'll pass for a boy. You'll just need to keep your face dirty." She pointed to a chair and picked up a pair of scissors sitting on the table. "I know this is going to be hard, but it's for your own good. Please sit."

With tears running down her cheeks, Eliza eyed the long strands of hair as they fell to the floor.

Colin came into the back room. "Since men tend to wear their hair long around here, maybe not cut it too short?"

What a wonderful idea. Would Sadie get upset if she hugged her husband?

"Look at the way it's curling the shorter it gets." Sadie handed her a mirror. "Men don't usually have such curly hair."

Right now, it was shoulder length and curling around her face like a picture frame, making her eyes seem bigger. She swallowed around the lump in her throat. "I'm afraid Sadie is right. Besides, it will be easier to keep clean if it's short." With a deep breath, she swiped away her tears. "Cut it all off."

"Now all we have to do is get her some gear." Gus grinned. "I guess I should say get *him* some gear. I guess we should start calling you Eli, too, shouldn't we?"

Sadie led them back into the main part of the store. "Good idea. Now, what does he need, Gus?"

The older man ran a hand over his beard. "Let's see, a bedroll, a change of socks and underwear, another shirt, boots, a . . ."

Eliza's heart dropped as Gus kept adding things to the list, including more food. She had to stop him. "Wait, Gus. I can't afford all this. As it is, if Mr. Swearingen should find me, I'll have to pay him back for what he spent on my trip out here and the clothes he gave me."

Gus pointed a finger in her face. "You think it cost him anything to get you out here? Why, those were his own coaches and second or third-hand dresses he has you gals wear. You owe him nothing." He shuffled his feet. "Besides, I can afford it and would enjoy the company. I don't want to hear another word about it. You'll be earning your keep."

Heat rose to her face. "What do you mean earn my keep? I won't . . . I mean . . ."

"Oh, Lordy, girl. I don't mean that." Gus frowned. "I mean helping me pan for gold and cooking and keeping our clothes clean."

Relief washed through her. She was about to apologize when the bell over the door jingled and a tall man, holding a rifle at his side, came into the store.

"Hey, Gus. How you doing, old man?"

"Well, I'll be. If it isn't Wade DesForge." Gus slapped him on the back. "What're you doing away from your claim?"

"Needed supplies. Getting sick of beans, beans, beans." He glanced over Gus's shoulder. "Who is this young man?"

"Where are my manners? Wade, this is my new apprentice, Eli. Eli, this is Wade DesForge. He has the claim next to mine."

"Apprentice? Since when do you need an apprentice?"

"I'm getting on in years. This young pup ran away from home and thought he could get a claim and work it on his own. Colin caught him stealing bread and, instead of setting Bullock on him, decided to have the kid work for me. Isn't that right, Eli."

Eliza nodded. "Yes, sir."

Wade laughed. "Kinda scrawny, isn't he?"

"Probably not any scrawnier than you were at his age."

"Which is?"

Gus didn't answer but stared at Eliza. "You gonna answer him, boy?"

So, now she was going from being called 'girl' to 'boy.' "Fourteen," she managed to squeak out. It was the age of one of her stepbrothers and the first one that popped into her head.

Wade slapped her on the back, sending her stuttering forward a couple of steps. "Guess he has plenty of time to fill out."

Colin set down a couple of wrapped bundles on the counter. "Think I have everything you asked for, Gus."

"Then we'd best be getting back to our campsite. What do I owe you?"

"That'll be ten dollars and fifty cents."

Ten dollars? Was he crazy? She was a stranger to him. How would she ever pay him back? She'd have to work as hard as she could. Since she was used to working on the farm, panning for gold shouldn't be too hard.

CHAPTER FIVE

Eliza

Eliza rolled from her bedroll and eased to her feet. Was there any part of her body not hurting? She'd been with Gus for ten days now and, instead of getting used to the hard labor, she was still struggling. Her back ached from bending over to pan. Even though the calendar said it was June and the weather was warm, the creek temperature hadn't caught up, making her hands chapped and raw from the water's chill. With her feet constantly in the water, they weren't much better. In the morning, her knees cracked as loudly as Gus's from squatting so much.

Despite the rigors of living in a tent, cooking over an open fire, spending eight to ten hours a day scooping a pan into the creek sand, then swirling it around, letting the water and sand swish from the pan, hoping a nugget of gold would settle on the bottom, evenings were the best. They sat around the fire where Gus told his stories. While they were enjoyable, some seemed too far-fetched to be believable. Being chased by a herd of buffalo and outrunning them? Unlikely.

Eliza flipped back the tent flap, stretched, patted her face with dirt, and breathed in the fresh scent of pine. It was probably the best scent around. She sniffed. Oh, wait. Maybe the aroma of cooking pancakes? When she'd first arrived at Gus's site, they'd agreed he'd make breakfast and she'd do supper. Her mouth watered and stomach growled at the aroma of freshly brewed coffee.

"Hail the camp," a voice called out.

Wade stepped into their clearing, making her heart skip a beat. He'd been at their camp a couple of times, sitting around their campfire and chewing the rag with Gus. He tried getting her to join in on the conversations, but what she knew about horses, mining, or the people at the other claims could fit on the head of a pin. So, except for the few personal questions she could answer without giving herself away, she kept her mouth shut.

But that didn't stop her heart from racing whenever Wade appeared. His deep voice sent delicious shivers down her spine, not like the scary ones Frawley created. She tried to keep her eyes from him. He never removed his hat, so she wasn't sure what color his hair was, but if his dark, neatly trimmed beard was any indication, it had to be almost black. In contrast to his dark hair, he had bright-blue eyes, which tended to hold laughter.

How could a person always be happy? With the exception of the few times her stepsiblings let her join them in their play, she couldn't recall a time when she'd ever been happy. What must that be like?

Eliza filled her cup with Gus's dark, rich coffee and stopped in her tracks. Why was Wade here during the day? He only ever came after working his claim.

Gus plopped a scoop of thick oatmeal into a bowl and handed it to her. "What brings you here during the day, Wade?"

"I wanted to warn you."

Her interest perked up at Wade's serious tone. Her stomach skittered at his close inspection of her face. Had she forgotten to apply dirt this morning? The thought of sleeping with a dirty face was appalling, so she washed it off every night before climbing into her bedroll. No, she recalled giving her skin a dirt rub as soon as she'd left the tent.

"About what?" Gus sat on his chair made from a tree stump and dug into his oatmeal.

"Swearingen is on a rampage. It seems one of his new girls went missing."

Gus gave her a quick glance. "What's that got to do with us?"

"He's having his men go from camp to camp looking for her."

Don't panic. Keep eating. Don't panic. The spoon of oatmeal went down her throat as if it were a boulder. She coughed and took a sip of coffee. "Maybe she left town," she managed to say.

Wade shook his head. "They checked the stage and questioned anyone they could find who'd ridden out of Deadwood. They've been to Lead, Scooptown, and Fort

Meade. So far, no one has seen her. Now they think she may be hiding out in one of the mining camps." He gave her a hard look again.

Why was he staring at her like this? Did he suspect who she was?

Gus refilled his bowl. "Why is he so set on getting this girl back? Doesn't he have enough?"

"Evidently, he pays for their passage out here and new clothes. He wants his money. They've been telling everyone she's a thief and a murderer."

"Murderer?" Gus frowned. "Who do they say she killed?"

"Someone named Sapphire. They found her body by the creek behind the Gem. They say she was stabbed in her room and her body dumped in the creek."

Fear such as she'd never known sent spirals of terror through her. Her hand trembled. Sapphire was dead? Who would have done such a thing to her? And all because the woman was brave enough to help her escape. This was her fault.

"Why would the girl kill this woman?" Gus paused from eating.

"I'm not sure if I believe Swearingen, Gus, but they say this Sapphire helped the girl escape and the girl killed her to keep Sapphire from talking. Doesn't make sense to me. Then there's a man named Frawley who has been spitting nails about the girl's disappearance since he paid quite a bit for an evening with her."

Gus shook his head. "I seem to recall someone named

Sapphire. She was quite a big woman. How could a girl drag a heavy body down the stairs and to the creek without anyone seeing her?"

"Like I said, I don't believe a word of it. Swearingen or someone is covering up the murder, but they're determined to blame this girl. Her name is Eliza."

Again, he stared at her. *He knows who I am. What should I do?* She tipped her hat lower and tucked her chin into her chest. *I need to get out of here.* She stood.

Wade held up a hand. "Wait."

Her breath caught, and she couldn't breathe. Her head spun. She was going to pass out. What did she do to deserve this? She'd tried to be a good daughter. Tried to keep out of everyone's way. Didn't talk back to her stepfather or her mother.

"Don't run off." He grabbed her arm.

"Let go of me." She tried to jerk away, but his grip was too tight.

"I know who you are. I want to help."

Gus jumped up and rounded on Wade. "Just why do you think you know who Eli is? He's my apprentice."

Wade let go of her arm, sighed, removed his hat, and ran his fingers through his hair. Just as she'd thought, it was as dark as night. Thick and wavy. Thoughts of running her fingers through the mass sent her back a step. What in heaven's name was she thinking? She should be running for the hills.

"Remember, I was there when you were at the store a week or so back. You introduced me to Eli then."

Gus nodded and folded his arms over his chest. "Yeah, so?"

"I'd seen Sapphire leaving Haywood's. When I entered the store, you suddenly had this apprentice, when I recall you saying you didn't need help. You, Eli, Colin, and Sadie were all acting skittish. When I heard about the missing girl, it didn't take much to put two and two together."

Heavens. She was doomed. Doomed to suffer Swearingen's wrath. Not to mention what Frawley would do to her.

"I'm not saying this young chap here is who you think he is." Gus narrowed his eyes at Wade. "But what will you do if he is?"

"Anyone with any eyes in their head can tell Eli wouldn't have been able to murder Sapphire and move the body. He simply doesn't have the muscles to do such a thing, and I respect . . ." Wade stared at his boots for a moment. "As for stealing from him, well, I doubt that, too. Look, if you are this missing girl, which I'm fairly sure you are, I want to help. Anyone who has the nerve to escape Swearingen has my utmost respect. The man is evil. I would never knowingly turn a female over to him."

Eliza let out a breath. "Really?"

Wade nodded. "His men aren't too far away. We need to do something and fast."

"Have they already been to your site?" Gus unfolded his arms, poured a cup of coffee, and handed it to Wade.

"No, but they're close."

Her brief moment of relief disappeared. "What should we do? I can't go back there. I'm afraid of what Mr. Frawley will do to me."

"Not to mention Swearingen." Wade tipped his hat back on his head. "I hear he doesn't put up with anyone, man nor woman, defying him."

For a few moments, Eliza soaked in the birds' songs, the wind through the pines, and the ripple of water in the creek while the men contemplated what to do. Having no idea exactly where she was or where she'd go if she could leave, she had nothing to suggest.

Wade finally broke the silence. "Gus, have you visited with any of the other miners in the area since bringing Eli here?"

"No. Been too busy panning." Gus scratched his beard. "Besides, I figured the less people who knew he was here, the better."

"Good." He turned in a circle. "Is there a place we can hide him and his gear?"

"There's a small cave not far from here. It's big enough to hide her—I mean him—and his things."

"Eli, get your things. Leave nothing behind."

Her insides jittery with fear, she ran inside the tent and piled up her bedroll and extra clothes, then moved Gus's things to her place. After stacking her belongings in her arms and giving the inside one last look, she left the tent.

In the short time she'd been inside, the stump she always used had been removed, her dishes put in the storage box, and her small footprints swept away, leaving no sign an extra person had been staying here. Wade was gone.

"Ready?"

She nodded and followed Gus into the woods.

The cave was deeper than she'd anticipated, but not high enough to stand. She spread out her bedroll and lay down.

"Now, don't say a word."

What did Gus expect her to do? Break into a song and dance? For the first time, a giggle threatened to burst forth. She swallowed and nodded. He covered the entrance with brush, encasing her inside the cave like a caterpillar in a cocoon. The scraping of brush across the ground told her Gus was getting rid of their footsteps.

Time moved slowly. Several times raised voices came to her. Was it Jonathan and his buddies? Was Gus able to lie to them? Since he was a great storyteller, probably. After all, she never knew if he was telling her a whopper or the truth.

Her stomach growled. A line of ants carrying leaves, grains of sand, and a dead fly marched across her bedroll. A robin landed on top of the brush, cocking its head back and forth as if trying to figure out where this mound of branches had come from.

Finally, after what seemed like half the day had passed, the brush moved. Bit by bit, light filtered inside. She blinked against its brightness.

"You all right in there?"

"Yeah. Is it safe to come out?"

Gus took her hand and helped her to her feet. "As safe as it'll ever be. I waited until they were gone for a while before coming to fetch you."

She stretched and, on impulse, drew the older man into a hug. "Thank you so much for helping me."

He stepped back and shuffled his feet. "Don't mention it. Besides keeping you out of the clutches of Swearingen, I like having you here. You're a hard worker and good company." He grabbed her bedroll. "Let's head back then try to figure out what our next step will be. I have a feeling he's not going to give up, and if he gets Bullock to believe him, the sheriff won't stop until you're behind bars."

Panning gold with Gus was the closest thing to freedom she'd ever felt. Even if she had to go up against the law, she'd fight tooth and nail for it.

CHAPTER SIX

Wade DesForge

If he could, Wade would have shot the men searching through his camp. Why did they have to dump out his coffee pot? Or rummage through his storage box, messing up his food? They were idiots to think a woman could hide in either place. Kicking his mining gear into the creek had been unnecessary. What did that have to do with anything?

He put the food back inside the box. Fools who were simply trying to throw their weight around, using scare tactics to show who they thought was in charge. At least they hadn't brought the sheriff with them.

Inside his tent, he straightened his bedding, smacked the dirt from his pillow, righted the table, and placed his extra clothes back on top of his trunk. He'd waited until the men had been gone for a bit before straightening up. He wouldn't put it past them to come back just to make sure he hadn't been hiding the girl in a sock or something.

How much of Gus' things had the men destroyed?

Then there was the girl. How was she faring? It took guts to dress up and pretend to be a boy. Right from the start he'd thought there was something off about him. Even if she was fourteen like he/she'd said, his features were too feminine to be a boy. Oh, heck. He might as well refer to him as her. This going back and forth between referring to Eli as a girl and a boy was making his brain hurt.

Wade went back outside and stared at the sky. He could still get in a few hours of panning before it got too dark to see. But did he want to? His heart wasn't into looking for gold like other men along the creek. Maybe that's why he'd found some nice nuggets—he didn't care. He was heir to the railroad company his father owned, so he'd never want for anything.

Building a railroad empire had never been in his plans. Thankfully, even though his father expected him to take over the company, he'd understood. In fact, it was his father who'd suggested going out west to search for gold. Or search for something. At thirty, it was time to figure out what he wanted in life.

He plopped down on a folding campstool and rested against the back. At least his money let him buy gear to make his stay in the wilderness more comfortable. A cot kept him from sleeping on the hard ground. Boots going to his knees kept his feet dry. Enough money provided decent food.

Hooking his fingers behind his head, he closed his eyes and let his mind wander to the girl. Who was she really? Was Eli short for her real name? Was it Elizabeth?

Eliza? Ella? Or something different? He was betting Eli was close to her real name. It would make it easier to answer to it.

What did she look like under all that dirt? What color was her hair? How long was it? He'd never seen her with her hat off. What did she look like under all that men's clothing?

They did have to figure out what to do with her. She couldn't reveal her identity. If the men along the creek found out a woman was panning, who knew what they would do. Too many men believed women were good for only one thing. He knew differently. His father had instilled in him a respect for women and their intelligence. His father always said no one could manage a household, raise children, take care of her husband, and be part of society without a brain and a good work ethic.

He itched to head to Gus's camp to see how they'd fared with Swearingen's men. He checked his pocket watch. He'd wait an hour and head over. As he drifted into a quick nap, an idea popped into his brain bringing him fully awake. He jumped up, saddled up his horse, and headed to town.

Wade

"You're sure about this?"

Wade rode back to his camp alongside Sheriff Seth Bullock. When he'd gone into town yesterday to speak with the sheriff, he'd had every intention of spending the night in his tent. But while explaining Eli's situation to Seth and his partner, Sol Star, in the back of their hardware store, too many shots of whiskey had been consumed. Getting on his horse was impossible, so he spent the night as a guest of Sol.

"I'm sure. I don't know what else to do to clear the lad's name." Wade ducked under a heavy limb, his horse picking his path between two pines.

Seth chuckled. "I thought you said Eli was a female."

"I know. I know. It gets confusing." He guided his horse around a puddle nearly the size of a small pond. "Maybe if I had seen her as one, it would be easier to use the right term."

"If my foggy memory serves me right, she and Gus have no idea I'm coming?"

Wade wanted to nod, but his head would probably fall off. He was never taking another shot of whiskey in his life. Well, maybe that was too severe. He wasn't taking a shot for at least a week or two. "No, they don't. Once I had the idea to seek your help, I wanted to come see you right away."

The campsite looked as it had when he'd left yesterday afternoon. At least that meant Swearingen's goons hadn't returned. He stopped and dismounted. "There's a lot of brush between here and Gus's. Let's walk over."

No one was in Gus's camp, so they headed to the creek. "Hey, Gus. I brought someone to see you."

Gus groaned as he stood and walked up the bank. "Hey, Wade. Why'd you bring the sheriff with you?"

"I'll tell you in just a minute. Where's Eli?"

"Around the bend." Gus put two fingers in his mouth and let out a piercing whistle. "That'll bring him running."

In a few seconds, Eli rounded the bend then stopped. He tipped his head toward Bullock. "What's going on? Who's this guy?"

Wade could kick himself. Now that he knew Eli was female, how could he have not noticed he sounded nothing like a fourteen-year-old boy? And even under her baggy shirt, the slight indention at her waist was easy to decipher. "You got any coffee, Gus?" Without waiting for an answer, he walked from the creek's edge to the camp's firepit.

"Eli, get us some cups, will you?" Gus ordered, following on Wade's heels.

Without taking her eyes from Wade and Bullock, she did as Gus asked, handed each one a cup, then poured the coffee. "Wade, who is this guy?"

The quiver in her voice showed how nervous she was. Explaining the sheriff's presence wasn't going to be easy. "Can we sit?"

At Gus's nod, he set his cup on the ground and rolled a stump over, while Bullock did the same. When they were seated, he began. "Yesterday, after those men left, I kept mulling over how to help clear Eli's name." He nodded to Eli. "By the way, what is your real name? I know it isn't Eli."

At her wide eyes, he went on. "Don't worry about the sheriff. I explained your situation."

Eli jumped to her feet, dropping her cup in the process. The coffee seeped into the dry ground. "How dare you. Is he going to arrest me?"

"Please sit down and let me explain." Wade motioned to a crooked log.

With a sigh, Eli did as he asked.

"Now what is your real name?"

"Eliza."

He'd ask for her last name, but he was lucky he got her first. "Okay. Yesterday I kept trying to figure out how to help you. We all know you couldn't have killed Sapphire."

Eliza narrowed her eyes at Bullock. "Even him?"

"Yes. Seth says there's too much evidence that a man committed the crime."

"So why are you here?" She narrowed her eyes at the sheriff.

Bullock set his cup on the ground and leaned his elbows on his knees. "I know Swearingen well. He's never going to give up until he finds you." He glanced at Wade. "Last night we talked it over and decided it was in your best interest to arrest you."

She jumped to her feet again. "Arrested? This is your big plan?" She rounded on Wade. "How dare you. You said you were going to help. You lied to me."

Wade held up a hand. "Will you please sit down and listen." He looked at Gus. "Can you please tell her to sit."

With another sigh and a glare at Wade, she plunked down. "Go ahead. Explain to me why I'm going to be arrested when I haven't done anything wrong."

"If Seth arrests you and you're in jail, Swearingen can't get to you. In fact, since he and his buddies are running all over the place searching for you, we can get you to town without him knowing, giving us a chance to investigate the murder. If he does realize who we have in jail, you'll be safe from him."

"Who is going to protect me? I can't imagine Mr. Bullock would sit in the jail keeping watch over me twenty-four hours a day."

Gus patted her knee. "I will."

"You can't leave your claim."

"Yes, I can. You mean more to me than some stupid gold. Besides, my aching bones could use a change of pace. Sitting around watching you could be just the thing."

"But, Gus, you can't keep an eye on me all the time. You have to eat and sleep."

Wade crossed his ankles. "I'll be there when Gus needs a break. In fact, he can do the day shift while I do the night."

If the anger shooting from her eyes could kill, he'd be dead in seconds. "You'll protect me like you said you'd help me? Excuse me if I don't believe you." She folded her arms over her chest and turned her back on him.

Bullock chuckled. "I told you this wouldn't be easy."

"I know. I know. Listen, Eliza. This is the only way. We need to have time to find the murderer, and you need to be safe. What if his lackeys come back here when Gus is gone? Or in the water and you're up here? What would you do? You weren't here before. Wouldn't they wonder why you're here now?"

"He's right, Eliza." Gus patted her knee again. "It's the safest place for you."

Seth stood. "We'll take you into town dressed as a boy, so your secret will remain safe."

"Oh. Aren't you guys brilliant?" Her sarcasm was loud and clear. "Since all I have in my possession are men's clothes, how else would I go into town?"

Seth shook his head and laughed. "Point taken. So, are you on board with this?"

Eliza turned back to them.

Wade's heart broke when tears rolled down her dirty cheeks, leaving white streaks. She wasn't going to make this easy, was she?

"I guess I don't have a choice." She walked to the tent.

Wade frowned. Was she going to hide? "What are you doing?"

"Getting my things."

Her things? What was she thinking? "You don't need anything."

She stopped and faced them. "Mr. Bullock, does your jail have bedding? A pillow? A change of clothes? A towel? Soap?"

Seth shook his head. "Point taken again. Get your things. We'll go back to Wade's camp. You can ride behind Wade." He glanced at Gus. "Can you come into town on your own?"

Gus snorted. "How do you think I've been getting into town all this time? Damn whippersnapper. Why . . ."

Sensing the older man was about to go into a rant, Wade took Eliza's bedroll from her. "C'mon, let's go."

CHAPTER SEVEN

Eliza

Arrested. Good heavens, she'd been arrested. Riding behind Wade had set her nerves on edge. Not because she was heading to jail, but because of his nearness.

Eliza sat on the edge of a cot in a room where the only light came from a window covered in bars. Expecting a tiny building, the large size and its similarity to a house came as a surprise. What hadn't come as a surprise was how it resembled the buildings in town seemingly ready to fall down.

She hadn't been handcuffed, so their ride through town didn't raise any eyebrows. There was no one else in the building when they arrived, so it was quiet. The inside had the scent of newly cut wood and the walls still had bark on them. With her bedroll on the cot's thin mattress, she should be comfortable enough for however long she was to be incarcerated.

The sheriff had brought her a surprisingly decent meal

of roast beef, potatoes, gravy, and green beans. He hadn't said who cooked the meal, and she didn't ask, but if all her meals were this good, she might never leave.

True to his word, Gus arrived not long after they had. Right now, he was in the front office with Bullock and Wade. Their deep voices echoed through the empty building. What were they talking about? Since they'd agreed not to lock her door as long as one of them was guarding her and no other people were in cells, she could join them, but her irritation was still strong enough, she just might take one of their guns and shoot them. Not that she knew how to use a gun, but she'd figure it out.

Would she ever be able to make her own decisions? Probably not. Men tended to believe they knew what was best for women—but look at what her stepfather had done to her. If it hadn't been for him, she wouldn't be in this position. If it weren't for Swearingen, she wouldn't be dressed like a boy. If it weren't for Wade, she wouldn't be in jail.

Wade stood in the cell's doorway. "How ya doing?"

How long would she be able to ignore the man?

"Are you going to pretend you can't talk like you did at the Gem?"

How did he know that? She scooted across the mattress, leaned against the wall, and folded her arms across her chest, pretending he wasn't in her presence.

"Just so you know, I'll be here tonight. From what we've garnered, Swearingen is back in town, but his men are still searching for you."

She sighed inwardly. If she wanted answers to her

questions, she was going to have to talk. "How long do you think it might be before he knows I'm here?"

"Unless Bullock, Gus, or I say anything, he shouldn't know. But once word gets out that we have someone in jail, people are going to wonder and talk. Already the person who made your supper is asking questions."

"What happens if men get arrested and put in here? I'm not sure how long I'd be able to hide my identity."

"Being as Deadwood is a rather lawless town, it'll happen sooner than later, but we'll cross that bridge when we come to it." He snapped his fingers. "I have an idea."

Before she could ask what, he left. She smacked her hand on the cot. Ooh, he was irritating. Handsome, but irritating. It wasn't long before the men came into the room. "Now what decisions did you make without me?"

Seth leaned against the metal door frame. "I'd been thinking about what happens when this place fills up. Tomorrow is Saturday, and the miners will come into town to whoop it up. We generally keep several prisoners in each cell. It would be hard to explain why one young pup like you would get a cell by himself. We need to get you out of here before then."

"Seth says there is a new house up on the hill he and Sol built to sell and is empty." Wade shoved his hands in his pockets and stared at his shoes. "He said we can use it."

What? "What do you mean *we* can use it?"

"Someone will still need to keep an eye on you. If word were to get out a female is living alone, well, men would be lining up outside your door thinking only one thing."

Oh, brother. She'd be right back where she started when she'd arrived in Deadwood. "How would anyone find out?"

"Unless you plan on not going outside for however long it takes to solve Sapphire's murder, someone will see you. It didn't take long for me to figure out you were a woman, and it wouldn't take long for a sharp-eyed person to do so, too."

Eliza ran a hand over her short hair. Even after ten days, it still came as a shock not to feel her long tresses. "This is so confusing. Someone will figure it out. No one will figure it out. Swearingen will take me, but only if someone figures it out. Why can't I just leave Deadwood?"

"Because his men are watching all the roads leading out of town. You and Sapphire put a dent in his ego. That's something he can't tolerate. Plus, he wants his money for bringing you out here."

"If I had it, I'd give it to him. But I don't, so I'm stuck." She blew out a long breath. "So, when do you move me?"

Seth pushed away from the door. "I'm thinking the sooner the better. Like tonight. I'm sure he's going to have his men return tomorrow for the weekend. His place gets too rowdy, and he needs all his men on hand."

Eliza slid across the cot. She scooped up her bedroll. Maybe the next place would have a real bed with sheets and everything. "Let's go, then."

Wade reached for her belongings. "Here, let me carry that."

"Why? Because I'm a girl?"
Wade's smile sent her heart tripping.
"Yeah, something like that."

Eliza

It didn't take long for Gus and Wade to arrive at a medium-sized house built on the hill. Believing it would raise eyebrows for a sheriff to be walking with them, he stayed behind.

Like all the other buildings, the outside was of rough-hewn wood, but had a porch with a surprisingly straight railing across the front. A dormer stuck out on the second floor. Maybe it was the female in her, but she imagined the house being yellow with white gingerbread trim and shutters framing the two windows on either side of a door. A white picket fence would encase the yard, with rose bushes mixed with daisies growing before the fence.

The porch steps creaked as Wade took them slowly. Was he afraid they would break? She wouldn't blame him if he was, but if his large body made it safely then so would she. Was that a deep breath he let out as he unlocked the door?

Eliza followed him into a small entryway. Doors to the left and right led to two empty rooms. Where was the furniture?

Wade peered over her shoulder into the first room. "Hmm. Seth said there would be furniture here." He headed down the hallway and opened another door on the left. "Ah, here we are."

This room had a couch, a small matching settee, a low table in front of both, and a tall secretary with a glass-fronted bookcase attached.

Wade walked to the door. "Let's check out the kitchen."

Gus and Eliza walked behind him.

The room was large and bright with windows on either side of the back door and both sides of the room. A black cast-iron stove was angled in a corner. An ice box stood at the end of a counter. Pots and pans, dishes, utensils, and various other items she couldn't identify were scattered on the counters, and a large wooden table sat in the middle of the room.

"Looks like Seth or Sol knew which room was important." Gus picked up a knife and ran a thumb over the blade. "Good thing they own a hardware store."

Unless there was food to go with all the kitchen stuff, Eliza didn't care what Seth had supplied. "I'm going upstairs to find a bed. I don't know about you two, but I'm exhausted."

There were beds in each of the three bedrooms. Without a thought, she chose one room, tossed her bedroll on top of the mattress, kicked off her boots, tossed her hat on the bureau, and plopped face down. In seconds, she was sound asleep.

RESCUING ELIZA

Eliza

"Wake up, sleepyhead. Breakfast is ready."

Eliza slapped her pillow over her head. "Go away, Sarah."

"I'm not sure who Sarah is, but I'm certainly not her. You can pretend to be a boy, but no way am I pretending to be a girl."

Wade's deep voice eased into her brain. She opened one eye. He was standing in the doorway, grinning. "What are you doing here?"

"Telling you to get up and eat before the eggs get cold."

Eggs? She rolled from the bed, pushed Wade to the side, and raced down the stairs. She hadn't had eggs since she left the farm. How long ago was that? Weeks? Months? With everything that had happened, it could be a year. In her stockinged feet, she slid across the kitchen floor and landed in a chair. In the middle of the table was a virtual feast. Scrambled eggs. Bacon. Biscuits still steaming from the oven.

Unlike she'd have to do at home, she didn't bother to ask permission nor wait until everyone else had eaten before she filled her plate. The bacon was crisp, biscuits flaky, and eggs flavored to perfection. With a quick prayer of thanks, she began shoveling food into her mouth.

Grinning, Wade sat across from her and filled his plate. "Hungry?"

Last night's supper had been good, but this was amazing. She nodded, swallowed a mouthful of eggs, and washed them down with a sip of coffee. "Who cooked this?"

"I did."

Her folk clattered to her plate. "You? But I thought men didn't cook."

He chuckled. "Didn't Gus cook at the camp?"

"Well, yeah, but this is different. You used a kitchen. Hank wouldn't even look at a stove, let alone cook something for us."

"Who's Hank?"

She bit into a slice of thick bacon to gather her thoughts. How much should she tell him? Would he even care what he'd done to her? "My stepfather."

Wade hooked an arm around the corner of his chair. "If you don't mind my asking, how did you end up at the Gem? You don't seem the type."

"I'm not. It's a long story."

"Since I'm here for a while, why don't you share it with me."

"Let me finish eating first."

He surprised her again by washing his plate and the pots he'd used while she ate. Who was this man? When her plate was empty, he washed it, too.

"Okay, now you're done. Tell me your story."

Chapter Eight

Wade

"Seriously? Your stepfather sold you to Swearingen?"

He couldn't imagine a man doing such a thing to his daughter, step or not. He had to have known what was going to happen to her. "I want to ask you something. Did you spend time with any of the men at the Gem?"

Even covered in dirt, her blush was evident. "If you mean upstairs, then no. Frawley bought me for a night, but thankfully, Sapphire, the Haywoods, and Gus saved me before anything happened."

Relief such as he hadn't known in a long time washed through him. "Thankfully is right. I've heard bad things about the man."

"He's full of himself and gives me the shakes." She hugged herself.

What did she look like under that dirt? It was hard to tell what color her hair was. She probably hadn't had a bath since leaving Galena. Poor girl. He tapped the table.

She shrank back. Was she scared? Had her stepfather

beat her? "Sorry, didn't mean to frighten you. I'd never, ever hurt a woman, but I have an idea. How would you like a bath?"

She squinted at him as if she didn't believe him. "What? A bath?"

Her sudden grin showed off white teeth, making his stomach flip. Except for one tooth overlapping another, they were straight. "Yes, a bath. You up for it?"

"Oh, heavens, am I ever." She paused, thumped her metal cup on the table, and narrowed her eyes at him. "And just where am I going to take this bath?" She thrust a finger at him. "And don't be getting any ideas."

Wade held up his hands at her angry tone. "No ideas other than knowing you'd appreciate getting clean. I bet it's been a while."

"You've got that right." Her eyes were cold. "You didn't answer my question. Where? I'm not going into town to use a bathhouse."

"I'd never make you do that. I found a copper tub on the back porch. I can haul it into one of the empty rooms down here. Do you have clean clothes to put on afterward?"

"I have a shirt and pants." She wrinkled her nose as if donning men's clothes again was distasteful.

"Good. There's a pump outside. I'll fill some buckets. You get a fire going in the stove, and we can get the water boiling."

Wade

Wade drummed his fingers on the kitchen table. How long did it take a woman to bathe? He was usually in and out of the tub before the water even had a chance to cool a degree. She'd been in there humming to herself for half an hour. She was probably all wrinkled by now. Every time the water splashed, visions of it running down her bare skin sent shivers down his spine and settled in his lower regions. He needed to get his mind back to the illusion she was a boy.

The door creaked open, and she was in the kitchen doorway stretching her arms in the air. "Oh, my that felt good."

His breath caught. His loins jerked. He swallowed around the lump forming in his throat. Good heavens, she was pretty. Her hair, which he thought was probably brown, was actually blonde and curling above her ears. Gus had told him how they had cut off a good two feet. It must have been beautiful and made a man want to run his fingers through it. Even now, as short as it was, his fingers itched to feel its silkiness.

High cheekbones, long lashes over blue eyes, a dimple in her chin, mouth full and shaped like Cupid's bow, and freckles over her nose all created a vision. He still couldn't tell what her figure was like beneath the baggy shirt and pants, but her bare feet were narrow and small.

She rubbed one foot over the other. "Is something wrong?"

"Um . . . No." Whew, he managed to say something without choking on his tongue. "You clean up nice."

She smiled.

Put her in a fancy dress and she'd be beautiful. Hell, she was beautiful in her boy's garb. "How old are you?"

Eliza came into the kitchen and sat across from him. "Does it matter?"

Hell, yeah it mattered. Right now, she looked as if she couldn't be more than fifteen. No way could he have impure thoughts about a girl that young. He wasn't that type of man. "I guess not, but I'm curious."

"I'm eighteen. I'll be nineteen next month."

That was a relief. He stood, pushed in his chair, and walked to the back door. He needed to get out of there before he did something dumb, like kiss her.

"Where are you going? Did I do something wrong?"

"You didn't do anything wrong. I need to get the buckets and empty the bathtub. Gus will be here soon to relieve me. Then I'll go check to see if Seth has learned anything about Sapphire's death." Before he said how her beauty rivaled the most perfect rose or something equally idiotic, he went outside. To be on the safe side and not be near her, he'd walk around the side of the house and use the front door to enter the house and empty the tub.

He had the tub empty when Gus came up to the house. "She get a bath?"

"Yeah."

Gus grinned and tucked a package he was holding under his arm. "So? What did you think?"

"About what?"

"Don't be obtuse. She's right pretty, isn't she?"

He'd forgotten how Gus had seen Eliza before her hair was cut and face smeared with dirt. "I guess."

His friend slapped his knee. "You guess? Man, you must be blind or a eunuch not to appreciate how pretty she is."

It was probably best to ignore the old man before he got any ideas. "What's in the package?"

"Sadie figured after a few weeks of acting like a boy, Eliza would enjoy dressing as a woman."

The empty bucket fell from Wade's hands and clunked to the porch floor. "Dress like a woman?"

"Yeah." Gus grinned and stared up at him. "You got an issue with that?"

"Um. No." He didn't have a right to stop her from wearing a dress; he simply wasn't sure he'd be able to handle knowing what her figure looked like.

Gus patted him on the back and muttered something sounding like *poor sap*. He climbed the porch steps then stopped. "You'd better head to the jail. Seth has some news for you."

Wade

"He what?"

"Somehow Sweringen found out Eliza escaped dressed as a boy. So, that's what he's looking for."

"Who told him?"

Seth shrugged. "Maybe one of his girls found out and told him under duress."

"Damn."

"Yeah." Seth fingered his bushy mustache. "Sadie told me she sent some women's things with Gus. Maybe it's a good thing she won't be dressed as a boy anymore."

"Yeah, but now he'd recognize her as a woman. Either way, she's in trouble." Wade groaned, frustrated he didn't know how to keep her hidden.

Seth sat behind his desk. "I was also told someone saw a man matching Jonathan's description down by the creek the night Sapphire was murdered."

Wade took in Seth's frown. "So, you think it was him?"

"Unless someone actually saw Johnny kill her, I can't do anything."

Wade punched a fist into his palm. "Do you think maybe one of Swearingen's girls saw anything?"

"Could be. I'm not sure how we'd know. They keep a pretty close watch on them, especially since Eliza got away. I'll have to think of something."

Wade raised an eyebrow.

Seth chuckled and shook his head. "And no. I'm not going there as a customer. My missus would kill me if she ever found out."

"But you'd be in there as the sheriff."

"Do you think for a minute Swearingen would let me go upstairs? He's too smart for that. He'd know I was up to something."

"Then I'm not sure what the answer is. I can't go in there at night, since that's when I guard Eliza." Wade stood. "I'd best get some shut-eye so I'm awake for tonight."

"What time do you head over?"

"Six. Gus is going to cook supper for us." Wade sighed. "Heaven only knows what he'll come up with."

Wade

It was as he feared. Eliza wearing women's duds was . . . Much to Gus's apparent mirth, he couldn't keep his eyes off her either. How had she managed to keep such a womanly figure hidden beneath the boy's clothes? While not overly large on top, there was plenty for a man to enjoy, and her waist tapered to full hips. Wade needed to do something to keep his mind off her.

He put a spoonful of what was surprisingly good stew into his mouth. Maybe he'd come up with something before he swallowed.

"Whatcha think of the stew, Wade?" Gus smirked.

"It's good. I didn't know you could cook like this, Gus."

"I didn't make it. Eliza did."

Oh. Oh. She was pretty, had a nice figure, was almost nineteen, and could cook. He was in so much trouble.

"She even made an apple pie for dessert."

His favorite. Apple pie. He was in double-down, I hear wedding bells, and see a passel of children, trouble. "Well, it's right delicious, Eliza."

Her cheeks turned a becoming pink. "Thank you. I helped my mother cook. No one ever complimented me, so I never knew if my cooking was good or not."

Her family, especially her stepfather, were idiots. He changed the subject. "What did you guys do all day?"

"I cleaned the rooms. Sets of sheets showed up from who knows where, so I made up the beds."

He wasn't about to tell her he'd had the sheets and blankets sent over. He was also going to keep it a secret that he now owned the house, and more furnishings would be arriving as soon as they were delivered to Deadwood.

Gus took another biscuit from a bowl and stared at Wade. "These are delicious, too, Eliza. You'd make a man a great wife someday."

Geez, old man. Don't be putting any ideas into her head, nor, as far as it goes, mine. Eliza stared at her bowl of stew. Great, now she was embarrassed. Could he smack Gus in the head without getting into trouble? "Do anything else besides clean?"

Eliza glanced up and grinned. "Gus taught me to play poker."

He glared at Gus. "You what?"

Gus shrugged. "Couldn't think of anything else to do. Now you two can play before Eliza retires for the night."

Don't think about Eliza and a bed. Don't. Just don't. He shoved a biscuit into his mouth. It was even better than what he made, and his were fairly good. Eliza glanced over his shoulder and frowned. "What's the matter?"

"I thought I saw someone at the window by the door. He was peeking around the edge, but I don't see him now. I must be imaging things."

As one, he and Gus jumped up and raced for the back door. Wade threw it open, ran down the back porch stairs, then around the corner of the house. Gus went the other way. They met at the front.

"See anything?"

Gus shook his head. "Damn. I can't imagine she was seeing things. Someone was snooping."

"I agree. But who?"

"I think I'd better stay the night with you. I can watch the back door and you can take the front."

Eliza came out the front door. "What's going on?"

A spike of fear hit him like a lightning bolt. "Get back inside. What if someone should see you?"

"I think someone already did." She went back into the house then turned back. "I'm in trouble, aren't I?"

CHAPTER NINE

Eliza

Gus locked the door behind her and Wade and followed her into the parlor where she sat on the edge of the settee.

"You're not in trouble with Wade and I, but I fear someone recognized you and took off to the Gem. I'm going to lock the back door."

Eliza folded her hands in her lap and chewed on her bottom lip. "But why would someone know to look here for me?"

Wade took a place on the sofa, draped his arm over the back, and hooked an ankle over his knee. "The only thing coming to mind is the comings and goings taking place up here. From what I understand, new houses on the hill aren't an everyday occurrence. Swearingen could have his men watching, and the new activity probably made him wonder who was living here."

She'd wonder the same thing if she were thinking like

Swearingen. "So, it's possible it was someone being nosy?"

"I hate to say it, but I doubt it." Wade shook his head.

Would her life ever be normal? Would she be forever looking over her shoulder, or dressing up as someone she wasn't? "You're probably not going to like this, but I have an idea."

Wade's frown didn't bode well. "Probably not, but let's hear it."

"Hear what?" Gus sat on the other end of the sofa.

"What if we set a trap."

Wade's frown deepened. "What kind of trap?"

"Maybe the person was just someone being nosy and won't go running to tell Swearingen or his men. I think we should let it leak out that I'm the missing girl staying here. Jonathan or someone from the Gem is bound to show up and either take me back or . . ."

Wade dropped his feet to the floor. "Kill you?"

His guess wasn't far off from her thinking. "Yeah."

"I won't allow it." He slapped his knee.

Was he kidding? Who was he to say he wouldn't allow it? "Um. I believe it's my decision to make, not yours. Get Seth and see what he says."

Gus shrugged. "It's not a bad idea. And we have Seth and other men we can trust watching the house. Maybe we can catch who killed Sapphire."

"I know. I know." Wade leaned his elbows on his knees and raked his fingers through his hair. "It's a good idea, but I don't have to like it."

Not that she wouldn't mind being taken care of by him. It was always hard to keep her emotions under control when he was around. She wasn't sure what all the stomach jumping, heart pounding, and sweating meant, but it happened every time they were in the same room, or when she thought about him. She was crazy. "No one asked you to like it, Wade. It's my life. You have no say over it."

Gus slapped his knees and stood. "I'll get the sheriff and bring him up here. On the way, I'll keep an eye out for anyone who might be spying on us."

It was their only hope—her only hope. Solve Sapphire's death and her freedom wrapped in one plan. "Be careful. I'll be waiting for your return."

Eliza

The next night after supper and playing poker with Gus, Eliza retired to her room. Instead of putting on the nightgown Sadie had given her, she switched to her boy's clothes. It would be easier to run away from someone in pants than a dress.

She was never going to be able to pay Sadie back for the clothes, nor Seth, Wade, and Gus for the food they'd bought. Then there was her debt to Swearingen, who wouldn't give up until he was paid back. She rolled over and punched her pillow. Waiting had her nerves tighter than a lasso around a calf's neck when they were branding.

Seth had agreed to the plan. He got one of his friends who'd never been to the Gem to go there and pretend to be drunk and talk about the girl in the house up the hill to anyone who'd listen. Now all they had to do was wait from one of Swearingen's men to show up. She figured it would be Jonathan.

Gus made a show of heading downtown. Wade had left earlier, then snuck back and was hiding under her bed. Seth had men stationed around the property, while he was in the next room waiting.

"Stop wiggling so much," Wade whispered. "You're going to squish me."

Eliza refrained from giggling. The feather mattress was soft, but close to the floor, making it difficult for Wade to crawl under. If the mattress should fall on him, she suspected all he would get would be a bruised ego.

"I'm sorry. I'm nervous." She leaned over the side and peered under the bed. "How are you going to get out from there to protect little ol' me?"

"Shut up," he whispered. "I'll figure something out. Now get back under the blankets."

A floorboard on the stairs creaked. Someone was coming. Someone who didn't know which boards to avoid. When her door opened, her heart picked up speed. Whoever was coming into the room could surely hear it. She evened out her breathing to look as if she were sleeping. She was facing the wall, so he wouldn't be able to see her trying to keep her eyes closed.

A large hand covered her mouth and pulled her over.

"Don't you dare scream, girlie."

She'd recognize Jonathan's voice anywhere. Deep, gravelly, evil. She nodded to let him know she wouldn't yell for help. He released her.

"You've given us a lot of trouble, girlie. Swearingen doesn't like his property going missing. He also doesn't like one of his girls helping another to escape."

"I'm sorry Sapphire had to be killed to help me. She didn't deserve that."

"She got what she deserved." He huffed.

Her mind filled with all the accommodations Sapphire had troubled herself with to protect Eliza. She didn't deserve punishment. She deserved an award. "Killed for being kind?"

Jonathan grabbed her arm and pulled her from the bed. "I see you're back in boy's clothes. I was hoping you'd be in a nightgown to make what I'm going to do easier." He tore her shirt in half. "You're a bit scrawny, but I'll still enjoy you before I kill you."

Eliza covered her breasts with an arm.

Jonathan yanked it away and covered them with his big paws.

Bile rose to her throat, making it difficult to speak, but she needed to get him to talk. "Like you killed Sapphire?"

"Ah, hell. She was just another whore who thought she was too good for the likes of me. It was a pleasure to choke her to death after we found out what she'd done with you. She's replaceable." Jonathan pressed a leg against her stomach. "You're going to like this, girlie. I promise you."

He shoved her onto her back on the bed, but before he crushed her, he disappeared. A loud crack filled the room.

Eliza jumped onto her knees and scooted into the corner of the bed. Expecting Jonathan to appear, she was surprised and relieved when Wade popped up.

He stood for a moment looking at something behind him before turning to her. "Are you all right?

Eliza pulled the edges of her shirt together. "Yes. He didn't hurt me. Where is he?"

"I believe he's knocked out."

"But how?"

"I grabbed his ankle and yanked his leg up. He hit his head on the bureau."

The door flew open, and Seth ran in. "I heard Jonathan confess, then a loud thud. You two okay?"

Eliza started shaking. She was almost raped and killed. If it hadn't been for Wade . . . A sob caught in her throat then burst out. "Th . . . thank you, Wade."

Her hero crawled across the bed and pulled her into his arms, cradling her like a baby. "Shh. It's all over. You're all right."

Never had she ever felt so safe, so secure. So . . . she couldn't describe how it was being in his arms, but she liked it. A lot.

"Good job, Wade."

Wade loosened his arms around her. She snuggled deeper into him. "How's Jonathan?"

"Dead. Broke his neck." Seth sat on the edge of the

bed. "That was quick thinking, Wade. Maybe I should hire you as a deputy."

"Nah. This was enough excitement for me." He kissed her on the temple. "I have other plans."

She stared up at Wade, curious how his plans could resolve Swearingen's demands that she pay him back for her freedom.

Chapter Nine

One Month Later
Eliza

"I told you over and over, Wade DesForge. I'm not going to live in this house. I can't afford it." She hefted her bag and stomped down the hallway to the front door. "I found a room at the boarding house."

"And I told you over and over, I own this house and I don't expect you to pay to live here."

"It's bad enough you paid off Swearingen for me and got me a job at Haywoods, but I won't live like a bought woman. I can't imagine what people have been thinking since I've been here. Why they . . ."

"Eliza, I've told you over and over not to worry what people think. It's usually those who protest the loudest who have the most to hide. Besides, people certainly can't think anything is happening between you and Gus."

"Hey, I resent that, you whippersnapper." Gus lifted his chin and smoothed his shirt. "Why couldn't there be anything between me and Eliza?"

Eliza held back a giggle at the rage in Wade's eyes. Would he go after Gus?

"Are you telling me there is?" Wade glared at the older man.

Gus held up both hands as if to ward off his friend. "Hell, no. But if you don't make your intentions clear with this woman, someone is going to scoop her up and carry her off into the sunset."

Wade turned his narrowed eyes on her. Again, she held back a giggle. It was rather fun seeing Wade jealous. Over the past month, he'd been nothing but a gentleman, but he was making his intentions stronger.

"Has anyone been bothering you when you're working at Haywoods?"

She'd gotten a job at the store, thanks to the owners. "Of course not. Colin would never allow it. Except for a few drunks Colin kicked out, the men who come into the store have been polite." She tapped her lip. "There is this one man . . ."

Wade pulled her up from the couch and into his arms. "If there is one man who . . . well . . . it's going to be me."

In front of Gus, he cupped her cheeks and brushed his lips against hers. Before she had a chance to wonder at the way her heart raced and her skin tingled, he stepped closer and deepened the kiss.

Gus cleared his throat. "I think I'll be leaving now."

Eliza barely heard the click of the door as Wade licked her lips and urged her mouth open. The instant his tongue touched hers, her body lit on fire. Her breasts ached. Heat pooled between her legs.

When he released her cheeks and pressed her pelvis against his, her legs went weak. She wanted to rip his clothes off. Tear hers to shreds. Lie back on the couch and let him make love to her. A moan built inside her.

Wade broke the kiss and put his forehead against hers. "We need to stop."

Stop? Was he kidding? Things were only getting more intriguing. She grabbed his lapels and tried to shove his coat from his shoulders, but he stopped her.

"Eliza. We can't. Not until we stand before a preacher."

"When will that be?"

Wade let out a shuddering breath. "Not soon enough."

Eliza couldn't help giggling at the frustration in his voice. Frustration she understood.

"It's not funny, Eliza." He stepped back then wrapped his arms around her.

Over his shoulder, she glanced out the window and pictured her white picket fence. Dreams did come true.

The End

ABOUT THE AUTHOR
TINA SUSEDIK

Tina Susedik is an award-winning, Amazon best-selling, multi-published author with books in both fiction and non-fiction, including history, children's, military books and romances. Her favorite is writing romantic suspense where her characters live happily ever after with a lot of problems in between. Tina also writes spicier romance as Anita Kidesu. She lives in northwestern Wisconsin where winters are long, summers short, and spring and fall beautiful.

Here are just some of her reviews for a few of her books:

The Balcony Girl: "Miss Susedik's love story is a delightful and charming mix of an old-fashioned western, a compelling mystery, and enchanting romance. Ind'tale Magazine." The Balcony Girl was first runner up in the 2020 Reward of Novel Excellence, Historical Category, 20th Century.

The Proprietress: "Ms Susedik hit it out of the park, yet again, with the third book in the Darlings of Deadwood series!! I loved it!"

Missing My Heart: "Fantastic storyline! This is the first book I've read by Tina Susedik, but definitely not the last. Great depth in her characters, excellent mystery plot, and not just a common romance. Loved the book!"
Love With a Side of Crazy: "This book has great

characters and a really good plot. For a topic like stalking that can get real creepy real fast - it doesn't. With humor spread throughout the book it adds enough to level out the seriousness. The mood of the book is basically happy and full of some good laughs. It really almost minimizes what could be crazy scary stalking and makes it just part of the plot. Humor keeps everything in perspective. I can honestly say that I have never read a book like this and thoroughly enjoyed it." "Book of the Year with Authors on the Air Global Radio Network."

How to find Tina:

Website: www.tina-susedik.com
Amazon: www.amazon.com/Tina-Susedik
Facebook: www.facebook.com/TinaSusedikAuthor
Instagram: www.instagram.com/tmsused
Bookbub: www.bookbub.com/profile/tina-susedik
Goodreads:www.goodreads.com/author/show/1754353.Tina_Susedik
Pinterest: www.pinterest.com/tinasusedik
All Author: allauthor.com/profile/tinasusedik
Newsletter:tinasusedik.us11.list-manage.com/subscribe?u=874ff86e3f10f756a138fbc3a&id=1cfdf516fc

The Glass Whisperer

AARON VOLNER

Marybelle Flint, reporter and substitute librarian, has always cherished the stories of monsters and magic collected by her late mother.

But when Deadwood's new electric lights bring a real, and coveted, magical creature into the library, she soon learns that her mother's stories may have been more than just legends.

Now, with a pair of shape-shifting bounty hunters tracking her, she must learn the skills to protect the library and uncover the truth about her mother. The man who can teach her is a handsome, spell-casting stranger who also wants the creature for himself. Her life after his lessons will never be the same... but her heart doesn't seem to mind.

CHAPTER ONE

1883, Deadwood, SD
Marybelle Flint

Marybelle placed herself squarely in the doorway to the library, crossed her arms, tapped an expectant finger on her elbow, and drew her eyebrow pointedly into a clean arch.

The maintenance man, Donnellson, huffed at her and rattled the crate of light bulbs in his hands. "Oh, come on. You expect me to haul these to storage?"

"Last I checked, that was part of your job, Donnellson." Marybelle didn't budge. If she moved an inch Donnellson would get the light bulbs into the library. Again. Then he'd leave them there for patrons to trip on, as though the library were storage space and not an important institution in Deadwood. Again.

Marybelle was only the substitute librarian for a few weeks, but no careless placement of technological rubbish would disrespect the space on her watch. Not if she had anything to say about it.

Donnellson snorted. "Does anybody use this little book room? Oughta do something useful with it."

"The city and your boss designated this 'little book room' as Deadwood's library. It isn't for stashing things you're too lazy to haul to where they're supposed to be."

"I'm having to replace these things all the time, Marybelle." Donnellson gave her a pleading look. "They burn out so much faster than the folks who installed them said they would. If I have to go all the way to storage—"

"You might have to spend an extra five minutes, you poor thing."

Although, Marybelle had to admit he was right about how often the bulbs needed replacing. Everywhere else in Deadwood, the newly installed electric lights lasted as long as advertised, but here in the Syndicate building, they'd burn out with aggravating frequency. No one knew why.

Before either of them could say another word, noise from the street drew their attention. Specifically, the sound of a horse screaming in terror.

The argument forgotten, Marybelle dashed for the front entrance. Across the street, she could see the terrified horse wasn't just any animal but her own mare. People gathered around the horse, but the wide-eyed animal fought her tether and kicked out in panic.

"What happened?" she asked one of the men watching.

"A wolf spooked her, but she's okay, Marybelle. Just scared."

"A wolf? It's the middle of the day."

"Damndest thing, I know. A red wolf came prancing

along through town like she owned the place, scared the bejeezus out of your mare here, and ran off. Folks are trying to track it now."

"Let me through. I need to calm her down."

But when Marybelle got through the onlookers, she found herself unneeded. The mare was already calming, helped by the gentle attentions of a red-headed man in a long coat. His skill with the animal was beyond anything Marybelle had seen. Everything from his words to how he moved was mesmerizing to the horse and the surrounding crowd.

When the mare finally settled, the onlookers applauded and then started to disperse. Marybelle approached, and the red-headed man noticed her.

"Is she yours?" he asked.

Marybelle nodded.

"I hope you don't mind my stepping in."

"Not at all, thank you," said Marybelle, stepping up to the mare and scratching her behind the ears in the place she liked. "Was she hurt?"

"Thankfully, no. The wolf got close, though. She'll be a tad skittish."

Marybelle hugged the mare's neck. "She'll get through it. She's a tough old girl."

"If I may, this town seems awfully small to need a horse to get around," the man added.

"She needs the exercise. Besides, my uncle left her to me," said Marybelle, releasing the horse's neck. She started to say more, then changed the subject. "I'm afraid I've little enough to thank you. But if you come back to the library, I can interview you for the papers."

"This town has a newspaper?" The man raised a skeptical eyebrow.

Marybelle laughed. "Several, actually. Although, the *Pioneer* seems to be on its last legs. I can make you famous for a day."

"Flattering as that is I—" The man's eyes flew wide. "Deadwood has a library?"

"Well, yes—"

"Where?"

Marybelle felt skepticism warring with vindication in her chest. Men showed far less interest in the library, overall. His excitement was a tad difficult to believe, if a welcome change. "Right across the street. #5 in the Syndicate building."

"Can you show me, please?"

She started to do just that when an ominous wolf howl just past the town border drew their attention.

The mare whinnied nervously, and Marybelle turned to her, scratching her behind the ears again and reassuring her. When she looked again, the red-headed man was gone. She glanced around for him, but he'd thoroughly vanished.

She turned back to the mare. "Are stallions as unfathomable as human men?"

As she crossed the street, Marybelle caught a man watching her from the shadows of a building down the road. Scruffy black hair framed a face she couldn't make out, save that it seemed unusually pale. She might not have noticed him if his gaze hadn't followed her so closely.

He stalked away, and Marybelle tried to put the odd encounter out of her mind.

When she stepped into the library, she clenched her jaw and huffed. For there, right where she'd tried so hard to prevent it from being, sat the carton of light bulbs. Before she could storm out in search of Donnellson, a patron asked for her help, distracting her with work.

In between patrons, Marybelle worked first on her freelancing for the newspapers, then later on her book project. She'd been told publishers still didn't care to print novels by women, but that didn't faze her. The editors of the papers had come around, hadn't they?

She worked longhand, even though the editor at one paper had offered to help cover the cost of a typewriter. While the machines seemed marvelous, she didn't want to owe a single paper that much and feel pressured to favor them over the others.

Eventually, it grew too dark to write, at which point she noticed it was also too dim to read the books' spines. Marybelle sighed as she got up to turn on the lights.

"If only the sun were this easy." She flicked the switch, and the electric lights shone to life. A little thrill passed through her chest. Much as she hated the box of bulbs that tormented her, electric lights were still a wonder.

Thought of the bulbs brought her gaze to the crate nearby. Perhaps she could move it into the hall to prove a point? Smack in the middle so that Donnellson couldn't miss it. She smirked and knelt to test how heavy it was. Something darted out of it and skittered across the wall.

Marybelle screamed and leaped back from it, straight into the chest of a stranger she hadn't known was there.

More screams accompanied her twisting and pummeling the stranger with open palms.

A pair of surrendering hands raised, framing a face with a dark-red beard to match the unkempt hair. Several seconds passed before her memory caught up, and she recognized the man in front of her.

"You're the gentleman from this morning," she said.

Before he could answer, boots thundered up the hallway. A banker from down the hall and another man barreled into the room, panting.

"What happened, Marybelle?" Their eyes fell on the stranger. "Did he touch you?"

"No," she said, stepping forward to put a hand on the banker's arm. "I'm fine. He startled me, is all."

"We're all perfectly safe here, gentlemen," said the stranger. "Though we much appreciate the fleet feet."

The banker grumbled something about how many years of his life Marybelle had just wasted as he and his compatriot shuffled away.

"And what can I do for you, now that we've rattled the whole building's nerves?" Marybelle asked.

"What was it that startled you?" the man asked, stepping past her and squinting at the wall.

Marybelle would have been irritated with him, save for his expression. His curiosity bordered on wonderment, with a hint of something like determination. She'd never seen the look on a grown man before, and she found she rather liked it.

She let him wonder momentarily, then said, "Just a spider, I'm sure. Were you looking for a book?"

"I was hoping you could guide me…" the man trailed off and glanced around the room. If he tried to mask the look of disappointment, he failed miserably.

"The library hasn't been around long. The collection is still growing," said Marybelle, glancing sheepishly at the hundred or so volumes the room sported. Funny, it always impressed Deadwood residents that the library existed at all. Where was this man from that a hundred books didn't impress him? And why did she care that it didn't?

She shook off the thoughts and continued. "Maybe I can still find you something?"

"Anything on local legends?" he asked, though, by his tone, he wasn't feeling hopeful of an answer.

Marybelle quirked an eyebrow at him. "You're searching for Indian stories?"

"Not necessarily, but that would be part of it, yes," said the stranger.

She made a show of glancing through the shelves, though she already knew she didn't have what he wanted. Not in the library collection, anyway.

"I'm afraid not. May I ask why you're looking—"

Marybelle stopped when she noticed the man's attention was no longer on her but riveted on the window. He held his hands as though trying to catch a fly. Of all things, he was sneaking up on a distortion in the glass. A whorl that caught the lamplight and distorted it. Perhaps he thought it was the spider that had startled her?

She watched him, equal parts curious and irritated at his wandering attention. He crept up on the window, hands growing closer together. Then he pounced. Unfortunately for him, his forehead beat his hands to the glass.

He cursed, grabbing at his face and stumbling backward into her desk, rattling and knocking over the contents. Including an ink bottle from which the cork fell.

Marybelle's heart wrenched as the black pool spread across the desk's surface.

"No, no, no!"

She rushed to the desk, righting the ink bottle and snatching away the papers, but she was too late. Every inch of her drooped as she lifted the first several pages of her book, and watched the ink, still spreading as it soaked them, blacking out her words forever.

"I'm so sorry!" The stranger suddenly realized what she was holding, and his eyes lit up. "You're a writer."

"Yes, I'm a writer. A working writer, thank you very much. Or rather, I am when I don't have bumbling oafs charging their way into my library and ruining things. We're closed. Get out, now."

"Wait, if you could just allow me—"

He continued to babble, but she was too angry to process the words, and she took him by the ear and dragged him from the library. After tossing him out into the hallway, she held up her ruined pages, then flung them at him.

"You might as well keep this. It's your handiwork now."

"But wait—"

Marybelle slammed the door on him and locked it

before he could utter another phrase. Hotness burned in her chest as she returned to the desk and looked over her work for the day. Nothing of the library's had been ruined, thankfully. A few papers had splotches, but nothing irreparably damaged. The ink had irrevocably marred only her own project.

Most of her work had survived, but she'd have to rewrite the missing pages from nothing but her memory.

Tears flooded her eyes, and she let them come as she sat hard and sobbed for a time. Only a few pages, perhaps, but she'd poured her heart into them, and it ached at their loss.

When she was all cried out, she dried her face, gathered her things, and got up to leave. She was about to cut the lights when something crunched beneath her shoe.

Marybelle moved her foot and squatted down, only to find herself thoroughly confused by what she saw. It looked like the tail of a lizard, only made of glass. The wider end, where it would attach to a body, was smooth. Thanks to her foot, the tip lay ground to shards.

The only explanation she could think of for how it had gotten there was that the red-haired stranger had dropped it. She derived a modicum of satisfaction from that thought. Now she'd ruined something of his, as well.

Marybelle pocketed the glass tail, then locked up and left.

On any ordinary night, Marybelle might not have even remembered crossing the street. But this day refused to be ordinary. When she emerged into the dark, she beheld a pair of golden eyes staring at her from the center of the road. She couldn't tell what they belonged to until the creature took a few steps toward her.

Marybelle's breath caught. A wolf. Not the same wolf from that morning, though. This one was as black as the surrounding night.

She spared a worried glance for the mare, who was clearly nervous but not panicking yet. Then she dug in her bag and pulled out her uncle's revolver. Thumb on the gun's hammer, she aimed the weapon and waited. Six bullets might be in the pistol, but she'd only have time to use one of them if the wolf attacked.

Gooseflesh ran the length of Marybelle's spine, but not because of the danger. Because of the wolf's eyes.

The predator's gaze carried more than mere hunger. Something in those eyes was calculating. Like the creature was studying her. Measuring her worth, even. She had seen that countenance on businessmen when they cut deals. Cold and ruthless. Predatory for its own sake. To see that look coming from a wild animal disturbed her.

Only mankind was supposed to carry that sort of malice.

Moments later, the wolf broke its eyes away from Marybelle and continued on its silent path down the street. She allowed herself to breathe again and felt the blood rush back to her face.

What happened to you that gave you those eyes?

Marybelle kept her gaze on it until she could no longer make out its shape in the darkness. She released the breath she'd been holding and dashed across the street to her horse.

She checked the mare but, to her relief, still found no signs of injury. Perhaps it'd be best to leave her stabled for the next few days when she wasn't actively riding her? Just because the wolves hadn't bothered the horse today didn't mean they wouldn't go after her another time.

"Fine animal."

Marybelle whipped around and had aimed the gun at the voice within seconds.

At the barrel's end stood an older woman, draped in a dress that had started cheap and plain and seen nothing but rough days since. She sported strawberry-blonde hair cut short and a pair of pale eyes that bored into Marybelle.

"You're going to help me with something," the strange woman said.

"Come by the library tomorrow. I'm off for the night."

"Your little library doesn't have what I need. Lovely as I'm sure it is, dear."

The condescending tone stiffened Marybelle's back. The stranger was old enough to be her mother, but just barely.

"And what is it you're looking for, ma'am?"

The stranger glared, and Marybelle almost stepped back beneath her gaze. Her eyes were familiar in a decidedly unwelcome manner.

"An old friend of mine. I know he's here, but I can't seem to find him."

It was Marybelle's turn to arch an eyebrow. "You must

not be looking very hard if you can't find someone in Deadwood."

"My friend has certain people he'd rather not drop in unannounced. He's good at lying low when he wants to stay hidden."

"Some folks might take that as a hint."

"All I need out of your mouth, dear, is whereabouts I can find him. Dark-red hair and a beard."

Marybelle bristled at the description, the image of the careless fool popping into her mind.

"I'm sorry to say I met that gentleman today. He won't be welcome back while I'm running the library. I'm afraid I can't help you."

"Did he take any books out?"

"Information about patrons and their selections is confidential," Marybelle said, parroting the rule she'd learned from the main librarian.

"Can you still call him a patron if he isn't welcome back?"

The mare let out a nervous whinny. When Marybelle looked, the animal had backed up the entire length of her now-taut lead. She was panting, and her legs were trembling.

"I need to see to my horse. I don't know where he is." Marybelle turned her back to the woman.

"You're going to let me know if he comes by again."

Marybelle looked over her shoulder as she untied the lead just long enough to say, "No, I won't. Have a good evening."

She relaxed when she heard the woman's footsteps walking away a moment later.

Marybelle decided to lead the nervous mare rather than try to ride her. About halfway home, she paused, ran a hand over her prickling neck, and peered about her into the dark. She'd just realized why the woman's eyes seemed so familiar, making her tighten her grip on the gun.

They reminded her of the black wolf's.

Chapter Two

Marybelle

Despite grogginess and the lingering pain of her lost pages, Marybelle felt better the following day. As she brushed out her hair and glanced over the papers on her tiny desk, her gaze fell on the leather-bound book she had inherited from her mother. With that glance, she remembered the first stranger she'd met yesterday, with the dark-red hair.

Her blood boiled at the thought of him.

And to think, I let him off with a tongue lashing.

She soured further when she remembered his request. Instinctively, one of her hands flew protectively over her mother's book. Of course, she had what he needed right here. That didn't mean she had to let him see it. Did it?

Marybelle set down the brush and took up the book. She always kept it out where she could see it. It was the only thing of her mother's that'd survived the fire. She brought it to her face, closing her eyes and savoring the aroma that always wafted from it: vanilla and the rosemary scent her mother had worn.

The book dedicated little space to Deadwood, because Marybelle and her mother had visited the South Dakota Territory infrequently during her childhood.

Infrequently, until the illness struck, at least. Then, Marybelle's mother had moved them there permanently. Her father and uncle had just set up shop in Deadwood, hoping to make good money in the wake of the gold rush. Though they'd never been particularly close, Marybelle's father had taken care of her mother those last few years for Marybelle's sake. Over time, Deadwood had become home for them all.

In that time, when she had the strength for it, Marybelle's mother had collected stories from the locals and added them to her book. Not history, but bedtime stories and wild tales of things that modern science couldn't explain. Myths and legends had always fascinated her mother.

She let the book fall open in her lap, a thing she rarely did. The page it naturally fell open to was the reason. A black paper stared up at her, blotted out years ago in an ink accident. Her mother's words, lost forever.

Marybelle could rewrite her own destroyed text, but her mother would never have that chance.

She kept her favorite passage bookmarked. Marybelle remembered the day her mother had written it. She'd dragged herself from bed to interview a transient bounty hunter about the ghastly tale, a story involving a glowing spirit from the hills that drove men to bloodlust. Though Marybelle didn't care for the story; it reminded her of the last time she'd seen her mother out of bed.

A sigh to wake the dead escaped her, and she added the book to her materials to bring to work that day. Librarians didn't swear oaths, but even substitute librarians might as well have. The man was still a patron. If she could help him, she'd do her best.

After dressing and gathering her things, she headed downstairs. In the front room, she found a crate of light bulbs and frowned deeply.

"Why so sour?" asked the owner of the boardinghouse.

"Why are those there?" Marybelle demanded, pointing at the crate.

"We'll be in the next round of light installations, and I wanted to be ready," said the landlady. "Why?"

God created light bulbs to torment me, didn't he?

"No reason, Mrs. Brown."

"Marybelle, before I forget, there's mail for you."

She stopped and blinked. Marybelle never got mail. She had no family alive to send her any. If the papers' editors needed something, they'd call on her or wait for her to drop by the office. "For me?"

"No, Marybelle, I said that for no reason whatsoever. A *gentleman* dropped it off this morning," Mrs. Brown teased. Marybelle would have reddened had she any clue what the missive said or who'd sent it.

She opened the parcel and removed a short stack of papers.

Her jaw nearly fell to the floor.

In her hand sat the opening pages of her book. The one she'd been writing on yesterday, destroyed before her eyes by the red-headed stranger's carelessness. Only now, the pages shone up at her, completely restored. No trace of the offending ink stains remained. She blinked several times to be sure what she was seeing was real. These were indeed her words leaping off the page at her.

Only she couldn't fathom how.

No note or letter explained, so Marybelle looked up at Mrs. Brown.

"What gentleman brought this?"

"Red-haired fella with a beard. Funny looking, if you ask me, but I suppose every lid has its pot, dear."

"It's not like that, Mrs. Brown. You'll tell me if he comes by again?"

Mrs. Brown assured Marybelle she would, and the reporter stepped outside, still staring at the pages in her hand. She paused just outside the boardinghouse door, still studying them and not entirely trusting her eyes. Yet there was no question that it was her handwriting.

Is he some kind of inventor?

Perhaps he was a scientist who'd been laughed out of the east coast for his crazy ideas and came west to prove he was on to something? Yet removing accidental ink wasn't a crazy idea. A side project, maybe?

The weight of her mother's book in her bag felt suddenly heavier.

If he could do it for my pages, then maybe...

Marybelle let the thought trail off, unwilling to let her

hopes get too high. A determination settled into her chest. Even if nothing came of it, she had to find him.

She followed her reporter instincts and started with the local watering holes. Odds were a visitor to town would have stopped in one. Those instincts proved correct but frustratingly less than helpful.

In every establishment, folks remembered seeing the red-haired stranger around town over the last few days. Yet no one recalled what he was doing in town or where she might find him. The closest she came to a usable lead was so ironic she almost burst out laughing.

"I don't know where he's staying, Miss Marybelle. I only saw him for a few minutes along the edge of town. You should ask that woman who's here visiting family. Got the blonde hair and dresses like she ain't got money nor time to care how she looks."

Marybelle had restrained her laughter and asked, "Whose family is she?"

"Come to think of it, I'm not sure who she's visiting. Never would say. She and her son seem to know him right good. They told me I shouldn't talk to that fella, that he wasn't a good sort. So you be careful if you go looking for him, Miss Marybelle."

The woman had a son? It was odd to picture. She hadn't struck Marybelle as the motherly sort.

With her leads dried up, she returned to the stable nearby the boardinghouse. As per her intentions the night before, she'd left the mare stabled today. She mulled over what she'd unearthed at the bars as she fed and brushed the horse. Mostly she'd learned the red-haired man stuck to the edges of town, only rarely coming into Deadwood proper. That might mean he was camping in the environs. Which, if true, explained why his presence had been so inconsistent since he'd arrived here but did little to help her find him.

A possibility struck her without warning. Perhaps he was helping a victim of the flood? Earlier that year, the rains and the snowmelt had contributed to a rage of water that washed away several of Deadwood's businesses. Some folks were still working on rebuilding. He might be a temporary worker in town to help. It was worth looking, anyway.

Marybelle checked the time and decided to chance riding the mare out. If the search took her outside the city limits, she'd need the animal to get back in time to open the library. She hurried up to her room to change into split skirts. Women were generally expected to ride sidesaddle, but Marybelle's mother had insisted she buck the tradition and ride in the more practical position adopted by men. Once, it had gotten her stares, but the town was used to it now.

Getting information from the flood repair teams proved difficult. Most refused to pause their workday to answer questions, and just as many were more interested in making lewd comments about her than being helpful.

"Haven't the papers had enough news about the flood?" one foreman asked her. "Once we finish this, you can do all the stories you want."

"I'm actually here for—"

"I don't care why you're here, miss. I have work that

needs doing, and you're wasting my daylight. Now run along."

Marybelle stormed off, her face flushed, but a workman caught her before she could mount.

"Wait, Miss Marybelle. I know where to find him."

A smile broke across her face. "You've seen the red-haired man?"

The workman furrowed his brow, looked down in thought, then sheepishly back to her. "Can't say, Miss Marybelle. We only exchanged a few words. I don't remember his hair color. But he said where to find him if you came asking."

She was too taken aback to respond at first. The stranger had told the flood crews where Marybelle could find him if she came asking? But he knew where she lived and worked. Why wouldn't he leave his message in one of those places? Something about this didn't add up.

Nevertheless, she got directions from the workman, thanked him, and nudged the mare into motion. The directions led outside of town, just as she'd suspected.

When she reached the edge of Deadwood, Marybelle paused. There were the wolves to consider. A shudder shot through her at the memory of meeting the black wolf's eyes. Yet odds were they'd moved on by now. After all, angry pursuers with guns had greeted them every time they'd approached Deadwood, and there was no game shortage that she was aware of. Why would the predators stay in Deadwood when easier prey could be had elsewhere?

A howl spooked the mare as if summoned by the thought, and the horse reared back.

"Easy, girl," Marybelle said, reaching for her bag to fish for her gun.

The horse turned to bring the howl into her line of vision, and Marybelle saw the creature emerging from between houses. Her blood ran cold. The wolf was like a slice of midnight walking the earth.

Before she could get the weapon free of the bag, the wolf charged, growling and snapping at the mare, which bolted ahead of it. Gun forgotten, Marybelle could only hold on for dear life.

The mare came face-to-face with a second hunter, a red wolf, just outside of town. The beast came snapping at her haunches, driving her toward a wooded area that bordered a steep hill. The terrain was treacherous and forced the horse to slow down as she ascended. Before long, the hunters herded them into an alcove, closed off by rock and trees, with nowhere to escape.

Marybelle's only solace was that it gave her the moment she needed to pull the gun from her bag.

Then the mare turned and reared, trying to put the force of her hooves between them and the wolves. Both predators were advancing with fangs bared, although the red wolf was clearly the leader, the black hanging back deferentially. Marybelle struggled desperately to get the gun into line for a shot around the neck of the panicking horse.

What happened next would haunt Marybelle's nightmares for many nights to come. For at that moment, when the red wolf should have struck them down, it instead sat back on its haunches and split open at the chest. And forth from its skin emerged the blonde woman, wet and steaming, her hair and dress plastered to her. Yet she seemed for all the world like she was merely out for a stroll.

"I don't much appreciate being lied to, young lady," the blonde woman said.

Marybelle tried to respond, but the terrified whinnying of the mare blocked her words.

The blonde woman turned to the black wolf. "Back off. She can't talk with that thing panicking under her."

With one last growl, the black wolf slunk off into the trees.

Calming the mare enough for Marybelle to be heard took several minutes, and even then, the horse was still panting in the blonde woman's presence.

"What are you?" Marybelle asked.

"Tell me what I want to know, and you won't have to find out. You said Jeremiah wasn't welcome back in the library, but then you spend all morning looking for him. It seems to me you're hiding something. You and he working together?"

"Who is Jeremiah?"

"You answer one more of my questions with a question, dear, and my skin goes back on."

Marybelle contemplated shooting the woman but still had the black wolf to consider. Could she end the beast before it got close enough to strike? Not likely.

"I know nothing more about the man you're looking for than I did yesterday."

"You're lying, librarian."

Before Marybelle could respond, an angry growl issued from the forest, followed by a pained yelp. Moments later, the black wolf backed into view from the trees. The beast was bleeding and baring its teeth at the red-headed stranger, also wounded and wielding a gleaming sword. Wolf and man lunged at each other, testing the other's defenses.

Marybelle noticed the fight had diverted the woman's attention. Now was her chance.

She kneed the mare into motion, swung the barrel of the revolver, and conked the blonde woman on the head as she passed. Then, pulling back on the reins, she fired two shots at the black wolf. One found its mark, and the wolf cried out in pain.

"Get on," she yelled to the red-haired stranger she suspected was named Jeremiah.

He dashed for the mare but, with Marybelle's help, only managed to drape himself belly down over the horse's rump.

"Better hold on back there," Marybelle advised as she spurred the horse into motion.

Chapter Three

Marybelle

"What by God are you doing with our Marybelle that she arrives at my doorstep in this state, sir?"

To Marybelle's detriment, Mrs. Brown blocked the boarding house door with arms crossed and a fiery gaze fixed on the bleeding stranger. His blood had soaked Marybelle's outfit when she'd helped him down off the mare. Marybelle tried to assuage the raging landlady's concerns. "I went for a hike and ran into some trouble—"

"Trouble usually comes tall and dark, but the red-headed variety gets the same treatment in my book." Mrs. Brown reached for something behind the door.

Marybelle remembered the broom kept inside the boardinghouse door and the many male skulls it had whacked in her time here. Marybelle spoke quickly. "He saved me from a wolf attack, Mrs. Brown."

The boardinghouse matron softened, then. "Well, get the boy inside, and I'll call for the doctor."

"No, please, no doctor," he said as they entered.

Mrs. Brown rolled her eyes. "You're getting a doctor, sir. I don't care how tough you think you are."

Marybelle looked at the man, a silent question in her eyes. They'd already discussed this earlier, but she wanted to be sure. His return glance told her he hadn't changed his mind.

"It isn't as bad as it looks," she said aloud. "I can patch him up just fine myself. No need to bother the doctor. I only need fresh cloth and hot water. If I need the doctor's help, I'll come get you."

The landlady declared them both fools but relented and said she'd bring up the supplies. Good as her word, she arrived with a steaming kettle and fresh material shortly after Marybelle got him up to her room and a glass with a small portion of liquor in it.

"I ripped up one of Mr. Brown's old shirts for you," the landlady said, setting down the makeshift bandages. Then she took her leave.

"I'm Marybelle. I take it you must be Jeremiah." She dropped her needle into the recently boiling water and rolled up her sleeves.

"Yes, I'm Jeremiah Locke. My apologies for our first meeting. I've never been good at introductions."

"What, you mean I'm not the only woman you waited until she was stitching you up to tell her your name? Here I thought I was special. Shirt off."

Jeremiah winced as he wriggled out of the shirt, revealing the bite mark on his side where the black wolf had gotten its jaws into him. Marybelle rather enjoyed the view but tried to be discrete about it. There would be plenty of time to admire his torso after she'd stopped it from bleeding.

As he tossed the shirt aside, Marybelle fished the needle from the kettle and dropped it into the alcohol. Then she wet a cloth and walked over to him.

"May I?"

"Please," said Jeremiah.

He drew in a breath sharply, instinctively moving away when the cloth touched his wound. Marybelle placed her other hand on his chest to keep him where he was as she wiped away the blood.

"I believe you owe me an explanation about who that woman and her…" Marybelle hesitated, unsure what to call the black wolf, "partner are."

She let a long moment of quiet pass, keeping her lips sealed until he started talking. It got awkward briefly, but her mother had taught her to always let the other person break the silence when she wanted information. A trick that often came in handy as a reporter.

"Ulma and Gareth are their names," Jeremiah said at last. Marybelle tried to hide the satisfied smile that broke on her face. "I'm afraid I don't know much more about who they are than that, but they're working for a business interest who wants the same thing I do."

"Which is what?" Marybelle tossed the bloodied cloth in the bin and retrieved the thread and needle. Thankfully, the wounds weren't deep enough to have punctured anything inside him. Stitches and bandages ought to be enough to get him on the mend.

"I'm afraid you wouldn't believe me if I told you."

"I just saw a woman burst out of a wolf's chest like it was her front door. You'd be surprised what I'm inclined to believe right now, Mister Locke."

She locked eyes with him and held his gaze as she brought the glass to his lips and had him take a swallow.

"You saw that," he finally said.

Marybelle laid a cloth soaked in the last of the liquor on the wound, drawing a pained gasp from Jeremiah.

"Yes, I saw that. What is she?"

"A shapeshifter of some kind, but one I've never seen. They must be of local origin."

Shapeshifter. A strange, uncommon term, yet one Marybelle vaguely recalled. She couldn't put her finger on why.

"So you've seen other kinds of shapeshifters, then?"

With these words, she started in on the stitching and let him explain as she worked.

"Yes, I've seen them before." With each pass of the needle, his grip tightened on the bedclothes, relaxing in between stitches, if only just. "I suppose it'd be more accurate to say I've met them before. Shapeshifters are people like you and me, aside from the ability to change form." Here he paused, gritting his teeth as the needle hit an especially sensitive spot. "Mostly across the pond, in my visit to Germany, but one or two in the States. They're more common than one would suppose, even in my line of work."

Marybelle shot him a look that made her question obvious.

Jeremiah fumbled for a moment, clearly trying to conjure the best way to say his next piece, before blurting out, "I run a preserve for magical animals."

She stared at him. After learning that people who could turn into animals were 'more common than one would suppose,' perhaps this revelation should have been less shocking. Still, she found herself dumbfounded.

Jeremiah was quick to offer further explanation. "Not for shapeshifters. They're not animals, after all. Well, half the time anyway. And even then, they aren't animals in the sense of—never mind. You know what I mean, I think. I assume you do. After all, you're quite intelligent and—"

"The point is, I acquired some land in the Wyoming territory, and I gather magical creatures there who've become endangered in the wild. Either they've been over-hunted, or another calamity has made them hard to find. We make sure they don't disappear from the world entirely. By we, I mean some friends of mine from the scientific community and a few native locals who believe in the work we're doing. They help me run it."

Marybelle said nothing. She blinked hard, then returned to her stitching, needing her hands to be doing something as she processed what she'd just heard.

On the one hand, it seemed preposterous. More than preposterous. Any other day, she'd have called the doctor, or the sheriff, right then. But today, she'd seen a woman step out of a living, breathing wolf's chest and start talking.

Jeremiah interrupted her thoughts, apparently uncomfortable with the lingering silence. "Of course, your original question regards why we're all here. Ulma, Gareth, and I. We're here because of a magical animal that's somewhere here in Deadwood. I want to collect it for the preserve, and they want it for their business partner who wants—"

Marybelle held up a hand, and he fell silent. She finished stitching the last hole in his bite wound before she finally spoke.

"Exactly how am I supposed to believe any of this?"

Jeremiah looked as dumbfounded as she'd felt only minutes earlier. "I thought— You told me you saw Ulma change. I suppose you haven't seen Gareth change, the black one, but,"—His eyes lit up, and he started looking around the room—"I can prove it. Your manuscript. Those pages I ruined. You got them back, didn't you?"

Marybelle looked toward her worn leather bag on the floor nearby. She fished out the pages and couldn't keep a grin from breaking out on her face to see them intact once again. In all the terrible excitement, she'd nearly forgotten the original reason she'd gone seeking Jeremiah.

"How did you do it?"

Jeremiah gave her a lopsided grin that sent a pleasant warmth worming its way from her chest down through her gut. Then he said, "If you've paper and ink, Miss Marybelle, I'd be more than happy to show you."

Marybelle fetched both from the desk drawer, dashing out a quick message of random words for the demonstration, which she picked up and gently blew on to dry it.

She turned to ask him a question and found him, the

shirt now returned to its place on his body, standing quite close behind her. Their eyes met for just a moment, his the bold green of a fallow field in summer, and the warmth in her grew hotter.

The fake message nearly fell from Marybelle's hands, and Jeremiah brought his own up under hers to steady it. His touch carried a gentle strength that felt calming and satisfying at once—no wonder he'd soothed her mare so quickly with hands like these.

"Your handwriting is beautiful."

Marybelle felt her neck blush despite herself. She would have covered it had her hands not been cupped in his and holding the note.

"I hardly think so," she said.

"Then you're sorely mistaken."

To change the subject, she took a breath and blew on the ink again.

"I'll do that," said Jeremiah, taking the note from her, "if you'll write something else out for me."

"Now?"

"We need it for the demonstration."

She raised an eyebrow at him. "And why can't you write it yourself, Mister Locke? Surely, beautiful handwriting isn't necessary for this little demonstration of yours?"

It was his turn to blush, and he turned nearly as red as his beard at the question. The way he turned his eyes away made her regret asking.

"My handwriting is abysmal. Unreadable, to be

honest. I've tried to improve it, but there's never any, no matter how hard I work at it. I couldn't last in school—"

She laid a hand on his arm to stop him. "I'm sorry I asked. What do you need me to write?"

Jeremiah told her what he needed, and it was bizarre. Words in a foreign language she didn't recognize and needed his help spelling.

When their note of random words was dry, Jeremiah asked her to light a candle and opened up the tiny stove that heated her room in the winter. Then, he laid the first note out on the desk, took the ink bottle, and poured a generous helping onto it that obscured it.

"Are you preparing to"—she fumbled over the words, hardly able to believe she was speaking them—"do magic, of some sort?"

"Precisely, Miss Marybelle. What better way to prove my occupation as a caretaker of magical animals?"

Marybelle, having expected a scientific process, felt her skepticism growing.

"Magic of the sort they hung women for in Salem?"

He shook his head while rolling up his sleeves. "Magic in the true sense, not the made-up or imagined sense. And for it, I need four things."

The reporter crossed her arms as she listened. Her posture didn't seem to faze him.

"The first is a physical representation of intent. In other words, the note, so kindly and readably provided by you."

"Readably isn't a word," Marybelle interjected.

Jeremiah coughed but otherwise ignored her and kept going. "The second is energy, of which we'll have plenty from this candle. The third is a physical conduit for the magic, which in our case will be my body. And lastly, a verbal declaration of intent serves the dual purpose of initiating the spell and inviting the magic into me as the conduit."

"So, you're going to read the paper and then burn it."

He blinked at her, then said, "Essentially, yes."

Marybelle took in a long breath. Her mind was at war with itself. Part of it, still enchanted by the miracle of her restored pages, wanted so badly for him to be serious. An inclination reinforced by the mental image of Ulma dripping and steaming from being inside the wolf's skin. Yet, her natural tendency was to assume he was putting her on for his own amusement.

She gestured at the blacked-out note. "Show me, then."

Jeremiah nodded, then began to read. As he finished reading, he held the note over the candle flame until it caught, and the fire began consuming the paper.

The first blow to her skepticism came when the fire touched the words, and they glowed green.

He tossed the paper safely into the stove, and the green light shot from it into his body. Not a second later, he stood over the inked note, his hands poised above, and Marybelle drew close to watch. He made slow, gentle hand motions over the note. Like he was pulling a thread from a spool. At first, nothing happened in response. Then, the ink on the page began to tremble and rise off the sheet in response to his movements. Slowly at first, and then all in a rush, it ripped free until it floated as a liquid cloud in the air between Jeremiah's hands.

The note sat there unassumingly, wholly restored to how they'd initially written it.

Marybelle bent close to the note, staring with widened eyes, then turned to Jeremiah. He still manipulated the ink in midair, the black liquid responding to his every gesture.

"Have I convinced you?" he asked.

She didn't answer but reached out a hand and touched it with her finger. When she pulled it back, her fingertip was wet with blackness.

"It's real," she said. No other words came to her.

Jeremiah beamed. He sent the ink spiraling in a stream up her arm with fluid motions. He sent it around her neck and head when it reached the shoulder before bringing it back to its resting place between his fingers.

"Would you mind opening the ink bottle?"

Her hands shook with such excitement that Marybelle nearly dropped the bottle but got it open. Jeremiah guided the ink into the bottle in a languid stream. Then his whole body seemed to relax.

A hundred things crossed her mind at that moment, but one thought rose to the surface and came bubbling out.

"Show me how to do that myself."

Jeremiah cocked his head to the side, clearly taken aback. "You want to do magic?"

"I want to do *that* magic," she said, running to her pack and pulling out her mother's book. She flipped it open to the blacked-out pages, the vanilla and rosemary smell coming at them in a rush. "Please tell me it will work on this. Please."

He examined the pages, then turned back at her. "What was it?"

"My mother's journal." At that moment, she remembered the stories toward the end and her intention to show them to him and see if they would answer his question. "You can read it all you want. She collected stories from locals in the back. There might be something to help you with Ulma and Gareth. But these pages here got ruined before she died. Please tell me it will work. Tell me I get to read them, finally."

A strange smile had come over him. "I'd be happy to do it for you, Miss Marybelle."

"No, I need to do it myself."

The smile faltered. "I'm not sure that's—"

"It's my mother, Jeremiah. Please let me do this for her. Please."

"An inexperienced spell caster could accidentally draw all the ink, not just the part you need removed. Are you willing to risk losing it all?"

The knowledge of that possibility sobered her on the idea, and she paused to think.

"Can we do it together?" she finally asked.

"Now, that is a fine idea."

As the rational side of her brain caught up to her, she posed a second thought. "Perhaps you should search for what you need in the Deadwood stories first? Just in case."

"Are you sure you can wait?"

She handed him the book but playfully grabbed a fistful of his shirt as she did and growled, "Don't you dare be slow about it."

"I wouldn't dream, Miss Marybelle."

While Jeremiah hunted through the rear portions of her mother's book, Marybelle wrote out the spell on another piece of paper. Waiting for him afterward was agony. She paced until the sweet release of his turning the last page and looking up at her.

"Anything?" she asked.

"I wish I could say yes, but it seems your mother never came across a legend about shapeshifters like Ulma and Gareth. Or if she did, I couldn't recognize it from these stories. But thank you for letting me study it."

Marybelle held up the paper with the spell and raised her eyebrows expectantly.

"Let's get started," he agreed.

It took several minutes for him to coach her on the pronunciation of the spell's words. When she asked how it would feel when the magic entered them, he shot her a mischievous smile. "I believe it'd be best for you to learn that on your own." Then, he took her off-hand in one of his, and they began.

A wave of embarrassment washed over Marybelle as they spoke the spell. Despite seeing the magic in action herself, a part of her still felt silly at the notion. Like they were school children playing pretend.

All such notions vanished after they touched the paper to the candle flame, and the fire hit the lettering. With the flare of green light from the letters, Marybelle felt a wave of euphoria and energy surge into her from the page until she brimmed with power. Her body felt alive for the first time, and she had to close her eyes against its immensity.

"Don't forget to breathe," came Jeremiah's soothing voice, "or you'll faint."

She deliberately took in several deep breaths and let them out slowly. "Is it like this every time?"

"I'm afraid you get used to it after a while. I wish I could experience it for the first time again. Try to open your eyes."

Marybelle pried her lids apart, and the world came into focus around her. Right away, she noticed colors seemed more vibrant. There were more of them, too. Variations in shade and hue she'd never seen on every surface. Even Jeremiah seemed clearer and crisper, and the effect highlighted for her just how handsome he was.

"Still breathing?" he asked.

Not realizing she'd been holding her breath, Marybelle let it out in a rush and sucked in another.

"How do you stay focused like this?"

"It takes practice. Are you absolutely sure you don't want me to do this for you?"

"It's my mother's work, Jeremiah. I have to be part of it."

"I understand." He drew her over to stand before the book. He waved a hand, and the text flipped open on its own to the blackened pages.

This time, when the smell of vanilla and rosemary

struck her, it was almost too much. Her eyes even watered a bit.

"Let me show you on this corner." Jeremiah let go of her hand and began the same smooth, slow motions he had on the note. "Slow and deliberate is the key with your movements, but they're less important than your thoughts. Keep your goal in mind at all times, or the magic will do unexpected things. You don't need to be able to visualize the page as it was, but anything you know about it will help the process. Envision her handwriting from the other pages. Recall a memory of her writing in it. Anything to give the magic a more concrete anchor to the original creation will make it work smoother."

As he talked, ink liquefied off the page as it had before. He only withdrew a bit before stepping back.

"I'll be right here. I'll step in if anything goes wrong," he said.

With another settling breath, Marybelle put out shaking hands and began the motions. Like she was winding a lead over her fingers.

"Slow down," said Jeremiah. "You'll make mistakes if you rush."

Though it felt like she was moving so slowly as to drive herself mad, she did as he bade. As she slowed, Marybelle followed his other advice and imagined the handwriting from the other pages. Her mother's loose, flowing script that somehow managed to be crisp at the same time. Imagining it jogged a memory of a sunny afternoon in Deadwood. A day her mother had been feeling unwell but still dragged herself to her desk to jot in the book. How at that moment, with the sunlight illuminating her dark hair and the pen shaking in her hand, she'd still looked serene and content. Losing herself in work had restored a bit of vibrancy amid an illness wearing her down to a shadow of herself.

And then it happened. Painfully slow at first, but undeniably real. Marybelle's motions drew the ink from the page, and she gasped as the first droplet floated clear.

"Keep breathing."

She barely registered the reminder as the spell's flow became more robust, and ink melted free of the paper in a steady flow. At first, nothing but a blank page showed underneath. For a terrifying moment, she feared that she'd made a mistake and ruined the page instead, but then a line remained firmly in place, and she relaxed.

The line was strange, though. It looked nothing like her mother's handwriting. Within a few minutes, she understood as the magic uncovered more lines.

"It's a drawing," she said. Tears filled her eyes. "I didn't know mother was an artist."

"Let me take over. You'd best compose yourself before you continue," said Jeremiah.

Marybelle relented, stepping back as he reached out his hands, took the ever-growing ball of ink from her, and continued with the process. She watched as he finished one page and half of another, tears dripping down her cheeks most of the time. Both pages were drawings above blocks of writing. The first was a creature she didn't recognize and another of a location she remembered from one of their trips. Happy memories flooded her mind at the sight of it.

When she felt ready again, she touched Jeremiah's shoulder, and he passed the mass of ink back to her with a smile. More confident now, she found it easier to maintain the mental images and the steady flow of the movements. The ink practically soared off the paper. Jeremiah turned the pages as she finished each, occasionally reminding her to slow down or breathe.

The work went too quickly for her to examine the pages carefully. Some of them confused her, but more memories came as well. Each solidified the task in her mind, and the flow of magic became smoother and more potent. When the last droplet came free on the final page, her heart was so full of love that the spell's energy paled in comparison.

Between her hands floated a ball of liquid blackness. She looked at Jeremiah, who beamed at her. Then, she tried to do as he'd done and manipulate the ink through the air.

The liquid strand hadn't moved more than a few inches when her grasp on the power faltered. Marybelle tried to hold on, but the spell's energy vanished, and with it gone, the ink dropped to the floor, splashing droplets back up at them.

She looked at the spilled ink, then at Jeremiah. A spot of black now dotted his cheek.

A giggle escaped from Marybelle's lips, devolving into a full-on laughing fit. The joy bubbled over even more, when she caught sight of the book and its words and drawings that she'd never seen.

Without warning, she threw her arms around Jeremiah and hugged him tightly. "Thank you. Thank you."

The words tumbled from her lips again and again. And then, those same lips pressed against his, brooking no argument as to staying there for as long as she pleased. His were soft and warm and shot a tingle of pleasure the length of her body, so she pleased for a good long time indeed.

A second later, her sense caught up with her, and she realized what she was doing. Embarrassment flooded her. Honestly, to be kissing a man she'd only met yesterday?

Yet, another part of her dismissed the embarrassment just as quickly. After all, if her mother hadn't gone kissing men she'd just met, Marybelle wouldn't be here to do the same. Instead, she grabbed the back of his neck to keep him right where she wanted him until the blush on her neck had subsided.

When she finally released him, his expression made her break out in giggles again. His shock at what had just happened was so adorable she could hardly stand it.

After a shake of his head and a few stammered starts, he said, "You're welcome."

I rather like that look on your face, she thought. *I'd like to see it again.*

"Does it look how you remember?" Jeremiah asked, stumbling over his words as he awkwardly changed the subject back to the book.

"I told you, I never got the see them. But that's her handwriti…"

Marybelle trailed off, her attention caught by the

drawing in front of her. It was… a unicorn? Why on earth would her mother have used space in the journal to draw a unicorn of all things?

She turned the page and found a creature sporting a lion's body and an eagle's wings. The next contained a lion with the upper torso of a woman and an eagle's wings.

"My mother was drawing magical creatures," she said, struck dumb by the sight. "Are these like the creatures you have on your preserve?"

"Some of them, yes." Jeremiah's voice carried the same wonderment Marybelle felt in her chest.

She started to turn the page again, but Jeremiah stopped her. His finger traced down to where her mother had inscribed her initials, *EF*. Never one for wasting time, she'd always signed with her initials rather than writing out her full name.

Jeremiah looked up at her with an expression she couldn't quite place.

"What is your last name, Marybelle?"

The question surprised her, but she answered, "Flint."

His eyes widened.

"You're Eloise Flint's daughter?"

A long pause.

"You know my mother's name?"

"Marybelle, everyone in my field knows your mother's name. Eloise Flint is an undisputed authority on magical creatures. She spent her life traveling the world researching them, and her writings advanced their care and conservation by decades. Without her, my preserve wouldn't be possible." He stopped, perhaps seeing the look on her face and registering the question a moment before it fell from her lips.

"I was with her when she traveled the world. Why don't I remember any of this?"

CHAPTER FOUR

Marybelle

To Marybelle's surprise, they found the answer on the last restored page. A journal entry revealing Marybelle's mother had just learned that she was sick and nothing could be done. Not wanting anyone to use her daughter for knowledge, Eloise had asked a friend to wipe Marybelle's memory of the supernatural before they came to Deadwood to live with her father.

"It must have been hard for her, not saying anything to you about it," said Jeremiah.

"She had other things on her mind." Marybelle didn't want to talk about this. Not until she'd had to chance to mull it over for herself.

"I don—"

"Do you think it might be in here?" Marybelle tapped the book.

"What?"

"The creature you're after in Deadwood. Do you think it's in my mother's book?"

Jeremiah shook his head. "It definitely isn't."

"And how could you possibly know that? Didn't you say these are her unpublished notes?"

"Well, yes, but the creature I'm seeking is brand new. The world has never seen one like it before."

That statement snagged Marybelle's heart and mind. Her mother's past choices forgotten for the moment, she leaned forward and said, "Tell me about it."

"It's a creature we call a salamander," Jeremiah began.

Marybelle blinked hard at him. "You do know that salamanders aren't magical, yes? They're just lizards."

"Most of them are, true, Miss Marybelle—"

"I think you can drop the miss now. All recent activity considered, Mister Locke."

Jeremiah reddened to match his beard. "Ah, yes. Well, then, Marybelle, salamanders start as just lizards, true. But sometimes, when a salamander dies, it's reborn as a magical version of itself shortly after."

"Only sometimes?" As she asked the question, she was turning pages in the book.

"The death has to involve sufficient energy to power the transformation, and most lizard deaths don't. Being crushed or digested is hardly energetic enough to pull off the trick. It usually takes fire. The unmagical lizards like hiding in logs, so they were first discovered by folks who'd burn their hiding places for firewood. But—"

Marybelle's finger came down on a page of her mother's book. "There are different types of salamanders, each with different traits depending on how the lizard died.

THE GLASS WHISPERER

Woodfire salamanders, gun powder salamanders. Even a firework salamander."

"Quite right," said Jeremiah. "And the one we're looking for was reborn inside a light bulb factory out east. An electrical fire caused its death, and the creature was reborn clear as glass."

It was then that Marybelle remembered the glass tail. She strode to her pouch and pulled it out. "It most certainly was."

"You had your foot on it"—his face looked like a young child who'd just learned he was getting ice cream—"so it's definitely in the library. Or, was when it lost its tail."

"Up for a hunting expedition, Jeremiah?"

"I believe I am, Mi—Marybelle."

"Good."

As they were leaving, she touched his shoulder to draw his attention, planted her lips against his for a long second, and strode into the hall like it was nothing. She couldn't keep the satisfied grin from her face when she spotted that deliciously adorable look of shock on his face again.

Back at the library, they hung a sign to inform patrons they were closed for the day and began hatching a plan for the salamander's capture.

Jeremiah already had one necessary component prepared: a clay jar borrowed from a retired associate. Infused with a bit of magic, it would keep the creature's power contained during transport. The trick was getting the lizard inside.

"I don't suppose Eloise's book mentions this?"

Jeremiah asked. "It was a rushed trip to procure the jar. All my friend could tell me was not to touch the salamander with my bare hands."

Marybelle flipped open the book to the section on salamanders and skimmed the text.

"They're attracted to the residue of whatever type of fire created them. You use ashes to attract the wood fire variety, gun powder residue to attract the gun powder variety." She wrinkled her nose. "What do you burn to emulate an electrical fire?"

Jeremiah's gaze turned to the crate of light bulbs left behind by the maintenance man. "Will anyone miss those?"

Marybelle smirked. "I certainly won't."

"Then I'm going to need another spell note."

After fetching water for safety, they pulled out a single light bulb from the box and set it in the middle of the library floor along with the clay jar. Jeremiah insisted Marybelle stand behind the desk, though what added safety that could offer was beyond her.

"I'll have to work quickly. A caster can't hold on to this type of spell for long."

After the note burned and Jeremiah's body took in the magic, his hair and fingertips crackled with arcs of electricity.

Marybelle could tell something was wrong as soon as he stretched out his hand. The way he moved wasn't right. Jerky and imprecise. His expression rapidly grew pained.

"What's wrong, Jeremiah?"

"This magic is stronger than I—"

Before he could finish, the power burst from him, unbidden, striking not only the bulb on the floor but also the crate of new light bulbs. He cried out as the bulbs began shattering en masse, and Marybelle ducked beneath the desk to avoid the cascade.

Finally, the crash of breaking bulbs subsided. Marybelle remained still for a long moment as a unique burning smell permeated the air, no doubt from the bulbs' filaments. Finally, she poked her head up above the desk to see what was happening.

Jeremiah lay sprawled on the floor, shards of glass and wood fragments all around him. The crate housing the light bulbs had fared no better than its contents.

Marybelle dashed out to him from behind the desk.

"Please tell me you're okay," she said, more to herself than him.

Just as she knelt next to him, something moved.

Marybelle's breath caught in her throat, and she froze. Only her eyes turned to where she'd spotted the movement.

There it was.

She'd never have noticed the salamander if it hadn't moved. Though four inches long, even without a tail, it was clear as glass and, when it held still, was practically invisible unless you knew it was there. Just as her mother's book had said, the remains of its creation fire had drawn it out. It stood with its head poked inside the debris of the light bulb, licking at the burned-out filament.

A groan issued from Jeremiah, and he moved suddenly to raise himself to his feet. Marybelle saw his hand shift close to the salamander. She tried to stop him but couldn't react fast enough.

Light flared from the body of the startled lizard, so bright she had to turn away. Then she heard the crackle of electricity and Jeremiah bellowing. Out of instinct, she tried to pull him back and felt the electrical shock enter her own body, making every muscle spasm for agonizing moments before the world fell black.

CHAPTER FIVE

Marybelle

Marybelle's head felt like her mare had been riding over it all morning. Opening her eyes was painful, but she forced them to do it anyway.

She was in her room, the landlady, Mrs. Brown, sitting at her bedside.

"What happened to Jeremiah?" Marybelle asked. Or rather, she tried to ask, for the words came out in a slurred garble.

Mrs. Brown was instantly at her side. "Thank goodness you're awake, girl. You had me worried."

She fetched a cup of water from a pitcher laid out on the dresser and helped Marybelle drink it.

When her mouth and throat were moist again, Marybelle repeated her question.

"He was resting with the doctor until his aunt came for him," said Mrs. Brown.

Drowsiness fled from Marybelle's mind, replaced by dread. "His aunt?"

"Sour woman. Said they were taking her nephew home to rest with them and wanted to speak with you as soon as you were up and about. She left a note, so maybe tomorrow you can—"

"Let me see the note."

"You should stay in bed, for now, dear."

"Show it to me, Mrs. Brown." Marybelle was already pushing herself into a sitting position and rolling her legs off the side of the bed.

The landlady heaved a sigh. "I should know better than to try to keep you off anything you've set your mind to. At least it's a man, for once. A good girl like you, still not married at your age." Mrs. Brown continued grumbling as she handed the note to Marybelle.

"I think I'll be fine now. Could you leave me to get dressed?"

The grumbling got louder, but Mrs. Brown complied.

Marybelle's attention was on the note the instant the door closed. The handwriting was poor but clear enough she could decipher the signature at the bottom.

Ulma.

Her breath quickened as she read the rest.

We know you're keeping it in the library. Bring the key to its hiding place. Come alone. No horse.

They'd searched the library while she was out, but they hadn't found the salamander or they wouldn't need her help. Her thoughts turned to the glass tail in her bag, and a mirthless smile crossed her lips. With proof like that, she at least had some leverage.

A plan formed in her mind. A dangerous one, and not one she'd have considered if a person's life weren't at stake. But at the moment, it was all she had.

She fetched her sewing kit and an older dress and sewed an inner pocket into the upper chest next to the left sleeve.

Then, she wrote the words to the electrical spell on a spare sheet of paper, folded it, and placed it in the pocket where she could get to it quickly. She practiced slipping the note out until she was sure she could do it without dropping it. By the time she finished both tasks, night had fallen on Deadwood. She removed her mother's book from her satchel and hid it just to be safe, then made sure her gun was within easy reach and headed downstairs.

As she prepped the hooded lamp that Mrs. Brown kept by the door, Marybelle noticed the landlady's crate of anticipatory light bulbs again. She considered, glanced around her, then snatched one from the box and stuffed it in her sack.

The frosty night had driven the town's residents indoors, heralding the coming of autumn and the aching bones that came with it. It seemed that she and the wolves would be left to their own devices. Marybelle did her best to shake off the chill, keeping one hand in her bag and on the handle of her pistol. When she was within a block of the Syndicate building, she pulled it out and cocked back the hammer before continuing.

Her wait for Ulma and Gareth wasn't long. The red she-wolf appeared from the shadows, teeth bared in a ferocious snarl.

Instinctively, Marybelle faced the creature and backed away into a space between buildings. Too late, she realized the pack maneuver they were using. Before she could move again, rough hands were on her, one clamping over her mouth while the other took control of her gun hand.

"I'll take that."

Gareth's breath smelled of strong drink and nearly made her gag. She fought him for a second, but his grip was too strong, and he soon wrested the weapon from her. After the gun, he yanked the lamp from her hand, cast it to the ground, and kicked dirt on it until the light went out.

In the dark that overtook them, Marybelle heard the eerie, wet sound of Ulma stepping out of her wolf skin. Then she whispered, "You stay quiet, or you'll be dead before any help gets here. Understand, girl?"

Marybelle nodded, and the next thing she knew, Gareth had released her mouth to force her hands behind her and begin binding them with coarse rope. Her heart sank in her chest as she felt the coils rounding her wrists. It hadn't occurred to her they might tie her hands. Now she had no means of getting to the spell in her hidden pocket.

They brought her inside the Syndicate building through a back door they'd forced open and down the hall to the library. A single candle burned on the desk. In the center of the floor still sat Jeremiah's jar for capturing the salamander.

"Where is it, girl?" Ulma demanded.

"Show me he's alive first," Marybelle retorted, trying to buy herself time. Though for what she couldn't say.

"She ain't got it, ma. Let's just finish with these two."

"Check my bag. You'll find proof there."

Gareth snorted but took the bag from her and fished around in it until he dug out the glass lizard tail. He tossed the satchel aside as a grin split his face.

"I'll be damned. Look at that, ma."

Ulma pointed behind the desk. "Bring her around."

When they rounded the desk, Jeremiah came into view. He lay on the floor, bound by the hands and feet and gagged to boot. His eyes grew wide when he saw her.

"Are you okay? Did they hurt you?" She tried to inch closer to Jeremiah.

A hand shoved her to her knees, and they brought the candle down off the desk so she could see him more clearly. His face sported bruising, but he otherwise seemed fine.

"There," said Ulma, "Now you've seen he's alive. Where's my lizard?"

Marybelle's mind was buzzing, trying to come up with a convincing lie. "You'll have to go—"

A loud pop startled them all, saving her from the need to finish the performance. Marybelle recognized it right away as the structure settling. The Syndicate building did it all the time, but Ulma and Gareth didn't know that.

"Damn it; someone's working late. Best find 'em and make sure they stay away until we're done. Come on, son."

"Shouldn't I stay and watch these two, ma?"

"They're both tied, Gareth. What are they going to do? Come on. We'll get this done faster with both of us."

Before they left, Gareth set the candle on the floor, leaned over, and took Marybelle's chin. He turned her face toward him. Then he pulled down his collar to show her a patched-up bullet wound.

"Still owe you, girl. I'll get mine."

Both shapeshifters stepped into the hallway.

Marybelle's mind scrambled. There had to be something she could do. She wondered if Jeremiah could reach the hidden spell, but the wolves would be back by the time he got it out.

At least I have fire, she thought with a rueful glance at the candle.

At that moment, a thought popped into her head. She looked at Jeremiah, then back at the candle. Then she swallowed hard. "Jeremiah, do I have to read the words to a spell? Or will just saying them work if the paper still burns?"

His brows furrowed in confusion.

She simplified it, realizing he couldn't answer easily with the gag in place. "Can I just say the spell, yes or no?"

He nodded his head yes, his brow still furrowed in confusion.

Marybelle scooted closer, leaned over, and kissed him on the cheek. The adorable look of surprise came over him again, and it brought a smile to her face despite everything. "If I don't make it, good-bye."

With this last, she bent over the candle and held the shoulder of her dress containing the secret pocket over the flame. She soon felt the heat pricking at her skin, but she stayed in place. Jeremiah began yammering through the gag, probably telling her to stop, but she'd committed.

She started reciting the spell just before her dress

caught fire. The pain was almost more than she could bear, but she pushed through and finished the recitation, feeling the energy flood into her a second later.

If the ink removal spell had been a creek running through sand, the electric spell was a river overflowing its banks. The sheer volume of power that flooded her was beyond imagining. She found her muscles jerking involuntarily and her heart racing as the pain in her shoulder blossomed into an acute agony.

Marybelle tried to direct the power, but it was like holding back the wind with a feather.

Without her trying, an arc of electric power shot toward her bag and the light bulb resting within it. She heard a pop, and seconds later, the distinct smell of a burned bulb filled the air.

The wolves returned at that moment, and above the roar of the fire ravaging her shoulder and the electricity, she heard Gareth shout out, "She's gonna kill us all!"

"Don't you touch her 'til that spell wears off, son!"

Marybelle tried again to bend the magic to her will, but all she accomplished was a flare of power that made all of her hair stand on end.

"You're done, girl. Just let it go," Ulma demanded.

"Come make me," she managed to get out.

A flash of movement caught her eye. For a split second, she'd spotted a shimmery reflection in a place there shouldn't have been. Marybelle looked closer, and with the magic heightening her senses, she saw it right away. The salamander, drawn by the burned-out light bulb and oblivious to the burning electric woman kneeling not three feet away.

She felt the electric power in her drawn toward the salamander. Fearful of scaring it off, she moved her burning shoulder away, screaming at the pain of the movement.

But she felt something else. A shift in the power's reaction to the salamander. As though one side of her body repelled the creature while the other attracted it.

She let go of any other attempt to control the spell and leaned her right shoulder closer. The magic responded by arcing into a miniature lightning storm around her. One bolt snagged the salamander and drew it toward her. She turned to face Ulma and Gareth, then pushed her left shoulder forward, and the creature hurtled toward them.

"Catch it, ma!"

"Son, no!"

Gareth's hand's closed on the salamander just as Ulma grabbed him to pull him back. Blinding light flared, both of their bodies convulsed, and a second later, they dropped limply to the floor.

Marybelle's last thought was of the clay jar and how she might get the salamander inside before the blackness enveloped her again.

Chapter Six

Marybelle

Marybelle's head throbbed, and her eyes refused to open, but she heard voices that told her she was somewhere safe.

When she finally dragged herself fully awake, she was in the home of Deadwood's doctor, laid out in bed with her shoulder bandaged.

Jeremiah sat in a chair at her bedside, leaning close to her with worried eyes. "How are you feeling? The doctor was concerned."

Marybelle shifted in bed, testing that everything still moved as intended. Though stiff and sore and, in the case of her shoulder, throbbing, it did.

"I think I'll survive 'til tomorrow." She could hardly believe the words as she said them, having fully expected the spell or the fire to do her in.

The fire. The books!

Her pulse leaped at the realization. "What happened to the libr—"

Before she could finish, Jeremiah's lips were on hers, and her breath was gone. His fingers wound into her hair to hold her close as he let the kiss playfully linger.

When he came up for air, a mischievous grin split his face.

"Marybelle, the look on your face right now must be why you keep doing that to me."

Her lips tingled and a thrill passed through her. She was struck in that moment by how safe she felt with Jeremiah. Whether it was his openness about who he was, or the warmth and connection carried by his touch she couldn't say. Yet, he was far more than a pretty face to her. She'd never felt for someone like she did for him. In much the way her spell had drawn out the salamander, Jeremiah's presence had drawn out something new inside Marybelle. A longing she didn't fully understand, but now yearned to explore. "Do it again."

And he did. Oh yes, he did. At one point, she heard the door to the room open, but they ignored it, and it quickly closed again.

When the second kiss ended, she placed a hand on Jeremiah's chest and pushed him back. "What happened to the library?"

"Ulma and Gareth weren't exactly being quiet about anything. And when the racket of your spell came into the picture, folks got to the building quickly. They rescued us and put out the fire before any significant damage occurred."

"Somehow, I doubt they'll ask me to substitute again."

"Do you want them to?"

THE GLASS WHISPERER

She ignored his question and asked, "The wolves? What happened to Ulma and Gareth?"

Jeremiah's demeanor darkened. "Gareth hasn't woken yet. They aren't sure if he will. Ulma, the marshals arrested. I'm not certain what will happen to her, and I don't think I care to know."

"The marshals came for her? How long have I been asleep?"

He squeezed her hand. "Too long."

She shuddered at the memory of the last seconds before she'd lost consciousness. "What about the salamander?"

Jeremiah released her hand and reached down to the floor by the bed. He lifted the clay jar up onto his lap and patted it lightly. "All cozy until we get to Wyoming."

A tension gripped her chest. She'd known Jeremiah had to return soon, of course. Getting the creature back to his preserve was why he'd come to Deadwood in the first place. But what did that mean for them? Was there even a them to concern herself with? Perhaps the last kiss hadn't meant for him what it meant for her. "When are you going back?"

Jeremiah's face grew serious. "Soon. I have to get it back there before they send more hunters after it."

That those hunters could catch up to him on the road back weighed heavily on her. He'd be traveling alone. She tried to remind herself that he had ways of protecting himself as she asked, "What if they send hunters to the preserve?"

"We have ways of dealing with them there."

Marybelle raised a playful eyebrow, even though she wasn't particularly feeling playful. Her wounds were already dragging her energy down again, and she was no closer to the answer she wanted. "How mysterious, Mister Locke."

He shot an equally playful sideways glance. "You have no idea, Miss Flint."

They laughed, and then he took her hand. "I won't be back in Deadwood for a while. I—"

"Me either, once I'm healed," Marybelle interrupted. It was time to get the heart of things.

"Oh, is that so, Miss Marybelle? And where are you going?"

She tapped a finger on her lips, pretending to be thinking hard. "I was considering the Wyoming territory. I've heard that there's work like my mother's that needs doing there. I'm keen to explore that field myself, now that I know more about it."

Jeremiah beamed. "It just so happens I know a place you could get started. With plenty of magical creatures that need to be studied."

"Are you sure, Jeremiah? Because wherever I end up, I have two conditions about which I will not take no for an answer." She gave him an earnest glance.

"What are those?" he asked, a hint of worry in his eye.

"First, I want to learn magic."

"You can learn it in Wyoming. Someone there is willing to teach you, and you seem to have a talent for it."

"And the second is far more important."

Jeremiah said nothing but bit his lip while she let a silence pass.

Her heart pounded through those quiet seconds, as she realized the enormity of what she was about to lay on the table. Still, she'd never been one to sit around and wait for things to come to her. When she wanted something, she went after it, just as her mother had taught her. What she wanted was to discover the hidden wonders of this strange new world now revealed to her. And to uncover those mysteries with the man who'd opened the door for her at her side. "I won't pick a place without someone to keep me warm at night."

He smiled and leaned in close, and a warm shiver passed through her as he met her eyes and said, "I can most certainly arrange that, Miss Marybelle."

THE END

ABOUT THE AUTHOR
AARON VOLNER

Aaron spends a lot of time creating interesting places in his mind and getting irretrievably lost in them. Fortunately, he manages to find his way back long enough to write books. He lives in the high desert of southwest Wyoming with his faithful dog, Andy, in a house full of plants from all over the globe. Writer by night, librarian by day, Aaron also enjoys reading, acting, gaming, crocheting, and golf.

Connect with Aaron

Website: aaronvolner.com
Facebook: www.facebook.com/aaronvolnerauthor/
Twitter: twitter.com/aaron_volner
Instagram: @aaronvolnerauthor
Pinterest: www.pinterest.com/aaronvolner0100/
Goodreads:
www.goodreads.com/author/show/17132493.Aaron_Volner
Bookbub: www.bookbub.com/authors/aaron-volner

Want more romance and fantasy adventure? Read:

BLOOD OF OLTHETTA

In a city where having the wrong blood can land you in jail, the law controls the press, and certain books are banned, the bookseller Patrick finds love with the beautiful, gun-toting journalist Elleira.

But then, Elleira vanishes. As the city guard arrest those close to her and burn the places she frequents, Patrick must scramble to uncover the reason behind it all. Why are the banned books, and people of a certain blood, so dangerous to the city's High Lord? What secret is so damning he would go to such lengths to protect it?

Patrick must dredge up answers if he's to find Elleira and expose the truth. But if he does, will the city, or the world, survive what he unearths?

Made in the USA
Middletown, DE
16 May 2022

65836234R00308